Daring the Pirates to Shoot at Them!

The two attack copters came screaming out of the night sky, the pirate camp dead in their sights. To the dark amusement of all, Crash changed the MP3 blaring out the psyops sounds to a hyperventilated version of "Ride of the Valkyries."

"Now comes the fun part," Nolan thought grimly.

He armed all his weapons. The .50-caliber machine guns mounted on his winglets came back as ready; same for the huge 30mm cannon sticking out of the copter's nose. Twitch had his M4 up on the portside weapons mount, fed by a continuous belt of ammunition. Gunner's huge "Streetsweeper" was ready, too.

In seconds, both copters were down to just ten feet off the deck. Nolan went in first, with Batman just behind him. Whiskey was daring the pirates to fire at them so they would know where to fire back. Any brigand who showed himself to shoot at Nolan would find himself in Batman's crosshairs an instant later.

It quickly turned nuts. The noise of the two copters flying so low was deafening, yet Nolan could still hear the energized strains of "Ride of the Valkyries" over the roar. Everything was loud and fast, and smoke and flames and flashes of light were going off in all directions.

But . . . something was wrong.

Nolan knew it right away.

———————————

Turn the page to see what people are saying about **The Pirate Hunters.**

"*The Pirate Hunters*—lots of action and adventure fueled by adrenaline."

"With clever plotting, scorching pace, and 'from the news' situations, Maloney's straight-ahead style makes the reader realize the high seas can be filled with unusual and unpredictable danger."

Praise for Mack Maloney's Superhawks Series

"Maloney's page-turning plots are what everyone would like to see in real life: direct, decisive action against Al-Qaeda killers, without ceremony or pretense. Maloney has his finger on the pulse of the nation. As he sends his Superhawks heroes into the global fight against terrorism, his grasp of modern technical detail combines with the most authentic presentation of terrorist forces, making this the top action series in the marketplace."

"Superhawks is a great adventure series . . . a perfect blend of rage, humanity, and occasional flashes of dark humor."

"Mack Maloney has created a team of realistic characters that pulse with patriotic fervor. He hasn't just crafted a great war story, he has set a new standard for action-packed thrillers."

Operation Caribe

Mack Maloney

A TOM DOHERTY ASSOCIATES BOOK
New York

This is a work of fiction. All of the characters, organizations, and events portrayed in this novel are either products of the author's imagination or are used fictitiously.

OPERATION CARIBE

Copyright © 2011 by Mack Maloney

All rights reserved.

Edited by James Frenkel

A Forge Book
Published by Tom Doherty Associates, LLC
175 Fifth Avenue
New York, NY 10010

www.tor-forge.com

Forge® is a registered trademark of Tom Doherty Associates, LLC.

ISBN 978-0-7653-6522-4

First Edition: February 2011

Printed in the United States of America

0 9 8 7 6 5 4 3 2 1

For Richard Kennedy, Gene Smith and Ed Metcalf,
Heroes of World War II

ACKNOWLEDGMENTS

Thanks to the usual suspects and especially to Sky Club for providing the soundtrack.

PART ONE

Saving the *Saud el-Saud*

1

THE OH-6J ATTACK helicopter circled the mega-yacht twice before landing on its stern-mounted helipad.

The copter was armed to the teeth with a .50-caliber machine gun attached to each side of its fuselage, small winglets holding mounted rocket pods, and a 30mm cannon that jutted out of its nose. The copter was painted ghostly gray; a decal on the pilot's door identified it as *Bad Dawg One*.

Six vessels were anchored around the mega-yacht. Crews from four Kenyan patrol boats, a French destroyer and a Spanish minesweeper anxiously watched the copter land. A U.S. Navy guided-missile cruiser, the USS *Robert J. Messia*, lurked nearby. A forest of antennas sticking out of its bridge was the only hint that the cruiser frequently engaged in intelligence operations.

An enormous black-and-green vessel ten miles away was barely visible in the haze. It was a supertanker of sorts, but it was not full of crude oil. Rather, it was an LNG carrier—as in liquefied natural gas. The ship was more than a thousand feet long, with five large geodesic dome shapes protruding from its deck. These domes contained 500,000 cubic feet of highly explosive LNG. The ship sat at anchor, no other vessels anywhere near it.

The rotors on the OH-6J finally stopped spinning and five men climbed out. They did not look like military types.

Each wore his hair long and sported a stubbly, rock-star beard. One had earrings dangling from both lobes; another's open shirt revealed tattoos of ammunition belts crisscrossing his chest. The copter's pilot had a black patch over his left eye. One man walked with a prosthetic leg. A fifth man was missing his left hand.

Colonel Omir Zamal of the *Al Mukhabarat Al A'amah,* Saudi Arabia's version of the CIA, was waiting for them. A large man stuffed inside desert battle fatigues, he was surrounded by heavily armed guards. Indeed, there were armed men scattered all over the huge yacht's upper decks.

Zamal's aide was standing next to him. At first sight of the five men alighting from the helicopter, he whispered to his boss: "Are these the people we've all been waiting for? Or have they just escaped from a carnival?"

Zamal approached the men and offered only the briefest of introductions; there were no salutes, no handshakes.

"What's the situation?" the man with the eye patch asked him.

Zamal indicated the huge LNG ship in the distance. "The pirates who seized it are definitely Somalis," he said in heavily accented English. "They killed six members of the crew when they came aboard, and now they're threatening to blow up the ship if their demands are not met."

"And what are the demands?"

"Two hundred million dollars," Zamal replied starkly. "In cash."

The man with the earrings let out a whistle. "Now, that's some serious coin."

"How much is the ship worth?" the man with the patch asked, studying the LNG carrier through an electronic telescope held up to his good eye.

"More than a billion dollars," the Saudi officer said. "With the LNG on board? Maybe another hundred million."

"They picked the right ship to swipe," the man without a hand said.

"These pirates were well-prepared," Zamal told them. "They brought lots of food and water on board with them. They also brought ammunition, military radios, batteries, even a satellite dish so they're able to monitor media broadcasts and listen in on military communications, including NATO radio traffic."

"They're smart," the man with the tattoos said. "And that's scary."

"It gets worse," Zamal said. "They've rigged the ship with explosives—lots of them. So blowing it up is no idle threat. And they did not plant these explosives in any haphazard fashion. They put them in just the right places to cause the most damage in the shortest amount of time."

"How do you know that?" the one-eyed man asked.

"Because they posted a video of it," Zamal replied. "On YouTube."

"You're kidding. . . ."

The officer snapped his fingers and his aide pulled out a BlackBerry. He punched up a video that showed a collage of shadowy figures placing explosives below the LNG carrier's decks.

"They must have studied the structural stress points of this type of LNG tanker," Zamal explained. "Our experts tell us those charges are planted in such a way that if they blow up, they'll instantly ignite the liquefied gas. If that happens, that ship will light up like the sun and everything will be gone in about two seconds."

"How many crew are left alive on board?" the one-eyed man asked.

"Just six now," Zamal said. "It's a highly automated ship. Computers and GPS take care of all the work. A single person can drive the whole thing."

"And how many pirates are there?"

"Five in all," Zamal said.

"And any idea *where* they are on board?"

"Again—they're outsmarting us," Zamal replied. "They came aboard wearing clothes similar to the crew. Heavy work shirts, overalls, bandanas, hard hats. They have the real crewmembers doing their routine maintenance tasks, so when we look through our long-range binoculars, we can see people walking around on deck all the time. We just don't know who's bad and who's good."

The one-eyed man studied the ship further. "And how much gas is in that thing again?"

"A half-million cubic feet," Zamal replied.

The man with the earrings whistled again. "If it blows, it will make a pretty big hole in the ocean."

Zamal nodded grimly. "Now you understand why we're all anchored so far away."

ZAMAL BROUGHT THE five men below and led them on a long trek to the front of the huge pleasure craft. It was like walking through a luxury hotel. They passed by gigantic guest areas, salons, spas and dining areas. Giant bedrooms led into lavishly appointed private lounges and Jacuzzi spas. One cabin featured an infinity pool looking out onto the sea. Another held a movie theater, complete with candy counter and popcorn machine. Still another had six billiards tables, and another, a complete tailor's shop. One of the largest cabins was a children's playroom. It was filled with a variety of toys, many of which were strewn about on the floor. Dozens of boxes, unopened on the shelves, held more.

"The owner is a big movie fan," Zamal explained, playing the unofficial tour guide. "He loves billiards and dressing well. And, as he has many wives, he also has many, many children."

They finally reached their destination: the captain's master galley. This cabin had the look of an ultra-exclusive, modern restaurant, all tablecloths and candles and tasteful chandeliers. The mega-yacht's owner, Prince Saud el-Saud, was waiting here. He also owned the hijacked LNG carrier, which bore his name. A small man with a huge mustache and glasses, he sat at the head of an enormous dinner table, wearing the traditional Saudi *thwarb* and *ghutra an iqal*, looking worried.

Sitting to el-Saud's right was a younger man, a Westerner wearing sunglasses and a bad suit. To his left sat an older African man wearing rumpled doctor's scrubs. He looked like he hadn't slept in days.

The five visitors fell into seats at the other end of the table. The Prince studied them up and down. He knew a lot about them; most people in this part of the world did, especially those who made their living moving cargo on the high seas.

They were Team Whiskey. Former members of the elite Delta Force of the United States military, they'd been part of the small army of American special forces who'd pursued Osama bin Laden in the mountains of Afghanistan immediately after 9/11. The rumors said Team Whiskey actually cornered bin Laden near the mountain fortress of Tora Bora and had him in their gun sights, only to be ordered by someone at the highest level of the administration in Washington to let him go.

When bin Laden escaped, Whiskey raised such holy hell with their higher-ups, they were eventually bounced from the U.S. military altogether. Their leader—the man with the eye patch—created such a stink, he was imprisoned for seven years on trumped-up charges and then forbidden to ever set foot on U.S. soil again.

Prince el-Saud had obtained dossiers on each man. The

team's leader, "Snake" Nolan, had lost his eye, and apparently part of his sanity, during that futile chase after bin Laden. "Crash" Stacks, he of the blond spiked hair and dangling earrings, was the team's marksman and could put a bullet up someone's nose from four miles away. "Gunner" Lapook, the tattooed giant of the group, was the weapons expert and door-kicker. When the team needed to do a forced entry, he always went in first. "Twitch" Kapula, a native Hawaiian, was the team's explosives man. Small and muscular, with dark skin and Polynesian features, he'd left his right leg, and part of *his* sanity, back in Tora Bora, too.

The fifth team member was "Batman" Bob Graves, the man missing his left hand. In a world where prosthetic limbs looked like real human appendages, Graves's false hand most closely resembled a Trautman Hook. An invention of the 1920s, it was two pieces of dull steel, each about four inches long. With its slightly bent tips, the hook's functions were limited to pinch and release and little more.

Team Whiskey had reunited six months before, and eventually reinvented themselves as an anti-piracy outfit. Banking on their special ops skills and far-reaching connections, they had delivered in a very short time results that were nothing short of fantastic. They'd fought two small wars against a powerful Indonesian pirate named Zeek Kurjan, finally killing him and destroying his large seafaring gang. They'd recovered a multimillion-dollar Indian Navy warship after Somali pirates had hijacked it near the Maldives. They'd saved a cruise liner full of Russian mafia bosses from a mass-poisoning attempt in the Aegean Sea, and they were believed to have been involved in the recovery of a unique multi-*billion*-dollar microchip buried on an uncharted island off East Africa.

Their success had brought them much wealth—and a

reputation for being able to handle virtually any job. They were also undeniably American in looks and demeanor. Hard-bitten, hard-drinking, cynical, bitter—and very tough. Though they were all in their late 30s, each man looked old beyond his years.

The prince finally addressed them. "I admire your past accomplishments. You've done some brave and amazing things in the past few months. In fact, from what I've heard, someone should make a movie of you. But I must be clear: We are in an entirely different situation at the moment, one that is only matched by the unusual circumstances that led me to ask you here."

"And what are those exactly?" Nolan asked him.

"That's my LNG ship out there and I want it back," el-Saud told them. "But obviously, considering the cargo it's carrying, there can be *no gunplay* involved in its recovery. One bullet in the wrong place and the whole ship and everything around it will explode like an atomic bomb. So . . ."

The prince nodded to his aides. They wheeled in a laundry cart carrying four enormous satchels. Each looked to weigh a couple hundred pounds at least.

"This is the ransom," he said. "Two hundred million dollars—all in five-hundred-dollar bills, just as the pirates demanded. All I want you to do is deliver this to them so I can get my ship returned to me."

The team was bewildered.

"You called us here just to deliver a ransom?" Nolan asked.

The prince nodded. "The pirates refuse to allow any military to be involved. No U.N. No Red Cross. I need someone I can trust to handle such a large amount of money. And besides . . ."

He let his voice trail off.

"Besides what?" Nolan asked.

"Besides, one of the pirates' demands is that *you* make the ransom transfer."

Nolan was taken aback. "Us, specifically?"

"Yes, by name," el-Saud said. "They are insisting that you and your associates act as the middlemen, or there is no deal."

"This smells like a setup," Nolan said.

"That's because it is," the prince said bluntly. "Like everyone else around the Indian Ocean, these pirates know who you are and what you've done. We're listening in on their radio transmissions. Your names have been mentioned; your history has been discussed. I don't have to tell you how these pirates feel about you. You've killed their brothers, their cousins. So, they're probably going to kill you once the ransom is delivered, just to increase their reputation in the pirate underworld."

Nolan almost laughed. "Let me get this straight," he said. "These mooks say the only way they'll release the ship is if *we* deliver the ransom to them. And the reason they want us to do it is so they can kill us and increase their street cred. Yet, we won't be allowed to take any firearms with us to protect ourselves?"

Everyone at the other end of the table nodded. "That's it in a nutshell," el Saud said.

"And actually, gunplay will be impossible," Colonel Zamal interjected. "The pirates are being very aggressive about searching anyone coming aboard. They even brought metal detecting wands with them. It would be impossible to carry a firearm aboard that ship."

"How do you know all that?" Nolan asked him.

For the first time, Zamal indicated the man in the doctor's scrubs. "They allowed Dr. Bobol here aboard to treat one of the pirates injured in the takeover. He went over in the Spanish ship's helicopter. Tell them your experience, Doctor."

"I was frisked three times," Bobol said. "Then I was buzzed with wands another three times. They did everything short of molesting my private parts and doing a full cavity search. They, on the other hand, are heavily armed and seemed quite willing to shoot me had I stepped out of line, stray bullets be damned. They have the frisking process down to a science. They will detect any weapons on you immediately—and when they do, they will kill you instantly, and not later on. I'm sure of it."

A silence descended on the room. Nolan thought for a few moments, then asked: "Are there any Americans aboard the ship?"

"No."

He turned to the man in the bad suit and sunglasses. "Then why is the ONI here?"

The man shifted uncomfortably in his seat. The team knew he was an agent from the U.S. Navy's Office of Naval Intelligence—his cheap suit gave him away. ONI was basically the CIA of the seas, and because of Team Whiskey's ex-Delta, expatriate status, the little-known agency had been a thorn in their side since they'd started their maritime security business. This also explained the presence of the shadowy USS *Messia* nearby.

"We are here on an unofficial basis," the ONI man said finally. "Purely in an advisory capacity."

"Put that through the bullshit meter, please?" said Nolan.

The agent's face turned crimson. "We're here because the gas in that carrier came from Qatar; Qatar's export partner is ExxonMobil," he admitted. "And we want to protect their interests. As well as those of the Saudis and, of course, the prince himself. But, for the record, the ONI feels it's an impossible situation we have here and, again for the record, we recommend you don't go through with it."

Nolan just rolled his eyes and turned back to the prince. "You expect to pay us for this job, right?" he asked.

"Ten million dollars if your efforts are successful," the Prince replied somberly.

Nolan thought about this, then said: "What if the ransom gets delivered, but we still get popped? We're just, what? 'Collateral damage?' Is that it?"

Again, the prince just nodded. "It is a truly impossible mission," he said. "And I can understand every reason you would want to turn it down. It seems lose-lose no matter how one looks at it. But I felt I owed it to you to ask."

Nolan looked at the rest of the team. Each man tapped his own ear twice.

Finally Nolan asked, "Can my associates and I have a few minutes to talk?"

THE TEAM WALKED toward the front of the boat, emerging onto the bow.

Zamal followed and kept an eye on them from a respectful distance. The five Americans were soon locked in an intense discussion.

The Saudi intelligence officer couldn't imagine what they were talking about. They were being offered a job that could only result in their deaths. What was there to discuss?

Yet, ten minutes later, they were back in the captain's galley.

"Twelve million," Nolan told el Saud.

The prince was shocked. "Are you certain?" he asked. "The chances you'll survive are almost nil."

"Then make it fifteen," Nolan said. "You'll only have to pay us if we succeed, so what difference does it make?"

The Prince thought a moment, then asked: "Seriously?"

Nolan looked at his colleagues. Each man touched his chin.

"Seriously," Nolan replied. "We'll take the job."

Once again silence descended over the galley. The prince and the ONI man plainly were shocked the team was going ahead with it. Even Dr. Bobol looked incredulous.

Again, Zamal broke the tension. "What do you need from us then?" he asked Nolan.

The Team Whiskey leader thought a moment, then said: "First of all, Doctor, please draw us a diagram of exactly where the pirates stood when you went aboard and while you were being searched."

"And second?" Zamal asked.

Nolan indicated the four large bundles of money. "We've got to put that into a few wooden crates and nail them tight," he said. "We know what it's like to carry loose bills on a helicopter."

WHILE THE OTHER team members visited various cabins within the yacht in preparation for the mission, Nolan climbed up to the bridge and got on the radio.

He called the pirates on the LNG carrier ten miles away. The gang's leader answered.

Nolan's first words were: "We've got a problem."

"Who is this?" the pirate asked in heavily accented English.

"The people you insisted deliver the ransom to you."

"You are the Americans? The Whiskey people?"

"Yes."

The pirate leader said something to someone off the mic. Nolan heard muffled laughter in the background.

"They have the ransom," Nolan told him. "I just saw them count it. Two hundred million in five-hundred-dollar bills."

More laughter.

"So—what is this problem?" the pirate leader asked.

"That much money weighs almost a half a ton," Nolan replied. "And we have only a small utility helicopter. Yet delivering it that way is the only option. We can't parachute it because that would require a large plane, and it would be a rough landing on that deck. And I understand you don't want it delivered by sea, is that correct?"

"Yes, it is," the pirate replied. "Do you have a solution, then?"

"We'll have to break it up into wooden crates," Nolan replied. "And deliver them one at a time. There's no other way."

A long silence on the other end of the line.

"How many people work for your company?" the pirate asked.

"We are five."

"Are they all with you now?"

"Yes."

Another silence, and then the pirate spoke again: "We'd be fools to trust you, so this is what you must do. Deliver the first crate—and leave your four men behind. Deliver the other crates—we make sure the money count is right, then the ship is yours and we let the crew go."

"Along with me and my men?" Nolan added.

"Yes—of course," the pirate said quickly.

"One hour," Nolan told him, again hearing more laughter from the other end. "You can expect us then."

Forty-five minutes later

COLONEL ZAMAL WAS standing outside the cabin where Team Whiskey was getting ready for their mission.

They'd requested this place as their prep room, a lounge that ran off the gigantic kids' play area.

"You only have ten minutes to get airborne," Zamal said, checking his watch and banging on the cabin door. "We must stay on schedule."

The door opened a crack; the man they called Batman stuck his head out.

"What time is lunch served on this boat?" he asked Zamal.

Zamal was thrown by the question. "Anytime the prince wants it," was his reply. "Why? Are you hungry?"

The man patted him lightly on the shoulder with his hook hand.

"No—not now," he said, closing the door again. "But maybe later."

FIVE MORE MINUTES went by. Zamal anxiously paced the passageway. He was more convinced than ever the Whiskey team members were crazy. It was almost a certainty that the pirates would kill them once the ransom money was paid. It was a no-win situation. Yet the team was going ahead with it.

Finally the cabin door opened again, and the five men came out. Zamal had expected to see them dressed in full battle gear, but the opposite was true. They wore no body armor, no military fatigues. Not even combat helmets. They were dressed as before: camo shorts, shirts, sneakers and baseball caps. And they were carrying no weapons that he could see. All they had in hand was Dr. Bobol's drawing and a letter of terms from the prince.

As they started up to the helipad, Zamal stopped them.

"My apologies," he told them. "But the prince insists."

With that, he frisked each member quickly. When Zamal declared them to be clean, they resumed walking toward the helipad, where the crates of money awaited.

Zamal started to follow but then glanced into the empty cabin. It looked unchanged, except for two things. It smelled faintly of ammonia, and in the wastebasket was a handful of torn plastic, the remains of some kind of packaging. Zamal took out the refuse and read the few words he could find on them: One was "Mega Blast." Another read "Zapper-500."

Zamal scratched his head, baffled.

"What on earth is this stuff?" he thought.

STRIPPED OF ITS weapons, the copter nicknamed *Bad Dawg One* circled the LNG carrier once before landing on the helipad in front of the ship's massive stern-mounted superstructure.

The five pirates were waiting. Just as the doctor's drawing had indicated, four of them were standing in what appeared to be prearranged spots, one at each corner of the helipad. Each was carrying an AK-47 and had a machete tucked in his belt. As predicted, they were dressed like the tanker's crew and had their faces covered with bandanas save for their eyes. The fifth pirate was stationed on the railing about eight feet above; he held an RPG launcher.

Batman was piloting the copter; Twitch was in the copilot's seat. Nolan, Gunner and Crash were riding in the passenger compartment in back, straddling the first wooden crate. They were all eyeing the pirates, especially their weapons. More than ever, Whiskey knew one stray bullet, and this corner of the Indian Ocean would go up.

They waited in the copter, engine running, until the pirates motioned them to get out, one at a time.

Again, just as the doctor had said, the team members were subjected to an intense search. One by one, the pirates roughly frisked them, once, twice, three times. Then they played the metal-detecting wands all over their bodies, paying special attention to their boots and belts, looking for small, hidden firearms. Batman's metal hand and Twitch's false leg set off the wands, but no weapons were found.

Finally cleared, Batman gave the boss pirate the letter, handing it to him between the metal clasps of his hook.

"This is from the prince," he told the pirate. "It contains the conditions we've all agreed to."

The pirate took the letter, put it under his arm, and then looked at Batman's hand appliance. He asked, "Crocodile?"

Batman shook his head and pointed to the pirate on the railing above and said, "RPG."

The pirate boss smiled, displaying a set of red-stained teeth. He put his AK-47 in his left hand and held up his right, showing that it was missing its index finger. He laughed and said to Batman, "Crocodile."

"Unlucky you," Batman said.

Then, in one swift motion, Batman flicked a six-inch razor out of his hook and slashed it across the pirate's throat.

At the same moment, Twitch yanked off his prosthetic leg to reveal a twelve-inch-long serrated bayonet. He brought it over his shoulder and down on the second pirate, splitting him open from his chin to his navel.

Gunner and Nolan instantly reached into their crotch areas, the one place they knew the Muslims would not search, and retrieved tiny plastic water guns. Both were filled with ammonia. They fired at the eyes of the third and fourth pirates standing about five feet away, causing both to drop their guns. Two kicks to the scrota, two kicks to the temples, and both pirates were dead.

The pirate up on the railing was looking down on all this in shock. The blood, the screams—it had all happened so fast. He finally pointed his weapon down at the team but hesitated. This gave Crash enough time to pull a Zapper-500 toy dart gun from his crotch, go into a three-point stance, and squeeze the plastic trigger. The dart, sharpened to a razor point, hit the pirate in the throat, puncturing his windpipe. The man gagged horribly, fell over, and drowned in his own blood.

And that's all it took. In a matter of seconds, the pirates were dead, victims of the Muslim prohibition of feeling another man's private parts. As a result, the ship and crew were safe. And the prince's $200-million ransom was still intact.

All without using gunplay.

Sort of.

"Lose the evidence," Batman reminded them.

Nolan, Gunner and Crash calmly walked to the side of the ship and threw their toy guns over the side.

Then, looking around and seeing a job well done, Batman said, "OK, let's get some lunch."

PART TWO

The *Other* Pirates of the Caribbean

2

THE FIFTY-FIVE-FOOT LUXURY yacht *Mary C* was in trouble.

Boaters traveling between Miami and the Bahamas just after sunrise reported seeing the vintage Rybovich sports craft spinning slowly in a circle off North Bimini.

A U.S. Coast Guard HC-130 patrol plane, returning to its base in Clearwater, Florida, flew over the yacht around 8 A.M. and tried to establish radio contact with it, to no avail. Attempts by the Coast Guard liason office in Nassau to contact the yacht also failed.

With most of its assets deployed elsewhere—a large storm had blown through the Bahamas just three days before—the Coast Guard asked any law enforcement agency with a vessel in the area to head for the *Mary C* and render assistance.

As it happened, a patrol boat belonging to the Palm Beach County Sheriff's Department was just six miles north of the wayward yacht. The twenty-two-foot Boston Whaler, newly purchased by the sheriff's marine division, was on an early-morning shakedown cruise, checking out its long-range GPS-based navigation system.

The boat had three deputies onboard.

They were sent to investigate.

THEY FOUND THE *Mary C* a half-mile west of where it had first been sighted. It had run out of fuel, so it was no longer going in circles. The deputies used a grappling hook to pull alongside, and then two went aboard, climbing onto its stern.

They called out for anyone onboard, but got no response. Three Daiwa sports rods, already baited, hung in place. Obviously some deep-sea fishing had been planned. Nearby, a case of beer was on ice, along with some vodka and orange juice. Somewhere a radio was playing salsa music.

The deputies called out a second time, but again, there was no reply. The sliding door to the expansive cabin was partially open. They peeked inside.

Nothing looked out of place. Breakfast food and coffee sat on a table surrounded by leather couches. A TV nearby was on, turned to a religious station showing Easter services but with the sound on mute. All the cabin windows were closed and doors were secured. There was nothing unusual on the floor, nothing broken or upturned anywhere.

The deputies shouted directly into the cabin. Again, no reply.

They drew their weapons and stepped inside. It was more of the same. Nothing was out of place. They walked through the sitting area to the galley. It, too, was clean. Glasses, plates, bottles—all secured and where they ought to be. The fridge was filled with food and the vessel had plenty of drinking water.

They moved into the sleeping area, half expecting to find a body or two on one of the beds, a murder-suicide perhaps. But everything in the sleeping area was also in order. It was empty, and while there were no wallets or money lying around, everything else was in its place.

This was getting weird. Both deputies were veterans of the sheriff's marine division. They'd seen a lot of odd things on the job, but nothing like this.

They returned to the rear deck, holstered their weapons and contemplated the situation. There *were* pirates in these waters, though not the typical kind. They were more like drug addicts and thieves who would board yachts, sometimes in force, and rob the passengers and crew. Most times, they murdered anyone onboard to eliminate witnesses. Coming upon these pirated vessels, though, it was obvious to law enforcement what had happened: Bloodstains, bullet holes in the hull, and signs of a struggle usually told the tale.

But the *Mary C* looked as normal as any boat at sea could look—except it was empty. Not even any towels on the rear deck to hint the occupants had been lost while swimming.

The deputies climbed up to the bridge to find the steering column had not been set to drive the boat in circles; it had just been left unattended with the yacht's engines pushed half-speed forward. The radio, located next to the controls, indicated the last message: A call to a recorded weather service had been sent two hours earlier. So the *Mary C* had been adrift since 6 A.M. or so.

"The *Muy Capaz*, maybe?" one deputy finally asked.

The Muy Capaz was a gang of Bahamian criminals who attacked luxury boats at sea to get cash and valuables. Their name, Spanish for "very capable," was a loose indication that, unlike other gangs, they strived to leave behind as few clues as possible whenever they committed a crime. Though pretty much drug-addled and shabby, the Muy Capaz nevertheless had been known to wipe down surfaces for fingerprints and to clean up bloodstains.

But if some kind of crime had taken place on the *Mary C,* then the boat had not just been wiped down but *scrubbed* down, sanitized and everything put back in its place with mind-boggling efficiency.

"'I'm not sure the 'Muy Capaz' is this 'capaz,' " the other deputy replied. "Something else happened here."

"Like what?"

"Like UFOs? An abduction?"

The first deputy barely smiled.

"Don't even joke about that," he said.

THEY TOWED THE *Mary C* a mile east, to shallow water, where they dropped its anchor. Then they called the Bimini police, reported what they knew and turned the whole matter over to them.

But no sooner had this been done than the deputies received another call from the Coast Guard. A second boat had been spotted adrift about five miles south of their present position.

Would they please investigate?

THE DEPUTIES CAME upon the *Rosalie* fifteen minutes later.

It was a sailboat, sixty-five feet in length, with two masts. A real beauty. It was moving west, a few miles off the Bimini resort of Alice Town. All its canvas was set, but it was obviously drifting.

It took some adept maneuvering by the deputies to catch up and grapple the sailboat. They climbed aboard and immediately lowered the vessel's sails and tied off the steering wheel. Then they searched it.

Unlike the *Mary C,* the sailboat did have some life aboard. There were two canaries and a cat inside the cabin. The cat was spooked, though, and hid as soon as the deputies appeared.

The lawmen searched the sailboat stern to bow and back again. Every cabin was empty, but not in disarray. There were no signs of struggle or conflict. As before, there was plenty of food and water onboard, and the fuel tank for the sailboat's small inboard engine was full.

As on the *Mary C*, there was no way to tell if anything valuable was missing. From the number of cabins that appeared to have been occupied, the deputies determined at least six people had been aboard the sailboat. But while there were no wallets or billfolds lying about, there were several iPods, TVs, and even a Bose music system still onboard, just the type of thing pirates would normally steal.

The ship's log, written in a woman's hand, indicated the sailboat had left South Rocks Cay just after dawn, heading for Miami. This meant it had been adrift for about two and a half hours.

"If this is the Muy Capaz," one deputy said, "then they're having themselves a busy Easter morning."

AS BEFORE, THE deputies towed the vessel into shallower waters, dropped its anchor and contacted Bimini police. And finally, the deputies were able to do what they had come way out here for: test their boat's new navigation gear.

But just as they were about to contact their headquarters at West Palm Beach, they received yet another call from the Coast Guard.

A *third* pleasure boat had been spotted drifting not twenty miles from the deputies' current position.

Once again, the Coast Guard asked them to check it out.

THE *PRETTY PENNY* was sitting dead in the water about twelve miles north of the Bimini Road when the deputies found it. It was a sixty-five-foot Alberta, its engine not turning, its one sail taken down. It was motionless, and the water around it was motionless as well.

By this time the deputies were very weirded out.

Pirate attacks on pleasure boats plying these waters were

not unheard of. It happened more often than people thought. It just wasn't widely reported because everyone involved— like law enforcement and the media—knew the area's economy would suffer badly if the tourists thought there really *were* pirates in the Caribbean. Or, at least close to it.

But again, these so-called pirates were usually slovenly drug addicts in boats looking for money so they could cop their next fix.

What was happening this morning seemed to be something different.

The deputies boarded the *Pretty Penny* and found more of the same. A large, expensive yacht, in perfect condition, with no signs of struggle or conflict—but with no one onboard.

They found all the cabins were in order. They found lots of exotic women's clothing—bikinis and thongs—neatly folded on several of the bunks. A pot of coffee in the galley's stove was still warm.

Ominously, up on the bridge they found a man's watch that had stopped at 0815 hours, approximately the same time as the last entry in the ship's log, which was a brief comment about the good weather.

By coincidence, the *Pretty Penny* had come to a stop over a submerged coral reef. The deputies played out the anchor line to fifty feet and dropped it, securing the vessel in place. They made yet another call to the Bimini authorities and then decided they'd had enough strangeness for one morning.

Citing their dwindling fuel supply, they radioed their HQ to say they were returning to West Palm Beach.

EASTER TURNED COLD and rainy over southeast Florida.

By 2 P.M., Del Ray Beach had emptied out, leaving only

a couple of municipal employees working the holiday to get a head start on picking up the half ton of trash the morning's bathers had left behind.

Using nailed sticks and plastic bags to gather the litter, the two workers made their way up to the north end of the beach where the sandy, flattened-out shoreline became rocky. They knew a place here where they could hide from their boss and smoke a quick couple of joints.

They were just about to light up when they realized a boat had washed up right near their hiding spot. It was a twenty-two-foot outboard with powerful engines and a lot of antennas and wires sticking out of it. The side facing them was caved in, the result of the boat slamming up against the rocks in the incoming tide. There was no one on the boat or anywhere around it.

The workers couldn't help but investigate, the thought of picking up a few loose items as salvage crossing their minds. But that notion quickly dissipated when they reached the wreck and were able to see the still-intact port side, which had been facing away from them.

Written on the hull was the name of the boat's owner: the Palm Beach Sheriff's Department.

The two workers quickly stuffed the joints back into their pockets.

"What the hell happened here?" one whispered.

3

MARK CONLEY WAS sitting in the new headquarters of Ocean Security Services, Inc., trying to drink his morning cup of coffee. He was having a hard time of it, though, because the phone would not stop ringing.

Located on the top floor of the Kilos Shipping building, the imposing gray-and-glass skyscraper that looked out on the ancient seaport of Aden, the five-office suite was now home base for Team Whiskey. The vast Kilos Shipping Company had given them their first security job, so it was natural the team would make their patron's thirty-story building their first official business address. It had been open for exactly a week.

Each of the suite's five rooms had a specific function. One was devoted to communications. Another was filled with computers for hacking and gathering intelligence. A third room served as a crash pad for the team when they were in town. A fourth held most of their exotic weaponry. The fifth was an office—actually, just a cover for the other four. The sign on the door read: KILOS IMPORT-EXPORT ANALYSIS DIVISION. The suite's door was kept locked at all times.

Conley was head of Kilos Shipping's Middle East security department. With more than a hundred of the company's ships plying the high seas, it was a full-time job for the middle-aged ex-NYPD cop. But with the surprisingly quick success of Whiskey's anti-pirating unit, Conley had become the team's de facto booking agent as well. Since he'd arrived here a half hour earlier, more than a dozen people had called the OSS hotline looking to buy Team Whiskey's services—and it wasn't even 7 A.M.

His first official duty this morning was to sign for a diplomatic pouch that had been delivered by courier from the Saudi consulate. Inside was an envelope sealed with red wax. When Conley opened the envelope, an international money-wire transfer slip fell out. It was documentation for Prince Saud el-Saud's $15 million payment to the team for saving his LNG tanker.

Attached to the slip was a plain banker's check for an additional $1 million—a tip for the team's efforts. Conley sipped his coffee and smiled. This was the third time the team had done such a good job that the client saw fit to pay a gratuity.

These two payments increased the team's fortunes to nearly $25 million, tax-free, all of it made in just the past three months. This growing pile of cash was in a special Kilos-controlled vault within the Port of Aden National Bank. Under armed guard 24/7, it was accessible only to Conley and the Team Whiskey members.

Taking a brochure Nolan had left for him from his desk drawer, Conley realized the team's bank account was almost large enough to enable them to buy what they considered their ultimate anti-pirate weapon: a used British Aerospace Harrier jumpjet.

"Someday," he thought, returning the brochure to the drawer.

AROUND 8 A.M., Conley reheated his coffee, hoping for a break, but getting no such thing. In the past hour alone there had been twenty more calls, all of them from people desperate to buy Team Whiskey's unique protection services.

Luckily, Conley didn't have to actually answer the phone. He saw the name and company of each caller on his computer screen. After noting each call, he forwarded it directly to his voice mail, where a computer program converted the voice message to text. This way, Conley could read over the job offers without ever talking to anyone. It was categorizing all the information that took time.

At least his method of triaging the offers was simple: The highest-paying jobs that would take the least amount of effort got the most consideration; everything else got a pass. As it was, Whiskey had been released from a U.S. Navy rehab hospital in Italy only a few scant hours before the Saud el-Saud job materialized. Each member was still suffering the aftereffects of their small war against Zeek the Pirate. Batman Bob Graves had lost his hand. Nolan had nearly drowned in the Indian Ocean during a climatic death match with Zeek himself. Crash, Gunner and Twitch were also nursing a bevy of smaller wounds.

Conley knew these things also had to be taken into consideration when choosing the team's next job. That's why one particular offer appeared so intriguing. The climate was good. The problem seemed manageable, especially when compared to taking on Zeek's pirate army or protecting the Russian mob. And the price was right. And Conley thought the team could wrap up the gig in just a few days—a week at the most.

Plus, it was on the other side of the world, also a positive. Conley believed getting the team out of the Indian Ocean for a while was not a bad idea. Technically speaking, what they'd been doing in the area lately—arming cargo ships, running unauthorized combat missions inside sovereign borders—wasn't exactly legal. With just a little push, any number of seafaring countries could have them locked up for a slew of maritime violations.

"Yes," Conley thought, checking the job's details again. "A change of scenery will do them good."

4

Five days later

SNAKE NOLAN HAD looked forward to crossing the Atlantic.

The weather forecast had promised no storms, calm seas, and warm winds for most of the five days it would take to complete the journey.

Besides bringing him closer to the country he loved but could not enter legally, Nolan had envisioned himself actually relaxing during the trip. Playing poker with the guys, watching DVDs, maybe even doing some reading. The fact that a large Kilos container ship, the *Georgia June,* was sailing along with them, acting as an enormous floating bodyguard, took some of the uncertainty away from the 4,000-mile voyage west.

That concern came from the team's own vessel. Rusty, oily, with a single stack and four cargo masts, it looked barely seaworthy. But looks could be deceiving. Technically, it was a DUS-7 coastal freighter, the type of ship used for short trips up and down coastlines, and not normally for transoceanic journeys. Just 120 feet long and twenty-four feet wide, it looked every bit of its fifty-plus years afloat. It was so battered, if it had washed up on a beach somewhere, it wouldn't have gotten a second look.

In the eyes of Team Whiskey, though, its shabby appearance was an asset. When they first went to war against Zeek the Pirate, Kilos Shipping had offered them one of the company's "workboats," a barely disguised, intentionally misnamed vessel that was actually a long-range mega-yacht, full of communications equipment and weapons, like something from a James Bond movie. Though high on the comfort scale, Whiskey knew such a boat would have made them too obvious when operating in Zeek's Indonesian home waters, an area full of container ships, supertankers, steamers and fishing boats. So, Kilos gave them the DUS-7 instead.

It was exactly what the team needed. Like the Kilos workboats, the small freighter, in its former life, had transported highly sensitive cargos to some of the company's shadier customers. To this end, the DUS-7 had a so-called rubber room hidden deep within its lower decks. It was a compartment where up to ten tons of cargo—usually arms and ammunition—could be sealed off behind false panels that even the most ardent NATO search party would miss. In this hidden storage cabin now sat Team Whiskey's small arsenal of weapons, communications equipment and various gadgets of the special operations trade.

The DUS-7 had another important attribute: With not one, but two propulsion systems, the old coastal freighter was much faster than it looked.

Its primary means of motion was a dual diesel-based system that turned twin screws and moved the ship at about eighteen knots in a calm sea. But because the old freighter was specially adapted by Kilos for cargoes that absolutely had to get there—"sensitive shipments," in the company's parlance—Kilos engineers had added a small gas turbine as a second propulsion unit. Hundreds of gallons of seawater sucked into huge tanks in the hold of the ship were condensed and, using power from the spinning turbine, shot out the back of the ship at high velocity in the form of jet sprays. When the ship needed some extra speed and the crew turned on these jets, it was like switching on the afterburner in an F-16. With this added power, the freighter could top forty knots, faster than some of the U.S. Navy's speediest warships.

Along with the ship, Kilos had also provided Whiskey with a crew of five Senegalese nationals. Widely regarded as excellent sailors, these longtime employees of Kilos Shipping were loyal, smart, funny, and could pilot the ship under even the worst circumstances. They also knew their way around combat weaponry. But because their names were just about impossible to pronounce, the team just referred to them as the Senegals.

And the team had a nickname for their ship, too.

They called it the *Dustboat*.

AS IT TURNED out, Nolan slept for almost the entire trip west.

From the day they'd set off from southern Italy, the location of their rehab stay, and where the *Dustboat* had been docked, and went across the western Mediterranean Sea, out past Gibraltar, and into the Atlantic, it was as if he'd been injected with a sedative. He'd sleep, wake up, eat—and then fall right back to sleep again.

He felt so odd, he asked Crash, the team's medic, about it during one of his few waking moments. Was something wrong with him? Yes, there was, Crash replied. There was something wrong with *all* of them. Since they'd started their new enterprise three months before, they'd been so busy, none of them had gotten anything resembling a good night's sleep. The closest thing to it had been alcohol-induced slumber, which inevitably came with a hangover.

Crash's diagnosis: Nolan was suffering from exhaustion. They all were.

And the cure?

Sleep—and lots of it.

Nolan enjoyed the new experience. No card playing, no DVDs, and definitely no reading. Just deep, peaceful sleep.

Until their fourth night out on the Atlantic.

He had slept that whole day, and had planned to do the same that night. But sometime just after midnight, he suddenly woke up—and this time, when he lay down again, he didn't instantly fall back to sleep. Instead, his mind started racing, and for him, that was not a good thing. When the past ten years of his life started going through his head, it was like a highlights reel stuck in fast forward. Except these weren't exactly his favorite memories.

That last day at Tora Bora. Their OK from Higher Authority to pursue bin Laden, the excitement of actually seeing him, catching up to him, chasing him down, only to be called back at the worst moment by the pissheads in Washington—it was a reoccurring nightmare that Nolan couldn't stop, or even slow down. The battle that followed, unauthorized as it was, cost him his eye and Twitch his leg.

The aftermath. While the others were given dishonorable discharges and immediately booted from the military, Nolan was laid out as the ultimate sacrificial lamb. He had no lawyer, no means of defense, yet he was still court-martialed, found guilty by a secret court, sentenced to prison indefinitely and banned from ever setting foot on American soil again.

Frequent escape attempts followed, which led to him being bounced from prison to prison—Gitmo, Sardinia and finally Baghdad. He busted out twice from the Iraqi prison and was found walking across the desert intent on getting back to Afghanistan, back to Tora Bora, as if there he could resume his pursuit of the mass murderer.

Once he was released by the U.S. military more trouble followed, and Nolan was eventually thrown back into prison, this time in Kuwait. That's where the rest of the team found him.

Frustration at their subsequent low-paying jobs as security cops in Saudi Arabia led them to form their anti-piracy unit, and there had been no looking back since. But still, all the good things that had happened in the past three months could not erase memories of the horrific events he had experienced in the past ten years. Jailed, homeless, a man without a country? Some scars ran deep, and some wounds would never heal.

And then there was the *Dutch Cloud*.

His four days of slumber had brought their share of odd dreams, but the subject of the *Dutch Cloud* was a real-life ghost story. At least for Nolan.

It started with the team's gig for the Russian mob, to protect a cruise ship trip through the Aegean Sea. Saving the Red Mafia bigwigs from a mass poisoning attack had been a bonanza for Team Whiskey. Not only were they paid handsomely for three days of work, along with a $50,000 tip; their client, a mobster named Bebe, had passed on to the team valuable intelligence, which helped them catch up to and finally kill Zeek the Pirate. And it was Bebe who told Nolan about the *Dutch Cloud*.

It was a seemingly mythical vessel, a phantom ship said to have gone missing shortly after 9/11 and endlessly sailing the seas ever since, its contents unknown and the subject of much speculation. Bebe said that if the team were to capture the *Dutch Cloud*, they would be in for a reward of $50 million, payable by none other than the CIA.

It sounded like drunken Russian bullshit—and in truth both Nolan and Bebe were highly intoxicated when the mobster told him the tale. But then Nolan actually *saw* the ghost ship. It happened while Whiskey was heading toward an island near Zanzibar to help recover buried treasure containing a billion-dollar microchip. One night, he had just awakened from an alcohol-induced dream, when he went out on the deck of the *Dustboat* in a gale and saw the spectral ship pass about a thousand yards off their port side, only to be quickly lost again in the storm and fog.

Or at least that's what he *thought* happened. Because when he woke up that next morning, brutally hung over, he found himself in the care of the Senegals, who for some reason had not seen what he thought he had just seen a few hours earlier.

Another strange memory.

NOW AFTER MANY days and nights of deep slumber, he was suddenly wide awake, feeling the Atlantic rolling the *Dustboat*, his heart pounding in his chest. He felt anxious, he needed air, and he was in no mood to contemplate what lay ahead or what had happened before.

So he rolled out of his bunk, grabbed a six-pack from his small fridge and went up on deck.

At the moment their guardian angel, the *Georgia June,* was sailing about a mile in front of them. The rest of the team was asleep and the Senegals were steering the ship. Nolan walked back to the stern alone, and the beer started going down fast. He quickly quaffed three beers and the darkness engulfed him, and that's when he saw it again.

The *Dutch Cloud*. It was moving north just as the *Dustboat* was moving west. It was about a thousand yards off the stern and looked just as it had the first time he saw it: a long, dark container ship, bearing one yellow, one green and one red light. Painted mostly black, it had a white bridge. But as before, the vessel seemed strangely lifeless, as if there was no one in control, no one on board.

It was a dark night with no moon, and Nolan didn't have his one-eye electronic telescope with him. He could see the ship with his good eye for only about ten seconds, and then it was gone, covered over once again by the darkness.

In fact, it disappeared *so* fast that he immediately wondered if he'd seen it at all—or if it was a figment of his imagination or a side effect of his clinical exhaustion.

Or maybe he was still asleep and dreaming.

HE WALKED UP to the bridge and was greeted warmly by the Senegals.

He hesitated to ask if they'd seen the mystery ship, since the last time this had happened, they'd seen nothing.

So he asked them instead: "Are we and the *Georgia June* the only ones out here tonight?"

"Just us and the sea monsters," one Senegal replied in his native French.

Nolan slumped into a seat and another Senegal passed him a cup of *mooch*, the slightly hallucinogenic liquor favored by many North Africans.

"Drink this and maybe we'll see some UFOs, too," one said to him.

Nolan hesitated—but only for a moment.

Maybe this is just what I need, he thought.

AS USUAL, WHENEVER Nolan drank mooch with the Senegals, he wound up laughing crazily and seeing the stars above light up in different colors—and this time was no different. And then, suddenly—*poof!*—the next thing he knew, it was morning and he was lying on the bridge's bunk.

He looked up to see the Senegals were now wearing brightly colored flower shirts, like those sported in the tropics.

One of them handed him a mug of coffee. At that moment, a rain squall passed them by and they were suddenly bathed in brilliant sunshine.

Then, suddenly, Nolan saw Crash go flying past the bridge window, head first, followed by a great splash on the port side. Gunner soon followed—with another huge splash. Batman went past the window next, and on his heels came Twitch, prosthetic leg and all. Two more huge splashes.

Nolan froze. Had his four colleagues had just fallen off the ship?

It was so weird, Nolan was convinced he was still under the influence of the mooch. He struggled to his feet, and through bleary eyes looked out the bridge window.

In front of him was a vision of heaven, a string of tropical islands that stretched forever in both directions. Blue water, white sand, and a breeze gently flowing through the palm trees.

That's when it finally dawned on Nolan.

His colleagues didn't fall off the ship—they were diving off the mast to swim in the warm, inviting water. And that could only mean they'd come to the end of their journey.

He just looked at the Senegals, who laughed at his confusion.

"Welcome, mon," one of them said in a bad imitation of Jamaican-tinged English. "Welcome to the Bahamas."

THEY WERE ANCHORED off a small pinprick of land called Denny Cay.

Located at the far eastern edge of the Eleuthera Cays, it was shaped like a quarter moon laid on its side. Barely a half-mile long and mostly covered in tropical flora, it had a white beach dotted by a handful of huts and a single finger dock that reached out into the crystal-clear water. Space for three small boats comprised the entirety of its harbor.

Paradise.

Anchored about a half mile farther offshore was the *Georgia June*, watching over them like a big brother, as always. Looking out the *Dustboat*'s bridge window, Nolan

could see some of the container ship's crewmen were diving off its bow, enjoying the warm waters, too.

So, why not him?

He hadn't been in the water since his near-fatal battle
with Zeek the Pirate. Having come as close as one possibly
could to drowning, Nolan wasn't sure he ever wanted to go
back in the water again.

But now, with the bright sunshine and the warm Bahamian breeze, he was suddenly obsessed with the idea of
jumping off the tallest part of the *Dustboat* into the crystal-
clear bay.

It was not to be, though. In the time it took him to race to
his quarters, get on a pair of old shorts, and then climb the
mast, a helicopter had appeared, and was circling the ship.

It was a large Bell 430, considered to be among the Ca-
dillacs of helicopters. It was painted blue and light purple,
the colors of the islands, with a splash of yellow up around
its engine cowlings, representing the sun.

"We got a meeting—and our ride is here," Batman said
just as Nolan reached the top of the deck. Then he looked
at Nolan and added: "Are you wearing *that*?"

WITHIN FIVE MINUTES after the copter landed, Team
Whiskey had climbed aboard. The pilots told them to strap
in, then they took off and headed south.

The team was used to doing things on the hush-hush—
and except for the gaudy air taxi, this gig was no different.
Conley had told them nothing about the job ahead, prefer-
ring to let them relax and recharge during the ocean crossing. The team assumed whoever they were meeting would
be high on the food chain of some intelligence agency or
military organization. And the request that they attend this
meeting in civilian clothes was par for the course. They

could understand someone not wanting them to stick out in their bright blue combat suits.

"Just as long as they pay us," Batman said as the chopper streaked through the air. "Preferably in cash."

The Bell 430 carried them over a long line of Bahamian outer islands. The team, after operating almost exclusively in the Indian Ocean and near the Java Sea, was enchanted as they looked down on the clear blue water at what seemed like another planet. They could actually make out the sea bottom in many places.

During the flight, Batman was particularly animated. He'd lived in the Bahamas just before Whiskey re-formed.

"If we can wrap this up quickly, maybe I can get back to my old digs," he said, nose pressed against the copter's window. "I could retrieve some expensive booze I left there. Maybe even crash there and do some bone fishing."

THOUGH THE FLIGHT took less than twenty minutes, they had flown a zig-zag course—another nod to security. They finally turned due west and were soon approaching the island of Oyster Cay, in Exuma Sound. About five miles long and half that wide, it was thick with lush, emerald-colored vegetation.

But instead of seeing some staid and hidden military-type building on the isolated island, the team saw instead what looked like a large saucer-shaped resort located on the island's highest point. The futuristic building was about ten stories high, surrounded by swimming pools, waterfalls, golf courses and hundreds of perfectly shaped palm trees.

"Are we in the right place?" Gunner asked looking down at the island. "This looks like a Disneyland for billion-aires."

"Yeah," Crash said. "If there was a Disneyland on Mars."

* * *

THE COPTER SET down on a helipad next to the saucer-shaped building. The team climbed out, expecting to find an escort to lead them to the meeting.

But instead of a person in uniform or a CIA spook type, they were met by a young woman dressed like a high-priced hooker from the future: micro-miniskirt, tight silver top, high heels, platinum blond hair.

"I think I've seen this movie before," Batman said. "Was it *Goldfinger* . . . or *Thunderball*?" Like the ultra-luxurious resort itself, the girl *did* look like something from a 007 movie.

She ushered them to the rear entrance of the saucer building. Again, here they might have expected to be searched or led through a metal detector, or some other security device. But none was in evidence.

Instead, the team was brought to a large glass-enclosed area that was a cross between an arboretum and an upscale singles bar, with palm trees larger and more carefully manicured than those outside. Tropical birds flew above and a light mist fell from the crystal ceiling; refreshing if almost indiscernible. Tables containing bottles of champagne and dishes of exotic food seemed to stretch on forever.

About a dozen women were sitting around the large rectangular table in the center of the room; others were chatting in small groups nearby. All of them were beautiful; some distractingly so.

As Batman put it: "If they ever make a movie about us, I want all these women to play themselves."

So the team members were surprised for a third time. Their hosts typically were a gang of military stiffs, CIA spooks in bad suits or some billionaire who wanted his ship back. The only males here were an elderly black gentleman wearing a bright white seersucker suit, sitting at one end of the table, and a bearded man in a pricey three-piece suit, at the other.

The bevy of beauties finally realized Whiskey had arrived. The team was directed to seats at the midpoint of the table, where they found a printed agenda, which included a list of the meeting's organizers. Only then did the team realize the people they'd sailed across the Atlantic to work for were not someone's military or the CIA.

They were travel agents. More accurate, they were public relations agents from some of the largest, most prestigious travel agencies in the Bahamas.

There were a couple dozen in all, known collectively as the Bahamian Association for Business Enterprise.

Reading this, Batman leaned over to Nolan and whispered: "They got the acronym right, anyway."

The person chairing the meeting was a stunning blonde with a lilting British accent. Her name was Jennessa, and she, like the others, looked like she belonged in a fashion catalog. She introduced everyone around the table, but Nolan, dazzled by her beauty, barely heard her.

She read a brief statement highlighting the recent successes Whiskey had enjoyed against international pirates: saving the Saud el-Saud LNG tanker; the battle to take back the Indian warship *Vidynut;* and the rest.

Her account didn't get into all the details of these actions, but it didn't need to. Team Whiskey was successful in thwarting pirate threats of all shapes and sizes, and that's all the consortium of travel agency reps wanted to hear. Because they had a problem. A *pirate* problem. And like customers stranded in a resort during a hurricane or enduring bad shrimp on a high-priced cruise ship, they were willing to pay anything to fix it quick.

"We have a huge predicament that's getting worse by the

day," Jennessa said, finally addressing the team directly. "A pirate gang has been preying on pleasure boats around the Islands. After these pirates attack, police agencies find boats adrift, valuables gone and passengers missing.

"These criminals are brutal, but they're also smart. They are very careful not to leave any evidence behind. No fingerprints, no footprints; no blood, no bullet casings. This is why they are called the 'Muy Capaz' gang. Roughly translated, that means 'very capable.' And it's apt. They know the more careful they are, the harder it will be for law enforcement to catch them or to prove anything if they do."

She pushed a button and a screen descended out of the mist of the ceiling. She began a PowerPoint presentation showing photographs of vessels suspected to have recently fallen victim to the Muy Capaz.

Most of the photos had the same eerie theme running through them: While they showed obvious ransacking of a particular vessel, each crime scene was devoid of any incriminating evidence. A few marked "ES" even showed boats that were in almost perfect order, as if photographed for a magazine spread.

Jennessa went on. "We're not really sure what the Muy Capaz do with their victims. They might throw them in the water, maybe with their hands and feet tied, ensuring they will drown quickly. Some of our waters have sharks or other flesh-eating fish in them. Plus, with the Gulf Stream, the currents around here can be so powerful, a body could wind up in the middle of the Atlantic in no time. Whatever the reason, no bodies have ever been found after a Muy Capaz attack. Not a one. And for some reason, the pirates always surprise their victims—and I mean *all* of their victims, because no one has ever so much as sent out a distress call in any of these cases."

She ran a few more slides.

"One thing the victims seem to have in common," she said. "They were all fairly wealthy, or at least well-off. They all either owned a very expensive yacht or they were chartering one at a hefty price. We don't have a clue of the kind of vessels the pirates are using."

More slides.

"There's something else unusual about the Muy Capaz. Their attacks seem to come in waves. They'll hit a few boats one night—usually no more than three—and then we don't see them for a while. But whenever they do it, they come and go like demons. No witnesses. No stray radio transmissions. Nothing. That's why Dr. Robert is here. He's an expert on this sort of thing."

Dr. Robert was the man in the natty three-piece suit. He was actually the best-dressed person in the room, the women included. He was in his early thirties and had a breezy arrogance about him.

He rattled off some credentials: a PhD in psychological profiling, a book called *The Superstitious Criminal*, appearances on many U.S. TV talk shows.

"I can tell you without equivocation that the way this gang operates is connected to a voodoo ritual of some sort," he announced, as if he were beginning a college lecture. "I can also tell you these attacks are definitely connected to the full moon. My research shows without question that this gang is more active when the full moon is near.

"I call it the 'Wolfman Complex,' which happens to be the title of my next book. For instance, the last time the gang hit was a week ago, on Easter Sunday. Three boats were attacked; the moon was full that night. The pattern runs roughly the same through the past year or so. Therefore, the pirates will be active again in about three weeks, which should give you gentlemen enough time to track them down and do something about them."

He pushed a set of five three-ring binders in the team's direction.

"It's all in there," he said. "My profile, my recommendations, my statistics—and a coupon for 10 percent off my next book."

With that, Dr. Robert gathered up his briefcase and his paperwork. Overhead, they could hear a helicopter coming in for a landing.

"And now, if you'll excuse me," he said. "I'm due back in the States this afternoon. I'm taping *Dr. Phil* tomorrow."

And off he went.

Jennessa resumed her slide show. The images began flashing by faster now. According to her figures, the Muy Capaz had attacked more than twenty yachts in the past year or so.

"But in the last few months they've been far more aggressive than before," she told the team. "And that's why we called you. As it is right now, most of these incidents have been given very little publicity by the Bahamian media. Most people like to think the reporters are simply being lazy, but we know, just as their bosses know, that just like shark attacks and hurricanes, making a big deal out of these incidents would not be good for anyone. The economy, the citizens who live out here, people who work out here, TV and newspaper advertising. *No one.* If news about these criminals was widespread—especially with all the nasty stuff we hear about the Somali pirates these days—the entire Bahamian tourist industry could crash and burn in a matter of weeks. That's why we're reluctant to even call them 'pirates.' Even though that's what they are."

There was murmured agreement around the table.

"Plus, technically, there are some sticky questions about the jurisdiction of these matters. Bahamian waters. International waters. U.S. waters. Who knows? And with no bodies, there's no way anyone can really take the lead in going after these killers, again not without making headlines. So, along with our friends in the Organization of American States, we've managed to assure a lot of the parties concerned that *we* will take care of the problem for them. That *we* will provide the solution. And that solution, gentlemen, is *you*."

She took a plain white envelope from her breast pocket. "We are prepared to pay you five million dollars to find these pirate people and eliminate them, quickly and quietly."

Jennessa motioned to the older black man sitting nearby.

"Our friend, Mr. Jobo here, is a member of the Organization of American States's law enforcement division. He has special arrest powers in the Bahamas and as a formality he will make you his deputies. But again, the only thing we ask is that you do this job quickly and quietly, as one of our biggest times of year—college Spring Break—is coming up."

Mr. Jobo stood up.

"I would never suggest to you how to do your job," he began in a thick Caribbean accent. "But be aware these Muy Capaz people are brutal murderers that the world would be better off without. So, if you find yourself up against them, take the steps necessary to protect yourselves at all costs, and I mean preemptively if you have to. Your rule of thumb should be: 'gloves off.' "

Then Mr. Jobo read a prepared statement, swearing in Team Whiskey as deputies of the OAS. It was more than a little awkward.

When he was done, he passed them a small leather case. Nolan opened it to find five police badges.

"These are for you," Jobo said. "Just to make it legal. We also have uniforms."

He passed them a duffle bag. Batman reached inside and took out the shirt and pants of an OAS deputy—they were ugly brown, with red piping. The bag also contained five nightsticks.

"Wear all that in good health and with good luck," the OAS man concluded. Then he sat down again.

Jennessa walked around to the team's side of the table and gave Nolan an envelope containing a bundle of documents and a half dozen DVDs.

"You will find a lot of information on the Muy Capaz in there," she told him directly, brushing up against him on purpose. "Some of it comes from Bahamian law enforcement sources, which won't be much help, and some of it we generated on our own. The gang's leader is a man named Charles Black. He's a descendant of authentic Bahamian pirates and he displays a lot of the same characteristics. Ruthless, bloodthirsty, perverted. We believe he's also involved in moving large quantities of drugs. In fact, we believe these pirate attacks are simply ways to get money to finance his drug operations.

"The Muy Capaz are also heavily armed, thanks to Cuban weapons dealers. They have a hideout somewhere in the islands that no Bahamian law enforcement agency has been able or willing to find. I think your main goal should be to find this hideout and nip the problem in the bud."

Jennessa smiled sweetly.

"Any questions?" she asked the team.

Twitch raised his hand. He was usually the least talkative member of Whiskey.

"Can you repeat those slides that were marked 'ES?' " he asked her.

Jennessa did as requested.

"They seem different from the rest," Twitch said. "The others show disarray—obvious signs of a struggle. If not blood, then at least evidence that the boat's occupants met with a bad end. Yet, these three vessels don't have any of that. They're neat as pins. Any idea why?"

Jennessa shook her head no. "Actually, those slides show the most recent attacks, the ones from Easter Sunday, thus the 'ES' tag. It was because of them that we finally decided to contact you. We believe this is proof the Muy Capaz have become more emboldened with this last wave. Three plea- sure boats were found drifting on Easter morning, no sign of their passengers, absolutely wiped clean and nothing out of place. Then, a police boat that had investigated all three was later found washed up near Palm Beach—its officers long gone. Now, with these three deputies still officially listed as missing, this hasn't become a 'cop-killer thing' yet, if you know what I mean. But again, in our opinion, these last few slides are telling us that the Muy Capaz is becoming more able, and more efficient in leaving no clues behind."

Twitch just stared at the slides as they slowly passed across the screen again.

"Or maybe," he said under his breath, "they're telling us something else."

5

IT WAS AN unusual airplane, a leftover from World War II, rebuilt and customized.

It started its life as an Arado Ar-95W, an amphibious biplane designed in the mid-1930s by the German military and sold to the Chilean Air Force just before the war. It had an art deco look to it, lots of curved surfaces and stainless steel accents. The large, front-mounted engine spun a huge

wooden propeller. Below its bi-wings was a large floatplane.

At some point, the plane's original thirty-five-foot fuselage had been stretched to forty-four feet and expanded to
accommodate a six-person passenger compartment. The
addition of an enclosed cockpit provided side-by-side seats
for a pilot and copilot. Four Plexiglas observation bubbles
were installed along both sides of the fuselage, making it
perfect for aerial sightseeing, and retractable landing gear
was added. The interior of the plane featured highly polished wood and gleaming aluminum, and was now equipped
with a quadraphonic sound system. The result was a seventy-
year-old hot rod that flew.

But the airplane's uniqueness didn't end there. The Ar-95W
was also foldable. Its wings, slightly swept back in the original design, hung on hinges that allowed them to be folded
back and down. The rear third of the fuselage was also
hinged and could be folded forward. The struts that held the
pontoons folded upward. Even the propeller was hinged to
be folded backward.

The odd, flexible design came from the notion that, had
the Ar-95W gone into mass production, it would have been
an ideal recon aircraft for German U-boats, because in its
folded-up position, it could be carried inside the submarine
itself.

So, the plane was very unusual.

But not any more unusual than its owner.

COLONEL CAT WAS in his middle forties, though his
long ZZ Top beard made him look older. He always wore
the same clothes: tattered island shirt, ragged shorts, dirty
sneakers and a long-sleeve denim jacket. He was well known
around the Fort Lauderdale airfield where he housed the
Ar-95W and all over the Bahamas. He had the Caribe look

and the demeanor down pat. If you wanted to go, he was the man who'd fly you to Margaritaville.

Colonel Cat hired out his unusual seaplane for a number of functions. He gave sightseeing tours of weird Bahamian locations, like the Stairs of Atlantis, the Tongue of the Ocean and the islands' mysterious Blue Holes. He would take people deep-sea fishing, flying out to an ocean location to fish right from the cabin of the plane. He also flew scuba enthusiasts to hard-to-reach dive sites.

A lot of his business, though, involved transporting people who had chartered yachts waiting for them in the Bahamas. Many of these customers were novice sailors not experienced enough to handle what could be a rough crossing over from Florida, a transit that involved fighting the fast-moving and unpredictable Gulf Stream. Other charter customers were people who might be carrying items they did not want airport security to see, or for whatever reason didn't have a valid passport. Some were just out-and-out criminals. Most wanted to travel without leaving a paper trail.

These special clients usually had money and weren't afraid to spend it, allowing Cat to charge premium prices for his shuttle service. In most cases the flight from Fort Lauderdale to the Bahamas took under an hour, and as an extra bonus Cat could land the customer right next to his chartered boat. He even helped with their luggage, whatever it might contain.

As Cat liked to say: "Discretion is my middle name."

HE HAD TWO customers this morning; they were typical in just about every way.

He was a sixty-ish married, wealthy banking executive from Ohio. She was a "hostess" at a bar on Miami's South Beach. She was one-third his age and stunning.

They had met only recently and were in a whirlwind romance of sorts. The executive had quietly chartered a yacht for three days out of Alice Town in North Bimini, intent on getting some alone time with his new paramour.

He'd seen Colonel Cat's ad in the local *Beach Scene Magazine* and called. Cat got the banker to agree to pay $1,000—cash—for a private flight over to Bimini and back.

CAT FUELED HIS plane and was ready to go from the Fort Lauderdale airport by 9 A.M. The happy couple arrived by limo a short time later.

He loaded their luggage. The banker was clearly drunk with lust. Cat couldn't blame him; the hostess *was* gorgeous.

They took off at nine-fifteen and were soon heading east. The hostess sat up front; the banker was behind her, massaging her bare shoulders as they flew. After a lot of small talk, Cat went into his pitch.

"If you have a few extra minutes, I can show you some interesting sights," he began. "Lots of strange things out here. Some people don't realize it, but the Bahamas are right in the middle of the Bermuda Triangle."

The couple agreed, and once over North Bimini, Cat began pointing out various places of curiosity. The Stairs of Atlantis. The area of ocean where the famous "Flight 19" was thought to have gone down. An oval reef formation called UFO Rock. And finally, an isolated island the locals called "Via-grass Cay."

The banker asked Cat the meaning of its name.

Cat explained the people who lived on the island had cultivated a strain of marijuana that, in addition to providing a long-lasting high, also was an herbal Viagra.

This was a full-blown symphony to the banker's ears. He quickly asked Cat how he could buy some of the weed.

Cat remained coy. He'd done this before.

"It's impossible to get," he replied. "The people who live down there are very picky who they share it with."

By this time, Cat had turned the plane back to the southwest and was heading for Alice Town, where the couple's chartered yacht awaited.

But the banker was insistent.

"There must be a way," he said, slipping five hundred-dollar bills into Cat's shirt pocket. "Am I right?"

THEY LANDED TWO minutes later. Cat taxied up to the waiting yacht and helped the pair unload their luggage, including the girl's sizable jewelry case.

As she climbed aboard the yacht, Cat pulled the banker aside.

Cat asked him: "Where will you be tonight?"

"We'll be moored near an island called Thomas Cay," the banker replied. "Do you know it? Real isolated. No one around to interfere."

Cat nodded. "I know the place. If I can snag a bag for you, I'll fly it in after dark. If I can't, I'll return this five spot when I fly you folks home in three days. Deal?"

"Deal."

They shook hands and Cat returned to the floatplane.

Waving merrily to the couple, he took off, circled the yacht once, then headed back to Fort Lauderdale.

HE MET HIS next two customers at 11 A.M.

They were a middle-aged couple from Arizona. He was an author; she was his research assistant. He wrote books on the Bermuda Triangle and its alleged UFO connection—but his latest book was in trouble. Because he had nothing really new to say on the topic and no photos of any consequence, he'd written the book at home in Tucson, fabricating all of it. His publisher had caught a whiff of the hoax and demanded an authentic book or a return of the hefty advance.

Desperate, the pair had hired a small research vessel to cruise around the Bahamas in an effort to find something— *anything*—to write about, all without wanting their publisher to know. They were especially looking for photographs of UFOs, which as hard as they might be to provide, were by now being demanded by the publisher.

The flight over to the Bahamas was a bit tense, though Cat gradually filled it with small talk about seeing strange lights in the skies over the Bahamas for years. In fact, he said, he'd taken many pictures of them himself.

By the time they touched down near the Great Harbour Cays, the author was begging to buy Cat's UFO photos at $250 an image.

"Tell me where you'll be tonight," Cat suggested, helping unload the couple's luggage onto their leased yacht. "I'll fly back with the photos. If you like them, then we can talk."

CAT'S NEXT CUSTOMER flew out of Fort Lauderdale at 2 P.M.

He was a professional sports fisherman from Alabama. A lucrative tournament was being held in the Bahamas in two weeks. It was going to be televised and would award large cash prizes. The fisherman wanted to get to the islands early and relax before the tourney.

Or at least that was his story. A few minutes after taking off, the fisherman admitted the contest was to be held at a yet-to-be-disclosed location somewhere off South Bimini. His plan was to go around the South Bimini islands in his rented boat looking for likely places and trying his best to get a feel for them. It was a violation of the contest rules—

which was why he'd hired Cat to fly him over. Again, no paper trail.

"I might know a better way," Cat told him.

"Which is?" the man asked.

"I'm flying a couple of that tourney's judges out here in a few days," he said. "And they've already faxed me a list of their destinations. One of them *must* be where the tourney is being held, right?"

The fishermen couldn't believe his luck.

"How much?" he asked.

"I couldn't take anything," Cat protested weakly.

"Consider it a tip, a bonus," the fisherman said.

"Tell me where you're going to be tonight," Cat said. "I'll fly out with the maps. You look at them, figure out the sweet spot—and then we can talk about a tip. Deal?"

The fisherman gave him an enthusiastic fist bump.

"Deal," he said.

Off Thomas Cay
Six Hours Later

THE BANKER WAS sitting on the stern of his rented yacht. The girl was up on the bow, at the opposite end of the boat, as far away from him as possible.

Night had come. The last of the sun's rays were disappearing over the horizon and the stars were coming out above. A half moon was rising in the east.

The banker took a long, sad sip of his scotch. "This was a big mistake," he thought out loud. Just as he had feared, his performance so far had been underwhelming.

Then he heard a noise off in the distance. He looked up and saw a light approaching from the west.

"Damn," he whispered. "Could this be the cavalry?"

He watched the light as it flew overhead and started a long slow turn down toward the isolated bay where the chartered yacht was anchored.

The banker was on his feet as the Ar-95W floatplane came down and skipped along the water. The girl was suddenly at his side.

The plane taxied up next to the yacht, so close the banker was concerned its long wings might actually clip the leased boat. But at that moment, he would gladly have paid for the damage. If the wacky pilot was carrying what he'd promised, it might just turn around this disaster yet.

The pilot skillfully maneuvered the plane so its rear hatch was nearly flush with the yacht's stern. The banker threw out a short gangplank; it just reached the rear door of the odd airplane. The hatch opened and the banker expected to see the bearded pilot walking out, hopefully carrying a bag of the good stuff.

What he saw instead were four men in ragged clothes pointing assault rifles at him.

The banker froze. The girl screamed. The first two men came across the gangplank and hit the banker hard, knocking him to the deck. Terrified, the girl ran through the cabin—two of the men chased after her. The banker tried to get to his feet but was knocked down again. This time, his assailant kept his bare foot on the banker's throat, not allowing him to move. The banker could see that, in addition to his rifle, the man was carrying a huge machete in his belt.

These guys aren't the police, he thought.

The next thing he knew, the banker was looking up at Colonel Cat. In the panic and confusion, the banker thought that somehow these armed men had hijacked the pilot and his plane. But then he saw Cat looking down at him and grinning darkly.

"How's your vacation so far?" Cat asked him snidely.

"I *trusted* you!" the banker screamed back at him.

"Sorry, dude," Cat replied. "I really am . . . but I got needs."

For the first time, the banker saw Cat was holding a small copper pipe with a silver bowl—a crack pipe.

"You're a fucking crackhead," the banker cursed at him. "Doesn't that figure."

Cat shrugged. "And I got a bad gambling habit, too. But you're a lame dick pothead. So what's worse?"

The banker was yanked to his feet and brought into the yacht's cabin. By this time, the other intruders had captured the girl and were holding her on the deck face up. One was forcing her to drink saltwater.

"What are you doing to her?" the banker screamed at him. *"Who are you people?"*

One of the intruders hit him hard with his open hand, sending him to the deck yet again. That's when the banker realized that all of the intruders, including the pilot, were wearing clear surgical gloves.

They don't want to leave fingerprints, he thought.

The girl was pulled up to her knees. The saltwater caused her to vomit heavily, expelling her large diamond ring, swallowed just moments before.

Two intruders then ransacked the yacht, going through the couple's luggage and finding money, BlackBerrys and more jewelry, all while the two others held the banker and the girl down on the deck with their bare feet.

The girl was looking over at the banker, absolutely terrified.

"Don't worry," he managed to tell her. "It will be OK."

THE GUNMEN TOOK just five minutes to go through the sixty-five-foot yacht.

They not only stole all the couple's valuables, they also

took the yacht's GPS system, its satellite radio and its flat-screen TVs.

They were incredibly efficient, despite their ragged appearance. Through it all, Colonel Cat sat on the stern, taking tokes from his crack pipe.

The ransacking over, the gunmen prepared to leave. Two carried their booty onto the airplane; Colonel Cat returned to the cockpit and started the engine. The banker and the girl were pulled to their feet. Both were praying the pirates would just leave. But that wasn't the plan.

At the point of two machetes, the banker and the girl were marched into the floatplane, and soon, the strange aircraft was airborne again.

CAT STEERED THE Arado northeast, heading toward the open ocean.

The pirate named Crabbie was sitting beside him, counting the wad of cash they'd taken from the yacht. Crabbie was the senior man of the group. The rest of the gang was in the passenger compartment holding down the banker and the girl.

"How far out do you want to go?" Cat asked the pirate.

Crabbie looked out the cockpit window; the half moon was glowing off the calm sea below.

"You have two more pigeons to visit tonight?" he asked Cat in heavily accented English.

"Yes—I think good ones, or at least as good as these two," Cat replied.

"Not too far out then," Crabbie said.

They flew for another five minutes; by this time they were more than a hundred-fifty miles north of Bimini, over the Atlantic Ocean, with no land in sight.

Finally, Crabbie looked back at the other pirates and nodded.

One opened the plane's rear door. It was only then that the banker and the girl realized what was about to happen.

The banker started fighting madly, but it was useless. The pirates were strong and it was obvious that they'd done this sort of thing before.

The banker gave it one last struggle, punching two of the pirates, but he was quickly overwhelmed. The pirates threw him out the open door. As he fell they could hear his screams, finally drowned out by the sound of the wind racing by.

The girl was next. She became hysterical, crying, promising the pirates anything, including sex, if they would only spare her life. But they weren't interested. They were in a hurry.

She began fighting, too, and they had to hit her a few times to subdue her. It took longer than it should have, but finally they shoved her out the door as well. As with the banker, they watched her fall, screaming, to her death.

Two victims, no witnesses. And no bodies to be discovered. The sharks and the deep water would see to that.

Crabbie patted Cat on the shoulder twice.

"OK, let's turn back," he told the pilot. "More treasure awaits."

6

COLONEL CAT WOKE up the next day, worn out and hung over.

He'd bought a large bag of crack after the third flight with the Muy Capaz, joining the pirates in a seedy Bimini bar once their work was done and smoking it all. He'd returned to Florida just before sunrise, flying the sixty miles from Bimini to Fort Lauderdale in a narcotic haze. Landing, putting the plane away, driving to his condo in Cooper City: it was all a blur.

He didn't mind helping the Muy Capaz—he had no conscience, no qualms when money was involved. But he couldn't keep falling into the same pattern of behavior that the pirates always did: get a bunch of money and blow it on drugs and booze before the night was through. That's exactly what happened last night.

His bedroom TV was on. Through bleary eyes, he saw nothing on the news crawl that mentioned any missing persons in the Bahamas. This was usually the way it went. It would take the owners at least a week to locate their chartered yachts; only then would they suspect something was really wrong. And by the time the Bahamian cops realized the Muy Capaz had struck again—well, it was a pretty good bet they wouldn't be calling a news conference to blab to the world about it. And because Cat never left a paper trail, when it came to who he flew and where, there was little chance anyone would connect him to the disappearances.

So, it had been clean and quick. If he just hadn't spent all his share . . .

He finally rolled out of bed only because his phone started ringing and would not stop. A pair of wealthy bachelors was answering his ad. They needed a discreet ride over to an isolated cay used by couples craving privacy.

Cat took the gig for only one reason.

He needed more dope.

AN HOUR LATER he arrived at Fort Lauderdale to find the customers waiting for him.

One man was large and dopey-looking; the other was small and muscular. They had a lot of luggage and were dressed like people who were experiencing the tropics for the first time, sweaty and sunburned. Prime pigeons.

Cat wearily loaded their luggage onto the plane, got the men settled into seats up close to the cockpit and took off.

As always, as soon as he turned east, he started up a conversation. They talked about the weather, the seas, the Bahamas themselves.

Cat gave them his usual spiel about the mysterious islands—but then, thinking they might enjoy a free tour above Via-grass Cay, called over his shoulder: "So, are you two a couple?"

The next thing he knew, cold steel was touching the top of his spine.

Crash Stacks leaned forward and pushed his pistol deeper into Cat's neck.

"A couple of what?" he asked him.

THE ARADO FLOATPLANE appeared over the tiny unnamed cay just after sundown.

The four hung-over pirates waiting on the sandy beach forced themselves to their feet. Shaky as they were, they retrieved their weapons from their Boston Whaler and watched the floatplane come in for a landing.

None of the pirates wanted to go out on another foray; they'd celebrated last night's crimes all too well, and now were paying heavily for it.

But when Colonel Cat contacted them and said he had another couple of Conchy Joes, real suckers, who appeared to have money, the pirates—now almost penniless again— knew they had to do the gig if just to recoup some of what they'd squandered the night before.

The floatplane taxied up to the deserted beach. The pirates waded out to it as the plane's rear door opened. The youngest pirate, nicknamed Jumbey, was assigned to carry the team's ammo. He had the clearest view of what happened next.

The first two pirates reached the open door and suddenly fell backward into the water. And just as suddenly, that water turned blood red.

At first, Jumbey thought his fellow pirates had hit their heads on the plane's door or something. But then their limp bodies floated past him, and he could see what had happened.

Both had been cracked on the skull.

Jumbey looked up to see two men standing in the plane's doorway, do-rags hiding most of their faces. They were aiming huge assault rifles at him and the remaining pirate.

Strangely, one of these men had a hook for a hand. The other wore an eye patch. Both were also wielding nightsticks, the weapons that had dispatched his two colleagues. But Jumbey knew these guys weren't cops. Not typical ones, anyway.

They look more like pirates than we do, he found himself thinking.

"Come toward us . . . slowly," the man with the eye patch told them. "Start fucking around and it will be the last thing you do."

Jumbey and the remaining pirate, the senior man known as Crabbie, were so stunned they could do nothing but follow the man's instructions.

As soon as they got within reach, the masked men dragged them into the plane, took their weapons away and began beating them severely. Jumbey was especially cut up by the hook hand, which the man used to hit him about the head and shoulders, slicing him badly with each blow.

The pummeling ended long enough for Jumbey to look

up from the floor of the plane to see Colonel Cat sitting in one of the passenger seats, his face also showing the effects of a beating, his hands tied in front of him with duct tape.

That's when the plane started moving again.

All Jumbey could think was: *Who's flying this thing?*

BATMAN LOVED THE Arado floatplane.

It handled like a well-preserved 1930s sports car—and it looked like one, too. He'd flown jet fighters before his days in Delta Force, and he'd spent a lot of time piloting helicopters since Whiskey went into the pirate-busting business. But nothing moved through the air like the foldable Arado.

He was behind the controls now as the plane slowly climbed past 10,000 feet, heading east toward the open sea. Its human cargo of two pirates and Colonel Cat, all three bound by duct tape, was stretched out in the back, squeamish and squirming, as the plane rose even higher into the night sky.

Many things had happened in the past twenty-four hours, not all of them expected. Thanks to the information give to them by BABE, Whiskey had boned up on the Muy Capaz, and now knew they were indeed smarter than your average pirate band. In addition to their attention to detail whenever they swooped down on a hapless vessel, careful to leave no evidence behind, the pirate gang apparently maintained a hideout so well hidden, the Bahamian cops had long since given up trying to find it. Even with the promise of a large cash reward, no one had ever come forward to reveal where it was. And while the local law enforcement was sure it was situated somewhere among the hundreds of tiny islands along Bahamas' outer cays, that's about all they knew.

Whiskey wanted to complete this gig quickly and then

maybe relax a little. So, they knew they had to do what the Bahamian cops couldn't or wouldn't do. They had to find the Muy Capaz hideout.

But they had to get on the gang's tail first. As it turned out, the DVDs BABE had given them also proved helpful in doing this. Not the ones containing information from the Bahamian cops' database; as Jennessa had said, those were practically useless. It was the information BABE had generated on its own—detailed records on past victims of the Muy Capaz—that held the key.

The tourist agency consortium estimated at least twenty people had met their end at the hands of the pirates in the past year. In their continuing effort to keep the lid on, the Bahamian cops had classified these people as simply missing persons or unrecoverable accidental drownings, basically making them instant cold cases. But BABE knew better.

Twitch found the pattern they were looking for. After going over the records of the missing victims, he noticed that more than half of them shared two things in common: one, they were leasing boats in the Bahamas at the time of their disappearance; and two, there was no record of how they got to the Bahamas in the first place. No tickets bought from regular commercial airlines, no evidence of passage on any cruise ships or ferries. But because these people were going to pick up their chartered boats, they *had* to get to the islands somehow.

A charter flight was one way to do this. So Twitch started a search of every small airline flying between Florida and the Bahamas. A whiz at busting through firewalls and hacking files from the Internet, he got into the flight records at Fort Lauderdale airport, and one name kept popping up: Colonel Cat.

It turned out that on more than a few occasions over the

past year, Cat had flown customers to the islands shortly before the Muy Capaz struck—in some cases, just hours before a pirate attack.

More damning, though, was that on those same occasions, the very thing Cat had tried to avoid—leaving a paper trail—actually tripped him up. Scuba divers, deep-sea fishermen, people wanting to fly over the mysterious Bimini Road—all these people paid him freely with credit cards or checks.

But the passengers Cat took up around the times of the Muy Capaz's crimes? They must have all paid in cash, because there were no receipts. No paper trail. The absence of evidence was the evidence itself.

Cat had outsmarted himself.

By connecting the dots on dates close to a Muy Capaz crime wave, Twitch estimated twelve of the pirates' victims might have been on Cat's antique airplane at some point.

That was more than half, and that meant it was more than coincidence. After that, the rest was easy. Whiskey hired Cat's plane, then beat the shit out of him, and he eventually sang like a canary.

So far, so good.

But then they realized not *everything* they'd heard at the BABE briefing was adding up.

For instance, while interrogating Colonel Cat, they'd discovered—much to their surprise—that the Muy Capaz had hit three more yachts just the night before, each time with Cat's help.

But there was no full moon the previous night; in fact, the moon was barely waxing at half. So much for the "Wolfman Complex."

Even stranger, at one point, when they were beating the daylights out of Cat, and Batman asked him how deeply was he involved in voodoo, the pilot actually laughed in their faces. He told them the only voodoo he was involved with went up his nose or into his veins.

Well, no matter, Batman thought now as he pushed the old airplane past 12,000 feet and continued to climb. Every mission had its twists and turns, its intangibles. Timeline or not, voodoo angle or not, they were still on a good pace to wrap up these Capaz monkeys, get paid by BABE, and then spend a little time enjoying the fruits of their labor on a warm beach somewhere.

So what if it didn't come all wrapped in a bow?

What in life did?

THE PIRATE NAMED Jumbey had never flown so high.

He'd been on Colonel Cat's plane on four occasions, going to and from raids on the yachts or while they were taking care of witnesses. But on those flights, he could clearly recall looking out the plane's observation blisters and seeing the ocean or land just below him, no more than a thousand feet away.

Now, they were flying so high, he couldn't see the earth—land or water—below him at all. It was also cold inside the airplane, and it was rattling and coughing and seemed to be bouncing all over the sky.

But creature comforts were the least of Jumbey's worries at the moment.

He was lying on the deck of the passenger compartment, still bleeding from his wounds, his hands and legs tied with multiple strips of duct tape. His head was jammed up right next to an observation blister; this was how he knew how high they were flying. But he couldn't move. He could barely turn his head.

At one point, though, he realized by the voices bouncing back and forth in the cabin that the man with the hook hand was flying the airplane. He also knew that, besides the man with the eye patch, there were three other masked men in the cabin with him. All five of them were huge, wore military suits and carried large weapons and nightsticks. Beyond the cold, the rattling and the terrifying altitude, it was these men themselves who were scaring the shit out of him. They seemed capable of anything.

Colonel Cat was tied up on the floor right next to him.

"How did they know about us?" Jumbey managed to whisper desperately to the pilot. "We were always so careful to keep it all secret."

"How the fuck do I know?" Cat spit back at him. "Maybe they're fucking psychics."

At that moment, Jumbey heard the man with the eye patch give an order to the three other masked men. Straining mightily to turn his head, Jumbey saw one man open the rear hatch of the airplane, while the two others grabbed Crabbie and dragged him over to the doorway. Jumbey and Cat were horrified.

"What's your voodoo name?" one masked man asked Crabbie. But the pirate had no idea what he was talking about.

The man smacked him hard across his face.

"Why didn't you wait until the full moon this time?"

Again, Crabbie was totally baffled by the question.

"I do not know what you mean," he told the masked man.

The masked men didn't ask Crabbie any more questions. One simply said to him: "You shouldn't have killed all those people, mon. You shouldn't have killed those cops."

Then the largest man of the three simply picked Crabbie up off the floor and threw him out the open hatchway.

There was a look of complete bewilderment on the pirate's face as he went out the door. Even as he was falling, everyone on the plane could hear him scream: *"What cops?"*

Then the masked men turned toward Jumbey.

The young pirate started crying.

"What do you want from me?" he yelled. "I've only been hooked up with these guys for a month!"

"Tell us where your hideout is," the large man demanded of him.

Jumbey became hysterical. "I don't know, general. I've never even been there. That's just for the senior crumbs."

The large man started dragging Jumbey toward the open door.

"Better talk now," he yelled at him.

But Jumbey could barely breathe, never mind talk.

"I don't know!" he screamed again. "I've never been there! I'm just a new fish. That guy you just tossed? *He* was a senior man. He was there all the time!"

At that point, all the masked men looked at each other. They just realized they'd thrown the wrong guy out of the plane.

"So much for wrapping this up quickly," one of them said.

The large man pulled Jumbey even closer to the open hatch. The wind was blowing madly. Jumbey looked down on the dark clouds and was terrified that he would have to pass through them before smashing into the water or the earth that he knew was somewhere way down below.

"Last chance," the big man told him. "You must know *some way* we can find your boss."

Jumbey looked out on the clouds again and, to his horror, imagined he could see Crabbie flying alongside the aircraft like a bird, bloody and laughing at him.

"I don't," he said, trembling. "I've never met him."

The man pushed Jumbey halfway out the door.

"You got three seconds," he growled. "One . . . two . . ."

"I don't know!" Jumbey cried again. "I'm just a minnow. A little fish!"

"Good-bye," the large man said.

He picked Jumbey off the floor and started to throw him out the hatchway.

"Badtown!" Jumbey finally yelled.

He was almost as good as gone—but then he felt the huge man pull him back in again.

"Badtown? What is that?"

"It's a slum," Jumbey said, trying mightily to catch his breath. "In Nassau. The whole city is a mess, but people call the worst part of it Badtown."

"Your hideout is in Badtown?" the large man asked him.

"No," Jumbey replied, still shaking all over. "Senior crumbs just hang out there sometimes when money is good."

"*Where* in Badtown do they hang out?" another of the masked men demanded to know. "It must be a big place."

Jumbey hesitated again—and the large man pushed him back toward the open door.

Finally Jumbey yelled, "The Tainted Lady."

"Tainted Lady?" the large man asked. "What is that? A boat?"

"Don't tell him!" Colonel Cat suddenly bellowed. "He'll kill us!"

"*They'll kill us!*" Jumbey yelled back at him.

He looked up at his would-be executioner.

"The Tainted Lady is a blind pig! A saloon, mon. There's a hidden room upstairs where the top guys hang out sometimes. That's all I know."

TWENTY MINUTES LATER, the floatplane landed in rough water next to an outer island so small it had just a single palm tree on it.

The masked men dragged Jumbey and Cat out of the plane and threw them, still bound in duct tape, onto the tiny beach. Then the masked men sloshed their way back to the airplane and climbed aboard.

Cat started screaming as he and Jumbey fought to rip the tape from their hands and feet. But there was so much of it, it was impossible.

"You can't leave us here!" Cat yelled. "When the tide comes in, this place will be gone!"

"Climb the tree then," one of the masked men told him.

"But . . . but we're so far out, no one will ever find us!" Jumbey yelled.

The large man yelled back. "Them's the breaks, mon."

"But—my plane!" Cat screamed.

The large masked man yelled from the open door. "Oh yeah—thanks! We'll take good care of it."

With that, the Arado turned back toward the ocean, and with a burst of smoke and sea spray, took off and flew away.

7

BADTOWN WAS WELL named.

Dominating the southern end of Nassau, just over the hill from some of the most glamorous resorts in the western hemisphere, it was a collection of hovels, tin shacks, drug dens, and cafés that attracted more flies than people. Much of Nassau was a slum; Badtown was its most treacherous part. When cruise ships docking here warned their passengers to exercise caution while walking in the outlying neighborhoods at night, Badtown was the place they were talking about.

A canal connected this place to the sea. It was the conduit through which much of Badtown's criminal activity

flowed. Pot. Crack. Meth. Jewels. Guns. Just about anything and everything was for sale to adventurous tourists
and addicted locals, if the price was right.

The busy season for Badtown's drug trade was approaching. American college students on Spring Break would
soon besiege the islands, and this meant dozens of pounds
of coke and hundreds of pounds of pot could be sold in just
one week.

These days, the people moving all these drugs around
were, more often than not, the most feared, if most secretive pirate gang in the islands: the Muy Capaz.

OF THE TWO dozen bars in Badtown, most were little
more than shacks with mud roofs. But one stood out, because it was made not of metal, but of stone.

It was as old as anything could be in this part of the Bahamas. Built more than two hundred years before by the
British Army to house prostitutes close to one of its many
forts, it was known then, as now, as the Tainted Lady.

The bar inside was as rundown as the building itself.
Made of rotting wood from a nineteenth-century schooner,
it was bordered by three shelves of bootleg liquor. There
were a few tables, a few chairs and that was it. Cigarette
smoke, pot smoke, spilled beer and blood combined to give
the place a unique aroma. It was always dark inside, no
matter what the time of day.

Just off the bar was a small room whose door was hidden behind a false wood panel. Few people knew the room
existed. Inside it tonight were four members of the Muy
Capaz. There were dressed badly even by Badtown standards, in stained, ragged shorts, dirty beach shirts and tattered straw hats. Each man had a gun in his belt and a
machete by his side. Several bottles of rum sat on the table.

The pirates had been playing Cuban Poker since midnight. At about 2 A.M., the secret door opened and four heavily armed men came in. Everyone in the room froze. The four men weren't rival gang members—they were bodyguards. Their sudden appearance could mean only one thing.

Another man walked in a few moments later. He was six-foot-two, with the build of an ex-boxer and the scars of an ex-con. He was dressed all in white, and his hands, cracked and rough, were an odd shade of red, as if they were permanently stained with blood.

He was Charles Black, the boss of the Muy Capaz.

This was not good—and the four pirates knew it. For Black to show himself in public was a rare event. He almost never left the gang's secret hideout. His presence here meant something was wrong inside the world of the Muy Capaz.

And that could be bad for everybody.

BLACK'S MAIN SOURCE of income was buying and selling large quantities of pot and coke. His suppliers were from Jamaica; the business was strictly cash up front. Whenever Black and his men needed an injection of funds to get resupplied, they did what pirates do: They robbed vessels at sea. Turning that booty into money, they bought the drugs wholesale, and then resold them to mid-level dealers, most right here in Badtown, for a good profit.

The problem was, Black and his men were pirates from skin to bones. Like their predecessors of centuries past, they had something in their genes that caused them to be quickly separated from any extra money they came across. Despite their reputation for moving like ghosts when it came to committing crimes at sea, they were terrible business-men. When they made a score, they would take the profits and hit Badtown hard. And whether their visit lasted several days or even a week or more, after a bender of booze, drugs, gambling and paying for the boom-boom, most if not all of their ill-gotten gains were gone.

This was why the gang was almost always broke, forcing them to knock off more yachts, to get some more seed money, to buy more stuff from the Jamaicans, to sell again, to blow the profits again. It was a vicious cycle. And had it had nothing to do with voodoo or the full moon.

The problem flowed from the top. Black himself was prone to recklessness when he was in the chips, and to foul moods when the well went dry. In the past year alone he'd murdered six people, three inside this very bar, all over money matters.

There was no way the local police were going to arrest him, though. The only reason they came to Badtown was to pick up their bribe money.

BLACK WAS IN an especially bad mood tonight.

The gang was again low on funds. A raiding party he'd sent out the night before had spent nearly all of its profits over in Bimini. Doubling their sin, the same four men had not returned from a raid they'd gone out on earlier this night. Again, the big selling week was coming up, and gang's coffers were seriously depleted. But even worse, the thought that his men might be holding out on him was enough to make Black's blood boil.

He walked over to the table where his gang members were playing cards and viciously slapped the first man he saw. The man fell to the floor, his nose broken, his mouth bloody.

"When I slap you, you goin' to stay slap," Black roared at his astonished victim. "You understand? Or do you need more cut lip?"

The man didn't reply; he just scrambled away.

Black took his seat, which was all he really wanted.

The pirate captain also commandeered the man's meager pile of money and began playing poker, but clearly, he was distracted. He was constantly checking his watch, waiting for his raiding party to show up with some much-needed capital. But as each minute ticked by, that possibility seemed more and more remote.

Into this swirl of dangerous vibes stumbled a man named Petey Chops. He was small and rodentlike, and he'd spent more than half his life in jail for murdering a child. These days he was a low-level drug mule for Black's crew; his forte was pushing powdered coke on American college students here on school break or for a long weekend.

Chops was supposed to be carrying a $10,000 payment for a load of coke Black's men had given him the week before. Tonight was the night to pay up, which was the reason Black had left his hideout in the first place. He wanted that money in his own pocket, no one else's. But when Chops walked in and saw Black himself in the flesh, he immediately tried to turn and run. Black's bodyguards stopped him at the door, though, and the pirate captain motioned them to bring him over.

By the time Chops reached the table and sat down, he'd turned ghost white. He also looked beat up. His eyes were puffy, his lips swollen.

"I'm sorry," he blurted out, not daring to look at Black across the table. "But I don't have your scratch."

Black glared back at him. "What do you mean?"

Chops was trembling. "I *had* the money. But I was rolled thirty minutes ago. Two guys in military uniforms. They took everything I had."

Black drank an entire glass of rum without taking his eyes off Chops. "I got rolled" was the oldest excuse in the book, and everyone at the table knew it.

"But it's true," Chops insisted. "I was leaving my crib and these two army dudes came out of nowhere. Masked faces, billy clubs. They hit me from behind, then dragged me into the alley and took my roll. Ten grand in tens and twenties. It was like they were waiting for me. It was like they knew I was coming here with your money."

Black never broke his gaze. The tension in the room was nearly unbearable.

He asked Chops, "So, when *can* you get us the money? Tomorrow? The next day?"

Chops's relief was so apparent, he nearly fell out of his seat.

"For sure, Captain," he said. "Tomorrow, for sure."

Black reached across the table and tapped Chops lightly on his face.

"Tomorrow," the pirate captain told him. "Or else."

More blood trickled from Chops's busted-up nose. But he didn't care. He'd somehow escaped with his life.

"Yes, Captain," he said, wiping the blood away. "I won't gin it up."

Black reached into his shirt pocket and came out with a joint the size of a cigar.

"Let's smoke this outside," he told the others at the table. "It's new stuff—from Panama. We don't want everyone out there to be smelling us."

Everyone at the table got up and filed through the secret doorway and outside via a short stairway that faced the dirty canal. Black's heavily armed motorboat was tied up close by.

The pirate king handed the Panama blunt to one of his men, who lit it with a huge cigarette lighter. He got the joint going and blew out a huge cloud of bluish smoke.

The man passed the huge joint to Chops. The dealer took

a long drag—but before he was able to exhale, another of Black's men had moved up behind him and suddenly had a leather belt around Chops's neck.

The pirate started pulling the belt tight, slowly twisting and turning it. Chops began fighting madly, but his fate was sealed.

"Examples must be made," Black told Chops nonchalantly. "You understand, mon?"

Chops collapsed to his knees, but his executioner yanked him back to his feet. The pirate kept twisting the belt tighter and tighter while Black and the others calmly passed the joint back and forth, looking on, unmoved.

Finally, the pressure was so intense, Chops's eyes popped out. Only then did the pirate let his lifeless body fall to the ground. Black took another long drag on the joint and then gave Chops a final kick in the stomach.

"He's lucky we didn't tear him to shreds first," Black said.

They took rope from Black's motorboat and tied Chops's body to a docking post. When the sun came up, his corpse would be visible for all of Badtown to see.

It was a clear warning: Don't cross the Muy Capaz.

THE PIRATES RETURNED to the hidden room and opened another bottle of rum.

Dispatching Chops had eased Black's frustration level a bit. But it left the gang with the same old problem: They still had no money. In fact, now they were another ten grand in the hole.

That's when Black's cell phone rang. It was one of his contacts in the nearby casino district. Could Black still get a large quantity of coke on just a few days' notice? The contact had three customers looking for a substantial deal.

They would pay up front, and were interested in regular large buys in the future.

It was just what Black needed.

He turned to the two senior pirates at the table, Doggie and Jacks.

"Clean up and head over the hill," he told them. "Sniff out a deal with these guys—and don't bitch it up. If spirits agree, tell them we can move up to a ton of stuff if they want us to."

DOGGIE AND JACKS walked into the lounge of the Regency Casino just before 3 A.M.

They'd changed their clothes to appear a little more presentable, but at best, they still looked like part of the casino's kitchen crew.

They spotted the contact sitting in a dark corner with three coal-black men. They were well-dressed, very refined looking, and spoke with strange accents. The pirates sat down and made small talk while an army of high-priced hookers paraded around the casino's main floor.

Finally, they got down to business.

The contact told the pirates the three men were looking for coke, meth, pot—and weapons. These were things the pirates could get with ease. The three men were also looking for someone to attack the vessels of their business rivals at sea. Again, the Muy Capaz were the people for the job. Best of all, the three would pay in cash, up front, for everything the pirates could give them.

It was the deal that the Muy Capaz had been awaiting for a long time.

Drunk and stoned and now dreaming of riches in their heads, Doggie and Jacks shook hands with the three men, sealing the deal.

Then Jacks asked, "Where are you blokes from? Antigua? Belize?"

The three men laughed.

"No, mon," one of them replied: "We are from Senegal."

8

The outer islands

THE NEXT NIGHT, Doggie and Jacks left the dock at the Muy Capaz's secret hideout and headed out to sea.

It was just past midnight. They were using Black's own twenty-four-foot sports fishing boat for this trip. In the boat's hold was a quarter pound of cocaine, just about all the pirate gang had left. They also had four ounces of methamphetamine, two AK-47s and a hundred rounds of ammunition. These were just teases for the three men who wanted to make the big score.

Doggie and Jacks were a bit on edge. Four of their fellow pirates had yet to return from a raid the previous night. But Doggie and Jacks weren't feeling uneasy because they thought something bad might have befallen their comrades—there was no honor among the Muy Capaz gang. Their fear was that the four might have been nabbed by some law enforcement agency higher than the paid-off Bahamian cops—the U.S. Coast Guard, for instance—and that the Muy Capaz's string of perfect crimes had been broken. While they were fairly sure the gang members wouldn't fold under interrogation for fear of what Captain Black would do to them if they did, Muy Capaz's ghostly street cred would definitely take a hit if the four missing pirates had been arrested.

The mystery of their missing colleagues was not enough to delay this deal, though. It was a rare day that the gang could find regular customers for pot, coke, meth *and* weapons.

This one was just too good to pass up.

THEY FOUND THE ship just where the three men said it would be.

It was anchored off a cay near one of the Bahamas' mysterious Blue Holes. This island was a part of the outer Eleuthera chain, an area that saw few visitors—not just because of its isolation, but also because it was believed the waters in this part of the Bahamas were haunted. It was a perfect place for this type of meeting.

Doggie and Jacks were surprised by the ship itself, though. Because the three men from the casino had seemed so refined and were so well-dressed, they'd expected to be meeting on an expensive mega-yacht or even something more luxurious.

What they found instead was an enormous container ship.

They saw the prearranged signal, four flashes from a red light, and were soon up alongside the huge vessel. A rope ladder was dropped from amidships and the two pirates climbed up. Doggie was carrying the coke and meth; Jacks had the weapons and ammo.

The three well-dressed gentlemen greeted them up on the rail, embracing them with monstrous bear hugs as they came aboard. No other crew members were in sight.

The three men took them to the ship's galley, where drinks were waiting for them.

"What is this?" Doggie asked them, looking at the amber liquid swirling around inside his paper cup.

"It is mooch," one of the three men replied in his thick

French-tinged accent. "Soothes the muscles and calms the nerves."

The pirates drained their cups and accepted the offer for a refill. Then the three men suggested they take a quick tour of the ship.

Walking along the cargo hold, the three men told the pirates that they could carry anything within the huge containers—tons of drugs, weapons, stolen merchandise. Even an airplane, one bragged.

Whatever the pirates could supply to them could be moved practically anywhere in the world, without fear of being caught by law enforcement because just about anyone they would encounter at sea could be paid off or disposed of.

"More money for you," one of the three men said. "More money for us."

The pirates were not only taking it in, they were getting physically excited. Everything the three men were telling them made great sense. By the time the tour was over, the formerly drab ship looked bigger and more elaborate than any seagoing vessel the pirates had ever seen.

When the three men asked if the pirates had any questions, Doggie had only one: He asked if they could have another cup of mooch.

DOGGIE AND JACKS left about twenty minutes later. They had a deal in place, a half-gallon of mooch in hand, and a bag of money as payment for the guns and drugs: ten thousand dollars in all, mostly in tens and twenties.

They started their boat's engine and headed off to the southwest.

A minute later, the helicopter known as *Bad Dawg Two* took off from the *Dustboat*, hidden on the other side of the cay, and headed in the same direction.

* * *

THIRTY MINUTES LATER, *Bad Dawg Two* was flying at 10,000 feet, extremely high for its type of rotary aircraft.

Batman was behind the controls; Nolan rode shotgun. They were bundled up in heavy flight suits, boots and gloves, essential as the copter's cockpit doors had been taken off, and it was extremely cold at nearly two miles up.

Gunner and Crash were shivering mightily in the passenger seats behind them. Both were wrapped in emergency blankets, but they were of little help, as each man was wearing nothing more than a wet suit and flippers.

"How did we draw the short straws again?" Crash asked, blowing on his hands, trying to keep them warm.

"I thought we lost a bet," Gunner replied.

"You'll be warm soon enough," Nolan told them over his shoulder.

He was peering into an instrument called an XFLIR. An upgrade on a typical FLIR, or Forward Looking Infrared Sensor, it functioned like night-vision goggles—identifying people, places and things based on their heat signatures, but over large areas. The "X" stood for the device's extraordinarily long range at night; at the moment, it was maxed out at three miles and change. That was the reason for their nosebleed altitude; they could cover more ground up here than flying closer to the earth.

They were passing over a string of tiny islands called the Sunset Chain. This was where they'd tracked the pirates' fast boat after it left the *Georgia June*. They'd kept a visual on the vessel despite their frosty altitude until it disappeared in among the dozens of minuscule islands and reefs in the chain. Somewhere down there, Whiskey was sure lay the Muy Capaz's hideout.

At first, what they saw was not very promising. The islands of the Sunset Chain looked practically deserted. Lots of oceanfront, lots of beaches, a few villages here and there—but nothing that would qualify as a hideout for a bunch of cutthroat pirates.

But then they flew over an island located about a mile off the northeastern edge of the archipelago, away from the others. Surrounded by thick reefs and rocky beaches, it was appropriately named Craggy Two Cay for the river that ran through it, cutting it in half. And though it was covered with heavy jungle and almost impossible to approach safely from any side by sea, the XFLIR almost immediately started picking up clusters of heat sources on it.

"We might have a bingo," Nolan declared.

He checked the flight computer's map and saw that this speck of land barely registered on the grid. There *were* a lot of boat wrecks on the reefs and rocks around it, however, some marked, some not. This alone ensured most vessels would avoid the place.

Nolan zoomed in as far as the XFLIR would go and started picking up individual heat sources. There were about three dozen in all, human figures moving about, as well as some livestock. He also saw fires burning, probably in barrels, and other unusual heat sources. Most important, though, he was getting a reading on a boat that had just pulled up to the beach near the camp. This was most likely the same boat that had carried the two pirates to the *Georgia June*. Its engine was still throwing off heat.

Nolan reported all this to those on board.

"Gotta be the place," Batman said. "So hang on."

IT TOOK THE copter just three minutes to spiral down to wave-top level.

They were soon flying off the eastern edge of Craggy

Two Cay. From here, the team members used their standard night-vision goggles to peer through the sea mist and into the island's jungle beyond.

The encampment they saw was not quite what they'd been expecting. Again, they knew the pirate gang had access to a lot of money. And though it seemed to go through their hands like water, they always had the ability to make more. But this place looked more like a city dump than a hideout. Shanty shacks were surrounded by mounds of trash and debris with empty and smashed liquor bottles everywhere. Piles of broken and rusted outboard motor parts covered the small beach that led from the camp to the river. Pigs were running free everywhere.

"Some Somalis live better than this," Crash said.

Nolan and Batman were sweating badly now inside their flight suits in the heavy, 80-degree night air. Crash and Gunner, on the other hand, were cool and comfortable.

But not for long.

The copter came to a hover just off the island's east-facing reef. The dividing river ran through this reef, past the pirates' camp, and then on to the other side of the island. Called a "bight," this was not unusual topography for the Bahamas. And it would be key for what happened next.

"Ready back there?" Nolan yelled over his shoulder to Crash and Gunner.

He heard two "Rogers," in reply.

With that, both men jumped out, hitting the water with a great splash.

Nolan waited until he received a thumbs up from them, then gave Batman the signal to go. The copter roared straight up, soon disappearing back into the night.

Crash and Gunner swam the hundred yards in through the channel. Their intent was to observe the pirates' hideout, SEAL-style. The mild current was going with them, so they soon reached a point about twenty-five feet off the camp's river shoreline. With their faces blackened and their eyes aided by waterproofed night-vision goggles, they started the recon.

What they saw was more of the same: lots of junk, lots of garbage, lots of engine parts and debris. There were fifteen shacks in all, arranged in a rough semicircle around a huge bonfire. Everywhere around the shacks the ground sparkled because there was so much glass from so many smashed liquor bottles. Amid all this refuse stood a tree holding a satellite dish used for receiving TV and radio broadcasts.

Crash and Gunner counted more than thirty gunmen around the camp. These had to be the hardcore pirates, Captain Black's senior men, the ones privileged enough to actually live, eat and breathe within sight of their bloodthirsty leader. Some were gathered near the bonfire, apparently gambling. A few were fighting each other with knives and fists. The rest were drinking by the river's edge, not far from where Crash and Gunner were quietly treading water.

The Whiskey members could see no signs of security, no lookouts, no sentries around the camp—which was good. But there was also a lot of firepower in evidence. Most dangerous were a pair of .50-caliber chain guns, one set up at each end of the camp. These nasty weapons were connected to ammo drums containing hundreds of rounds. It was obvious they were put in place to fire at any boats approaching from either end of the bight. But set up on tripods, they could just as easily be trained upward and used against a threat from above.

The pirates also had an open-sided shack filled with AK-47s hanging on racks for easy access. A similar structure next to this armory was full of weapons still in their packing crates. Gunner figured these were arms the pirates had for sale.

There were also stacks of rifles and shotguns set up next to shacks, and many others scattered haphazardly on the ground.

"There must be five weapons for every guy here," Gunner said to Crash.

"At least," Crash replied.

Most important, the camp was built close to the edge of the jungle. There were dozens of places in the shadows of the flora where gunmen could hide during an attack.

"This will have to be an exercise in drawing fire," Gunner said. "We'll have to tease them out if we want to get them all."

"Roger that," Crash replied.

Gunner took a lot of pictures with the team's waterproof digital camera and then they both resumed swimming down the bight. When they reached the far side of the island, the team's copter was waiting for them.

As soon as the pair climbed in, Nolan asked, "Well, what's the 411?"

Gunner replied, *"Muy desorganizada."*

Then Crash added, "But still *muy* dangerous."

9

The next night

NOLAN WAS AT the controls of *Bad Dawg Two*.

It was just before midnight. Not twenty-four hours after Gunner and Crash had completed their recon of Craggy Two Cay, Whiskey was on its way back, this time in force.

They were flying low, just above the wave tops, coming from the north. Batman was off Nolan's left wing in *Bad*

Dawg One; Crash was with him, manning one of the door guns. Gunner and Twitch were riding with Nolan, their M4s hooked up to extended belts of ammunition. Some of the photos Gunner had taken of the pirates' secret camp were taped to Nolan's flight panel. He'd studied them closely and knew the numbers they told: more than thirty hardcore pirates were probably at the camp, along with two big chain guns and a lot of assault rifles. The advantage, six to one in the pirates' favor, didn't bother Nolan. Back when they attacked the base of Zeek the Pirate in Indonesia, Whiskey had been outnumbered almost *eight*-to-one, and had still come out on top.

It was the target's makeup that troubled him. The Muy Capaz camp was so cluttered, it offered dozens of concealed places from which the pirates could fire. This meant Whiskey had no choice but to come in low, destroy the two big chain guns first, then draw the pirates' fire and take out anyone who fell in their sights. Nolan was well aware how dangerous this would be. One round in the wrong place, like in his engine, or his skull, and the show would be over, just like that.

So in planning the mission, the team had to come up with a few tricks, things to knock the pirates off kilter before they came in so low and exposed.

Gunner suggested building a stinkpot, a weapon designed hundreds of years ago. A concoction of saltpeter, limestone and a spice called asafetida, plus lots of dead fish, it was packed in a container drenched with kerosene and lit by a fuse. When detonated, it created such a stench, it could cause waves of debilitating nausea almost immediately.

A stinkpot was now tied to Nolan's right side strut. Made to Gunner's specifications, it was contained in a fifty-gallon milk can they'd requisitioned from the *Georgia June*. If they could drop the stinkpot at the beginning of the attack,

Whiskey was hoping many of the enemy gunmen would be too busy vomiting to fight.

But this was not their only psy-ops weapon. *Bad Dawg One* was equipped with an external loudspeaker. Typically employed for crowd dispersal or talking to hostage-takers, the loudspeaker was connected to an MP3 player in the copter's cockpit that could play any recording at earsplitting volume.

To this end, Crash had made an MP3 loop featuring a mélange of unsettling sounds: people screaming; wounded and dying animals; horns blowing, drums beating. It was a primal cacophony, like a soundtrack for a war movie. Whiskey hoped this, too, would add to the pirates' confusion.

Batman had chipped in by making several dozen flash bombs, using soda cans as his weapons jackets. Filled with phosphorus and aviation gas, they would not only make an ear splitting noise when they exploded, they would produce a flash of light so bright it would blind anyone nearby.

These were all good ideas. But in planning the attack, the team sensed they needed one more thing, something almost cosmically unsettling. Twitch had pointed out that back in the old pirate days, the most powerful weapon the brigands had was their flag—the skull and crossbones. When the pirates would come up on a ship, sometimes all they had to do was run up their Jolly Roger and the victim would simply give up. Fear could be a powerful weapon in battle. But what would instill such fear in these particular modern-day pirates?

Twitch made figuring that out his personal mission.

Their preparations for battle had taken the team most of the day. But as the sun went down and they began suiting up for the attack, one important question remained: what if, after hitting them with the stink bomb, the psy-ops recording, the flash grenades and Twitch's secret weapon, the pirates wanted to give up?

The thought had crossed Nolan's mind more than once during the day. Back in Indonesia, Whiskey had trapped dozens of Zeek's men on a sandbar and mowed them down with a fusillade of .50-caliber machine gun fire. It was distasteful, but in the end, necessary. Zeek's men were murderers, rapists, and sadists. The *Muy Capaz* were no different. Besides, eliminating them was what Whiskey was being paid to do.

So before they took off, Nolan had told the team: "Remember what Mr. Jobo said. 'Gloves off.' Those are his words. Those are our specs. So, that's what we gotta do."

THE DAY HAD passed in surreal fashion for the pirates on Craggy Two Cay.

The four brigands who'd gone out on a "flying raid" two nights before had not returned. And while it was not too unusual for gang members to simply give up the pirate life and vanish, it *was* odd that four would jump ship together. What's more, no one had been able to get in touch with Colonel Cat. Had his plane crashed two nights ago? The pirates had heard nothing on their shortwave radios about any aircraft crashes on the islands. Had their colleagues been caught by the authorities, then? No one knew—and that was making everyone feel uneasy.

On the other hand, the deal that Doggie and Jacks had made the night before with the men from Africa had the potential to change Muy Capaz's financial situation forever. If they could line up enough drug and weapons dealers and start a pipeline flowing, they would make so much money, they could spend scads of it in Badtown for weeks at a time and still have plenty left over.

So, it had been a day of yin and yang. Still, the pirates had spent it as they usually did: sleeping, gambling, fighting with each other, drinking and doing drugs. The only defensive action Black took was to post a half dozen men down on the east beach of the cay, near the mouth of the bight that split the island in two, something he did in times of heightened security at the camp.

The job of these six men was simple. They were to report anything unusual coming their way from the ocean side, the likeliest route for any attack on the hidden camp.

And something odd *did* arrive around midnight.

Not from the sea, but from the air.

ONE MOMENT, THE six pirates on the beach were passing a bottle of rum and only casually checking the horizon.

The next moment, hellfire fell upon them.

The noise came first—and it was incredibly loud. People screaming, animalistic wails of agony, people shouting over radio static. It was suddenly all around them. Then the night lit up with incredibly bright explosions, dozens filling the sky.

Then came the helicopters. The pirates weren't sure of the number, but it sounded like hundreds of them. Two streaked close past them; they looked dark and menacing, loaded down with bombs and guns. But there was another thing: The emblems on their fuselages were unmistakable: the red-white-and-blue insignia, with the star in the middle?

These were Americans. U.S. military gunships sent here to attack them. Between all the noise and the flashes of light, it was as if the 82nd Airborne itself was suddenly descending on Craggy Two Cay.

The six pirates on the beach were instantly terrified. They'd never run into anything like this before.

They had no desire to take on the helicopters. None of them even shot back. Instead, they dropped their weapons and ran into the jungle, heading at top speed back to their encampment.

NOLAN'S WAS THE first copter to arrive over the hidden pirate base. Flying very low, he slowed down just enough for Gunner to light the stinkpot's fuse and kick the malodorous weapon out the copter door; then they streaked away. The bomb landed with a splat right in the middle of the camp's huge bonfire. It exploded instantly, hurling its contents over a wide area.

"Bada bing!" Gunner yelled.

Nolan pulled the copter up and over the camp, making way for Batman and *Bad Dawg One*. It streaked underneath them, MP3 blaring, flash bombs still falling from its weapons points. Batman immediately opened up with his forward cannon and took out the chain gun on the eastern edge of the camp. Then came a quick turn, another cannon barrage, and the western edge chain gun was destroyed as well.

Nolan flew over the hideout a second time. Flipping down his special night-vision telescope, he scanned the ground below. Lots of heat sources were moving about—and for a moment, it seemed like more than just three dozen people running around. But one thing was clear—the pirates seemed in a panic.

Their plan was working.

Both copters now backed off and started a slow orbit 1,500 feet above the treeline. A small white mushroom cloud was rising over the camp, the aftereffect of the stinkpot explosion. Crash's MP3 was still blaring as well.

Again Nolan studied the camp below. So much smoke covered the target area, it was hard to distinguish the heat signatures of the pirates from the residue of the flash bombs.

But that was not surprising. Everything was unfolding as they'd hoped.

The team gave the stinkpot bomb two more minutes to do its work. Then Nolan and Batman turned their copters over and began to dive again.

"Now comes the fun part," Nolan thought grimly.

He armed all his weapons. The .50-caliber machine guns mounted on his winglets were ready to fire, as was the huge 30mm cannon sticking out of the copter's nose. Gunner and Twitch both had their M4s up on the starboard side weapons mounts, connected to continuous belts of ammunition.

Both copters were soon down to just ten feet off the deck, quickly slowing to half speed. In this dangerous maneuver, they wanted the pirates to fire at them and reveal themselves, so Whiskey would know where to fire back. Nolan was in the lead, with Batman a little behind and off to the right. Anyone who showed himself to shoot at Nolan would find himself in Batman's sights an instant later.

The noise of the two copters flying so low was deafening—but Nolan could still hear Crash's soundtrack booming between his ears. The attack quickly turned nuts. It was loud and fast and full of smoke and flames and flashes of light going off in all directions.

But . . . something was wrong.

Nolan knew it right away.

No one—not a single pirate—was shooting back at them. In fact, he could see nothing at all moving around the camp.

The pirates were not a disciplined army; there was no way they'd *all* taken cover and were keeping their heads down.

Nolan completed his pass and did another quick infrared scan of the camp. He saw heat sources strewn all over, but none of them was moving. It was almost as if they were all dead already.

His radio suddenly came to life. It was Batman.

"You see what I see?" he asked Nolan.

"I think I do," Nolan replied. "It's already a ghost town."

Batman radioed back: "But there's no way we greased *any* of these guys already. We just got here."

Nolan's head started spinning. The gig had been almost too easy up to this point. Now this curveball—and he had no idea how to explain it.

"We got to find out what's happened down there," he radioed back to Batman.

Batman clicked his radio mike twice.

"Roger that," he told Nolan. "See you on the ground."

A MINUTE LATER, the two copters had set down in a field just west of the small camp.

The five team members climbed out and checked their equipment. They were all dressed the same: black camouflage battle suits, flak jackets and oversized battle helmets. Each man was carrying an M4 assault rifle equipped with a night scope, and each was breathing through a gas mask. Each man was wearing his OAS badge as well.

But they were also wearing huge American flags on their backs. This was their version of the Jolly Roger. They'd believed nothing would put the fear of God into the brigands like seeing the Stars and Stripes coming at them.

That's why Twitch quipped, "Maybe we *scared* them all to death."

Whatever happened, though, the smell was awful.

"At least your stink bomb worked," Crash yelled through his mask to Gunner. "It smells like one skunk crawled up another skunk's ass and died."

Could that have done it? Nolan wondered. Had the smell from the stinkpot been so overwhelming, it had actually killed all the pirates?

He didn't think so. It *had* to be something else.

The team formed up on the edge of the hideout, then put about twenty feet between them. Weapons ready, they began walking into the encampment.

They moved slowly, sweeping the camp with their night-vision goggles, ready for anything, working their way through the stink and fog.

But they could see no movement at all. No one was trying to run. No one was throwing up from the putrid cloud. No one was shooting or resisting them in any way.

Nolan gave out a loud, short whistle—the signal that the team should be wary of booby traps or an ambush. But as they moved cautiously into the camp, their weapons pointing in every direction at once, it was soon obvious there *was* no opposition.

They found the first pirate in the middle of the camp. He was lying face down near the huge bonfire, not far from where the stink bomb had hit.

But he hadn't been shot, or burned or "stunk to death."

His throat had been cut. Even stranger, his right ear had been cut off.

"We sure as hell didn't do that. . . ." Twitch said through his gas mask.

They came upon four more pirates in front of a shack nearby. They, too, had had their throats slit, and one ear removed. Behind the shack were two more. Both had their necks sliced open, both were missing an ear.

It went on like this for the next five minutes. The team found groups of pirates in the shacks and in the jungle nearby. None had been shot or hit by ordnance. All of them had died from getting their throats slit. Each one had had an ear cut off.

This was totally baffling and bizarre. The Whiskey guys were all veterans of some of the heaviest missions of Delta Force. They rightly thought they'd seen it all.

But they'd never seen anything like this.

They moved down near the river that ran past the camp, and here they found the six men who'd run back to the encampment from the beach at the beginning of the attack. Their throats, too, had been slashed, and one ear had been removed from each of them. The blood from their hideous wounds was turning the river bright red.

The team finally stopped and had a muffled conversation through their gas masks.

"They're *all fucking dead*?" Crash was yelling. *"All of them?"*

"Every one, so far," Batman said. "And none of them went pretty."

"But how?" Crash asked.

No one knew. . . .

"Are we going to get blamed for this?" Twitch wondered loudly.

Nolan just shook his aching head. *Blamed?* An odd choice of words, he thought.

They stayed together, checking each hut and finding many more bodies, all of them with their necks cut open, each with an ear sliced off.

Finally they reached the last shack—the one occupied by Captain Black himself. There were four pirates piled up near the entrance. All were dead from knife wounds to the throat, all missing one ear.

But one pirate inside was still alive. It was Black himself.

Crumpled in the far corner of the rickety structure, his throat was severely cut and his right ear was missing. He was bleeding heavily all over his white clothes, but somehow he was still breathing. They gathered around him. Medic kit in hand, Crash desperately tried to stem the flow of blood from his wounds, but couldn't. He looked up at the others and just shook his head.

Black could barely speak, his words coming out in a bloody gurgle. Still, he tried.

"Are you blokes the cops?" he asked them weakly.

Still talking through his gas mask, Nolan yelled that they were part of the OAS.

"Never heard of you," Black gurgled back.

Nolan knelt down beside the dying pirate. He *had* to know what transpired between the time the team first dropped the stink bomb and when they started the aborted attack on the camp, five minutes at the most.

"What happened here?" Nolan asked him. "Why is everyone dead?"

The pirate could only shake his head. "I don't know, mon," he replied with great difficulty. "We was drunk and high. Asleep. Passed out. Then, a stink bomb comes in. Weird screaming. I woke up, but I couldn't see anything. And I couldn't breathe because my fingers are on my nose."

He coughed once, ejecting a small river of blood.

"Next thing I know, all my men around me are dead— and my own throat is cut, and my ear is gone. I didn't see nobody. I didn't hear nobody."

Another cough, more blood.

"Ghosts," Black struggled to say. "We were killed by ghosts."

But Nolan didn't believe him. He couldn't. It didn't make any sense. He believed Whiskey had actually stumbled upon some weird mass murder-suicide. It was the only rational explanation.

Batman knelt down beside the dying pirate as well. He lit up a joint, pulled up his gas mask, took a drag, then lifted Black's head off the bloody floor and put the joint to his lips. The pirate drew in deep.

"Want to get clean now while you can?" Batman asked him.

The pirate nodded yes, a bubble of blood coming out of his open throat.

Batman shouted behind him: "Who's got the fucking video camera?"

Gunner was soon beside him, a small video camera in hand.

"Get all of this," Batman told him.

He turned back to Black.

"You guys knocked off all those yachts, right?" Batman asked him.

Black nodded slowly. "Just trying to make some scratch, you know, general?"

Batman gave him another puff of pot.

"And all those people?" he asked. "You threw them into the sea?"

"Couldn't have any witnesses, you know?" Black said. "It's bad luck. But a lot of their stuff is here. You can have it. No good to me now."

"You might have gotten away with it," Batman said, taking another hit himself under his mask, "if your pilot hadn't been a junkie and had been more careful."

"Always a pain in the ass, that guy," Black said after another toke. "I hope he crashes someday."

Batman nodded. "Yeah, me, too. But you know what really screwed you? Taking those yachts on Easter. And killing those cops, man? That was fucked up. That's what got everyone pissed off, and set everything in motion against you. That's why they called us in."

Black accepted another weak puff of the pot—and then a strange look came across his face.

"We done all that you say before," he coughed, fading fast. "But no three yachts on Easter Day, mon. And definitely no cops. That was not us. We were all drunk on Easter. We could not move. That was someone else."

"Bullshit," Gunner said, still recording it all. "He's freaking stoned even as he's checking out."

But now Nolan wasn't so sure.

"If it wasn't you guys," he asked Black. "Who did it?"

But the pirate captain could no longer reply. His eyes were going up into his head, his body was starting to convulse.

Batman threw the joint away and started shaking him.

He repeated Nolan's question: "If it wasn't you on Easter, who was it?"

Black came back to life for just a few more seconds. Long enough for him to manage a weak grin.

"No idea, mon," he said. "Guess the big joke is on you."

Then, he died.

10

THE BRIGHTLY PAINTED Bell 430 helicopter appeared above the *Dustboat* around noon the next day.

With help from two of the Senegals, the copter landed on the coastal freighter's empty helipad and four people stepped out.

One was Mr. Jobo, the OAS officer the team had met at the beginning of the mission. Jennessa and two other women from BABE were with him.

The women, dressed in very sexy island wear, with perfectly coiffed hair blowing in the breeze, were carrying a huge ice bucket full of champagne bottles and glasses.

Batman was immediately on hand to greet them. Jennessa gave him a warm hug and took out the first bottle and popped the cork.

"You did it!" she said happily. "You rid us of those horrible Muy Capaz people."

Batman nodded weakly. "Apparently," he replied.

"We got the report this morning," she said happily. "The Bahamian police are already crawling all over that island. They're finding all kinds of things: weapons, drugs, IDs and personal effects from a lot of the missing people. You guys did in three days what those idiots have been pretending to do for years."

Batman didn't reply this time—he just sipped his champagne.

"So, it's my pleasure then," Jennessa went on, "to give you this . . ."

She handed him a cashier's check for $5 million.

". . . and this," she added, giving Batman a huge kiss on both cheeks.

Then she shook his hand and said, "If only all our vendors were as good as you."

But Batman was still uneasy. "We usually provide a post-action debrief after a job," he told her. "It lets you know what we did and when. And how your money was spent. It also gives details of what went on."

Jennessa just laughed.

"No need," she replied, adding with a whisper: "However you did it, that's fine with us."

Mr. Jobo agreed.

"You did the whole world a favor," he said in his booming voice. "And especially our little piece of the world here. You know?"

Batman pulled Jobo aside.

"Look, there's something you might want to know," he told the OAS officer. "Those guys are gone, but—"

Jobo put up his hand and stopped Batman mid-sentence.

"Are they gone forever?" he asked. "Buried in a mass grave out there?"

Batman hesitated—but then nodded yes.

"And was that not the point of your mission? To get rid of them?"

Batman nodded again.

"And you were paid?"

"Yes—we were . . ."

Jobo pounded him on the back. "Then celebrate, my boy. You deserve it."

"But some strange things happened on that island," Batman told him. "Things we really can't explain."

Jobo put his arm around Batman's shoulder. "My friend— strange things are *always* happening out in these islands. And some of them no one can *ever* explain, even if they take a hundred years to try. The more time you spend out here, the more you will come to understand that."

Batman thought this over. The pirates were dead. The BABE consortium had paid them. And the OAS representative was being quite clear he didn't want to know or care how the pirates met their end.

So . . .

"End of mission, end of story?" Jobo asked him.

Batman finally managed a smile.

"You learn quick," Jobo told him.

Batman turned and clinked glasses with Jennessa.

"All's well that ends well," he told her.

She smiled and kissed his cheeks again.

"Exactly," she replied.

Crash, Gunner, Twitch and the Senegals had all joined them by now. They, too, were getting their glasses filled by Jennessa's gorgeous colleagues.

"I guess our vacation starts today," Crash said.

* * *

THE LITTLE CELEBRATION went on like this for a while. It was a perfect day. The warm winds were blowing, the crystal-clear water was lapping gently against the *Dustboat*'s hull, the sun was shining brightly.

Everything seemed ideal.

But not for Nolan.

He never joined the others. He spent the whole time up on the bow where the team's helicopters had been brought, scraping off the oversized United States insignia they'd added before the assault on the pirates' hidden camp.

His body language made it clear that he wanted to be left alone, and the members of Whiskey understood.

Flying the U.S.-marked copters and wearing the American flag on the back of his battle suit had been a reprieve of sorts for Nolan. For a little while, it was as if he were serving in the U.S. military again. Fighting for his country again.

It seemed like such a little thing, but it was hugely important to him.

Now that the mission was over, ending strangely or not, getting rid of the emblems was his job—no one else's.

"What's with him?" Jennessa finally asked Batman. "Doesn't he like champagne?"

Batman just shrugged. "It's a long story."

Jennessa shook her head. "He's really handsome, you know," she said with a sigh, immediately taking the wind out of Batman's sails. "Good build. Rugged looks. Has he ever done any modeling?"

"Only for the Army," Batman replied with a sinister laugh.

It was true: When Nolan was an officer cadet, his picture had graced some Army recruiting posters.

"Well, the eyepatch adds just the right amount of mystery," Jennessa went on, refilling Batman's glass. "So please, tell him for me, no matter what he does, don't ever do anything to screw up that face."

PART THREE

The Sugar Men

11

MARK CONLEY ARRIVED at the Kilos building an hour before sunrise.

Coffee in hand, he took his seat inside the OSS suite, glanced at his computer screen and let out a long sigh. More than three dozen requests for Whiskey's services had come in overnight. Representatives from the governments of Japan, Saudi Arabia, Brazil and Spain were inquiring about the team's availability. Companies from Greece, Taiwan, Sri Lanka and The Netherlands were also hoping to book them. They'd even received an inquiry from someone at a company in Los Angeles that simply said, "Call me."

"We should just franchise this thing," Conley thought aloud as he began the process of transferring the voice messages to text. "Then they can take over this whole freaking building."

A letter was waiting on his desk. It was postmarked the Bahamas, three days before. Inside was a funds transfer slip from the Royal Bahamian Bank of Nassau to the Kilos-controlled OSS account in the First National Bank of Aden. The transfer was for five million dollars. An attached note read: "Wish you were here." It was signed by Batman Bob Graves.

Wiseass, Conley thought.

The day went on. Conley split his time between OSS stuff

and his real job of running Kilos Shipping's Middle East security department. By 11 A.M., he was ready for lunch.

He left the Kilos building and headed for the docks. There was a falafel stand down there that actually sold hot dogs. *Hebrew National* hot dogs, yet.

Conley ordered his usual: three pups and a Saudi Arabian Pepsi. Packing it all in a brown paper bag, he headed back to the office.

Upon crossing San'nah Street, though, he found his way blocked by a huge black limousine.

As he approached, the limo's rear door opened. A large man inside was beckoning to Conley.

"Hello, friend of my friends," the man called out to him.

He was wearing a thick wool suit and had hands the size of baked hams. His skin was pasty white, his teeth were gold and yellow, and his nose appeared to have been broken so many times, the cartilage didn't know which way to go next. Judging by the bulge under the man's suit coat pocket, he was packing a firearm the size of a small cannon.

Conley knew who he was right away.

"Comrade Bebe, I presume?" he asked.

"And you are ex-Big Apple cop?" the man replied. "Good to meet you."

Bebe was the Russian gangster who'd hired Whiskey to provide security for a cruise ship full of Russian mobsters during a trip through the Aegean Sea not two months before. As unlikely as it seemed, the gangster took a liking to the team and had provided them with crucial information about how to finally track down and kill Zeek the Pirate.

Conley had heard so much about Bebe from the team members that he would have known him anywhere.

But what was he doing here, in Aden? In a limo that barely fit through the narrow streets? And in that suit? It was almost 95 degrees and it wasn't even noon.

"Ride with me," he said to Conley. "I'm just needing a few minutes."

Armed only with his hot dogs and soda, Conley climbed into the limo and it sped off. Bebe took his lunch bag from him, looked inside, and then passed him an envelope full of photos.

"Do you know this man?" Bebe asked him.

Conley studied the photos. They showed a slight, well-dressed Asian man going in and out of various buildings, walking along the street, sitting in a park. All of the photos were candids, as if the man had been under surveillance, and the locations ranged from slums to typical Chinese streets to a building that looked nothing short of Shangri-la.

The photos were blurry in spots, but that didn't matter. Conley knew who the man was: Sunny Hi.

He was one of the most dangerous criminals in the world, yet virtually unknown outside Asia. Boss of the Shanghai crime syndicate, Sunny Hi commanded an underworld organization so vast, its tentacles had a stranglehold not only on all of China, but on every other country along the Pacific Rim as well. Drugs, money laundering, prostitution, arms sales, murder for hire—Sunny Hi was so powerful, the ruling elite in Beijing reportedly kissed his ring whenever he requested a private meeting with them.

At his core, Sunny Hi was a pirate. His gang started out hijacking ships in the South China Sea, killing their crews, unloading the stolen cargo on the black market and then selling the commandeered ships themselves. Weapons and heroin dealing followed, as did white slavery and contract hits, and finally, a thriving business in child prostitution. His personal fortune was said to be more than $70 billion. His immediate gang numbered in the thousands; his activities affected, directly or indirectly, millions of people around the world.

But he was famously known never to have had his photo taken, or even be seen in public, which was why Conley was surprised to see so many images of him now.

"He is usually like a bug who crawls out only at night and in places where you cannot see him," Bebe explained. "But more of late, he shows himself in the daytime. He even walks streets with his wife sometimes. He is trying to make it look like he's leaving the criminal world behind because something grave has happened in his life. But it's all show when it comes to his business. Inside dope says he's as evil as ever."

Bebe singled out a photo that showed Sunny Hi looking down into the cargo hold of a ship that was literally full of young females, several hundred at least, presumably being shipped out for prostitution around the Asian continent. They looked like cattle, and judging from the demeanor of some of the heavily armed guards also caught by the interloping camera, anyone who resisted was most likely beaten or killed, just to make an example.

"Sunny Hi has been scum of Earth," Bebe concluded. "And when you hear that coming from man like me, you know I'm serious. I mean—criminal or not, we all have to make living, no? But selling these girls? Killing those who resist? Torturing their families? Even I know these things are wrong."

Bebe lit up a cigarette.

"This man affects maybe one quarter of people on planet right now," he went on. "In five years, maybe half. In ten years, the way Chinese dragon is behaving, who knows? Maybe he will control entire world?"

Conley put all the photos back in the envelope and tried to hand it back to Bebe. But the Russian insisted he keep it.

"I know you and your friends have major beef with Sunny Hi," Bebe told him. "He was money man behind the departed Zeek. Plus, you and friends know this man is capable of many bad things. So, *you* must stop him somehow. Especially now that he loosens up, showing himself more in the light."

Conley was more than a little surprised.

"Us?" he asked Bebe. "Why *us*?"

The gangster smiled, displaying his mouth full of dingy, gold-capped teeth.

"Because these days, you are superheroes," the Russian said. "And no one else will dare do it. No country. No mafia. No military will go after him. They are afraid or too busy elsewhere. Fate of world is in your hands."

With that, Bebe signaled his driver to stop. The limo door opened and Conley realized they were back where they started on San'nah Street.

"Take my word for this," Bebe went on. "Now is time to whack this monkey. It won't be easy. Will be very dangerous, in fact. I will be in touch with more information on his location, but I know foolproof plan is needed here because this man is not stupid. He is very, very smart. But you must help world. Save kids. He is pirate. You are pirate killers. Think it over."

Conley stepped out onto crowded San'nah Street. Bebe waved to him, then closed the door and the limo roared away.

Only then did Conley realize Bebe still had his hot dogs and soda.

The Gulf of Siam
One week later

THE *HONG SONG STAR* was a mid-sized, Kilos-owned freighter home-ported in Ko Si Chung, Thailand.

Sailing off the Thai coast, one day out of port, the

freighter was overtaken by pirates. Ten of them in all, they approached in a large motorboat, hooded and armed with machine guns. Climbing a ladder left unattended on the bow, they quickly rounded up the crew and seized the bridge without firing a shot.

In all, it took less than five minutes for the *Hong Song Star* to fall to the hijackers. In its cargo hold was 12,000 tons of sugar, worth about eight million dollars. Or at least that's what it said on the ship's manifest.

The pirates immediately locked the crew in the engine room, giving them plenty of food and water and DVD players for entertainment. There they remained while the hijackers repainted and renumbered the ship. By the next morning, the freighter had been rechristened the *Ocean Song*.

At noon that day, the crew was brought back up on deck and fed a hot meal. While they ate, a fleet of Vietnamese fishing boats approached in the distance. Confirming with the freighter's captain that all was OK, the pirates put the crew overboard in life rafts. The Vietnamese fishermen picked them up within minutes. The master of the fishing fleet immediately radioed the International Piracy Center and reported what had happened.

Meanwhile, the hijacked ship disappeared into heavy fog to the east.

Only once the Vietnamese fishing boats were out of the ship's sight did the pirates finally take off their masks.

There were ten of them in all: the five Senegals and the five members of Team Whiskey.

"If hijacking ships is really *that* easy," Batman said, throwing his mask into the sea, "maybe we're in the wrong business."

AN HOUR LATER, a Chinook helicopter appeared over the ship.

Flying out of a secret Royal Navy installation near Singapore, the copter hovered about fifty feet from the freighter's stern while two men slid down an access rope, both landing with a thump.

One was Dr. Alan Stevenson, the ex-Special Air Service physician who had hired Team Whiskey almost two months before to retrieve the mother of all microchips after it had been buried on an island off Zanzibar. The second man was also ex-SAS, a surgeon named Dr. Mace.

The Senegals helped them to their feet and picked up their heavy bags. Stevenson gave a thumbs-up to the copter pilot, and the huge aircraft flew away.

Both doctors were quickly brought below.

Two hours later

BATMAN KNOCKED TWICE on Nolan's cabin door and went in.

He found his friend sitting on his bunk, eye patch in place, staring into space.

"Are you ready for this?" Batman asked him.

"As ready as I'll ever be," Nolan replied.

Batman said, "I mean, are you *sure* you want to go through with it?"

Nolan shrugged. "No, I'm not—but I'm going to do it anyway."

Batman shook his head. "You realize we're not so deep into this thing that we can't call it off. Who would know?"

Nolan shrugged again. "Well, *I'd* know. And so would all the people this guy has terrorized or will terrorize. It's a long list."

Batman started to say something but stopped. He knew it was virtually impossible to change Nolan's mind once it was made up. Still, he felt he had to at least talk to him about it.

He pulled out a joint, lit it and offered Nolan a toke. Nolan just waved the smoke away.

"Don't let those SAS guys see you smoking that," he told Batman.

Batman laughed. "Who do you think I got it from?"

Nolan retrieved a beer from his fridge and opened it. "Just what I want to hear," he said glumly.

He still hadn't gotten over the strange incident in the Bahamas a week before. The non-attack on the Muy Capaz hideout kept replaying over and over in his mind, taunting him, making him more uneasy than usual. Things just hadn't seemed the same since.

Batman started up again. "We're talking about something pretty drastic here," he said. "I've been thinking about it since we dreamed it up. We've all done undercover stuff before, as well as the disguise thing—but never to this degree. You're the group leader. Nothing says you *have* to go."

Nolan drained his beer and opened another. He hadn't been sleeping well lately either, always a bad sign.

"We've gone over this a hundred times," he told Batman wearily. "*Two* people have to do this gig. Twitch can pass for just any race on Earth and he speaks a bit of the language—so, aside from the fact that he's freaking nuts, we're lucky there. But he can't go alone; someone has to watch his back. Gunner would be perfect, but he's just too big for this part of the world. Crash admits he wouldn't be able to keep his mouth shut, and neither could you. So, that leaves me."

"Leaves you doing a charity gig, you mean," Batman reminded him. "They'll be no payday for this one. No tip. In fact, it's costing us money."

Nolan drank his beer. "We already got a pile of money

in the bank. It won't hurt us to do a freebie every once and a while."

"OK, Charlie Chan," Batman finally told him, taking another toke and then stubbing out the joint. "It's your fortune cookie."

Nolan finished his second beer, crushed the can and fired it into his wastebasket.

"Just show me the weapon," he told Batman.

Batman took a small plastic case from his pocket. He opened it to reveal a tiny white ball, no larger than the head of a pin. Nolan had to get his good eye up close to it to even make it out. "You sure that isn't a head louse or something?" he asked.

Batman picked up the tiny ball with his fingertips. "It's ricin, compliments of your friend, Bebe. One of the most lethal poisons on earth. If you look closely, you can see it's embedded in a tiny sphere of wax. Now, that wax outer coating is tough, but it will dissolve in about a second in the presence of heat. So, if this goes into hot food or drink, it will work in a few minutes. But if it's somehow injected into the blood stream, it will work almost instantaneously."

Batman put the tiny ball back into its case and gave it to Nolan.

"Uric acid will neutralize it," he said. "But even then, it's still hazardous. So, be careful with it at all times. It's very nasty stuff."

FIVE MINUTES LATER, Nolan and Batman walked into the ship's makeshift sick bay.

Stevenson and Mace were waiting for them. Both physicians were wearing scrubs, rubber gloves and untied surgical masks. Both looked particularly grim.

The first thing Mace did was show Nolan a large syringe, big enough to treat a horse. It was filled with a clear fluid.

"This is methoxsalen," Mace said. "It's an anti-*vitiligo* drug. It's been around for years and has no side effects—except the obvious reaction. With your permission?"

Nolan rolled up his sleeve and allowed Mace to inject him. He was then led over to a hastily prepared operating table and asked to lie down. Mace and Stevenson tied up their surgical masks while Batman retreated to the corner.

Nolan's eye patch was removed. He could see the doctors wince as they looked into his empty, damaged socket.

Mace retrieved another syringe, smaller, but filled with a hideous-looking red fluid.

"This will help a bit," Mace said. "Not a lot, though."

He injected it just below Nolan's jaw. It felt like a dagger going in, but the pain was quickly replaced by a dulling sensation. In a few seconds, Nolan felt paralyzed from his neck to his nipples.

Out of the corner of his good eye, Nolan could see Mace was holding a large sewing needle and a long string of black thread.

"Are you ready, Major?" Mace asked him.

Nolan couldn't speak—so he just gave a weak thumbs-up.

The procedure began.

THE FIRST PART of the operation lasted just fifteen minutes—but that was the only good thing about it. Even though his neck muscles were numb, Nolan still felt the pain every time the sewing needle pierced the skin above his throat and tightened it just a little more. It was like someone was slowly strangling him.

Once the surgeons had finished, they produced a small paint can and a pair of brushes. They stripped off Nolan's clothes and proceeded to coat his entire body with a solution from the can.

"Highly diluted nitric acid," Mace told him. "Normally this would turn pale skin to bright yellow, but when used in conjunction with the methoxsalen? Well, let's just see what happens."

The ten-minute application filled the room with a nauseating odor. Then the doctors performed two more suturing procedures, this time on Nolan's eyes. Because no painkiller could be used so close to his optic nerves, he again had to take the sting each time the surgical needle went in and out of his skin.

Next the doctors brought in a portable dentist's drill. Like everything else in the operation, it was courtesy of the SAS special equipment division.

Mace hooked up the drill to its battery pack and proceeded to bore a tiny hole about the size of a golf ball dimple into Nolan's number seven incisor. Into this, Mace inserted a tiny one-way radio. This would allow anyone on the other end to hear every conversation going on around Nolan—an ironic twist, it would turn out. This procedure could not be done with Novocain, though, as any residue might interfere with the radio's signals. So, once again, Nolan had to endure the pain.

When that was done, Mace used yet another large syringe to inject Nolan's lips with a massive amount of collagen.

It was at *that* point Nolan realized Batman had been right. This *was* absurd. If he were married, if he had a wife and kids, or just some significant other, he would never have considered doing any of it.

But in reality, he had nobody—and thus, nothing to lose. Maybe *that* was why he was going ahead with it.

Truth was, he wasn't really sure himself.

* * *

AT LAST, ALL the cutting and sewing was done.

Mace looked down at Nolan, flashing a small light in his good eye.

"Still with us, Major?" he asked.

Nolan could barely nod in reply.

Mace showed him one last hypodermic needle.

"Novapol," the surgeon said. "It will help you sleep."

The SAS surgeon injected him yet again, then said, "Count backward, slowly, from one hundred."

The two doctors then replaced the surgical light with an ultraviolet lamp. Nolan could feel its heat burning his body almost immediately. He could also see Batman, still standing in the shadows, staring at him with a look of revulsion on his face.

Counting down as Mace suggested, Nolan passed into unconsciousness before he reached ninety.

24 hours later

NOLAN WAS OUT cold for an entire day. When he finally woke up, the *Ocean Song* was four hundred miles closer to its goal.

Stevenson and Batman were there when he opened his eyes. His first words to them were, "I dreamed about someone losing a nuclear submarine."

Stevenson gave him a quick once-over and pronounced him no worse for the wear.

But then Batman came up with a mirror.

"Ready for this?" he asked Nolan.

"Just get it over with," Nolan managed to say.

Batman put the mirror up to Nolan's good eye—but Nolan did not recognize the person looking back at him.

His face was darkened and jaundiced. The corners of his eyes—both the good and bad one—had been stretched to an oval shape. His lips were hideously puffed out, as was his nose. He didn't look Asian exactly, which was the whole point of this. But he certainly didn't look Caucasian anymore, either.

The most shocking thing about his appearance, though, was the long, ragged line of stitches stretched across his neck. All Mace had done was put harmless, if painful, sutures into his skin. But looking at them now—puffed out and intentionally untreated—the result was monster-ish. Nolan looked like someone who'd barely survived a brutal throat slashing.

Before Nolan's world came to an end at Tora Bora, before he was even commissioned as an officer, his picture had appeared on Army recruiting posters. His image had been selected because he embodied everything the Army wanted its recruits to think signing up was all about: You become all-American and handsome, heroic and hunky. That's how ruggedly good-looking Nolan had been.

Now, not only wasn't he all-American-looking—he was actually grotesque.

In other words, his disguise was complete.

He was ready to murder Sunny Hi.

12

THE *OCEAN SONG* sailed into Shanghai Harbor just after sunset the next day.

It glided past the newer parts of the city's sprawling downtown, heading for an older section of the bustling port. Ships of all shapes and sizes passed on each side of the repainted freighter. From junks to huge container ships, no one gave it a second look.

Until, that is, a military patrol boat intercepted them about halfway to their goal. It was heavily armed and carried one of Shanghai's many harbormasters. A curt radio call ordered the freighter's crew to get their papers in order, including a summary of their cargo. They were about to be boarded.

The *Ocean Song* slowed to a halt and the harbormaster and an officer of the Chinese Navy came aboard. The Senegals greeted them, displaying false transit papers forged by the SAS and brought aboard by Stevenson and Mace. The papers claimed the ship was registered in Kuala Lumpur under a Honduran flag. The sugar, they said, came from Santos, Brazil.

The harbormaster studied the paperwork—but it was only a cursory inspection. Wrapped up inside was a bundle of cash: five thousand dollars in new U.S. twenty-dollar bills. The visitors were soon gone, and the *Ocean Song* was once again on its way.

Passing the last of new Shanghai, its towering buildings looking more futuristic than anything else in this part of Asia, the freighter floated further up the Yangtze, finally reaching Old Harbor. This area resembled Shanghai of the 1930s: dark, dank, shadowy, crowded—and *very* dangerous. A few similar-sized ships were at anchor here; others were tied up to the creaky, decaying docks nearby. A low mist hung over everything, and foghorns bayed a mournful tune.

Beyond the docks was the ancient walled city of Old Shanghai. The thick harbor mist had spilled over to its extremely narrow streets and innumerable back alleys. Lines of electrified Chinese lanterns hung everywhere, strung from dull, gas-fired streetlights. But only the glow from the numerous neon bar signs was able to cut through the fog, and then just barely.

It was now 7 P.M. on Friday and the streets were crowded as usual. The many saloons along the docks were already in full throat. Occasionally the sound of a drunken laugh or a pleasant squeal rose above the dull roar, issuing from either the bars or the brothels many housed upstairs.

The *Ocean Song* quietly tied up at an isolated spot along the old pier.

Phase One was now complete.

"REMEMBER, YOU MUST not talk," Batman said to Nolan. "You cannot say a word. You're supposed to be some-one who's had his vocal cords severed. You've got to stay in character or this whole thing will be screwed."

They were all sitting in the ship's galley: the five members of Team Whiskey, the two SAS doctors and the Senegals. As the operation's commander, Batman was conducting one last briefing before launching the strange mission. He was hammering home the details like a football coach before the big game.

"I know you can understand a little Chinese," he told Nolan. "But, if you let one word slip, English or other-wise, they'll hear your American accent and that will be a death sentence. Any kind of talking will also screw up that radio in your tooth. It might be worth about a million dollars, but we won't be able to hear anything else if you're talking while it's transmitting, because your voice will over-whelm its tiny microphone. And if we can't hear anything else, we won't know what's happening. Understand? So, *no* talking—no matter what."

Nolan nodded, but numbly. He could barely talk as it was. His mouth, his eyes, his throat—he ached from the neck up.

But he knew what Batman was saying was of paramount importance.

The idea behind his bargain-basement facial surgery was to transform him into an Asian tough guy, someone who, by his repulsive looks alone, would deter people from messing with him—and by extension, with Twitch. The *faux* suturing around his neck, mimicking a grisly wound, was done simply to obviate the need for him to talk, as Far Eastern languages weren't exactly his strong suit. The ironic thing was that Twitch, though very Asian-looking due to his Hawaiian ancestry, rarely said more than two words to anyone, friend *or* foe. Yet he'd be doing all the talking for the mission.

Batman started up again, now addressing both Twitch and Nolan.

"OK, just to review, here's what we know thanks to Bebe and the SAS. At midnight on the first day of every month, Sunny Hi attends an event that everyone calls the *Ba Xi,* or 'the Game.' He never misses this thing, as it's a real bonding session with his original pirate gang. But it's also the only time he accepts new recruits into his organization. Anyone wanting to join up has to pay some kind of tribute to him, just to be considered worthy. And because it also happens to be his son's birthday, he'll be in a more responsive mood, and possibly lower his guard a bit."

"Now, we think the Ba Xi is a high-stakes poker game, or whatever passes for poker over here, but we're not entirely sure. But as midnight is now just four hours away and that starts the first day of May, we're sure it's being held somewhere tonight."

He checked the last page of his notes.

"It's important that you link up with your contact as soon as possible. From what the SAS intelligence guys were able to tell us, he will know more about the Ba Xi and how you can get close to it, and therefore get close to the target. Obviously, the nearer you can get to Sunny Hi, the better the chances of success. But it's not going to be easy. He's always heavily guarded. We'll need a whole lot of luck on our side."

Batman looked at his watch.

"As of this moment, the clock is ticking," he said. "It's now 8 P.M. on the dot, and we figure that bribe to the harbor patrol has a life of about a half-day. So this thing has got to be done before sunup tomorrow so we can get the hell out of here. And *that* means you've got exactly ten hours to get in and get out. So, set your watches—and get back here by 0600 hours at the very latest. If you don't, we'll all be toast."

A grim murmur of agreement went around the galley.

Lastly, they went down their equipment checklist: Twitch was wearing his trusty transponder wristwatch; it would emit a radio pulse every few seconds, telling the team where he and Nolan were at any given moment. The Senegals reported that the tiny radio in Nolan's tooth was coming in loud and clear. Both Nolan and Twitch had a diagram of Old Shanghai's confusing street grid drawn in ink on their shirtsleeves, this because even Google Earth had a hard time getting a clear image of the area's urban confusion. Twitch was also carrying five thousand dollars in cash, for bribes and to buy into the Ba Xi if it was a poker game. Most important, though, the pinhead containing the ricin super poison was jammed up under the nail of Nolan's right index finger.

Batman concluded the briefing with one last comment to Nolan.

"And, whatever you do," he said, "*don't* bite your nails."

NOLAN AND TWITCH got off the ship by riding atop a large crate being lowered to the dock by the Senegals. Hooked up to the forward cargo winch, the crate was marked: USE ONLY IN EMERGENCY.

Once down, Twitch checked his transponder watch. It was now 2010 hours. They had less than four hours to somehow crash the Ba Xi.

They were both wearing heavy crew jackets and black stocking hats, as the fog was cold and wet. They had no weapons other than the pinhead of poison; even the knife that Twitch usually kept inside his prosthetic leg had been left behind. They'd have to depend on their wits, their street smarts and their intuition.

They had one last glance up at Batman, Gunner and Crash standing on the rail.

Then they pulled their jacket collars tight and walked into the mist.

THE DARK STREETS of Old Shanghai were even narrower than they imagined. They were jam-packed with people, motorbikes, handcarts, discarded produce crates, fish barrels and the occasional car or truck. Trash was piled high everywhere. Telephone poles, thick with wires that resembled drooping black spaghetti, lined every street. The electrified Chinese lanterns and the blinking neon signs added a weird glow, but did little to dispel the misty gloom. And everything, including the people, seemed to be covered with a thin, oily sheen.

The constricted streets were also home to hundreds of overcrowded *jiubas*, small Chinese versions of a Wild West saloon. Each jiuba was filled with drunken locals, rowdy sailors and Shanghai hookers, all watched over by massive, heavily armed bouncers. Bad eighties music seemed to be blaring from each one. The combined sound was deafening.

NOLAN AND TWITCH followed the street maps inked on their shirtsleeves. After fifteen minutes of walking through a sea of people, they came upon a particularly dark alley. At the end of it was a jiuba called the Sea Witch.

This was where they were supposed to meet their contact.

The place was much smaller than any of the saloons closer to the docks. Instead of a giant bouncer watching the door, a middle-aged female dwarf stood out front, smiling broadly and giving anyone who wandered by a piece of candy from her straw basket.

The tiny woman let out a yelp, though, when she spotted Nolan approaching.

"My poor disfigured travelers," she said in barely recognizable English. "For you, special candy."

Instead of taking two pieces from her basket, she handed Twitch two pieces of candy from her pocket.

"Special," she repeated, patting him affectionately on his rump. "Special candy for you and your friend."

They went down the steps to the subterranean bar. The only illumination came from a few candles scattered about the place. A macaw, looking down on them from a perch above the rear door, screeched when they walked in.

Only one other customer was in the bar. He was sitting at a table in the far corner, leaning over a glass of beer.

He was Asian and seemed to have an overly large head. He was totally bald and sported an extremely long Fu Manchu mustache. He was either doped up or drunk, and his eyes were barely open. He was dressed as they were, like a seaman, and was smoking a cigarette right down to the nub.

This was their contact.

They walked over to the table. He looked up at them and visibly shuddered at the sight of Nolan's distorted features.

"Do I owe you two money?" he asked. It was the code phrase.

"You have already paid us," Twitch replied, using the counter-phrase.

The man indicated they should sit down.

"I speak a little English," he said to Twitch. "And I hear you do, too. So we can talk. But, what about your friend here? What's his story?"

"He is my cousin," Twitch replied. "Doesn't speak at all. He lost his voice in a dispute with a knife in Rangoon. But he never had much to say anyway."

"And his eye?" the contact asked, grimacing at the sight of the empty socket.

"Another dispute—long ago, in Calcutta," Twitch said. "He can barely see at all, but I consider him a good-luck charm—and good protection. Can't be too careful these days."

The contact nodded and tapped Nolan twice on his forearm.

"Don't worry, my friend," he said. "For people like you and me, there's not much to see in this world anyway."

The surly bartender delivered a pitcher of beer and two more glasses to the table. Twitch poured himself a glass and downed it in one gulp. Then he said to the contact: "Tell us about the Ba Xi."

The contact sipped his own beer. "Ah, the Game."

"It exists?"

"It does."

"And Sunny Hi still plays?"

The contact slapped Twitch hard across the face. Twitch barely flinched, but his cheeks glowed beet red.

"*Never* speak his name in my presence," the contact told him in an angry whisper. "Or to anyone else in this city. It's a good way to get yourself killed. He is simply known as *Shang Si*—The Boss. Understand?"

Twitch replied through gritted teeth: "My mistake."

The contact lit another cigarette. Twitch drank a second glass of beer. Nolan, sitting stone-cold mute through all this, had not touched his own drink. He felt the dangerous mission would be best done with clear heads. Twitch obviously thought otherwise.

The contact went on. "So, yes—the Ba Xi exists. And your timing is good, and here's why: The Boss's son's birthday is nigh, and he is accepting presents in his name. You arranged for a tribute, I hope?"

Twitch nodded. "A cargo hold full of sugar," he replied. "Twelve thousand tons of it."

The contact let out a long, low whistle.

"An impressive gift," he said. "Do you have a dollar figure on that?"

"Almost eight million," Twitch told him.

The contact smiled. "*Very* impressive. That will get you noticed, especially if you say it's a present for his son. But who did this sugar belong to originally?"

"Who knows?" Twitch said. "We found it, floating around at sea."

They clinked beer glasses. Then Twitch reached inside his pocket and came out with ten hundred-dollar bills. He discreetly passed them to the contact.

"What do we have to know from here?" he asked the man.

The contact pocketed the money. "You must go to a jiuba called the Red Lantern, twenty blocks north of here. Pay your way in. Talk to the people who always sit in the last booth. You can't miss them—they're identical twins. And don't be intimidated by their firearms, even though they will be in full view. Say *shengri liwu*—birthday gift. Then tell them what you told me. If they like you, they will pass you on to the next station."

"And what if they *don't* like us?" Twitch asked.

The contact smiled darkly. "Then say your last prayers—

because you'll be chopped up and fed to the fishes by morning. In fact, that might happen to you anyway. There are people in this town who will kill you just for sport. Or maybe because they don't like the color of your coat, or the look of your hat. Or maybe they're hung over or need a fix. Or maybe they just haven't killed anyone in the past hour or so and they're bored. But they might also be looking for a spare kidney or an eye or two. Stealing body parts has become a very big business here. Humans hunting humans is what it is. Your liver is worth more than a kilo of cocaine. Your kidney is worth its weight in gold. The old city is an extremely treacherous place to be these days, so you must be careful at all times. You might never know when your last breath has arrived."

The contact finished his beer, a sign the meeting was over. But Twitch had one last question.

"The Ba Xi," he said. "What is it? Poker? Blackjack? Craps? Is it a 'game' at all?"

The contact smiled again. "The 'Ba Xi' *is* a game—but it's not poker or blackjack or craps."

Twitch was surprised. "What is it then?"

The contact began to reply, but suddenly they heard a dull thud. The contact pitched forward, landing face first on the table. A large kitchen knife was sticking out of his back.

Nolan acted instantly. He swept the candle off the table, plunging half the jiuba into darkness. At the same time, the bartender pulled a gun from under the bar and started firing. One round hit a candle hanging from the ceiling—its ricochet killing the macaw in the process. Now it was completely dark inside the bar and raining feathers to boot. Two more rounds went through the curtain behind the table from where the knife had come. But was the bartender shooting at the contact's murderer—or at Nolan and Twitch?

They didn't stick around to find out. Nolan yanked
Twitch off his chair and together they ran for the door. But
on reaching the top of the stairs, Twitch collided head-on
with the woman dwarf. She went straight up in the air, only
to hit Nolan face first on the way down. Nolan literally saw
stars as he fell halfway back down the jiuba's stairway.

He pushed her away and crawled back up the steps, just
as they heard more gun blasts going off inside the bar.
Twitch finally got Nolan back to his feet and they ran out
of the dark alley.

Reaching the main street again, they stopped to catch
their breath amid the bustling crowds. Bent over, hands on
his knees, Nolan was spitting out streams of blood—and
something else.

The woman's tiny skull had caught him square in the
teeth, shattering his number seven incisor and destroying
the tiny radio imbedded within. Nolan studied the minuscule remains in the palm of his hand.

"Hey, didn't they say that thing was expensive?" Twitch
said, still out of breath. "Will we have to pay for it?"

As this was happening, a young girl appeared out of the
crowd. She walked up to them, smiled broadly and put a
flower in each of their lapels.

Then she said in broken English: "Welcome to Shanghai."

13

NOLAN AND TWITCH pushed their way through the
crowded streets for the next twenty minutes, running when
they could, and constantly looking over their shoulders for
anyone in pursuit.

In truth, though, Old Shanghai was so jam-packed with

people, an entire army could have been following them and they wouldn't have known.

Had the knife that killed the contact been meant for one of them? Had the bartender been defending them or was he in on some plot? More important, would the rest of Whiskey realize the tooth radio had been destroyed? Or would they think, after hearing all the gunfire via the one-way transmitter, that Nolan and Twitch had been killed?

These things had no answers, and Nolan knew it was just a waste of time dwelling on them. It was almost 9:30 P.M. Midnight would bring May first and, presumably, the start of the Ba Xi. The minutes were slipping away.

As an ex-Delta guy, he knew that few missions went off exactly as planned. In those cases, knowing how to improvise, especially when some of your equipment broke, might be the key to success.

Turning back now was not really an option. Hunted or not, radio or not, they would press on.

USING THE DIRECTIONS from their late contact and their shirtsleeve street guides, they found the Red Lantern fifteen minutes later.

The jiuba was tucked into another narrow alley. There was no diminutive woman watching the door here, though. Two massive bouncers guarded the entrance instead. Twitch approached them and started a conversation in local Wu Mandarin, but the goons were clearly distracted by Nolan's presence, no doubt due to his swollen lips, the uncovered eye socket, the disturbing stitches across his throat—and now, the bloody, busted opening where his tooth once was. He looked more frightening than dangerous.

Twitch finally uttered the magic words—shengri liwu—while pushing five hundred dollars into each man's hand.

One of the bouncers made a cell phone call, had a brief conversation, and then waved Nolan and Twitch into the bar.

The Red Lantern was barely big enough to hold a half-dozen tables and a few small booths. Two Asian men wearing sunglasses and business suits were sitting side by side in the last booth, a pair of Uzis on display in front of them. They were indeed identical twins. Both even had facial scars in almost the same locations.

Nolan and Twitch walked to their booth and boldly sat down. The two men didn't seem surprised to see them, but were startled by Nolan's appearance.

"What's with this guy?" one twin said to Twitch in Wu. "He's a mess."

"He's my cousin," Twitch repeated. "Bar fights took his eye and his vocal cords."

"He looks one step away from the grave," the other twin said. "It's upsetting."

Twitch didn't miss a beat. "He's much better off than the man who tried to slit his throat," he said. "As well as the person who took his eye—and the one who just took his tooth. This is a dangerous city. Everyone needs a little protection, no?"

"Sure," the first twin said. "If you plan on scaring people to death."

One of the men signaled the bartender. He arrived shortly with four glasses and a bottle of *baijiu*, the potent clear liquor also known as Shanghai vodka. The twins poured drinks for themselves and one for Twitch. They started to pour one for Nolan, but he put his hand over the empty glass.

Twitch still had no such qualms, though. "My cousin doesn't imbibe," he said. "So, I drink what he doesn't."

The three of them downed the baijiu. The twins winced

as the strong liquor hit the back of their throats, but Twitch showed no reaction. In fact, he refilled his glass and drained that as well.

The twins were astounded by Twitch's constitution. They took another measure of him. One asked him, "What size suits do you two wear?"

It was such an odd question—but Twitch was quick in reply. "I got no idea," he said. "I've never owned a suit. And neither has my cousin."

The twins just shrugged as Nolan shifted in his seat. He was able to follow most of the conversation, and was trying hard not to show his impatience. But suit sizes? Time was running out.

They finally got down to business.

"So, we hear you have a present for our boss's son?" one twin asked.

"For his birthday, yes," Twitch replied.

"And what is this present?"

"A ship full of sugar," Twitch said. "Eight million American dollars worth."

This raised the eyebrows of both men.

"Quite a gift for such a young boy," one said.

Twitch laughed. "He can have the whole damn ship," he said. "It's just come into our possession temporarily. And we don't need it anymore."

The twins smiled.

"A ship, *and* a valuable cargo?" the other asked. "Naturally you want something in return."

Twitch nodded. "We want into the Ba Xi," he said.

The twins glanced at each other.

"Are you sure?" one asked. "Or is that the vodka talking?"

"I'm very sure," Twitch told them. "We can't wait to play."

The twins did a simultaneous shrug. Then one said: "Just for the record, exactly *who* do you think our boss is?"

Twitch winked. "I know enough about him not to speak his name."

The men considered this, then said: "Wait here."

They picked up their weapons and left Nolan and Twitch alone in the booth. Nolan was painfully aware they were both woefully exposed to a bullet to the skull, or maybe a meat cleaver to the back. Yet he also knew they could not show the slightest fear or the jig would be up. So, Nolan did his best to stay frozen in place.

Twitch, on the other hand, downed two more shots of the powerful baijiu.

THE TWINS FINALLY returned to the booth.

"We checked it out," one said. "Your ship is called the *Ocean Song,* correct?"

Twitch nodded.

"And it's down on the docks in the Old Harbor?"

Twitch nodded again.

"Then your offer of a gift is appreciated," one gunman said. "Our boss is very impressed."

"So we get into the Ba Xi?" Twitch asked.

"That's a good possibility," the man replied.

Nolan showed no emotion, but he knew this was a big step in reaching their goal.

"However," the other gunman added. "There will be a fee of sorts."

Twitch was unfazed. "Name it," he said, fingering the wad of cash in his pocket.

"Your watch," the twin said.

Nolan and Twitch froze. The watch contained their hidden transponder, the only way those back on the ship could keep track of them, especially now that the radio was gone. The watch was intentionally designed to appear cheap and crummy-looking. Why would the twin want it?

"I've had this watch for years," Twitch told him calmly. "And it's not very impressive."

"But it's just my style," the man insisted.

Twitch was smart enough not to put up a fight. He took off the transponder and simply passed it to the man.

The gunman put it on and studied how it looked on his wrist.

"And another thing," he said. "The cargo of sugar and the ship it is on. It will have to be moved to another location. But no worries. One of our crews will take it over in a couple hours."

Nolan felt sudden fear—there was no way they could have anticipated this wrinkle. But Twitch stayed in character.

"Not a problem," he said nonchalantly. "It's all yours."

One twin wrote down an address on a table napkin.

"Go here," he said, passing the napkin to Twitch. "Tell them you talked to us."

Then, the twin gunmen looked at them as if to say, *That's it.*

Nolan and Twitch got the hint. Twitch downed one more drink, and they stood up and walked out of the Red Lantern without saying another word.

Once they were out in the alley, though, Nolan's anxiety level went up a notch. Improvising was one thing, but their problems seemed to be mounting up with every new move. They'd just lost their transponder—and maybe a whole lot of precious time as well if the twins made good on moving the *Ocean Song* before midnight. And because his tooth radio was also gone, there was no way to tell those back on the ship what happened.

So, should they abort the mission and get back to the *Ocean Song*? Or carry on and hope the rest of Whiskey could handle an unannounced visit from the twins' pirate crew?

Nolan's gut told him this: Because they were already inside Sunny Hi's underground network, if they disappeared now, it might raise all kinds of suspicions, which could be disastrous—*especially* for those back on the boat. And even if they returned to the *Ocean Song*, they probably couldn't get out of the harbor safely before the Shanghai mob knew something was amiss.

Adding these things together, he knew they had to keep going. But they had to do it double time.

GUIDED AGAIN BY their shirtsleeve maps, they fought their way through the crowds, pushing people over when they had to. Still, it took thirty minutes to get to their next destination.

It was a nondescript building on a particularly slummy side street. A canopy of wet laundry hung from dozens of lines overhead. A pack of wharf rats feasted on piles of garbage nearby.

Nolan knocked on the door. It opened to reveal a surprisingly well-appointed apartment with clean white walls, expensive furniture and exotic plants everywhere. Calming music was playing over the sounds of gurgling water. Perfume filled the air.

One word came to Nolan immediately.

Cathouse.

As if on cue, four beautiful Chinese girls dressed in short white see-through tunics, appeared. None of them looked older than twenty.

Sitting on a couch off to the side were two burly Asian men, obviously hired heat. The two looked at Twitch quickly without triggering a significant reaction. He was not a threat. But at the first sight of Nolan, stunned by his appearance, they nervously fingered their shoulder holsters

One man asked harshly, "Who sent you here?"

"The twins," Twitch replied.

The goon made a phone call. After a brief conversation, he said blandly, "OK, go—courtesy of the Boss."

The girls led Nolan and Twitch deeper into the room. Here were two tubs full of steaming, sudsy water.

"Hot water relax," one girl kept saying, pointing to the tubs. "Fun time is good for you."

Twitch needed no prompting. He made a beeline for one of the tubs, pulling two of the girls along with him.

But Nolan knew right away this was *not* good at all. It was clear that taking a bath was a prelude to anything else that happened in the cathouse. But with the goons on hand, he and Twitch were in no position to decline, especially since it was all courtesy of Sunny Hi himself.

The problem was, the poison pinpoint was still jammed up under Nolan's fingernail—and he was sure that the hot water would affect its wax enclosure. If that happened, and the ricin inside dissolved, it would quite possibly kill him and the hookers attending his tub.

The goons were watching him intently. Anyone who hesitated in this situation would doubtless arouse their suspicion. But what could he do? He'd run his left hand along the top of the water and indeed, it was almost scalding.

He looked at Twitch and nonchalantly tapped the side of his tub. Twitch got the message right away, deflating his enthusiasm. He gave a slight shrug, as if to say: what can we do?

Nolan had no choice. If he didn't want to kill them all, he had to neutralize the poison pinpoint.

He indicated to the hookers that before climbing into the tub, he had to relieve himself. They giggled and pointed him to the restroom.

He went inside and carefully removed the pinpoint from

under his fingernail. Batman had told him the poison could be neutralized by uric acid, and there was one place where lots of uric acid could be found: urine.

Nolan retrieved a cup from the sink, dropped the poisoned pinpoint into it, and then peed on it. The pinpoint turned from white to red, the sign that it had been neutralized. He reluctantly flushed it all down the toilet.

Then he sat on the edge of the sink and put his aching head in his hands. Could it get any worse? He and Twitch were now in the middle of hostile territory without the weapon they'd come here to use, without their radio, without their transponder and without any kind of Plan B.

Plus, the clock continued to tick down.

Why didn't we just stay in the Bahamas? he thought grimly.

AS SOON AS Nolan was out of the restroom, all he wanted to do was flee the cathouse and figure out what to do next.

But then he saw Twitch had climbed into his tub and was getting soap applied all over his body. His prosthetic leg was leaning against the nearby wall.

Nolan was instantly furious. They had no time for this!

But then he saw the two goons eyeing him again. On their silent commands, the two other hookers accosted him, led him to the second tub and stripped him of his clothes, all with little protest. He had to give the girls credit—his face was grotesque and his body was grossly discolored, yet they didn't give him a second look. They treated him as if he was the All-American poster boy of his youth.

He followed their instructions and eased himself down into the steaming hot water. And it *was* soothing—for about two seconds. Then another disturbing thought popped into his head. Was there a chance his skin coloring, the acidic wash on the outside, would be affected by the hot water and soap?

He immediately studied his arms and legs through the mountains of suds. To his great relief, the diluted acidic skin dye was holding its own.

The next couple minutes were a weird combination of anxiety and repose for Nolan. The warm water felt great, as did the hookers' hands roaming all over him. It would have been so easy for him to just give in, lie back and let the party girls do their thing.

He had to remember that kicking up a fuss now would surely arouse the goons' suspicions. As it was, the gunmen were no longer in sight; Nolan guessed they were probably searching their clothes, as part of their job of making sure he and Twitch really *were* OK.

But tempted as he was, Nolan had to stay strong, keep his wits about him and try to get out of this place, in one piece, as quickly as possible. He glanced over at Twitch, hoping he was staying strong, too. But what he saw instead was his colleague obviously succumbing to temptation. He had settled very deeply into the tub and, his immediate woes apparently forgotten, was obviously enjoying every move the hookers made. In fact, Twitch seemed particularly enraptured at the very moment Nolan looked at him.

Nolan just shook his head. Here he was, feeling like he was stuffed into someone else's body, in pain from head to toe, with all kinds of bad outcomes swirling before his eyes.

And there was Twitch, flying high on Chinese vodka, getting a hand job.

BATH TIME AND all it entailed lasted more than thirty minutes.

When it was all over, their clothes were returned to them

washed, dried, ironed and folded—a smokescreen for them having been searched.

Nolan and Twitch had dressed quickly, but found the two goons were waiting for them once they were done. The gunmen silently looked them up and down. Then one took out a tape measure and, without a word, quickly measured Nolan and Twitch, both height and shoulder width. Nolan and Twitch just stood there, totally baffled.

When it was over, one goon handed Nolan a slip of paper with an address on it. Then he said: "Good luck, Frankenstein."

Seconds later, Nolan and Twitch were back out on the crowded, dirty street. It was now almost 11 P.M. That had taken *way* too long. Time was really slipping away.

Nolan read the address the goon gave him and they went to check it on their shirtsleeve maps. Only then did they realize the washing process had destroyed their Shanghai street grids. All that remained were two blurry ink stains.

But even worse, Twitch realized all their bribe money was gone, too, stolen from his pants pockets

"Those motherfuckers," he roared, turning back toward the cathouse before Nolan stopped him. "Those fucking thieves . . ."

Was God just playing tricks on them now? Nolan wondered. They had no radio, no transponder, and now no assassination weapon, no maps or bribe money. It was like they were suddenly walking around lost and naked.

Now they had to strongly consider just making a run for it. Get back to the ship and try to get out before all hell broke loose.

But again Nolan believed they were just *too deep* into this thing for that. With the promise of the sugar and the ship, and now the gift of sex from the Boss himself—for all he knew, not showing up at the next station might result in half of Old Shanghai gunning for them, and the rest of Whiskey as well.

So, they no longer had a choice.

They *had* to continue on.

LUCKY FOR THEM, their next stop was just a half-block away from the cathouse.

They found the place by pure chance. They'd stumbled along for a few steps, past a gang of armed men lurking in a nearby doorway, and suddenly the address written on the slip of paper was in front of them. It was another rundown apartment building.

Nolan knocked on the door, and yet another beautiful Asian girl let them into yet another apartment. But this one was dark and full of shadows. There was no music, no perfume. And while the apartment was packed with people, they weren't hookers. They were gritty armed men—Sunny Hi's foot soldiers, no doubt. They were all sitting on the floor, smoking something from glass pipes.

An opium den—with lots of weapons in sight.

The gunmen were chattering and getting high. But when they saw Nolan, some began laughing hysterically.

"Xie mian ju!" one yelled. "Take off the mask!"

"Wu dai zuo meng shi zher!" another yelled. "My bad dream is here!"

So much for the intimidation factor, Nolan thought, picking up a few key words. He quickly retreated to a dark, unoccupied corner, while Twitch began a long, rambling conversation with one of the stoned gunmen, a man with a crooked mouth. Nolan couldn't hear much what they were saying, other than this man knew they were making their way to the Ba Xi and at first seemed to promise help. But by the time the dialogue ended, the gangster was holding up a bag of white powder and shaking it in front of Twitch's nose.

All Nolan could think was that the powder was cocaine or heroin, and the guy wanted them to buy or sell it.

But Twitch told him differently.

"They want us to *snort* some of this stuff," he said, joining Nolan in the corner. "It's ketamine. Also known as Chinese LSD. It's intended as a gift, and is a lot stronger than opium."

But Nolan shook his head furiously. His expression said it all: *no fucking way.*

Twitch grabbed him by the arm. "We got no choice, Major. If we don't play nice with these guys, if we don't prove that we are like them in every way, we'll be in big trouble. Believe me, he was quite clear on that point."

Nolan could only glare back at him. He wanted to scream at Twitch that they were *already* in big trouble. They were stuck in the process of trying to get close to Sunny Hi, yet they no longer had the poison to use on him. So, there *was* no point in trying to get closer. But if they tried to drop out now, Sunny Hi's men would definitely smell a rat and, yes—they would wind up as fish food, as would the guys back on the boat.

It was a classic catch-22.

The goon with the bag poured out a line of ketamine on a nearby table. With the gunmen looking on, Twitch accepted a rolled-up dollar bill, bent down and snorted the line. The gunmen cheered. They seemed to like Twitch.

Then the gunman handed the rolled-up bill to Nolan and poured another line on the table. Nolan had no choice. He bent down and snorted it as well.

The gunmen merely grunted in satisfaction for him, the monster. They went back to smoking their glass pipes. Meanwhile, Twitch and Nolan slid down the side of the apartment wall, landing in awkward sitting positions, to await the drug's reaction.

Time went by. A few seconds. A few minutes. A few hours. Nolan couldn't tell. Everything was spinning, and nothing was making sense.

At one point, one of the gunmen approached him and asked in crude English, "Do you pee regularly?"

Nolan tried to ignore him, but the man persisted.

"How about that one eye you got," the man said. "You got good vision in it? How's your blood sugar these days?"

Finally, Nolan just pushed him away and the man retreated back to the clutch of gunmen smoking their opium pipes.

The next thing Nolan clearly remembered was looking up at the drug den's slowly rotating ceiling fan and watching it dissolve into a swirl of colors.

Reds. Blues. Greens. Yellows. Going round and round.

The colors grew in intensity, taking on the brightness of the sun. Nolan could see the moon and the stars, too, a little galaxy floating above his head. And then, *poof!* It was gone.

He was sitting across from a shuttered window; he could see his reflection perfectly. The puffed-up face. The strangely shaped eyes. The missing tooth. The vaguely yellow skin. That line of infected sutures along his neck. What was really going on here? Who the hell *was* he? Did he live here? Was he from here?

Orders or not, he had to ask someone, anyone. He opened his mouth and began to speak . . . but nothing would come out.

He tried again.

Still nothing.

He went to touch his lips, his throat, his tongue. But his fingers only passed through empty space. He felt nothing.

His spirits crashed. He began to get dizzy again. Someone sitting to his left tapped him on the shoulder and passed him a cigarette. Though he didn't smoke, Nolan accepted it, took a long drag and handed it back.

"Thanks, mon," the person said from behind the cloud of smoke.

The voice sounded familiar. Nolan waved away the smoke and was astonished to see Charles Black, the Muy Capaz pirate leader, sitting next to him, slit throat and all.

Black leaned over and whispered: "Don't worry, mon—I can't talk, either."

Then he got up and disappeared into the shadows.

Suddenly, there was a knock at the drug den's back door. The gunman who'd laid out the ketamine for them yanked Nolan and Twitch to their feet.

"Fun's over," he told them. "Time for me to take you to the next stop."

He steered Nolan and Twitch to the back door and opened it. They staggered outside and found themselves in yet another smelly, unlit alley.

An SUV was waiting here, its engine running. It was black, all its windows were tinted.

The man with the crooked mouth opened the SUV's rear door and waited for Nolan and Twitch to climb inside. But just as he was climbing in himself, two shots rang out. A dark figure in the SUV's passenger seat had put two bullets into the gunman's forehead, knocking him back into the alley.

Then the SUV's rear door slammed shut and it sped off into the night.

14

NOLAN COULDN'T BELIEVE what was happening.

Nor was he sure he *should* believe it. Because of the ketamine making its way through his system, he was having a hard time telling reality from drug-induced fantasy, real life from hallucination.

Have we just been kidnapped? he thought.

It was as if Twitch heard him, because he roared back in reply: "Who the fuck would kidnap *us*?"

Yet here they were, in the back of the SUV, roaring down the dark and dirty alley, prisoners of somebody.

The man who shot the drug den goon turned around and pointed his massive handgun at them. Two more men, hiding in the storage area behind, pulled strips of duct tape tight around their necks awkwardly, adhering them to the rear seat. All four of their captors were laughing hysterically.

Nolan just couldn't absorb how the driver could go so fast, through such narrow alleyways. The buildings and the faces and the handcarts and the Chinese lanterns were all going by in a mind-blowing blur, broken only by the occasional flash of a neon sign, which to Nolan's distorted vision seemed like the sun exploding.

It was terrifying and crazy—but was it real?

"You fuck up!" the man with the gun was yelling at them in slurred English. "You hurt my grandmother? You bite her on her ass? You have big mouths. Now, we gonna make you pay!"

Once again, Nolan was unable to process any of this. Grandmother? Biting someone's ass? What the hell was he talking about?

The man never stopped screaming at them. "You don't

eat her candy? You don't *like* her candy? We *make you* eat her candy!"

That's when Twitch went ballistic

"We fucked up?" he screamed back at the gunman. "*You* fucked up, you mean! Your grandmother's a whore!"

Nolan was horrified. Without thinking, he screamed at Twitch to shut up.

But nothing came out.

He tried again—but just like back in the drug den, nothing happened. He tried a third time. Nothing.

Nolan was stunned. Panic washed over him.

He really *couldn't* talk.

The gunman, meanwhile, had turned beet red. "You're gonna kick my ass, Joe?" he yelled back at Twitch. "Then how about this?"

He pointed his gun right at Twitch's brow—but then that's when the SUV driver yelled, "Don't shoot him in the eyes!"

The man raised his aim slightly—and began to pull the trigger.

But somehow Twitch was quicker. Despite the tape holding him to the seat, he grabbed the gunman's hand, clamped his teeth onto it and would not let go. The gunman screamed in pain, and Twitch only bit down harder. The gun fell out of his hand and went beneath the front seat. Not missing a beat, Twitch grabbed the gunman from behind and around the throat. He pinned him against the front seat with his left hand, then began pummeling him viciously with his right.

"I banged your grandmother!" Twitch was yelling at the man as he pounded him on his face and the top of his skull. "And she was a lousy fuck—for a midget!"

Twitch reached in his coat pocket, retrieved the candy

the dwarf had given them back at the Sea Witch and jammed it into the gunman's mouth.

"Here's your fucking candy!" he bellowed at the man, choking him. "You eat it, asshole! How do you like it?"

The man fought back fiercely—and all the while, the SUV was still speeding through the narrow alleyways and the three other kidnappers were laughing hysterically.

But an instant after Twitch forced the candy into the man's mouth, the victim screamed in excruciating pain. A huge red bubble exploded from his nose. Blood began foaming from his ears and lips. He let out one more scream—and then died.

That's when all the laughing stopped. Even Twitch was shocked.

"That fucking candy?" he gasped. "That little bitch tried to poison us? Why?"

Before anyone could say a word, there was a huge *crash!* Something had hit the rear of the speeding SUV with such force, the impact shattered the back window and crushed one of the two men who'd restrained Nolan and Twitch from behind. It had also ripped the duct tape holding Nolan and Twitch to the seat. The other man tried to climb over the seat to get away, but a second, more powerful impact hit, propelled him into the front windshield, cracking his skull.

It was only then that Nolan realized someone was behind the SUV and trying to run them off the road.

He grabbed Twitch and they both fell to the floorboard. The man driving the SUV had retrieved his dead partner's pistol by this time and was firing over their heads, shooting back at the pursuing vehicle.

Nolan was able to look up into the passenger side rearview mirror. He could see a white Ford Bronco right on their bumper, and its two occupants with wild looks in their eyes. Who were these guys? Were they gunmen from the opium den? Were they associates of the goons in the cathouse? Or friends of the Ugly Twins?

They were pushing the SUV along the narrow alley now. The noise was earsplitting. The SUV was filled with smoke. Nolan was doing his best to protect himself and Twitch. But his colleague was lying so limp, Nolan suddenly wondered if he was even still alive.

He started pounding Twitch hard on the back.

"Stop hitting me!" Twitch finally yelled up at him. "For Christ's sake, let me enjoy this!"

Nolan almost hit him again, this time right in the jaw.

Can this get any more fucked up? he thought.

He looked back up at the rearview mirror and saw a strange sight: the expression on the Bronco driver's face had suddenly changed from fierce determination to utter fear.

What's the matter with him?

He found out an instant later.

The SUV rocketed out of the alley and onto the main street, just in time to broadside a fully loaded produce truck that had turned into their lane. The collision was so violent the SUV flipped over and started skidding along the sidewalk, creating a storm of sparks and broken glass. The interior filled with chunks of cabbage, celery and water beets—that is, until the SUV went through the plate glass window of a nearby butcher shop. This added chickens and chicken parts to the vegetable stew swirling around them. An instant after that, the pursuing Bronco slammed into the rear of the SUV for good, killing both its driver and his passenger and sending the SUV even deeper into the butchery, throwing chunks of bloody red beef into the mix.

Only then did the SUV finally come to a stop. Lying against one door and looking up at the other, Nolan could see all their kidnappers were now dead. He kicked out the side door's window, shattering it into millions of pieces.

Boosting Twitch out this opening, he watched as he slipped down the outside of the wrecked SUV, falling to the dirty street below. Nolan followed, slipping as well, and landing heavily on top of his colleague.

They were bruised, battered and bloodied—but Twitch was laughing again.

"Free at last, motherfucker!" he bellowed. "Thank God almighty, we're free at last."

Or so they thought.

The collision had sent everyone on the crowded street running for cover. Knowing this was the break they needed, Nolan tried to get Twitch to his feet, but they both kept slipping on the greasy, gas-stained pavement.

That's when a white and orange van roared up to the scene, lights flashing, siren blaring.

An ambulance . . .

"This must be my ride home," Twitch laughed, still flat out on the street.

A man got out of the vehicle. He was dressed in hospital scrubs and had a surgeon's mask covering his nose and mouth.

He grabbed Nolan around his shoulders.

"You OK now, Joe," he said to Nolan. "We fix you up good."

The man took a damp cloth from his pocket and put it under Nolan's nose. It had the unmistakable stink of chloroform.

The last thing Nolan remembered the man saying was: "Breath deep, Joe. Count backwards from one hundred . . ."

NOLAN WOKE UP to the smell of blood.

It seemed to be all over him, in his mouth, his neck, his hands.

He was lying in the back of the orange and white van, the

sound of its siren blasting in his ears, his body wracked with pain. His good eye was bleary and he could barely turn his head. But still, through the van's back window, he could see the reflection of the trouble lights spinning on top. He was also being tossed around violently as they were traveling very fast—again. He had no idea how long he'd been unconscious, but guessed it was only a few minutes. Twitch was sprawled beside him, still out cold.

Though groggy and aching badly, Nolan was nevertheless formulating a new plan. It would be a simple one. Once they got to the hospital, he would grab Twitch and run. Back to the ship to regroup and escape. There was nothing wrong with this approach. When the shit has unquestionably hit the fan, you take what you've learned, correct your mistakes, adjust your tactics, and live to fight again—that had been the old Delta Force way. Translation: They would come back to whack Sunny Hi another day.

Nolan opened his eye again. His vision cleared a little and he realized some things didn't seem right. Neither he nor Twitch was on a stretcher, and no one was attending them. They weren't bandaged; no IVs were stuck in their arms. And hanging on the interior walls of the van were not medical devices, but rows of carving knives and meat cleavers.

What the hell kind of ambulance is this? Nolan thought.

He saw more unusual things around him. Styrofoam coolers. Bags of ice. Boxes of rubber gloves—not the kind surgeons might wear, but industrial-strength gloves that a clean-up crew might wear.

That's when it hit him.

Jesus Christ . . .

How tall are you? How much do you weigh? Do you pee regularly? How's your eyesight?

He painfully reached around his back and made sure there wasn't a gaping hole where his kidney should be. He did the same thing to his good eye, as nonsensical as that might have been. He was bruised and battered and still under the influence of the Chinese LSD—but he knew what was happening here.

Your liver is worth more than a kilo of cocaine. Your kidney is worth its weight in gold.

Humans hunting humans . . .

Looking for body parts.

He started shaking Twitch, but this only alerted the two men riding up front in the van. The man in the passenger seat looked back at him and saw Nolan was awake. He tapped the driver and pointed back at him. The driver grunted once and sped up, turning up the volume of the siren as well.

Then the first man started to crawl back toward Nolan. He was holding a large carving knife.

Again, Nolan could barely move, could barely see, and was without a weapon. The man with the knife looked fierce, determined and capable of carving him up. This would not be a fair fight.

But then—Nolan heard a strange pinging noise.

In his altered state, he didn't recognize the sound at first.

Ping . . . ping . . . ping.

It was loud enough to stop the man with the knife from crawling into the back of the van, at least for a moment.

Ping . . . ping . . . ping.

Then a shaft of light fell on Nolan's face. It was alternating blue and red. Another shaft of light appeared—same colors, same frequency. Then came another and another.

Nolan looked up at the van's walls and saw a dozen holes that weren't there just a few seconds ago.

There was more pinging, and more holes appeared. They were big enough to stick a finger through and they were smoking around the edges.

Ping . . . ping . . . ping.

Nolan managed to sit up a little—and that changed the whole acoustic dynamic.

Suddenly the pings sounded more like bombs going off and the holes were getting bigger and bigger.

Bang! Bang! Bang!

Even Nolan was able to figure this out. Someone was shooting at them.

The driver increased the already-breakneck speed, but it did no good. In seconds, the van had been absolutely perforated by some kind of high-powered weapon.

The plan to relieve Nolan and Twitch of their kidneys, their eyes and their spleens had been interrupted. And now there was much confusion inside the van. The driver was no longer expertly cruising at high speed through the narrow streets; he was in a full-blown panic, weaving wildly around people, trucks and other cars.

A brutal crash—Nolan's second this long night—seemed just microseconds away.

Shanghai? he thought. *What an odd place to die. . . .*

Suddenly the van's windshield disappeared in an explosion of glass. The driver took the full brunt of the incoming barrage of bullets. Torn to shreds, he died instantly. His partner did the only sensible thing. He pushed his door open and jumped out.

But the van kept going.

And people kept shooting at it.

It seemed to take forever, but then came one more mighty crash. Nolan and Twitch were thrown to the roof of the van and then slammed back down again. Dirty water began filling the interior. It immersed the two front seats and stopped. From what Nolan could see, they had come to rest in a small canal.

Now he could hear people yelling—and the gunfire had yet to stop.

That's when Twitch finally woke up.

"Are we at the hospital yet?" he asked simply.

The back doors of the van suddenly flew open and Nolan saw the faces of two Asian men looking in at them, guns drawn. Nolan was sure they were Shanghai gangsters, goons who would probably finish them off for good.

But after wiping the grit from his eye, Nolan was surprised to see the two men were actually uniformed police officers.

And surprisingly, they weren't repulsed by his distorted features or his mightily disheveled condition.

In fact, they seemed very concerned.

"You have twisted face," one cop said to him in broken English. "You cannot talk. You can barely see?"

Nolan could only shrug.

Then the cop looked at Twitch and said, "And you have big mouth and talk like a mental patient?"

Twitch nodded slowly.

Both cops got very excited.

One said: "You are the *Shatang nan ren*?"

Twitch had to think a moment. "The 'Sugar Men?' " he finally asked.

"Yes . . . you are them?"

Twitch shouted back: "Yes, we are!"

The cops immediately put away their guns and started laughing.

One said, "Where have you crazy guys been? We've been looking for you all night."

THEY WERE SOON speeding through the crowded streets of Old Shanghai again.

Nolan was holding on for dear life, the g-forces pressing him against his seat. Even Twitch was nervous, his knuckles turning white—this from a guy with a permanent Hawaiian tan.

The cops were crazier than the opium addicts, crazier than the kidnappers, even crazier than the ambulance-driving body snatchers. They were driving at least 90 mph on the tiny, crowded back streets of the old city, sending hundreds of people diving for cover and leaving a long, oily contrail in their wake.

There was no way Nolan or Twitch could ask the cops to slow down or even ask where they were going, because while one cop was driving like a madman, the other was shouting nonstop into the car's two-way radio: *Shatang nan ren!*

The Sugar Men. We have the Sugar Men.

Only one thing was for sure—they weren't heading for the docks. In fact, at one point, Nolan glimpsed a part of old harbor as they were screaming down one particularly narrow street, and they were heading in the opposite direction.

We'll never live through this, he kept thinking as the police car went even faster. *After all this, we don't have a chance.*

Nolan detected a glimmer of hope, though, when the cop car climbed out of the back streets and onto an elevated highway, pointing them toward the new part of Shanghai. But any thoughts the policemen would suddenly drive more safely up here were quickly dashed. If anything, the man behind the wheel became crazier—topping 110 mph and weaving in and out of heavy traffic like a drunken Indy 500 driver. He even used the car's heavy front bumper—intended for moving disabled cars off the road—to push cars out of their way.

The wild ride came to a sudden end, and not with them wrapped around a light pole or crushed beneath a tanker truck. The cops took an off-ramp and screeched to a halt in front of the Shanghai version of a Mister Donuts coffee shop.

"Cops? Doughnuts?" Twitch moaned. "What are the chances?"

The cop manning the radio jumped out, ran into the shop, and returned not with doughnuts or coffee, but with a tiny plastic bowl of sugar.

He gave the bowl to Twitch as if it were made of gold.

"You must have this," he said again in bad English. "You must have this with you."

Before Twitch could ask why, the police car took off again and resumed its mad dash through the crowded, twisting streets.

Salvation came just three miles later—a distance the cops covered in about two minutes. The police car stopped at the top of a towering hill that overlooked the slums of Shanghai. A huge house teetered on the edge of its cliff. It had an ornate gate out front and a driveway that seemed a mile long.

"Who lives here?" Twitch asked.

"Your friend," one cop replied. "The Shang Si. The Boss."

Nolan and Twitch just eyed each other. Sunny Hi.

The cop doing the driving got out and spoke to someone inside the huge house via an intercom on the gate. Then he waved Nolan and Twitch over.

They climbed out of the cop car just as the huge gates started opening. Beyond were a half-dozen armed men, none of whom looked happy.

"Go ahead," the cop urged Nolan and Twitch. "They're expecting you. Give them that cup of sugar and everything will be OK."

With that, the cop returned to his car and roared away, lights flashing, siren wailing.

Nolan didn't know what to do. The guards were eying

them very suspiciously. Yet if he and Twitch chose to leave now, he doubted these guys would just let them walk away.

It was the catch-22 all over again. They were suddenly back inside their secret mission, again with no support, no communications and, most distressing, no weapon. And no longer any good reason to be here.

Nolan and Twitch finally walked through the open gate and were met by the small army of bodyguards. They were searched three times, but all they had on them at this point was the little bowl of sugar and the clothes on their backs. Still, the frisking process took more than five minutes, interspersed with a lot of back and forth on the bodyguards' walkie-talkies.

Finally, the guards simply told them to go.

Nolan and Twitch walked up the long driveway, a journey that took them almost five minutes. It was like walking into a dream, colors everywhere, trees swaying in unison. Water fountains rising up from nowhere, throwing up huge sprays in the mist and then disappearing just as quickly. Piped-in music was all around them, wafting on the breeze.

At last, they found themselves at the front entrance to the house, looking at two wooden doors so tall they seemed to get lost in the stars.

The mansion itself looked like something on the California coast. A palatial, two-floor beach house, half of it leaning out on stilts dug into the side of the tall hill. It had huge windows all around, most of them looking down on the expanse of Old Shanghai below.

It was impressive, no matter who owned it.

Nolan noticed one odd thing, though: a large pipe at the bottom of the house that went straight down like an elevator shaft until it disappeared into the shadows and dull lights below.

Escape hatch? he wondered.

They knocked, meekly. The huge door opened on its own. They took a peek inside and were relieved to find no drugged-out gunmen or hookers here, at least not in plain view. Instead they found themselves gazing at a grand entranceway with a long, curving path passing through a vast multi-story indoor garden. Only at the end of this pathway could they see the actual front of the house.

They stepped into the garden room, which seemed as big as Grand Central Station—but of course, both of them were still tripping mightily. The ceiling and walls were made of brilliant, emerald-tinged glass. Exotic plants were everywhere, and a stream of sparkling water fell from a balcony two stories high. A pond the size of an Olympic swimming pool sat halfway down the pathway. Spanned by a bamboo bridge, the pond was filled not with plain old koi, but with strange and exotic saltwater fish such as wrasse, flame angels and cat sharks.

Dozens of cameras looked down at them from every angle, and no doubt the place was thick with hidden microphones, too. Nolan nudged Twitch and put his finger to his lips as casually as he could. Twitch got the message. Definitely no talking here.

A servant dressed in ancient Mandarin-style silks met them on the bridge. Old and gray, with a long, stringy beard, he seemed to have walked out of a 1930s movie.

He bowed. They bowed back. He bowed again, then said in Wu: "My employer is looking forward to meeting you."

He made no comment on their rather ragged condition. He took them out of the garden, through the front entrance of the house, and into a grand room that looked like a real Mandarin throne room. The soaring columns, the gilding, the artwork and architecture—it was as if they'd been transported back in time to ancient China, except for one thing.

In one corner of this huge room was a McDonald's hamburger stand.

Nolan had to close his good eye for a moment. Was this real—or was the ketamine tricking him?

He opened his eye again—and yes, sandwiched between the giant ancient Yuan Dynasty pottery and the pair of authentic terracotta soldiers from the Huang era was a McDonald's. It had a small counter with two uniformed servers behind it. A huge menu board hung over their heads, and behind them were smoky grills and the crackling oil to make the fries. Off to the side was a self-service soft drink dispenser.

The servant turned to them and smiled. "My employer believed his son would have loved this. So he built it here for him."

Nolan was so amazed that he almost didn't notice the servant's use of the past tense when referring to Sunny Hi's son.

A beautiful Asian woman walked by them, holding a packet of french fries. The servant bowed to her; Nolan and Twitch politely nodded. The woman smiled at them, sadly, then disappeared deeper into the house.

The servant said to them: "My employer's wife. It's been hard on her."

They left the throne area and were led through a series of rooms. One was a library full of books, dark polished wood and low-lit lamps. It looked like something at Oxford, yet everything was built at half scale, as if it had been designed solely for a young child.

The next room featured a home movie theater and a massive array of video games that were all up and running. But again, judging by the cartoonish wallpaper and the types of video games on display, this room, too, appeared to have been intended for a child.

After this was a sizable gymnasium with a soccer net on one end and a baseball batting cage at the other. Yet walking through it, Nolan noticed plastic wrapping still on the baseball bats, and that the twine on the soccer net was so tight it had obviously never been used.

They were finally led to a large but very subdued nursery. There were a few toys scattered about, the largest a life-size, overstuffed teddy bear gathering dust in one corner. The walls of the nursery were covered with minimalist murals of peaceful Chinese forests, mountains and rivers. Calming music was being piped in from somewhere.

Next to a large window stood a pearl-white, king-size bed, with sides like a crib. Two nurses stood in the shadows nearby.

Sitting in a chair next to the bed was the *Shang Si* himself, Sunny Hi.

He was younger than Nolan had imagined him. This man, who until only recently had refused to be photographed, who reportedly tortured and killed anyone who dared point a camera in his direction, was maybe a couple years shy of forty. If this man had achieved so much at such a young age, Nolan thought, maybe by the age of fifty or so, he *would* be running the world.

He was dressed plainly, in a shirt and slacks and Italian loafers. He was unremarkable facially, and seemed if at all only slightly buff. He really didn't look like much of a pirate. But looks were frequently deceiving.

There were no introductions; none were needed. Sunny Hi knew who they were by now. But how ironic, Nolan thought. This was how the mission was *supposed* to play out. Their job had been to get as close as possible to the mob boss. But no way did they think it would be like this—in a nursery— and without any weapons or assassination device, with no way to get out and no way to call for help.

At a gentle wave from Sunny Hi, the servant disappeared, as did the nurses. This left Nolan and Twitch standing there, uncomfortable beyond belief, with Twitch still clutching the tiny bowl of sugar.

Nolan gave Twitch a subtle nudge. He stumbled forward, holding out the sugar bowl like a magi offering a cup of myrrh.

"A present," Twitch said in English, adding quickly, "A birthday gift—for your son."

He said the last word almost with the inflection of a question, sending a chill down Nolan's spine. He was certain this room was under surveillance by heavily armed goons. He was also sure that, with one wrong move, both he and Twitch would be reduced to a pile of ash in a matter of seconds.

Sunny Hi motioned them forward. He took the bowl from Twitch—and seemed genuinely affected. Nolan even saw the man's eyes well up.

"There's many tons more where that came from," Twitch told him. "In a ship we brought for you. It's down on the docks."

Sunny Hi nodded almost absentmindedly, his eyes still gazing on the tiny bowl of sugar. He was getting mistier by the second.

"Your present means a lot to me," he said, in near-perfect English. "Only true friends would think of giving this to me."

He bowed again—and Nolan was more confused than ever.

Finally Sunny Hi said, "Would you like to see him? My son?"

They could only say yes.

The pirate indicated they should come over to the bed. He drew back a blanket and revealed not an infant, but a young boy. He was at least five years old, maybe older. But it was obvious he had health issues. His arms and legs were moving, but not in any coordinated fashion; they seemed disconnected from one another. His skin, too, looked unhealthy, pale and weak. He was wearing a soft plastic helmet to protect his skull.

More shocking, though, the boy's left eye was glazed over and apparently blind, and he had a small scar running across his neck, the result of some childhood operation.

The boy looked up at them with a kind of confused, blank expression, as if he could see them, but just didn't know what to do about it.

Then he started to cry—which made Nolan and Twitch *very* nervous.

But Sunny Hi immediately took a pinch of sugar from the bowl and put it to the child's lips—and suddenly, the boy went from crying to smiling, and then to gurgling, more as an infant would.

"Sha tang," Sunny Hi said, looking down at his son. "That's his nickname—Sugar. Because it's the only thing I can give him to make him know that I love him."

Nolan's knees got shaky. He looked over at Twitch, and wasn't surprised to see him wiping his eyes. The last thing they expected was *this*.

Working the sugar with his tongue, the child turned away from his father, looked directly at Nolan—and started laughing. He held his hands out as if he wanted Nolan to pick him up.

Nolan froze—he wanted nothing to do with this.

But Sunny Hi was beaming. "He *never* wants anyone to hold him," he said. "He doesn't speak, and neither do you. His eye doesn't work, and neither does yours. His neck, his skin. He must see you as a kindred spirit. So . . . please?"

Awkward didn't come close to describing the next few minutes. Nolan picked the boy up and held him in his arms and the kid became extremely animated, laughing and touching Nolan's bruised and swollen face.

Sunny Hi was astonished—and so was Twitch.

"I waited for him all my life," the pirate boss said softly. "I built this house for him. Not everything works out as you've planned, though. But I've never seen him laugh like this. This birthday is a very special day for me—and him."

Nolan eventually put the boy back down on the bed. Sunny Hi gave him one more fingertip of sugar, and the boy went right off to sleep, a smile on his face.

Sunny Hi then looked at Nolan and said, "You have given me a gift worth more than all the sugar in the world.

"Now, I must repay you."

15

SUNNY HI LED them out of the nursery and into a large, well-appointed office one room over.

The office was something a Wall Street executive would love. Clean desk, a battery of computer terminals, more artwork.

Again, not very piratelike.

Sunny Hi checked his watch. It was exactly midnight—after the long, strange trip, Nolan and Twitch had made it here right on time.

Sunny Hi then made a cell phone call and had a quick, hushed conversation. This done, he went to a wardrobe in the corner of the office and took out a full-length black leather coat, a small, tight-fitting black beret, and a pair of enormous wraparound sunglasses. He put on the coat and the beret and adjusted the dark glasses just so. In those few seconds, he went from caring family man to some dark and dangerous character.

He noticed Nolan and Twitch's reaction to his transformation.

"Don't be alarmed," he said. "My job is all about image. But no matter what I look like—you two will be my friends forever."

He led them to a hidden door in the far corner of the office, next to the computer terminals. On the other side of the door was an elevator. Three enormous bodyguards were already on board, waiting.

Sunny Hi stepped on; Nolan and Twitch followed. One bodyguard pushed a button and the elevator started going down.

They were still descending two minutes later. It occurred to Nolan that they were riding inside the pipe he'd spotted before they'd entered the gigantic house.

When they reached the bottom, Sunny Hi opened the elevator door—and Nolan found himself looking out on the worst Shanghai jiuba yet.

It was small and smelly, with only one light, a dim, pulsating bulb hanging from the middle of the ceiling. The bar itself was tiny, and there were very few bottles of liquor behind it. Yet there were at least fifty people jammed in here. Most were pirates, no doubt.

They cheered when Sunny Hi stepped out of the elevator.

"This was where my gang got started," he said to Nolan and Twitch. "This little place, with a lot of these same people. They are my friends, too, and I never forget my friends or my beginnings. That's why I built my house directly above this place. So I could always come back down here and remember how it all began."

Nolan scanned the room again, this time studying all the armed men gathered here. They looked like the road company for an old-time buccaneer movie. All shapes and sizes, scars, weird beards, bald heads, loop earrings, tattoos. Most interesting, though, they were all races and colors—and apparently languages. In other words, Nolan could have blended into this place with little more than his eye patch and a few well-placed fake tattoos.

Son of a bitch, he thought. *This whole nip-tuck thing wasn't even necessary.*

The three enormous bodyguards immediately formed a phalanx in front of Sunny Hi and led him across to the bar, Nolan and Twitch in tow. The crowd parted for the head pirate, but not with as much speed or reverence as Nolan would have expected.

He's one of them, Nolan found himself thinking. *And they are like him. Pirates, to the end.*

Sunny Hi brought them to a small table circled by chairs filled with boisterous pirates holding fistfuls of money. Two Asian men were sitting at the table, and at first, Nolan thought they were playing cards. But while the table did have a deck of cards on it, it also held a pistol and a small bowl full of bullets.

That's when he finally caught on.

The Ba Xi. The Game.

It wasn't poker, or blackjack, or craps.

It was Russian roulette.

Sunny Hi cornered the man in charge of taking bets. He indicated Nolan and Twitch. "These two men are my friends. They will bet the maximum on both parties in each round, courtesy of me. Understand?"

The betting chief understood. What this meant was, no matter the outcome, Nolan and Twitch would win. And judging by how much money was in evidence, any win would be a substantial amount of cash.

The room quieted down. With Sunny Hi on hand, the

game—and the drama—could begin. The two men at the table were trying to stare each other down. One wore a red bandana, the other a black one. Both were sweating and breathing heavily. A man sitting nearby was acting as a referee. On a sign from Sunny Hi, the man cut the deck of cards, coming up with a red eight. The crowd erupted in cheers.

The man wearing the red bandana got to spin the weapon. He did so, but the muzzle wound up back pointing at him. His face fell as he took the gun, put in one bullet, spun the chamber and put it to his temple. More yelling and cheering from the crowd. Much money changing hands. Then the referee shouted: *You xi!*

Play!

The man pulled the trigger.

Click.

The crowd cheered wildly. With much relief, the man with the red bandana pushed the pistol over to his opponent. This man picked it up, spun the cylinder and put the muzzle up to his head.

The crowd went crazy again. More money went back and forth. The ref yelled the command again. *You xi!*

The man squeezed the trigger.

Click.

Another wild cheer from the crowd. Money was falling like confetti.

The man with the red bandana picked up the pistol again, and a new twist was added. He took a second bullet from the bowl and inserted it into the chamber. Now with two live rounds in the six-shot pistol, the chances that the gun would go off were one in three.

The crowd was at fever pitch. The man spun the chamber and put the gun to his temple. More money, more screaming, with Sunny Hi leading the chorus.

The man squeezed the trigger.

Click.

The bloodlust in the room rivaled the thick, smoky air. The man with the black bandana picked up the gun and spun the chamber. Thousands more dollars changed hands. The man put the gun to his head and squeezed the trigger.

Blam!

Half the man's skull wound up on the wall nearby. The crowd cheered wildly and even pushed his corpse to the side to collect their winnings. Two kitchen boys appeared, threw the dead man onto a stretcher and started to carry him away. Another worker did a rough cleanup of the gore on the wall and the floor nearby.

Then the drinks flowed again.

Sunny Hi turned to Nolan and Twitch. "This is my gang," he boasted. "Anyone who wants to be a part of it must be willing to take risks. Because with those risks come vast rewards."

They watched as the stretcher bearing the dead man passed them and disappeared through the kitchen door.

"Besides," Sunny Hi said, "the worst thing that can happen is that you'll die an interesting death."

At that moment, though, Nolan was still looking for a way out of this mess. It was like a bad dream running on a loop inside his head. *No* weapon. *No* plan. *No* way to complete the mission. Again, their Delta training told them that in situations as extreme as this, the prudent thing to do was to just withdraw and try again another day.

Twitch, though, had other ideas.

"I'll play," he told Sunny Hi.

The gangster was surprised—Nolan was floored.

"I didn't mean to suggest," Sunny Hi began stammering. "You are my guest, and—"

But Twitch cut him off.

"No—I *want* to play," he said. "Right now."

Nolan tried to grab Twitch, to stop him from doing this, but it was too late. Twitch had found a red bandana and had wrapped it around his head. The crowd went insane—the visitor wanted to play, and they found this tremendously exciting. All Nolan could do was watch.

Twitch sat down at the table. The crowd re-gathered around him. Another pirate was pushed forward and sat down across from Twitch, putting on a black bandana. This man was about three times the size of the diminutive Hawaiian and looked drunk and heavily stoned.

Twitch contemplated him, then suddenly yelled: "Let's go all out!"

His opponent was confused. He screwed up his face and asked: "All out?"

Twitch laughed manically, then took the gun placed before him and filled the chamber until it held not one bullet, but five.

"Yes—all out!" Twitch yelled again. "Reverse Russian roulette!"

The crowd was thunderous with delight. Once again, thousands of dollars changed hands in seconds. They gathered in even tighter. But this was strange—so strange even Sunny Hi looked a little on edge.

Without the slightest bit of hesitation or fear, or feeling, Twitch hissed at his befuddled opponent: "Do you feel lucky today, punk?"

It was at that moment that Nolan knew Twitch, already unstable, had completely lost his mind.

The gun was placed in the middle of the table. A card was drawn to see who would spin the weapon. Twitch won. He spun the gun violently. His huge opponent looked extremely nervous. The tension in the bar was almost unbearable.

The huge handgun stopped spinning, its barrel pointing at Twitch's opponent.

This man was now sweating profusely. He suddenly had no stomach to play this revised game.

But when he went to reach for the pistol, to the surprise of everyone in the room, Twitch beat him to it.

"Let me show you how it's done!" Twitch yelled, knocking the man's hand away. He picked up the gun, spun the cylinder, put it up to his temple and squeezed the trigger.

Nolan couldn't look.

It took forever, but then finally he heard . . .

Click!

The crowd roared. Money began flying around the room once again.

Twitch then passed the pistol to the man on the other side of the table.

The man was shaking mightily, sweat pouring down his face. He picked up the gun, spun the cylinder and put the muzzle up to his own temple.

He began to squeeze the trigger—again, Nolan just couldn't look.

Click!

It was unbearable. Nolan was trying to get Twitch to look at him, but his colleague's eyes were insanely fixed on his opponent.

The room never stopped going crazy, with money changing hands and much yelling and screaming. Standing right next to Nolan, even Sunny Hi was transfixed as Twitch picked up the gun again and put it to his temple.

But at that moment, Nolan realized something: Twitch hadn't spun the revolver's cylinder. That meant a bullet *had* to be in the firing chamber.

Twitch began laughing crazily again, never taking his eyes off his opponent.

He began to squeeze the trigger.

And finally, Nolan couldn't help himself.

He screamed: *"Fuck, no!"*

And this time, something actually came out.

But it was too late.

Twitch pulled the trigger, but the gun was no longer against his temple. It was up on Sunny Hi's forehead. The bullet hit the gangster right between the eyes. His head came apart as he was thrown backward, toppling over the table and collapsing it.

Then, with eerie calmness, Twitch fired one bullet into the head of each of the gangster's three bodyguards standing nearby.

With the last bullet, he shot out the room's only light.

RUNNING.

That's all Nolan could do. The light went out, gunfire erupted, bullet trails streaked through the room, and the next thing he knew, he was running. In fact, Twitch was yanking him along as if he could see where he was going when no one else could.

They went out through the kitchen—the lights in here had gone out, too. A stream of bullets followed them, smashing into bottles, pans, kettles, glasses. So many rounds were ricocheting around them, it looked like a laser light show. Combined with the sound of people screaming and cursing in many languages, it was deafening.

Nolan had no choice but to follow Twitch's lead. They found themselves running through endless hallways, up and down stairs, coming to blind corners, turning back, trying to stay as low as possible as a continuous fusillade went over their heads.

Finally, somehow, some way, Twitch found a door. He hit it without slowing down, breaking it off its hinges.

They were outside.

They stopped a moment to catch their breath. They were

on a typical Old Shanghai street, twisting, turning, smelly and full of trash. A maze of alleys surrounded them. Instantly there was an armada of SUVs behind them, and *many* people were firing lots of weapons at them.

Again . . ..

But this time, something was different. They had no idea where to go . . .

Then Twitch sniffed the air.

"Follow me!" he yelled to Nolan. "The water is this way!"

And for the first time in the whole fucked-up night, it seemed like one of them actually knew what he was doing.

So off they went.

They ran and ran and ran—dodging bullets, people, cars, diving for cover, keeping as low as possible whenever they could. And Nolan stayed glued to Twitch's tail. It was his show now.

They ran for five minutes nonstop. Then they turned a corner and suddenly were running past the Mister Donuts coffee shop.

Then, two blocks down and over one, they were running underneath the elevated highway.

Gunfire still rattled behind them, but it was getting more distant with each block.

Every place they came to looked familiar. Somehow, Twitch knew when to turn and when to run straight.

They ran past the butcher shop their car crash had destroyed. The street in front of it was filled with crushed vegetables and chicken feathers. They ran a few more blocks and found themselves passing the Red Lantern, its two massive bouncers barely noticing them run by. Twenty blocks later, they were running past the Sea Witch, pausing just long enough for Twitch to curse at the female dwarf still sitting by the door.

"You little bitch!" he screamed.

And then, somehow, they reached the waterfront—and found that the *Ocean Song* was gone.

Nolan and Twitch finally stopped running, collapsing on the pier, violently out of breath.

"Those asshole twins," Twitch gasped. "They must have been serious when they said they were taking the ship."

Nolan couldn't believe it—yet it was the only explanation.

But where was the rest of Whiskey?

Behind them now they heard not only the unmistakable roar of many SUVs heading in their direction, but also the wail of sirens.

The gangsters *and* the cops were chasing them.

"And the way those guys drive," Twitch said, "they'll be here in thirty seconds."

In fact, they could already see the cascade of headlights heading their way.

That's when they spotted the remains of the large crate lying on the dock in front of them.

Stenciled on one of the wooden pieces were the words: OPEN ONLY IN EMERGENCY.

Then, amid the cacophony of sounds, they heard a voice: "Hey! Up there!"

They both looked over the side of the pier, down onto the water—and saw what might have been the most beautiful sight ever: the Arado Ar-95W seaplane.

All unfolded, engine turning, ready to go.

Batman stuck his head out of the cockpit and yelled up at them. "What are you waiting for? You got half of China on your ass!"

At that moment, the sky opened up and the rain came down in buckets amid glaring lightning and booming thunder.

But it was still not enough to drown out the sound of the small army of gangsters and cops racing toward the docks.

Nolan and Twitch immediately jumped. They hit the water at the same time, creating a mighty splash just off the seaplane's left wing.

As soon as they surfaced, the Senegals were leaning out of the plane's rear hatch, yanking them aboard.

"What the fuck happened?" Crash yelled as they were pulled into the seaplane's passenger compartment.

"We greased the bastard!" Twitch yelled back. "But nothing went like it should have!"

"Join the club," Gunner said. "Or did you not notice the fucking boat was gone?"

"Yeah we know," Twitch said. "These two identical-looking assholes had it moved by their gang. They're the same guys who got my watch."

Gunner and Crash looked at each other for a moment.

"Someone has your watch?" Crash asked. "Because we've been watching the transponder's receiver all night and we thought you guys were just sitting in a bar someplace."

Twitch made as if to hit them, but then just laughed.

"It's a long story," he said.

"Well, luckily we had Plan B here," Gunner said, tapping the interior of the seaplane. "We kept this thing in the crate up on the dock. When those assholes came to take the ship, we just left quietly, and off they went. Then we unfolded this thing and we've been waiting for you ever since."

"Yeah, well, wait until those assholes find out all that sugar is really sand," Crash added.

Stevenson and Mace quickly checked out Twitch and Nolan. They declared for the moment neither looked worse for the wear.

Twitch ran a towel over his head, drying himself off, and then passed it to Nolan.

"Are you all right, Major?" Twitch asked him. "It's OK to answer me now. It's OK to talk."

Nolan dried off his face and wiped his good eye. Everyone jammed inside the plane was looking at him. So he opened his mouth—and to his great relief, words did start tumbling out.

"Thank you, brother," he said to Twitch with a croak. "Thanks for getting us out of there and saving my life."

They gave each other a bear hug.

"Anytime, Major," Twitch told him. "Though I got to admit, it wasn't as much fun as I thought it was going to be."

Batman had started taxiing the airplane out into the harbor by this time, but it was hard to see, the rain was coming down so hard. The only illumination he had to navigate by was coming from the frequent lightning flashes.

But now, mixed in with those flashes, were streaks of tracer fire. Back by the docks, three separate groups were shooting at them: the gangsters who had been chasing them all along; their old friends the Shanghai police; and now the military boat that had been cruising the harbor, the same one they paid off earlier.

Sirens were going off. Bells were ringing, Klaxons screaming.

They got to the middle of the harbor somehow, though.

"I just hope all the wood in this thing really does make it a low-tech stealth plane," Nolan yelled ahead to Batman in the cockpit. "If not, we'll have half the Chinese Air Force on our tail."

"We're going to find out," Batman yelled back to him, gunning the seaplane's huge engine.

They were dangerously overloaded, with a dozen people crowded onboard. Still, Batman managed to get the plane up out of the water.

Through a huge barrage of gunfire and lit by the nonstop lightning flashes, the plane climbed into the storm and escaped over the horizon.

PART FOUR

Team Whiskey and
The Phantom Pirates

16

IT WAS A slow night in Morrisville.

The clock atop the only church in the tiny southeastern Virginia hamlet clanged twice. Morrisville had only four policemen; two were on patrol tonight. The bell's toll signaled that their coffee break was over.

Parked near the town ball field, officers Perry and Tripp had just finished their thermos of black, no sugar, when they got a call from their dispatcher. A citizen claimed to have seen four men climbing into the Morrisville National Bank through an open window.

Perry and Tripp didn't believe the report. They couldn't imagine anyone breaking into their tiny bank. There was so little money inside, stealing it didn't seem worth the effort.

Still, they drove the quarter mile to the bank on Main Street, and as they were rolling by, happened to see the silhouette of a man passing in front of the bank's side window.

Maybe the bank got a night cleaning crew? Perry wondered. Tripp said no—Morrisville was so small, if the bank had hired a night cleaning crew, it would have been front-page news.

They parked their cruiser around the corner on Elm Street and approached the bank on foot. They did not draw their guns. Peering through the bank's front window, sure enough, they spotted three more dark figures inside.

Curiously, these people weren't near the bank's tiny vault;

rather, they were gathered around its main computer terminal, looking intently at its low-lit screen.

Perry and Tripp moved to the rear entrance. Here, they found the open window, its alarm wire disconnected. There were greasy palm prints all over the sill, along with remains of the snipped wires. Below the window, large chunks of grass had been torn up, caused by the men climbing in.

There was a large briar hedge at the rear of the bank. Perry and Tripp stepped behind it and waited. The four men climbed out the open window a minute later.

Perry and Tripp finally drew their weapons and showed themselves. They ordered the men to the ground. The intruders hesitated. Each was dressed in black, ski masks and baseball caps.

They stayed frozen for a moment, looking bewildered that someone had actually caught them. Finally, they obeyed the officers' orders and lay down on the damp grass.

But Perry and Tripp were still baffled. The whole thing didn't seem real.

Perry began thinking these people might be terrorists, possibly *homegrown* terrorists.

He reached down, intent on pulling the ski mask off one of them. But then he heard a thump and saw his partner's body crumple beside him. He turned just as the butt of a rifle came down on top of his head.

Then everything went black.

When both cops woke up about ten minutes later, the four men were gone. The bank window was closed. The greasy handprints had been cleaned off, and even the pieces of grass that had been torn up had been replaced and tamped down.

It was as if nothing had happened at all.

17

Eleuthera
The Bahamas

THE ULTRA-LONG-RANGE BUSINESS jet landed at Rock Sound International Airport and taxied over to the lone terminal.

Despite its impressive name, the airfield was tiny, with just a single runway long enough to handle large passenger planes.

Located on one of the more northeastern islands of the Bahamas, the airfield was primarily used by sportsmen who wanted to avoid the hustle and bustle of the more populous parts of the islands.

This was fine for the ten passengers aboard the private jet. The aircraft had been leased to Kilos Shipping's Import-Export Analysis Division. On board were Team Whiskey and the five Senegals—and the fewer people who saw them here, the better.

They'd just completed their third trans-Atlantic crossing in a month, and their second trip to the Bahamas, concluding a fourteen-hour nonstop flight from Aden. But this time, their stay in the islands would be brief.

They were here only to recover the *Dustboat*. With the *Georgia June* as their escort once again, they would sail the little coastal freighter back to Aden, where they expected to return to what they did best: providing anti-pirate protection for shipping in and around the Indian Ocean.

They were all still exhausted from their mission to Shanghai. Their low-level escape from China in the Arado seaplane had been uncomfortable, but uneventful; no one had pursued them. Once out of Chinese airspace, the seaplane made a series of mid-ocean stops, rendezvousing with pre-positioned Kilos vessels to take on fuel until they finally made it back to Aden.

Nolan had gone back under the knife there. Stevenson and Mace removed the hidden stitches around his eyes, and the not-so-hidden ones around his neck. They also replaced his missing incisor with a single false tooth. By this time, the skin-darkening agent had also started to fade, and he was back to wearing his eye patch.

But he felt awful. His muscles, his bones, his brain. He felt as if he'd played a game of tackle football without pads. The Shanghai mission had been a success. The world had one less super-criminal to worry about, and a major force in Asian piracy was now gone. But Nolan was so blown out, physically and mentally, after his one night in Shanghai that he wasn't sure he'd ever be the same again.

The plan now was to lease a helicopter, which would bring them back to the tiny island of Denny Cay, where the *Dustboat* had remained. A mini-hurricane had roared through the Bahamas while the team was on the other side of the world, a harbinger of things to come when hurricane season started in earnest on June first, not that far away. But from all reports, Denny Cay had survived unscathed.

ONCE REACHING DENNY Cay, the team planned to get the *Dustboat* ready for its long journey home, which would begin the next day.

That idea vaporized, though, as soon as the team filed off the plane. Instead of finding their baggage inside the terminal, they were met by two Bahamian policemen who said the team had to report to the airport's security office. Here, they found not a Bahamian security agent sitting behind the desk, but a middle-aged, balding man wearing a bad suit and cheap sunglasses.

They groaned when they saw him. He was Agent Harold Harry of the Office of Naval Intelligence, the seaborne version of the CIA. Simply put, the ONI had been a thorn in the side of Team Whiskey's anti-pirating business from just about day one.

"I thought they fired your ass," Batman told him bluntly.

"They did," Harry replied. "But once you guys got my dickhead partner canned, the brass had to bring me back."

Harry was drinking a cup of coffee. He tipped it their way in a mock toast.

"Thanks for that, by the way," he said. "It means I'll get my pension back as well."

Nolan was in no mood for this—none of them were. Anytime the ONI showed up, they always tried to get Whiskey to do something they didn't want to do. Not happy that ex-Delta guys were operating a paramilitary business right under their noses, the Navy intelligence group had harassed the team throughout their first few jobs in and around the Indian Ocean, threatening them with arrest or worse if they didn't spill the beans about their operations and tactics. At one point they even suggested that, for geopolitical reasons, Whiskey *not* go after the murderous Zeek the Pirate. In fact, the team believed it was Harry's young protégé who'd been responsible for arranging a near disastrous air attack on the *Dustboat* by two unwitting Navy F-18s. So, there was no love lost between the two groups.

"We're busy," Nolan barked at the ONI agent. "So—you gotta check our passports or something?"

Harry turned serious.

"No," he said. "Actually, I want to hire you."

The entire team laughed, even the Senegals.

"The freaking ONI wants to hire *us*?" Crash said in astonishment. "You wanted to kill us not two months ago."

"Look, I apologize for that," Harry said, his voice turning

grave. "But an extraordinary situation has come up. It's the strangest thing I've seen in my twenty-five years of doing this—and every available special ops group is needed, including you guys."

Batman studied him with much skepticism.

"What's the gig?" he asked. "Have you hooked up with one of the casinos? Someone using slugs in the slot machines?"

Harry didn't smile.

"You need to come to a top-level intelligence briefing," he told them. "It will all be explained there."

It took a while for this to sink in for the weary team members. They just wanted to get to Denny Cay and get some rest before the long sea voyage back to Aden.

Batman finally shrugged dismissively and said, "OK—have your people call our people and maybe we'll work you into our long-term schedule."

But Harry shook his head. "No, I mean now," he said. "This briefing starts in an hour. We have two copters waiting out back. One to fly you guys to the briefing, and one that will bring your crew back to your ship."

That was it. Whiskey started to walk out of the room. They had no interest in staying in the Bahamas, and certainly no interest in working for the ONI.

"Thanks, but no thanks," Batman called over his shoulder.

Harry stood up and said: "I want to reemphasize this is a very urgent national security matter. And if you sign on, you can name your price."

But Batman still waved him off. "We got enough money already," he said.

Harry didn't miss a beat. "How's three million sound?"

The team came to a halt.

"Not as good as five," Batman replied.

Harry didn't hesitate a moment. "Five it is then. And

we'll get you a special license to buy that Harrier jumpjet you've been drooling over?"

Without prompting, all five members of the team said, "Done."

THE HELICOPTER FLIGHT lasted about an hour, flying generally south, but with lots of security-mandated zigs and zags along the way.

Finally, Team Whiskey found itself approaching a tiny, isolated cay. It was so remote, there was not another island in sight, a rarity in the Bahamas.

Doing some rough triangulation, Nolan guessed they might be somewhere between Cat Island and San Salvador. But after all the aerial twisting and turning, they really could have been anywhere. Wherever this island was, it was well hidden.

There were a few ordinary utility boats anchored off the island; several other helicopters had landed on the tiny beach as well. But there were no exotic "Cheeseburger-in-Paradise" accoutrements here. The cay had but a single building: a plain gray concrete structure that looked like nothing so much as a giant fallout shelter poking out of the thick tropical jungle.

Their copter landed on the hard beach. The team unloaded and followed Harry up the hill and into the bunker-like building.

There was one big room inside, with a large table and a huge video screen behind it. There were thirty-six seats around the table. Nolan noted eleven were empty. Intelligence types wearing civilian clothes occupied the others. Bad suits. Cheap sunglasses. It was always easy to spot the spooks.

Hastily written name cards were placed in front of each chair. All the usual suspects were represented: NSA, CIA,

National Reconnaissance Office, DIA, Office of Naval Intelligence. There were even four representatives on hand from Blackwater, now known as Xe, the controversial private military security firm.

What the place *didn't* have was champagne, exotic food, palm trees or mist falling from the ceiling. And certainly, no gorgeous women. It was the exact opposite of the BABE meeting.

"I wonder if this is a trap," Twitch said under his breath.

When Whiskey walked in, everyone looked up. They took their assigned seats at the far end of the table, leaving five chairs still open.

There was some hushed discussion among the spooks, and finally they decided to start the meeting without the missing party.

A man in a plain white shirt, a dark tie and sunglasses stood up and, without any introduction, started the briefing. Nolan tagged him as CIA right away.

"We have three major national security problems happening at the moment," he began. "These problems are classified under Level Code Red, and I'm assuming everyone here has that clearance."

The Whiskey members stayed frozen. They hadn't been given any security clearances since their days back in Delta nearly ten years before. But they weren't about to tell anyone that now.

"My friend here from the NRO can confirm this," the CIA man went on, "but the Director of Intelligence has determined that there is unusually big trouble brewing in North Korea, on the Pakistani-India border, and, of course, in Iran—all at the same time."

The screen behind him came alive with a map of the world. By way of confirmation, it displayed a blinking red dot in the vicinity of Pyongyang, the capital of North Korea; the suspected nuclear weapons plant at Bushehr, Iran; and the Kashmir region on the India-Pakistan border.

"Each of these flashpoints involves potentially unsecured nuclear weapons," the briefing officer went on soberly. "And what we've been told is that, though unrelated, at any moment, any one of these crises could go in any direction, with rogue elements trying to get control of either nukes or nuclear material for immediate use.

"These are three very unstable situations, and as you can imagine, the Pentagon and the President are struggling to prevent a catastrophe—or even three simultaneous catastrophes.

"However, this is *not* what we are here today to talk about."

The map on the screen behind him changed to show a grainy aerial photograph of a submarine.

"This is the Russian training sub, *Irktisk*," the briefer went on. "It's old and it carries no weapons. As you know, a so-called mini-hurricane went through these environs a few days ago, and we heard through back channels that this sub, on its way to either Cuba or Venezuela for training purposes, might have been lost or damaged in the storm. The Russians are trying to get their act together to look for it, something they insist they do on their own. But so far, they're just telling everyone it's 'overdue.'

"Of course, this is all top secret and sensitive, too—but *it* has nothing to do with what we are talking about here either, other than to say that if you see pieces of wreckage with red stars on them in your travels over the next few days, don't get alarmed, just call the Russians—I'm sure they'll appreciate it."

There was nervous laughter from around the room. "Their problem!" one person said.

The screen changed again, and now they were looking at something completely different and surprising.

It was an image of a skull and crossbones. The Jolly Roger. The universal symbol of pirates.

The CIA briefing officer pointed to the Jolly Roger and said, "*This* is why we are here."

At that, Batman leaned over to Nolan and said, "Finally, it's getting interesting."

"I'll make it simple," the briefing officer went on. "The Director has been made aware of chatter that a gang of pirates is planning a huge operation in the Caribbean or off the U.S. East Coast sometime in the next three days. We are talking about a high-priority target. A supertanker. A big cruise ship. Maybe an LNG vessel. Whatever it is, it will be extremely valuable and/or volatile—and will pose a great danger if anything goes wrong. The chatter says these pirates intend to ransom it—and destroy it if their demands are not met.

"And, before you ask, we have no idea who these pirates are. Or where they're from—other than they are *not* the type of local Bahamian pirates this area sees on occasion. These people are planning to hijack a capital ship, not some yacht or sailboat. They plan to hold it for ransom, not just ransack it for drug money.

"Now, for reasons we can't get into at the moment, we can't divulge the exact source of this intelligence. And while we're fairly sure they're not Somalis operating thousands of miles away from home, anything is possible, including an al Qaeda connection.

"But again, the chatter is fairly specific. Something is going down in the next forty-eight to seventy-two hours."

He looked out on the people gathered. Then he said, "Our job here is to prevent it from happening."

He let that sink in. Then he began again.

"The trouble is, with these other flash points happening around the world, our SOF groups are spread thin—so much so, there aren't any regular special forces units close to home who are able to work this threat on such short notice. That's why we have some asymmetrical units here."

He nodded toward the Blackwater reps and Team Whiskey.

"This will be a Band-Aid approach, because it has to be," he said. "And there will be two simultaneous investigations. One will be coordinated on land by our friends in the FBI and Homeland Security. The second, which we'll call the Sea Mission, will be honchoed by the Navy and involve Team Whiskey, Blackwater and—"

He cast a glance toward the five empty seats at the table. Just as he was about to say something else, the door to the bunker opened and five people came in.

They were wearing black camo and were walking tall and straight, almost as if they were marching. They all wore the same kind of buzz-cut hairstyle, and in a way they all looked alike, too: blondish hair, huge guns for arms, small fish tattoos on their necks. More tats evident on their shoulders. They exuded a real grim-jawed superiority.

SEALs, Nolan thought.

No doubt about it.

They took their place at the table right next to Whiskey and nodded in the general direction of the briefing officer. They gave no explanation for their tardiness. Judging by the looks on their faces, they believed none was necessary.

For good or bad, in many ways the SEALs were what Whiskey was not. Clean cut. Ripped. Disciplined. A sense of purpose on their chiseled faces.

"We used to look like them," Nolan found himself thinking. "We used to *be* them."

The briefing officer did a quick recap of the problem— the three flash points, the pirate threat, and as comic relief, the tale of the missing Russian submarine.

He then addressed the group as a whole again. He began by saying that the land mission would use a place in Miami as its HQ and that the sea mission would be coordinated from a "secure ocean base," whatever that meant.

At that point, the rep from Blackwater suddenly asked to be heard.

"We've thought this over," he said. "And we're going to pass on this."

The room was surprised, to say the least. The briefer was shocked.

"You're passing?" he asked. "Why?"

The Blackwater rep shrugged. "I don't think we will have enough information to actually fulfill our role," he said cryptically.

At that point, Twitch whispered to Gunner: "Maybe that means they already know too much."

Without further explanation, the four Blackwater guys got up and walked out.

At that point the CO of the newly arrived SEAL team leaned over and shook hands with Nolan.

"So, you're the famous Team Whiskey?" he asked.

Nolan just nodded.

"Commander Dogg Beaux," the SEAL CO said. "Team 616. I'm looking forward to working with you."

18

A NAVY SEAHAWK helicopter finally got Team Whiskey to Denny Cay.

It seemed like a long time ago when they were last here; actually, it had been less than two weeks.

Nothing had changed, despite the mini-hurricane that had

blown through the islands not long before. The half-mile-long cay, looking like a quarter moon laid on its side, still had its shimmering flora, its pure white-sand beach, its handful of huts and small finger dock. The *Dustboat* was rolling in the gentle waves just off the island. Anchored about a half mile farther out was the *Georgia June*, as always ready to watch over them like a big brother.

In other words, for Whiskey, this place was paradise.

But they were staying for only a few minutes.

The CIA briefing officer had given the team three things: a set of coordinates to reach the Secure Ocean Base, or SOB; an order that it was necessary to take down the *Dustboat*'s cargo masts; and a very tight timetable.

The team had to get to the SOB in exactly five hours, just as night was falling. It was about a 220-mile trip to the semi-secret location, which was somewhere west of Denny Cay between the Berry and Bimini Islands and identified on civilian maps as Blue Moon Bay. The team had little time to do more than throw their gear aboard the *Dustboat* and get under way.

Having arrived here earlier, the Senegals had the ship ready to go. Whiskey climbed on and the Senegals revved up the ship's diesel engines and its gas turbine-assisted water jets.

Within a minute of leaving Denny Cay, the small coastal freighter was making forty-two knots, heading west.

THERE WAS A problem, though. The team was still utterly exhausted.

From the time they pulled off the fake hijacking of the *Ocean Song,* to the entire Shanghai adventure, to their escape from China, their hopscotch flight back to Aden, to their fourteen-hour flight back to the Bahamas, none of them had gotten more than a few hours' sleep. Now they were about to take on yet another mission. So, the idea was that the members would get as much rest as possible while the ship was making its way to the SOB.

But Nolan especially found sleep unattainable. He'd collapsed on his bunk as soon as they were under way, hoping sweet slumber would come. But his psyche would just not allow it. The upcoming gig was strange enough. But he had another problem he hadn't told anyone about: He was still having flashbacks from his night in Shanghai.

They started back on the long flight to Aden aboard the Arado. Jammed into one of the seaplane's tiny passenger seats, he was just nodding off when he had a vision that he was back in Shanghai, being chased, being shot at, being butchered alive with a meat cleaver. The flashback lasted only a few seconds, but he was startled awake, and afterward, he found it impossible to fall back to sleep.

The same thing had happened to him a half-dozen times since, and it happened again shortly after the *Dustboat* left Denny Cay. He'd dropped off but was jolted awake just a few minutes later, again after seeing a flash of him and Twitch in the back of the horrible meat wagon. He knew better than to try to sleep after that. So he grabbed a six-pack from his cabin's tiny refrigerator and climbed up on deck.

The *Dustboat* was moving through the calm clear water like a speedboat on steroids. The Senegals had just finished the process of lowering the cargo masts—though they still didn't know why the CIA briefing officer asked the team to do this. The weather was perfect, although way off to the east sat a line of very dark clouds. Nolan got a chill just looking at them.

He took up a spot up on the bow, away from everything else. He drank his beer and looked off to the west and was soon filled with a melancholy feeling. Just as he could see dark storm clouds on the eastern horizon, in the opposite direction, he saw a sky full of magnificent cumulus, gigantic, billowing white formations, bathed in the warm afternoon sunlight.

While studying these clouds, Nolan thought he could also see, way off in the distance, after the water fell off, the edge of another world. He imagined this thin line on the horizon to be the coast of the United States.

The place from which he was banned for life.

He spent the longest time looking at it. Was it real, or was it just a mirage, a fata morgana, his overtired mind playing another cruel joke on him?

He didn't know, but as he tried to figure it out, one thought kept coming back to him: What if he jumped off the boat right now and just started swimming. Would he make it? Could he swim twenty miles? How about 200 miles?

If he could, then he would indeed step foot on U.S. soil again—and there would be no one to stop him.

ON THE OTHER hand, Batman had no trouble getting to sleep.

Soon after they left Denny Cay, he went into a deep slumber and stayed that way for four solid hours, positively Rip Van Winkle-like compared to what the team had gone through in the past couple weeks.

He credited his talent for sleeping to his ability to relax when the time called for it. But, of course, he also had a secret weapon.

Now, he rose from his bunk, refreshed, and went up on deck.

The air was warm and the *Dustboat* was roaring along, closing in on its semi-secret destination. He walked back to the stern near where the team kept its pair of helicopters. He wanted to take a few puffs of a joint in peace.

But he found Gunner and Crash sitting back here. Instead of sleeping, they had dropped a couple speed pills and had polished the team's pair of helicopters. Now they were lounging on the helipad deck.

Batman took his couple puffs then pinched out the joint and walked over to them. They were hovering over a small paperback book, reading it, unusual in itself. They were so engrossed, Batman was sure it was pornography.

But then he saw its title: *Mysterious Secrets of the Bermuda Triangle,* and just groaned. "Jesus, not again."

Gunner and Crash had a past when it came to things like this. During the team's campaign against Zeek the Pirate, Batman, Gunner and Crash had landed in a huge Indonesian graveyard to collect funeral flowers they needed to work a psy-op mission against Zeek's confederates. Batman had previously read a book on the numerous superstitions of the Indonesian people. The trouble was, Gunner and Crash had read the book as well, and had become obsessed with the many ghosts, gremlins and goblins of Indonesian lore. That night in the graveyard, both men were in a near panic whenever the wind blew or a dog barked, and especially when the clock began ticking off the minutes to midnight, which, in Indonesia, was when the nastiest demons came out to play. It was all Batman could do to get them to complete the mission.

Now they were reading again, this time about all the supposed paranormal mysteries pervading the Bermuda Triangle.

"Where did you get this?" Batman asked them.

"From the Senegals," Gunner replied. "They believe all this stuff."

Batman laughed. "Yeah, maybe when they're drinking mooch they do. Anything seems possible on that stuff."

"But there's got to be something to it," Crash insisted. "It can't *all* be bullshit. Take a look."

Batman leafed through the book. Not only did it document supposed disappearances of boats, planes and people in the so-called Triangle, it claimed the huge area of ocean was also a convergence site for UFOs, sea monsters, massive rogue tsunamis, electromagnetic time warps, and wormholes to other dimensions.

Even worse, according to the author, the points of the triangle were Bermuda, Miami and San Juan, Puerto Rico. This put the Bahamas, the very seas the team had been operating in, right in the middle of the accursed area.

Batman just groaned again. "Please, guys—don't start this crap again."

But they just laughed at him. "Like you didn't see this stuff in action back in Indonesia?"

Batman said nothing.

He just tossed the book back to them and headed amidships again to smoke the rest of his joint.

THE *DUSTBOAT* REACHED the SOB's coordinates just after sunset, right on schedule.

The entire team had convened on the bridge, curious as to what the so-called Secure Ocean Base really was—especially since it wasn't technically even in the ocean, but rather in a large bay. The betting was it would be another nameless island, similar to the one where the crisis meeting had been held earlier in the day.

So they were surprised to find nothing at the coordinates but a huge, if unremarkable, ship.

It wasn't a cargo vessel—not exactly. Though the ship was festooned with cranes and lifts and winches, its deck was crowded not with cargo containers, but with sonar buoys, service boats and what appeared to be scientific equipment of various shapes and sizes. The vessel was about 800 feet long and perhaps ninety feet wide. While outsized, it seemed as plain as could be, right down to its fading blue paint job.

"Oceanographic ship, maybe?" Batman guessed.

"Oil exploration vessel," Nolan opined.

"A spook ship in disguise," Twitch said, his words barely audible.

The *Dustboat*'s radio crackled to life. An eerie voice began transmitting instructions to them on how to rendezvous with the odd ship. They were told to maneuver behind it and await further instructions.

On the OK from Nolan, the Senegals followed the instructions and within a couple minutes, the *Dustboat* had lined up behind the slow-moving ship, bobbing gently in its low-level wake.

That's when the back of the ship suddenly started to open.

Twitch's guess had been correct. This vessel was a modified LSD. The rather unfortunate U.S. Navy abbreviation came from its hull designation, Landing Ship (Dock). In other words, it could flood its rear compartment and allow smaller vessels to float inside.

The Navy used LSDs in its so-called Gator Navy, those small fleets of ships whose duty was to put U.S. Marines on shore, invasion-style. The back of such a ship would open up and discharge air-cushioned landing craft that could carry to shore anything from tanks to artillery to Humvees to the Marines themselves.

But this ship looked much larger than any Navy LSD the team had seen.

The *Dustboat*'s radio crackled again, telling them to stand by. The back of the ship was suddenly lit by a bank of searchlights. The team could now see the vessel's internal dock, which was big enough to accept at least two good-sized vessels.

An instant later, the radio came to life a third time. The

same voice, now with a ghostly quality, started relaying instructions on how to dock inside the huge ship.

"Now I know why they wanted us to take down the cargo masts," Batman said.

The closer they got, the smaller the floating dock seemed, especially since another vessel was already tied up within.

"Are we really going to fit?" Crash asked.

Nolan turned to the Senegals. They were the experts.

"Est-il trop serré?" he asked them in their native language. "Is it too tight?"

The man at the controls grimaced and replied: *"Nous saurons bien assez tôt,"* as in "We will know soon enough."

What followed was five minutes of nail-biting as the Senegals fought the ship's suddenly rolling wake to slip into the confines of the LSD's interior dock.

They made it, somehow—but with only a few inches to spare. As soon as the *Dustboat* was inside, the ship's aft hatch closed behind them. They floated up to the dock, where men in unmarked Navy work clothes helped tie up the boat. The other ship was bobbing on the other side of the dock parallel to them, but the team couldn't tell what kind of vessel it was because it was draped in loose plastic similar to shrink-wrap.

Agent Harry was waiting for them on the dock.

"Welcome aboard the USS *Mothership*," he said, with a straight face. "This is a Security 5 vessel, so I don't have to remind you, if anyone ever asks, you were never here."

"But what *is* this ship?" Nolan asked him. "There's nothing this big in the Gator Navy."

"I guess you'd call it a super LSD," Harry replied. "We built it for the Israelis years ago, so they could move their nuclear-armed submarines through the Suez Canal. We intentionally made it look like an oceanographic survey ship. They'd put their subs inside here at one of their

Mediterranean ports and then they'd sail down the canal, to the Red Sea and then into the Persian Gulf, right under the eyes of the Egyptians and everyone else, without anyone knowing what was going on. The Israelis built their own a few years ago, so they gave this one back to us."

Nolan was amazed by the story. They all were.

"Freaking Israelis," Nolan said. "Always thinking . . ."

TEAM WHISKEY FOLLOWED Harry up a series of ladders to the top deck of the strange ship.

From there, they were escorted to the vessel's Combat Information Center, or CIC. The ship might have looked innocuous on the outside, but inside it rivaled the U.S. Navy's most modern vessels. Its design and equipment was universally high tech and the crew, all of whom were dressed in sharp but unadorned combat suits, exuded confidence and élan.

They walked into the CIC to find SEAL Team 616 already there, the five doppelgangers taking all the good seats up front. Nolan wondered if they owned the plastic-wrapped boat they'd seen tied up below.

A SEAL team with its own ship? he thought. That might be a first.

They had a quick round of introductions, something the two groups weren't able to do properly in the rush after the briefing on Bunker Island. It was mostly an exchange of grunts and nicknames. Snake, Batman, Crash, Gunner and Twitch meet Bowdog, Smash, Monkey, Elvis and Ghost. Whiskey was wearing its old-fashioned blue battle suits, a gift from the Russian mob before the team took on the cruise liner security gig. The suits were poorly made, thick, and fairly uncomfortable, but they were all they had. The SEALs, on the other hand, were wearing what looked to be brand-new black camouflage battle fatigues—a slick, very stylish modern design. In the fashion war, the SEALs definitely had Whiskey beat.

The CIC had room for only about a dozen people, so it was a tight squeeze. Much of the space was taken up by literally *tons* of futuristic surveillance and spy gear: There were twenty-two VDT screens jammed in here, each one monitoring some trouble spot around the world. It was obvious the ship was heavily tied into the U.S. intelligence services' galaxy of spy satellites, as many of the monitors were marked NRO—for the National Reconnaissance Office, possibly the most secretive of all of America's spy agencies.

Three uniformed Navy officers stood on a slightly raised platform in front of a Plexiglas situation board. Devoid of any rank insignia or nameplates, each man wore a gold crucifix on a chain around his neck. They were all in their mid-50s, all looked extremely serious and determined— and, in a strange way, they all looked alike, too. Buzz cuts, slightly windburned faces, tough as nails, and well aware of it. It was clear from the start that they would be running the show.

Nolan knew that for reasons of security, there'd probably be no formal introductions, so he had no idea what to call these people. Sensing this, Agent Harry leaned over to him and whispered: "These three guys are the superstars of the new ONI surface warfare special ops division. They're experts in kissing the right asses, from every big shot in the Pentagon, and right up to the Joint Chiefs. People either call them 'The Three Kings' or 'The Three Stooges.' Take your pick."

Whatever their handle, they started off the briefing with a bang.

"Everyone here knows the situation," the officer in the middle said, beginning the briefing. "So there's no need to read you the Bible again.

"But I will tell you this: This mission ain't for those chicken-shit civilian types. *This* ship is all about finding things, sometimes things that no one even knows are there. And I promise you, we're gonna find these pirate assholes before those civilian pansies move into their luxury suites in Miami. Any questions?"

The SEALs let out their version of 'hoo-rah!' "

Whiskey remained silent. Except for Crash, who whispered to Gunner: "Hey, *we're* civilians, aren't we?"

Nolan just groaned under his breath. He already missed the spooks on Bunker Island.

"This will be an exercise in sharing," the King went on. "We will all have total access to all intelligence concerning shipping activity in the Caribbean and southern East Coast area for the next three days. We are lucky in this regard because, except for the USS *Carl Vincent* due in Norfolk in two days and the boomer sub, USS *Wyoming* arriving about the same time in Kings Bay, Georgia, we are free of any major U.S. Navy ship movements within the crisis time frame. Everything else is routine commercial shipping: LNG ships, supertankers, cruise ships, probably thirty potential targets in all.

"All we have to do is identify, through the use of good, solid intelligence, which of these ships is the target, and how the pirates plan to get aboard. If we achieve these two objectives, we got this bitch in the sack before she can get her panty hose off. Any questions?"

There were none.

"Now, if it gets hairy, we have the authority to reroute any shipping from Cuba up to Virginia in accordance to this mission. In other words, if we need a clear area of open sea to make some noise, we can make that so.

"We will also have support from Naval Air Stations from Jacksonville to Norfolk. This will include P-3 maritime patrol planes, C-130s on loan from the Coast Guard, and I'm told, TR-1 high-altitude recon platforms. Plus the usual array of recon satellites. We also have a total of thirty non-capital surface ships at our disposal up and down the entire East Coast.

"And finally, we will be launching small drones from this ship, while larger Predator and Reaper drones will be launching from McDill, Langley and Charleston air force bases.

"So, we will have a lot of eyes in the sky and feet in the water. Believe me, once we spot them, these pirates won't have a chance."

He produced two folders. He handed one to Commander Beaux and the other to Nolan.

"What we need from your two teams is HUMINT— good old-fashioned human intelligence. These folders contain your mission points; we believe these are good places for you to start. Hopefully, they will provide leads that will produce results. But just like the fairy ground team in Miami, it's paramount that any intelligence you come across is passed on to us here as quickly as possible, so we can disseminate it to all interested parties.

"In conclusion, if there is a successful pirate action so close to the United States, just in future resource allocations alone—for anti-pirate patrols up and down the East Coast and things of that nature—it will break the Pentagon's piggy bank. And the fact that we have those three other hot spots happening around the world all at the same time makes this entire matter that much more pressing.

Whenever it rains, it tends to pour, but I'm sure everyone in this room knows that already."

He looked up at both groups.

"Are there any questions?"

Nolan was already looking through his file. It contained the coordinates of a Bahamian island where a resident claimed to have intelligence on the possible pirate hijacking of a large vessel off the East Coast. It appeared the team's mission was to find him and get the information from him. It seemed simple. Almost too simple.

"Nothing here," he finally replied.

The SEALs, meanwhile, had been furiously taking notes, writing down just about everything the King had said. They also appeared to be surreptitiously recording the meeting with their video camera.

Commander Beaux was still going through his team folder, which appeared bigger, thicker and more detailed than the one for Team Whiskey.

"Everything is nominal here," he finally said.

The King was about to wrap up the meeting when he stopped and said: "There's just one more thing. It occurred to us that Whiskey has more experience in finding and fighting pirates than SEAL 616. So, we're recommending that one of the Whiskey members accompany the SEAL team. This person would jump over and join 616, and keep Whiskey informed of what they are doing."

The room fell silent. Nolan never expected anything like this—and looking over at the SEALs, he could tell that neither had they.

Before anyone could say anything, Crash spoke up: "I'd be glad to do it."

Crash was a former SEAL. He'd spent two years with them before joining up with Delta Force and Team Whiskey. After the misadventure at Tora Bora played out, he was drummed out of the service along with the rest of them and had been doing private mercenary work until Whiskey got back together. But he'd never made any secret of the fact that the SEALs had been his first love.

"Sounds good," the King said.

He turned to Commander Beaux. "That square with you, Commander?"

To his credit, Beaux didn't hesitate.

"Great idea, sir," he said. "We'd love to have him along. He'll be an asset—and we'll learn from him, for certain. Plus, he can work our camera."

And just like that, Crash got up, walked to the front of the CIC, shook hands again with his new mates, and then went out the door with them.

As he was leaving, he looked over his shoulder to Whiskey.

"See you in the movies," he said.

19

TEAM WHISKEY'S STAY on the *Mothership* lasted less than three hours.

The briefing itself was just thirty minutes, start to finish. But there was another reason the *Dustboat* had to visit the Super-LSD.

The Three Kings wanted to install a secure antenna on the little coastal freighter. This device was deemed essential, as it would allow the team to communicate with the *Mothership* anywhere in the mission operations area without fear of messages being compromised. Looking like an extra crow's nest, the antenna was installed atop the *Dustboat*'s bridge and wired to bypass its existing onboard communications system. This way, no stray or unintentional messages about the secret mission could leak out.

Arriving back in the *Mothership*'s docking bay soon after the CIC briefing to wait for the antenna's installation, the four remaining members of Whiskey were surprised to see the mysterious shrink-wrapped vessel had already departed. They were sure now it was the SEALs' mode of transportation.

"Those guys are in a hurry, aren't they?" Batman said dryly. "I guess they want to get to the good part quickly."

Twitch just shook his head and said, "Yeah, something like that."

The *Dustboat* finally set out just before midnight.

Backing the freighter out of the enormous *Mothership* again took all the Senegals' expertise. Once it was free, they opened up the ship's two diesel engines and kicked in its turbine-assisted water jets. Then with the team gathered on the bridge, they turned northeast and were off.

As they were leaving, they spotted a darkened vessel about a half-mile to the south, shadowing the *Mothership*. Studying the vessel through their night vision goggles, Nolan and Batman were surprised to see the flag of Blackwater USA flying from its mast.

"For people who weren't interested," Batman said, "these guys seem pretty interested."

AGAIN, WHISKEY'S MISSION was to get to an island known as North Gin Cay and find a resident who'd claimed to have information about the impending pirate attack.

North Gin Cay was located at the far northeastern tip of the Abaco Islands. It was a string of cays that met the Atlantic with names like Strangers Island and Double Breasted Cay.

The trip by boat would take about five hours, or about

five times as long as it would have taken by helicopter. But the Three Kings had emphasized that security was the most important aspect of this mission. And Whiskey's assignment was a pure intelligence-gathering operation. This meant they had to arrive on North Gin Cay without making too much of a fuss. Landing in a heavily armed OH-6 gunship would certainly attract attention.

Upon arriving on the island, the plan was for the team to pretend to be a crew from a typical coastal freighter while quietly seeking out the informant. The mission file contained precious little information about this informant, though. He had approached an off-duty U.S. Navy officer earlier in the week and said something to him about pirates—"real pirates" and not the typical local gangs. This led the officer to contact ONI, and in turn spurred ONI to tell the Three Kings.

If the informant could be found and if he appeared legitimate, Whiskey would reveal itself and get whatever information he had. If not, the mission would qualify as a fire drill, nothing more.

As the team members joined the Senegals in drinking a pot of coffee on the bridge, they tossed around theories as to why Whiskey had been given this specific assignment. The team *did* have experience dealing with undercover informants—after all, that's what had led to their disastrous mission at Tora Bora. They were also good at presenting themselves as non-military types, again key to the mission's overall security. And they had successfully tracked down one of the islands' most notorious local gangs just weeks before. But it still seemed like not a lot of work, especially for $5 million.

"Just as long as the check clears," Batman said, repeating the team's mantra. "That's all that matters."

* * *

THEY PLOWED ON through the dark night, making good time, as all three of their power plants worked smoothly. Once their course was laid in, the Senegals started a game of French poker, and Gunner and Batman joined in. Nolan got behind the ship's helm and took over the steering. Twitch agreed to keep one eye on the navigation instruments.

At that point, Nolan noticed Twitch was reading a book. *This is a first*, he thought. He couldn't help but ask him what it was.

Twitch just showed him the cover: *Mysterious Secrets of the Bermuda Triangle*.

Batman overheard the exchange, shook his head and went back to playing cards.

"Crash gave it to me right before he left," Twitch explained. "We're sailing right through the middle of this freaking Triangle, and you know, some pretty strange stuff has happened out here."

No sooner were those words out of his mouth when there was a tremendous *crash!*

It felt like the *Dustboat* had hit a brick wall, shaking violently from one end to the other. Everyone was thrown to the deck; the poker table and all the cards went flying. The instrument panel erupted in a barrage of madly blinking trouble lights.

"God damn, we just hit something!" Batman yelled.

"Or something hit us!" Twitch yelled back.

Alarms sounded all over the ship. The engines coughed, and smoke billowed out of their air vents. Then came another tremendous crash over their heads. The ship's electrical system blinked once—then all the lights went out.

A moment after that, all three engines quit for good.

Though stunned and battered, the team recovered quickly. Batman and Gunner scrambled down to the engine room, while Nolan and Twitch ran forward to see what had happened.

Twitch stopped momentarily to grab some trouble lanterns, so Nolan was the first to reach the bow.

He leaned over the railing to see a substantial dent in the port side of the ship, about six feet off the nose.

But ten feet directly below the surface, he saw a green glowing light. As he stared at it, it took on a saucer shape and began sparkling, even though it was submerged. It began spinning incredibly fast, taking on a solid shape. Then, in an instant, it was gone, streaking off underwater toward the open ocean.

By the time Twitch arrived and directed the light into the water, all he could see was swirling waves and the huge dent in the ship's nose.

"What did we hit?" he yelled at Nolan.

But Nolan couldn't reply. Had what he'd just seen been real? Or had it been another flashback—even though he was awake?

Twitch played the light in all directions, but they saw nothing but the dark water. No rocks, no islands. No other boats. Nothing.

Nolan finally spoke. "God damn. I think I'm still going crazy from that shit we had in Shanghai."

"Why—what did you see?" Twitch asked him.

Nolan didn't want to say it—but he had to. "Something . . . bright green. It was a circle, under the water. It was there one second, then gone the next."

"Like a saucer?" Twitch asked.

Nolan snapped at him: "Don't *use* that word. I don't know what the fuck it was."

Twitch collapsed next to him and put a hand on Nolan's shoulder. "If it makes you feel any better, sir," he said, "I'm still going crazy from Shanghai, too. I've been seeing weird things since we got back here. Why do you think I was reading that crazy book?"

Nolan looked Twitch straight in the eye; the man was almost crying. He grabbed him and said, "Listen—we tell no one. That's an order."

Twitch was all in agreement. "No worries there, sir," he said.

Suddenly, Batman was up on the outer bridge railing, yelling down at them. "The engines are seized! And the radio is totally fucked up. What the hell did we hit?"

"It had to be a submarine or something!" Twitch yelled back.

"Or something," Nolan repeated.

"Well, whatever happened, we're screwed," Batman yelled back. "We were heading north, now we're floating due east— and that's open ocean out there!"

At that moment, Twitch fixed his lantern not on Batman, but on the bridge roof just above his head. In the beam they saw the newly installed secure antenna was now tilted at a 45-degree angle, dislodged by the violent collision and hanging as if caught in a freeze fame.

Before they could say or do anything, the antenna resumed its fall, smashing to bits on the bridge roof, its pieces spilling into the sea and taking the ship's old antenna with it.

This meant they had no engines, no power and no way to contact anybody, secure or not.

And now they were drifting out to sea.

20

"WANT A PEEK?"

Crash drained the last of his coffee and climbed up to the control deck. There was a periscope here, similar to those found on modern submarines.

But the SEALs' mysterious vessel was not a U-boat.

Commander Beaux adjusted the periscope to Crash's height and stepped aside. Crash pressed his eyes against the focal piece and saw the faint outline of a city twinkling in the distance.

"Is that Miami?" he asked.

Commander Beaux laughed.

"You're off by about ninety miles," he said. He pushed the periscope's zoom button, made another adjustment, and let Crash look again. This time the scope was focused on a sign painted on a beach wall. It read: BIENVENIDO A LA HABANA.

Welcome to Havana.

Crash was astounded.

"You can get *this* close?" he asked Beaux. "Don't they have a twelve-mile limit? Or military sea patrols?"

"I'm sure they do," Commander Beaux replied. "But what difference does that make when you're invisible?"

This was no idle boast.

The SEALs' vessel *was* invisible. At least to radar. And at night, under the right circumstances, it was pretty much invisible to the naked eye as well.

Its official name was the IX-529; it was later christened the *Sea Shadow*. Simply put, it was a seagoing version of a stealth fighter jet.

About 160 feet long and almost half that wide, it shared some design features with the F-117 Nighthawk. It was all angles, with no curves and no vertical surfaces, an overall shape that tended to make radar signals slide off instead of bouncing back to a receiver. Under optimal conditions, the *Sea Shadow* presented a radar signature no bigger than a seagull.

Technically, it was a catamaran. It had twin submerged hulls, each with a propeller, a stabilizer and a hydrofoil. The hulls were connected to the rest of the ship by two angled struts. With a draft of fifteen feet, it sat so low that it looked like it should have sunk the first time it hit the water. But this odd design actually made the IX-529 highly stable even under the worst conditions at sea.

Inside, the stealth vessel was tight but not uncomfortable. There was enough room to support a crew of six. It had a head, a shower, a small galley, six bunks and a fairly elaborate control deck—but that was about it. It carried no weapons—no torpedoes, no deck guns, no missiles.

But it didn't need any. The IX-529 *Sea Shadow* was not built to be a warship. It started out as an experimental platform to prove the basics of seaborne stealth. After its life as an experimental craft was over, it bounced around a bit and was put in storage until the Navy finally turned it over to the SEALs, who then turned it over to Section 616. The first thing they did was boost its power plants. The result was that the odd vessel could now travel close to fifty knots.

The 616 guys referred to it as "the bus," a way to get them to places where they could really do their thing.

And at the moment, it had brought them very close to Havana Harbor.

THIS WAS WHERE the SEALs' "taxi" came in.

It was called the Advanced SDV, as in the SEALs Delivery Vehicle. It was carried by a special brace above the *Sea*

Shadow's twin hulls. Essentially a mini-submarine, sixty-five feet long and eight feet high, it looked like a pregnant torpedo with a steering cockpit in the front. It could carry as many as a dozen SEALs to a target in a pressurized dry compartment. A sixty-horsepower motor could move it along at almost ten knots.

It had its own periscope, communications mast and GPS navigation system, plus SONAR and terrain mapping gear for spotting mines. It was, by far, the coolest piece of special ops equipment Crash had ever seen.

This was the plan: While the SEAL nicknamed Smash remained on the *Sea Shadow*, Commander Beaux would lead the rest of his team on a mission right into the heart of the Cuban capital's harbor.

The reason? Docked in Havana at the moment was an old Russian container ship that, according to intelligence reports Commander Beaux said he had secured for Team 616, was under the control of people other than its original crew.

The ship, the *Deshovshi*, had a shady past. It had been involved in various smuggling schemes over the years, and had been caught carrying contraband weapons, drugs, and stolen items including luxury cars and big-screen TVs. It had left the Russian port of Murmansk five weeks earlier and skirted the coast of England, France and the west coast of Africa before turning west and heading for the Caribbean.

Turning up in Havana the week before, somewhere along the way, its original Lithuanian crew had either left the ship voluntarily or had been thrown overboard. In any case, another crew had taken over.

According to Commander Beaux, the people on the *Mothership* believed this new crew could be harboring the phantom pirates—perhaps Africans, or possibly Eastern

Europeans, or even Muslim terrorists—who were planning the big strike.

It was up to the SEALs to find out who was crewing the *Deshovshi* and what they might be up to.

BEAUX HAD NO problem with Crash going with them. Although he'd left the SEALs and the U.S. military nearly ten years before, he was still in good shape, had maintained his skills, and was itching to go back into action with his old outfit. Besides, as Commander Beaux said, they needed someone to work the video camera.

When the time came, Crash happily climbed into a wet suit and, trailing the others, slipped out of the *Sea Shadow*'s bottom hatch and into the small SDV submarine it carried below.

Once he was sealed inside, the SDV was dropped into the water, dove to a depth of thirty feet and was on its way.

THE RIDE INTO Havana Harbor filled Crash with an excitement that almost bordered on sexual. Commander Beaux sat up front, steering the tiny sub, while Ghost acted as the navigator. Crash sat in the watertight compartment in back with Elvis and Monkey. It seemed odd to him, but they passed the time telling him about some of the 616's previous exploits, keeping him entertained. It was the stuff of movies or a TV show. With each tale, Crash felt something unexpected welling up inside him. It was at this moment, traveling under the water toward Havana Harbor, that he realized how much he'd missed being part of the SEALs.

It was 5 A.M., and morning fog was gathering when the SDV arrived in the harbor. There weren't many legitimate cargo ships present, but there were many Cuban naval craft in evidence, as well as a broken-down Russian Navy cruiser that was supposed to be leading the search for the missing submarine, the *Irktisk*. The SDV glided beneath them with ease.

Commander Beaux steered the tiny sub up to the mysterious *Deshovshi*. At that point, Crash, Elvis and Monkey put on their scuba hoods and masks, checked their air tanks and waited as their compartment was flooded. Then they swam outside.

They met up with Commander Beaux, also in full scuba gear and carrying a waterproof satchel. On his instructions, Crash started recording with the team's underwater video camera.

With the SEALs and Crash swimming about fifteen feet below the surface, Commander Beaux reached inside his waterproof bag of tricks. He took out what looked like an electronic stethoscope and attached it to the hull of the container ship. He hooked up a set of earphones for himself and the rest of his team, and in seconds they were listening in on conversations taking place inside the vessel, this while Crash videotaped it all.

By manipulating various dials on his stethoscope, Commander Beaux was able to go from one conversation to another. Using sign language, he indicated to Crash that the people on board were speaking a variety of languages: Russian, Spanish, and a lot of English. From this, Beaux pantomimed for the camera, he counted a dozen people on the ship, either on the bridge or in a cabin just beneath it.

Now came the hard part.

Commander Beaux signaled the others that their recon was complete—they were now going aboard. While Ghost kept the sub close to the side of the Russian ship, Beaux, Monkey, Elvis and Crash swam up to the surface, next to the vessel's stern.

Beaux threw a hook rope up to the railing and rappelled up to the back of the old container ship. Once on deck, he motioned for the others to follow. Crash was the last to climb aboard, making sure he got the others doing their thing on video before he went up himself.

Fortunately, it was dark on this part of the ship, and the growing fog was helping hide them as well. Lucky for them, the 616's video camera was equipped with an infrared night vision lens.

Commander Beaux explained to Crash that they'd decided to plant an explosive in the ship's engine room and detonate it with a time-delay fuse. That way, if this was the pirates' attack ship, it would be disabled and marooned here in Havana Harbor. And even if it wasn't, then at least there would be one less shadowy ship sailing the world's oceans. It was a win-win situation.

On hearing this, Crash again became tremendously excited. He was armed, as they all were, with an M4 that had been encased in waterproofing.

"Can you secure this end?" Commander Beaux asked him.

"Absolutely," Crash responded.

"Just keep the camera running," Beaux reminded him.

Then the three SEALs disappeared into the gloom.

The minutes went by. Crash found himself shaking, but in the most pleasant way. Adrenaline was rushing through his body like a succession of tidal waves. It wasn't a foreign feeling, because he'd done some pretty hairy things with Delta and the pirate-busting Team Whiskey.

But he recognized this particular sensation as the same one he used to get when he started his special ops career with the SEALs, nearly a decade before.

Shaking . . . but liking it.

At last, Crash spotted the trio of SEALs moving back toward him. He finally exhaled. The team had been gone for just five minutes, but it seemed like five hours. Beaux told him they'd installed ten pounds of plastic explosive in the ship's engine room with a timed fuse. This meant it was time to make their getaway—quick.

They hurried back down the hook rope, dove underwater, scrambled back inside the SDV and then raced out of Havana Harbor. They were about a quarter-mile away when they heard the timed explosion blow off the back end of the container ship. There were high fives all round.

Success . . .

SEAL Team 616 had put the mystery vessel out of action for at least the foreseeable future. And Crash was very impressed.

These guys are good, he thought. Really *good.*

21

Aboard the Dustboat

DRIFTING . . .

But for how long?

They couldn't tell.

Gunner was the only one onboard with a watch, and it had stopped the moment of the unexplained collision.

They were still moving eastward, though, toward open water, amazed that whatever happened to them was violent enough to knock them in an entirely different direction.

Down below, in the darkened engine room, Batman was banging a huge hammer fiercely on the side of the diesel engine compartment.

He didn't know what else to do. Nothing was jammed in the engine or transmission stations. Nothing was overheated;

the temperature gauges all read normal. There was no smell of smoke, at least not down here.

Everything in the engine room seemed in working order—except, nothing was working.

Gunner was holding the trouble light for him. "My old man used to say, it's not how hard you hit it, it's knowing where to hit."

"But this just doesn't make sense," Batman said as he pounded away. "I've had gremlins in aircraft, but on a boat?"

Just as those words came out of his mouth, the diesels exploded back to life.

Batman was so surprised, he was knocked back on his ass. The lights blinked back on. The generators started humming, and electronics started popping back to life all over the ship.

Batman stared at Gunner and then at the hammer.

"Did I do that?" he asked in astonishment.

He and Gunner ran back up to the bridge to find the Senegals flipping switches and getting the controls back in order.

Everything was suddenly working again—and most important, the steering controls were back on line. They ran a diagnostic through the control panel and everything came back green. It was as if nothing had happened at all. Yet they'd lost at least an hour's time, and they knew this only because Gunner's digital watch was working again, and when it blinked back on, it wasn't zeroed out. Rather, it showed that more than an hour had passed since it had blinked off.

NOLAN AND TWITCH had spent all this time out on the bow, looking for other submerged objects they might be in danger of hitting. But they had barely spoken a word between them.

Now that the ship had come back to life, they hustled back up to the bridge.

"Who found the 'On' switch?" Nolan asked Batman.

"That's the big mystery," Batman replied. "Everything seems to be working OK now, but the diagnostics said nothing was broken in the first place. Yet the GPS says we drifted more than twenty miles out into the Atlantic."

Nolan looked at the Senegals and just shrugged. The African seafarers all shrugged back.

"The sea is a strange place," one said in broken English.

"Especially *this* sea," Twitch said under his breath.

At Nolan's request, the Senegals re-engaged the engines and the *Dustboat* started moving forward again.

They reoriented themselves, turning the small freighter 180 degrees to a westerly heading, back toward the Bahamas.

They had hoped to reach North Gin Cay before daybreak, but the unexpected stoppage had thrown that schedule out of whack.

"Just lay it on," Nolan told the Senegals. "We'll worry about the fuel situation later."

They immediately pushed the diesels and the gas turbine water jets to full power. Suddenly, the *Dustboat* was back to roaring along at more than forty knots.

And everything seemed to return to normal—for about thirty seconds.

That's when one of the Senegals directed Nolan's attention to their sea surface radar screen.

Though they were supposed to be out in the middle of nowhere, with no land anywhere near them, the surface radar was showing a large land mass not a quarter mile dead ahead.

"What the hell is that?" Nolan asked, incredulous.

They all tried to look straight ahead of them, but even

with night vision gear, a sudden mist was preventing them from seeing much beyond a few hundred feet.

"This is crazy," Gunner said, looking at the GPS physical map. "We're still out in the ocean. There's not supposed to be anything out here."

"Unless the GPS is fucked up," Batman said.

Nolan ordered, "All engines stop!"

He closed his eyes and could envision them running up onto some rocky beach or reef and wrecking the *Dustboat* for good.

The Senegals complied immediately, killing all power and disengaging the engines.

They came to a dead stop in the water.

But no sooner was this done than the land mass they'd detected on the sea surface radar screen faded away.

"What the fuck?" Batman cried. "That was just there, solid as rock—and now . . ."

Nolan couldn't believe it. None of them could.

"Now it's gone," Twitch said.

That's when the lights went out again.

CRASH WAS STILL shaking with excitement when the SDV returned to the *Sea Shadow*.

The stealth ship had been sailing in figure-eights for the past hour about fifteen miles off Havana, staying hidden in the darkness and fog.

Commander Beaux reattached the SDV to the *Sea Shadow* via the special brace located between the submerged hulls. Smash lowered a ladder from the vessel's main compartment, and the team climbed back up into the stealth ship.

They were ecstatic. Commander Beaux declared the mission a success and very well done. Crash was extremely impressed by 616's professionalism. They appeared uncannily smooth throughout. None of the bumps that Whiskey seemed to encounter anytime they went out to do a job.

Crash rarely felt nostalgic—but at that moment, climbing out of his diving suit, toweling off, he once again felt a pang of loss that he was no longer part of the SEAL brotherhood. Looking back on it, pre-9/11, pre-Tora Bora, he realized that's when he'd been the happiest.

The IX-529 was quickly out of Cuban waters, using its high-powered propulsion system to put a lot of distance between itself and the hostile island.

They soon had the coffee percolating and broke out some freeze-dried chow. As Crash listened in and Ghost drove the boat, the SEAL team discussed the mission in all aspects, critiquing themselves on the minutest details.

When the post-mission analysis was over, Beaux turned to Crash and asked, "Just like the old days?"

Crash laughed out loud.

"Hardly," he said.

Aboard the Dustboat

THEY COULD SEE nothing around them but water.

None of the onboard interior lights were working. Their trouble lights were few in number and quickly getting dim.

The *Dustboat*'s main engines were still working, but the ship could only crawl along, because they had no idea where they were going.

The GPS was out, as was the sea surface radar. Their steering worked, though they weren't sure why. And while the diesels were running, the gas turbine-powered water jets were not.

No one had a clue as to what was going on. Even the star patterns above them looked out of place.

Nolan returned to the bow and shined his failing flashlight in all directions, trying to make sure they didn't hit anything again.

One of the Senegals was with him now, scanning the water as best he could, too.

At one point, Nolan spotted a series of circular waves breaking right in front of them. He quickly handed the trouble light to the Senegal, then leaned out over the bow railing to make sure these waves weren't being caused by rocks or a reef.

Stretching out as far as he could possibly go, Nolan looked down at the water . . . and saw an enormous eye looking back up at him.

He staggered backward.

"Jesus!" he started yelling. *"Jesus!"*

He unstrapped his pistol and began firing into the water.

The Senegal grabbed his arm.

"C'est une baleine," he was saying. *"Baleine . . ."*

Nolan stopped shooting.

Baleine.

A whale.

He collapsed to his knees and dragged his hands over his head.

A fucking whale?

Is that what they'd hit earlier?

Batman was suddenly beside him, alarmed by the gunshots.

He saw Nolan was in a bad way, so he hastily lit up a joint and passed it to him.

"Take a puff, man," Batman told him. "You gotta calm down."

Nolan did so, but only because Batman insisted.

"Now, listen to me," Batman said to him. "I think the worst thing that could have happened was those guys bringing that freaking Bermuda Triangle book on board."

Batman took a long drag on the joint.

Then he went on. "But I read some of it. And all this stuff can be explained."

He looked out at the water.

"We hit a whale," Batman said. "There's hundreds of them out here. And the mysterious landmass that disappeared? A fluke of electronics. Losing the electricity? Could have happened anytime, anywhere."

"How about the fucking green light I saw underwater right after we hit whatever we hit?" Nolan asked.

Batman shrugged, hearing this for the first time. "A formation of luminous fish," he said. "We're in the fucking tropics, dude. They got schools of fish down here that are brighter than Times Square."

Nolan finally let out a long breath. He felt his whole body droop. Batman gave him a friendly tap on his shoulder.

"Everything has an explanation, Snake," he told Nolan. "An *earthly* explanation."

But suddenly Nolan wasn't listening to him anymore.

He was looking at a spot up the night sky, directly off the port bow.

"Then, tell me something," he said. "What the hell is *that*?"

Batman followed his gaze, and then swore softly.

Two bright white objects were flying toward them about 100 feet above the surface of the water. They were bathed in an eerie glow.

They weren't missiles—they were moving too slowly. But they weren't aircraft, either. They had no wings, no tails, no sign of any propulsion equipment.

But they *were* flying side by side, in a perfect formation. That was the weirdest thing.

They looked like torpedoes.

Flying torpedoes.

Everyone on the ship saw them. They watched as they went right past the bow, no more than twenty feet away, before finally disappearing over the eastern horizon.

"Please explain that?" Nolan groaned.

Batman was stumped—but only for a moment.

"It's that place," he said. "AUTEC or something. It's where the Navy tests its new torpedoes—that kind of stuff."

He pulled out the Bermuda Triangle book.

"It says here it's on Andros Island," he said. "They call it the 'Underwater Area 51.' They test new torpedoes and God knows what else. We must be near it or near one of their outlying ranges."

Nolan laughed nervously. "They test *flying* torpedoes?" he asked.

Batman thought about that a moment. Then he tore the book in two and threw it overboard.

An instant later, all the lights on the ship blinked back on.

22

THE *DUSTBOAT* FINALLY reached North Gin Cay three hours after sunrise.

They were way behind schedule. The plan had been to reach the island under the cover of darkness. But that idea was dashed by the freakish events that had slowed the trip.

Nolan had spent the rest of the night up at the bow, trouble light in hand, sweeping the waters in front of them.

He saw more weird lights in the sky, weird shapes in the water, and their electronics—especially their compass and GPS units—continued to behave erratically throughout.

But as long as he knew there was some kind of rational explanation for these weird happenings—or at least most of them—he could live with the strangeness. At least until the sun came up.

So now, they were here. North Gin Cay looked like all the other islands of the outer Bahamas. Beautiful, isolated, a seventh heaven—but also a little mysterious, a pinprick of green in the middle of the bright blue sea.

They were approaching a small harbor on the east side of the island that was protected by a lagoon. The harbor was filled with sport fishing boats and yachts. There were a dozen buildings in the small seaside town nearby. Half of them appeared to be restaurants with outdoor bars attached, and all of the structures had a few years on them. North Gin Cay was part of the Old Bahamas. It was authentic, and seemed a million miles away from the megaresorts on the bigger islands.

The *Dustboat* passed the lagoon and anchored on the north side of the island. The team had covered the boat's weapons with tarps and fishing nets before sunrise. They'd also erected a fake wooden housing over the two helicopters. And the team had donned brightly colored island shirts, borrowed from the Senegals.

Nolan and Batman paddled ashore in a rubber boat, landing on a small beach of pearl-white sand. Palm trees swayed, and a warm breeze blew off the ocean. After the night they'd just experienced, it would have done them a world of good to collapse on the sand and take a snooze under the sun.

But they had a job to do.

They trudged along the beach, finally reaching the small

town. Nolan and Batman needed haircuts and were sporting beards—their usual look. They immediately fit in with the small crowd of sports fishermen, natives and Jimmy Buffett wannabes.

Their mission statement said the informant hung out at a bar called the Smoking Conch. They walked down the dusty sidewalk, passing a handful of souvenir stands, diving shops and boat rental places. They came upon a number of "art works" along the way: weird metal things, basically trash welded together, glinting in the bright morning sun.

The first saloon they came to was attached to an upscale restaurant called The Sky Club; it was the biggest structure in town and had some interesting music coming from within. They passed it by and checked out three more bars with exotic-sounding names, but nothing called the Smoking Conch. They finally reached the end of the street—but, no Smoking Conch.

They asked a woman pushing a food cart where it might be. She looked them up and down and laughed. Then she pointed through a small cluster of palm trees to a broken-down structure beyond and said, "If you really want to know . . ."

Nolan and Batman looked at the place and groaned. It seemed like something transported here from the worst slum in the world.

As they started walking toward the rundown bar, the woman called over her shoulder: "Leave a trail of breadcrumbs."

FOR SOME REASON, Nolan had envisioned meeting their informant in the bar of a fashionable restaurant on an exclusive resort island. He'd even imagined the informant might be someone who'd once been a Special Forces operator himself.

But this place, the Smoking Conch, was light years away from what he'd had in mind. Built of corrugated metal and flotsam, it was amazing only in that it was even standing, that's how ramshackle it looked.

At the front door they were greeted by the sweet smell of marijuana smoke.

Batman breathed in deeply. "Maybe this is my kind of place after all," he said.

They went through the swinging saloon doors to find a dark, cloudy, smelly dive—with about a dozen patrons, even though it was barely nine in the morning.

Taking seats at the bar, they ordered a couple drafts, then showed the bartender a sketch of the informant, wrapped in a twenty-dollar bill.

"Cops?" the bartender asked them.

"Do we look like cops?" Batman replied.

The bartender, all tattoos and nose rings, laughed. "Yeah, you do."

Batman peeled off another twenty.

The bartender pointed to a booth in the darkest corner of the place, where a man sat, head in one hand, sound asleep and snoring loudly.

Batman looked back at the bartender. "Am I going to want my money back?"

The bartender quickly pocketed the two bills.

"Yeah, probably," he said.

They took their beers and walked over to the booth. The man had Rastafarian dreadlocks and clothes, and reeked of ganja.

Nolan gave him a nudge, but this only caused him to snore more loudly. Batman nudged a little harder. Still, no effect.

Batman finally pulled the man's arm out from under him, causing his head to hit the table.

This woke him—but just barely.

"No weed to sell 'til noon, mon," he said groggily, adding: "What time is it?"

Nolan and Batman sat down across from him.

"We don't want any weed," Nolan told him.

The guy finally looked up at them and said, "Cops?"

Nolan pulled out the photo of the Navy officer the guy had first spoken to. "We're friends of a friend of yours."

The guy somehow recognized the photo. He sat up, his eyes brightening slightly.

"Oh, yeah," he said. "You want to talk about the people who got taken away by the UFO?"

Nolan and Batman just rolled their eyes.

Batman turned back to the bar and yelled to the bartender, "We're going to need a couple more beers over here."

HIS NAME WAS Ramon. He was Jamaican, though he'd lived in the Bahamas for many years.

He was somewhere between thirty and fifty years old, Nolan guessed. It was hard to tell. But whatever his age, one thing was for sure: he'd spent a lot of time smoking weed.

He was an artist—of sorts. He did sculptures by welding metallic sea junk together. This was the stuff Nolan and Batman had seen earlier, walking through the tiny village.

And Ramon had a story to tell, though it wasn't quite the same story he'd supposedly told to the visiting Navy officer a week before. Either it had gotten garbled in the translation, or Ramon was telling Nolan and Batman a new tale entirely.

But what a tale it was.

Ramon was also a handyman of sorts. He helped clean some of the restaurants in town, he repaired decks, he could cut chum, and when business was good, he helped out on the sports fishing boats.

His story began after one recent fishing trip. The boat's owner brought his customers into North Gin Cay for a post-trip drink. But because the local marina's fuel tanks were dry, he asked Ramon to take the boat to a nearby island and gas it up.

Ramon set out, but halfway to his destination, the boat ran out of fuel. He drifted for a long time, unable to control his direction. He passed many islands, some with people on them, some without, but he had no means of signaling them, as the boat's batteries were also dead, killing the radio.

At one point, he almost drifted out into the Atlantic, but a violent storm blew up and forced him back in among the islands.

Night fell and, tossed by the storm's wind and waves, he spent a terrifying several hours bailing out the boat and trying his best to reach land.

Finally, the gale washed the boat up onto an island he'd never been to before. He took refuge in a small village of native Bahamians, all of whom were women, children or elderly men. The island was one of many in the isolated northeast Abaco chain that had seen no development and attracted no tourists. Many of the people who lived there worked on other islands nearby.

When Ramon asked where all the men were, he was told by the women that one day all twenty of the island's males were hired by three men in black clothes who said they needed a forest cut down on an uninhabited island nearby. The job would take a week. That had been a month ago, and the men had still not returned. When the women reported the situation to a passing Bahamian police boat, the police went to the island in question and found it deserted—and treeless. But the trees hadn't been cut down; the island didn't have any in the first place. There'd been no vegetation on the island over five feet tall to begin with.

When the police returned with this news, the only explanation they could give the women was that either professional pirates had kidnapped their men to work on a ship or a UFO had taken them away. The cops basically told them, "Take your pick."

With the men gone and the women frantic, some of the elderly people on the island began telling stories they remembered from their youth, similar tales of large groups of people being led away by strange men in black—maybe pirates, maybe not. At the time, these were disappearances not considered unusual, because strange things were *always* happening in the Bahamas. The elderly people kept telling these stories over and over again, and at the end of the three weeks, half the people on the island believed a UFO had taken the men away—and the other half believed it was pirates.

The next day, using gas given to him by the women, Ramon found his way home. When he returned to the island a few days later to repay the women, it was deserted. The women and their families had all left for parts unknown.

This story took three rounds of beers and a couple smoke breaks for Ramon to complete. He spoke very slowly, with a deep Jamaican accent, and frequently lost track of where he was, which meant he had to go all the way back to the beginning and start over again.

But just a few minutes into the tale, Nolan was convinced that this was either a massive practical joke being played on them, or that the ONI was punishing them by putting them through some kind of weird security check. There just was no way they could take this guy, or his story, seriously.

That is, until he offered to show them the island where the woodcutters were *really* taken.

"It exists?" Nolan asked him. "You know where it is?"

"I can find it," Ramon assured him. "Bring me out in a boat and I will sniff it out."

Nolan and Batman just looked at each other. What all this had to do with some catastrophic pirate attack, they had no idea. Their mission was to find this guy, get the information he supposedly had in his irreversibly stoned brain, and then follow up on any usable intelligence. They weren't sure if going on a search for the missing woodcutters really applied.

"But, hey, we get paid no matter what we do," Batman said to Nolan as Ramon took another smoke break. "And believe me, I don't mind taking the ONI for their money, especially after what they did to us a couple months ago."

"I'm with you there," Nolan agreed.

"So we kill the day by taking a little boat ride," Batman went on. "What's the big deal? We've got the perfect excuse for fucking off—the ONI's nifty antenna fell overboard and we didn't want to use an unsecured line to let them know. Plus, we need the rest. *Plus,* we're in the islands—that's how everyone does it out here. We'll look for these missing guys, we'll write up whatever we find, and *then* we'll sail back to the *Mothership.* Unless *you're* in a hurry to go back and deal with those guys right away."

Nolan shook his head fiercely at that idea.

"Not me," he said, draining his beer.

Batman did a fist bump with him.

"Good man," he said, ordering two more beers. "Besides, by the time we get back, those SEALs will have probably caught the real bad guys anyway."

23

Ten miles off Miami Beach

THE *PERSIAN BREEZE* was bound for New Jersey.

The mid-size LNG carrier had 20,000 cubic yards of natural gas onboard. Loaded in Yemen, the LNG was due at a holding facility in Logan, New Jersey, not far from Philadelphia, in two days. At the moment, the ship was on schedule.

Though it was registered in Panama and licensed in Liberia, the *Persian Breeze* was actually owned by a Yemeni businessman. Its crew was comprised mostly of Iranians, but they all had fake visas that showed them to be Lebanese or Egyptian. They'd avoided any interference from NATO or American Navy ships during their trip to the U.S. East Coast, which was good, because the *Persian Breeze* was carrying more than just natural gas.

It was now 1100 hours and the captain, having finished his late-morning meal, came up on the bridge. He checked the ship's course and scanned the long-range weather console. They would be moving through some rainsqualls for the next hour, but then they were promised calm seas and good weather up the Florida coast and all the way to New Jersey. The captain was hoping they would arrive in Logan sometime the following evening.

Returning to his quarters, he called for his first mate. The man arrived, and together they unpacked a sea bag the captain had secured under his bunk.

Inside was more than 100 pounds of pure, uncut morphine.

At present it was in the form of boulder-size blocks, brown and sticky. The blocks were the result of the first refining process from the poppy fields in Afghanistan. Cooked down to morphine, the opiate became highly transportable. Once the morphine reached New Jersey, an illicit lab in Camden would further refine it, eventually turning it into pure heroin. When this heroin hit the streets—after being cut with plain powdered sugar—it would be worth close to $100 million. For the trouble of moving the illegal cache to New Jersey, the captain and his crew would split $2 million.

Their task now was to break the blocks into one-pound bricks, then package the bricks in plastic wrapping and label them.

As this process began, the captain and the first mate smoked some hashish. Their scale was a simple bathroom scale—there was so much morphine in the shipment, weighing it was just a formality. After weighing a brick, the first mate would wrap it in bright red cellophane. Then their last job was to assign each brick a number.

It was so easy they could do it stoned.

THE WEIGHING AND packaging took about an hour.

By the end of it, they were able to produce and package a total of 105 bricks.

The plan now was to secret the bricks in the ship's NGC wash box. NGC stood for natural gas cleansing, a procedure performed every time an LNG carrier unloaded its cargo. The wash box, where the tools used for the cleaning were kept, was probably the dirtiest place on any LNG carrier. Usually covered with metal filings and gooey wax, it was the perfect spot to hide the morphine.

The packaging complete, the captain and first mate celebrated by drinking a cup of Syrah wine. The captain had just drained his and was pouring them a refill when he looked up to see a shadow cast against his cabin door.

Someone was approaching, which made the captain angry, because he had standing orders that no one could disturb him during this phase of the smuggling operation.

He was about to yell something to the wayward crewman when the first mate grabbed his wrist and pointed to the porthole right above the captain's head.

A person dressed entirely in black, wearing goggles and battle helmet, was looking in on them. Another figure appeared in a second porthole as well; he was similarly dressed in black.

"What's going on here?" the captain cried out. These were definitely not his crewmen.

The next thing they knew, the cabin door flew wide open and both the captain and the first mate were looking into the barrels of two M4 assault rifles.

The shadow on his cabin door turned out to be a man in full combat array, soaking wet from top to bottom and holding a huge weapon.

"What is this?" the captain demanded. "Who are you?"

But the captain immediately knew the answer when he saw the patch on the man's shoulder. It showed a U.S. flag and an eagle sitting atop an anchor.

The captain's heart sank. "Navy SEALs?" he gasped.

"That's right," the man with the gun said. "Now hit the deck, both of you."

Crash was the third man into the captain's cabin after Commander Beaux and Ghost. Monkey and Smash were outside, looking in the portholes and making sure none of the other crew interfered. Once again, Crash was working the video camera.

He couldn't believe they were actually on the LNG ship. They had come up in back of it during one of the rainsqualls, invisible on radar and to the naked eye as well. Exiting the *Sea Shadow* by the top hatch, they hooked on to the tanker's rear railing and climbed up even as the rain soaked them. Then they quickly skirted the bridge and found the captain's cabin.

Commander Beaux had suspected the LNG carrier as being up to no good after carefully going over every ship transiting through the trouble zone. But though Beaux's intuition appeared to be correct, the Iranians were apparently up to something other than pulling off a massive sea hijacking. Still, it had been another seamless operation by the 616.

Beaux now went through the stack of morphine bricks, breaking off a piece and placing it on his tongue.

"Figures," he said, his image and words being picked up by the video camera. "These mooks think it's easy cash taking this junk into our country. They're giving the Mexican and Chinese cartels a run for their money"

What happened next Crash found very interesting. Had this been a Whiskey operation, he could see anything happening to this ship, from the crew being beaten, to the ship being sunk. That's just how things went with Whiskey.

But Crash was sure Commander Beaux knew better. Such things would only interfere with their main mission of finding the phantom pirates before disaster hit. So in Crash's eyes, Beaux did the most professional thing he could do.

He asked Crash to follow him as he picked up with ease the 100-pound bag containing the morphine bricks. Beaux carried it out of the cabin and out onto the deck, where Monkey and Smash were now holding the rest of the crew. Crash set up the video shot, and with a mighty heave, Beaux tossed the bag over the side. At least $100 million in dope now belonged to the sea.

Then they returned to the cabin and, camera still running, Commander Beaux picked the captain up off the deck.

"You're a very lucky man," Beaux growled at him. "I

could have you and your men locked up for the rest of your lives. But there are more important things happening right now—so I'll just leave you at the mercy of the people you were supposed to deliver that junk to."

At that point, Commander Beaux had the rest of 616 search the ship for weapons. They found a few handguns and some ammunition, which also went over the side. Then he and the SEAL team ran back to the ship's stern, intent on leaving the way they came.

They went down the access rope one at a time. Commander Beaux and Crash brought up the rear, covering their egress. Waiting their turn to climb back down to the *Sea Shadow*, Commander Beaux asked Crash: "So, how does it feel being a ghost?"

"Feels good," Crash replied truthfully. "They say you can't go home again. But I've just done that—or at least temporarily."

"Why temporarily?" Beaux asked him.

"Because I'm an old man by your standards," Crash replied. "Plus, I was drummed out of the military to the point where they won't even let my ex-CO step foot on U.S. soil again. There's no way the Navy would let me back in."

Beaux slapped him on the back.

"I'll make a deal with you," he said. "I admire what you guys have done in this sea security business. Give me details on how you pulled off your missions, and when this is over, I'll put in a good word for you to get back in to the SEALs."

Crash nearly fell off the railing to the water below.

"Really?" he asked.

Beaux nodded. "Really."

24

NOLAN WONDERED IF he needed some suntan lotion.

He was stretched out on a beach chair atop the *Dust-boat*'s bridge roof, the sun beating down on him merci-lessly. He had his shades on, and a wet cloth was covering his head. But he could still feel his skin getting a little burned—and this was a good thing.

He believed the last of the methoxsalen injected into him for the Shanghai adventure was finally leaving his system. The diluted nitric wash had already faded away. So if he *was* getting a sunburn, that might mean he was on his way back to being just another pale white guy again—at least on the outside.

It was almost 3 P.M. They'd been cruising around the astonishingly clear waters of the outer Abaco island chain since before 10 A.M. Ramon, their stoned informant, was in the ship's control room below, studying maps, looking at GPS readouts and having intense discussions with the Senegals—who he was convinced were from Jamaica, de-spite their repeated denials. This was all in an effort to find the island he believed the missing woodcutters were actually taken to, maybe by pirates, maybe by a UFO.

But at the moment, Nolan really didn't care. The sun felt warm and healing. The flashbacks of Shanghai were finally dissolving, along with his fake stitches, and all thoughts of the weird events from the night before. He'd spotted a num-ber of U.S. military aircraft flying off in the distance. Navy P-3 Orions and Air Force C-130s, they seemed to be doing crisscrossing patterns as part of the overall search for the phantom pirates, he guessed. So at least *someone* was doing something constructive. But if, as Batman believed, Whiskey had been sent out here on a fool's mission, then for $5 million, fools they would be.

He just wished they'd brought some Coppertone.

THERE WERE VERY few islands in the Bahamas that had anything taller than palm or black mangrove trees growing on them.

A few, though, were dotted with the *juniperus barbadensis,* a type of conifer, or the *ficus aurea*, better known as the strangler fig. Both trees could grow to substantial size.

By Ramon's distorted thinking, the native Bahamian women who'd lost their menfolk had probably gotten the name of the work island wrong. That's why the cops had found a cay with no trees on it. Only islands where *juniperus barbadensis* or *ficus aurea* grew would be logical places for anyone wanting to cut down a "forest of trees." And Ramon was sure he knew of just such an island close by North Gin Cay. It all sounded good—but they'd been going around in circles ever since he'd come aboard.

Nolan could hear everything being said on the bridge right below him—and Ramon truly was trying to find the island he had in mind. But he kept saying that he was lacking in "inspiration," as he called it, and that was making the search more difficult.

Half asleep and pleasantly disengaged, Nolan wasn't sure just what Ramon meant until one of the Senegals finally poked his head up over the roof and, in a slightly exasperated voice, told Nolan, *"Son inspiration est l'herbe."*

His inspiration is in the herb.

Without moving an inch, Nolan replied: *"Informer l'homme Chauve-souris."*

Tell the Batman.

Within a few minutes, Batman had passed a little inspiration on to Ramon. Ramon lit it up, indulged in it, and instantly had them going at full speed toward the northeast.

NOT TEN MINUTES later, they were approaching an isolated cay at the end of the outer Abaco chain.

It *was* an odd-looking place, flat, oval-shaped and maybe a half-mile around. There were no buildings or any other sign of habitation on it. A huge lake in the middle was fed by a long channel running through it from the sea. The lake was 100 yards wide at some points, narrower at others, and was roughly rectangular in shape. Judging from its blue water, it ran fairly deep.

The island was also home to some "blue holes," the underwater cave systems found on many Bahamian islands. And just as Ramon had said, the place was thick with patches of tall overhanging trees that didn't seem particularly Bahamian. There were so many of them, they practically hid the lake from view in some places

Appropriately, the island's name was Big Hole Cay.

THEY LOWERED A boat, and Nolan, Batman and Ramon motored toward shore.

The closer they got to the island, the more deserted and lifeless it seemed. So when they finally arrived on the beach, they were surprised to discover a lot of tools scattered about the sand. There were some axes and saws and ropes, and dozens of shovels, rusting in the sun.

"Looks like the equipment made it here," Batman said. "But was anything ever done with it?"

It was hard to tell. They could see no felled trees, no stumps, no piles of sawdust. And no evidence that any wood had left the island.

"This is a good sign," Ramon told them. "There is supposedly a creature that lives on islands such as this. It's called a chickcarnie. It has three toes, red eyes and the body of a bird. Anyone who disturbs its nest gets very fucked up, as in nothing is left of them but a few bones."

"Charming," Nolan said.

They left Ramon with the boat and walked deeper into the forest. That's when they came upon something very odd.

The channel that fed the island's big lake had a fairly narrow opening coming in from the sea. On reaching its banks, Nolan and Batman discovered what looked to be a recent effort to widen this opening. On both sides, they could see substantial portions of sand, mud and vegetation had been freshly removed, enlarging the relatively slight gap from about fifty feet to 100 feet or more.

It was only a small area where this work had been done, maybe 200 feet along each bank until the channel widened out on its own before emptying into the big, tree-shrouded lake. But it must have been arduous work for whoever did the labor, because all of it would have had to have been done by hand.

So, had the missing woodcutters actually been hired to widen this channel's opening? Was that the reason for all the rusty shovels?

"This channel's mouth was already fifty feet wide," Nolan said, looking at a year-old Google photo of the place. "Why would anyone want it to be a hundred feet across? No one's building anything here. This place is about as isolated as you can get. It's hardly been touched by civilization at all."

"It doesn't make sense," Batman agreed. "There's more water than land here—plus before you built anything, you'd have to cut down all these freaking trees."

They walked back to the beach to find Ramon lighting up again.

Batman peeled off ten fifty-dollar bills for him.

"We *did* see something weird out there," Batman told him. "We're just not sure whether it means anything or not. I mean, let's face it: those woodcutters could be over on South Beach right now, paying for the boom-boom. Or maybe they're sleeping with the fishes. Or living on Mars. Who knows? It's strange."

Ramon took the bills, counted them out, and then put them in his pocket.

"Like I tell you, mon, lots of things are like that out here," he said after blowing out a lung full of smoke. "Some things more stranger than others."

"Like what?" Nolan asked him. He couldn't resist.

Ramon pushed back his dreadlocks and said, "Like that submarine I found."

25

SEAL TEAM 616—plus one—had spent most of the daylight hours on a remote island at the end of the southern Exuma chain, not far from Cat Cay.

They had dashed here under the protection of the rainsqualls after completing the *Persian Breeze* boarding. The perfect hiding spot for the *Sea Shadow*, the team had told Crash they'd used this place frequently during past ops in the Bahamas. The island held a sheltered inlet on its eastern side with lots of strangler figs on every bank. These overhanging trees provided enough camouflage to cover the stealth boat.

Crash slept on the beach throughout the afternoon, exhausted after his recent adventures. The other team members napped as well, a typical upside-down day for them.

The men of Team 616 were primarily creatures of the night; there was no doubt about that now. They moved silently, through the shadows, atop the waves, just another weird thing cruising around in the Bermuda Triangle these days.

It wasn't until the sun started to go down that the crew returned to the IX-529 and prepared to take to the seas again.

In the ship's control room, Commander Beaux unfurled a set of plans on the lighted table. They looked like designs for a skyscraper; in fact, Crash had to use the video camera's wide-angle lens to capture it all. Only then did he realize he was looking at the drawings from the wrong angle. Once he scanned the designs horizontally, it dawned on him that he was looking at the schematics for a cruise ship. A gigantic one.

"This is an *actual* ship?" Crash asked.

He could see hundreds of cabins, restaurants, swimming pools, typical features of modern cruise liners. But this ship also had things like a pool where people could surf, a twelve-story rock-climbing wall, art galleries, movie theaters, huge casinos, a concert hall, even its own symphony orchestra.

"It's called the *Queen of the Seas*," Commander Beaux said. "It just started cruising the Caribbean a few months ago. It can hold almost 4,500 passengers, and there's about the same number of crew."

Crash was astonished the ship was so big.

"Bigger than the *Titanic*," Ghost said.

Crash laughed. "I don't know if that's a good thing or not."

"You'll get a chance to judge for yourself," Commander Beaux told him. "We all will."

Crash was confused. "You mean?"

Beaux nodded. "It's our next mission point," he said. "This is the biggest target floating around the Caribbean at the moment. And from what we can tell, they have zero in the way of worthwhile security. There could be undesirables running all over that ship right now. Or, all it would take is one passenger, or better yet, one member of the crew to help four or five people aboard—and, boom, you've not only got a huge pirate problem, you've also got a huge hostage problem. Considering what's happening out there right now, and the fact that this behemoth is fairly close by, I'd think we'd be remiss if we didn't look into it."

Crash just shook his head.

Wait 'til Whiskey hears about this.

LESS THAN AN hour later, the IX-529 was under way, beginning its pursuit of the massive cruise liner under a clear, star-filled sky.

Crash was riding up top in the open hatch as the ship left its protected spot in the cay's tiny inlet. He was serving as the vessel's lookout; his job was to yell down to the control room should they have to avoid anything nearby, especially other vessels.

Finding the *Queen of the Seas* wasn't any harder than punching up Google on the *Sea Shadow*'s main computer. The massive cruise liner had just left its Fort Lauderdale base of operations two hours before, heading for an overnight cruise to Puerto Rico.

The SEAL team was just forty miles to the north—and thus started a dash that got them up to nearly fifty knots, with the vessel's power plants working full out for the first time since Crash had hooked on with 616. He thought the *Dustboat* could move well atop the water. With the *Sea Shadow*'s engines at all ahead full, he felt like a ghost flying *above* the water. Silent. Stealthy. *Invisible.*

It might have been the most exciting half hour of Crash's life.

* * *

THEY SPOTTED THE huge cruise liner just south of Hollywood, Florida, in the process of turning southeast, toward Puerto Rico.

It was now almost 8 P.M., and with no moon, it was perfectly dark for 616 to do its thing.

Ten minutes of intricate maneuvering followed, this while Crash kept lookout on top of the mast, Smash, Elvis and Ghost monitored the IX-529's battery of exterior video monitors, and Beaux and Monkey steered the ship. All the pieces fell together, and they were soon riding in the cruise liner's wake, heading to a particularly dark part of the seas.

There was no need to use the SDV this time; in fact they'd left it behind, hidden in the small inlet. After Smash drew the short straw on who would have to stay onboard the *Sea Shadow*, the four remaining 616s, plus Crash, scrambled aboard the massive ship using their rope ladder hooked on to the service balcony at the bottom of the hull. They were all dressed in tourist wear, clothes that 616 for some reason already had on board. These duds were so bad— they all wore white belts and white loafers—they were guaranteed to mix in smoothly with the 4,500 passengers currently on the ship.

Once aboard, Elvis volunteered to stay near the service balcony, a laser designator in hand. Using this device, he could stay in touch with the *Sea Shadow*, which was soon riding about a half-mile off the cruise ship's massive stern, and signal it when it was time for the team to leave.

The other four moved on, stealing into a hallway and then blending in beautifully with the other passengers. Crash was videotaping as always. Ghost, being the electronics wiz of the group, was carrying his small toolkit in a beach bag, along with a laptop.

They walked the length of the ship, mostly on the sixth

deck, which was the main deck. It was fantastic in all respects. It literally had neighborhoods—groups of stores, eateries, businesses and attractions, all claiming little corners of the massive concourse. There was a re-creation of New York City's Central Park, with plants and trees and paths and a small lake, complete with rowboats. One restaurant could raise and lower itself three entire decks. There was a sports zone that included two surf simulators, a huge pool and a baseball field.

A place called Boardwalk featured a carousel and dozens of restaurants, bars and shops. Crash even spotted a tattoo parlor, causing him to think: Who would get a tattoo while on a cruise ship? There was also a large outdoor theater and another enormous swimming pool.

They finally reached the front of the ship and used an elevator to get all the way back down to the lower deck. From here, they took a stairway to the very bottom of the vessel, which was strictly a service deck. Following the plans Commander Beaux had secured from somewhere, they found a room marked "AV Central."

They picked the lock, slipped inside and secured the door behind them.

The room inside was a jungle of wires, power cords and AV junction boxes. Crash continued videotaping as Ghost somehow picked out one huge control panel among many. With admirable dexterity, he unscrewed the panel cover to reveal a fantastic array of coaxial cable and tiny LED bulbs.

It looked like an incredibly complex slot machine—all flashing lights and spinning numbers.

"This ship's got more TV monitors than Mission Control," Ghost said. "But this is definitely the main buss. Everything branches out from here."

As Monkey watched the door, Ghost studied the spaghetti swirl of cables, located a thick yellow one and traced it down to the bottom of the panel. He took some clip connectors from his toolkit and, with the hand of a surgeon, squeezed them so the points would pierce the yellow cable. He waited a moment; when the power lines didn't short circuit, he let out a whistle of relief.

"Glad we didn't blow a fuse here," he said directly into the video camera. "Might be hard to explain."

For the next five minutes, Ghost fiddled with the small laptop, which he had interfaced with the clip connectors. He explained that the numbers flashing on the laptop's screen represented every camera and monitor on the huge ship. He was collecting information on each one of them, letting it all drain into his laptop. Once this was done, he attached a small black box to the clip connectors and stuffed everything back into the panel.

Then Ghost took out his BlackBerry, pushed a few buttons, made a few adjustments and showed the screen to Crash and the others. Incredibly, they were looking at a live video image from the Central Park section on the ship's sixth deck. Ghost pushed another button, and now they were looking at the surf park. Another push and they were inside the ship's casino. Another push and they were looking out on the bridge of the super ship, which looked like a Star Trek movie set.

Just like that, Ghost had wired the entire ship so that 616 could see whatever the people running the cruise liner's security cameras, all 1,722 of them, were seeing.

"Now if anyone tries to take over this ship, we'll be watching them?" Crash said.

"And we'll be here before they know it," Ghost said. "Except for one thing."

He pulled out a small device that looked like a poker chip with a small blinking light.

"The only thing we can't control is where the ship is

going," he went on. "We need a way to keep an eye on its movements."

He held up the device. "This can intercept any signals coming and going from this ship via satellite transmission. It's like tapping into their GPS system. With this in place, we'll be able to monitor everything happening on-board, *plus* we'll know where it is at any moment. But—"

"But what?" Crash asked.

"But it has to be installed," Ghost said. "Near the navigation system's satellite dish. At the very top of the ship."

Crash didn't hesitate. "I'll do it," he said.

Ghost glanced at Commander Beaux and raised his eyebrows.

"I'm not sure that's a good idea," Beaux said. "If something goes wrong—"

"Nothing will go wrong," Crash insisted. "Remember, I haven't been sitting on my thumbs since I left the job."

Commander Beaux looked at his watch. "We've got about fifteen minutes before we have to leave," he said.

Crash snatched the device out of Ghost's hand. "Then let's stop wasting time," he said. "Just tell me exactly where this thing goes and I'll meet you back at the ingress point."

Commander Beaux looked at the others and just shrugged.

"OK, then," he said. "But while you're at it, make sure you keep that camera rolling."

CRASH MADE HIS way up the twelve decks, using the stairwells whenever the elevators were too crowded.

He kept track of the time the whole way. Attaching the device would take but a few seconds. It had an adhesive on its back, and it didn't have to be attached directly to the satellite dish. According to Ghost, anywhere within a few feet of it would do the trick.

During his ascent, his brain was swirling with thoughts

of what he'd done in just the past twenty-four hours. When he'd been part of the SEALs ten years before, he'd gone on black ops, been to exotic places, had some close scrapes and had seen things he never thought he'd see. Joining Delta only intensified these types of missions—right up until the disaster at Tora Bora. He'd done mercenary work after that nightmare was over, spending time in Sri Lanka and other places before Whiskey started up again—yet it was never the same.

But now *this*? The short amount of time he'd spent with the 616 made him feel like he was in the middle of a real-life action movie, and everyone around him was an actor. The team itself was right out of Hollywood casting. They had no fear. They knew their way around all the latest gadgets. They were intelligent and not prone to doing stupid things in the middle of an adrenaline moment. Yet 616 had no compunction about doing what *had* to be done, either, including stealing aboard moving ships, friendly or not, in the dead of night or in the midst of a wild rainstorm.

Crash never thought anything would be as good as his original SEAL deployment, or his time with Whiskey. But this? This was something else. This went above *and* beyond.

In fact, there was almost subtle beauty to the way the 616 operated, more art than science. For instance, the huge cruise liner was not an American vessel. To impose the SEAL's brand of security measures on it might cause political problems that no one needed at this point. Plus, the pending pirate attack was a highly classified matter, and it was important that it stay that way. The sight of SEALs running around the *Queen of the Seas*—or even reports of such activity—would definitely be bad for everyone.

Yet, if this worked—if the big ship *was* the phantom pirates' target, and if the 616 stopped the hijackers somehow—Crash was sure the United States would get the credit somewhere along the line. And he knew that's exactly how it should be.

He looked around at the crowds of passengers and was struck by the surreal aspect of all this. Here he was, among them, unseen, blending in. He was here to protect them, like a guardian angel. They all were.

It felt good to play his part.

HE FINALLY REACHED the top deck and quickly located the so-called Pinnacle Chapel.

He went inside and was glad to find it empty. He paused for a moment, taking in the religious surroundings.

Guardian angel.

Not a bad description.

He went out a side door and found a service ladder that led to the top of the chapel. And sure enough, there was a sat dish here, just where Ghost said it would be.

Crash quickly attached the device to its stand, as close as possible the dish itself. Once applied, it looked as if it had been part of the hardware all along.

His job done, he turned to go, but was suddenly struck by his surroundings. He was at the top of this gigantic ship, at its highest point, under the stars, looking out on to the sea.

It was magnificent.

He resisted yelling out the famous line from *Titanic*.

Instead, he just videotaped everything he could.

Then he said to himself: *Crash, old boy, you're living quite the life.*

26

THE HELICOPTER KNOWN as *Bad Dawg One* cut through the wind and spray of the rainstorm and began a shaky landing approach to the *Dustboat*.

It was midnight. Batman was flying the copter; Nolan and Ramon were with him, though of the two, only Nolan was awake. They'd spent most of the past eight hours looking for an island where Ramon claimed that, during his Odysseus-like journey a few days before, he'd spotted what he thought was a submarine washed up on shore.

But after searching through the late afternoon and most of the night, they'd found nothing even close to what he'd described. It was another wild goose chase, one that had nothing to do with suntan lotion and relaxing, and everything to do with wasting lots of aviation fuel.

They really should have known better by now. Just like when they were looking for the island of trees earlier, Ramon had been barely coherent during most of the search. He'd indulged in so much of Batman's inspiration between refuelings and liftoffs, he'd wound up with an old Rand McNally map on his knees, either mumbling or sound asleep as they flew over island after island after island, until they all started to look the same. More than once, they wanted to just push the guy out the passenger door and let him swim home. That's how frustrating it became.

But there were two reasons Whiskey had stuck with him. First, the intelligence he'd given them on the missing woodcutters and Big Hole Cay had panned out in a way. Technically, his long, rambling story *had* been "pirated-related," so the team had followed through on it, just as their mission statement said they should. Of course, what, if anything, they'd uncovered related to *real* pirates, or the phantom pirates everyone was looking for, they didn't know. They'd simply followed the specs to the letter, which they would write up in a report and present to The Three Kings—along with their bill.

But there was another, more mercenary reason they'd put their faith in Ramon again.

It had to do with the Russians.

Batman had laid it out for Nolan just before they took off on their long, crazy search mission.

"Forget all about the ONI and the phantom pirate stuff and the UFOs for a moment," he'd said. "The Russians are missing a submarine. That's a fact. It might be old, it might be small, it might be an irrelevant training boat, but they probably want to know what happened to it. They're probably looking for it right now with their spy satellites, but they can't search for it for real until they get their own S&R units out here—and knowing the Russians, that will take a while. So, look at all the hassle, the money, the manpower we'll save them if we locate it first. I think there's a good chance the Russians will pay us big time if we wind up finding it for them."

Nolan knew exactly where Batman was coming from. It was always about the money with him, which wasn't necessarily a bad thing. But he had wondered if it was wise to spend any more time out here, while so much else was going on. They had already frittered away almost an entire day before Ramon finally got inspired and led them to Big Hole Cay.

"But think about it," Batman had continued. "If we find that sub, I'm convinced the Russians will not only pay us for the coordinates, I'll bet we can get Bebe to drive our fee into the stratosphere. He's got to have some pull with the Kremlin, right?"

Again, Nolan couldn't disagree. In just three months of

operation, using Batman's financial philosophy, Whiskey had made more than $25 million, tax-free. It was hard to argue with that kind of success.

But it always came back to one problem: Ramon himself. His head was just too much in the clouds—pot clouds, that is. They flew around for miles with him. He kept spotting isolated islands and swearing that was the one where the sub was washed up, only to get there and find it either inhabited by a high-end fishing resort or empty of anything but coral, sand and a lot of sea birds. It was like flying a helicopter with a drunk driver as navigator—when he was awake, that is.

Finally, they'd agreed to make midnight their cut-off point, and just as they were reaching that time limit, the massive rainstorm moved into the area.

That was enough for them. They headed back to the *Dustboat* for good, willing to chalk it all up to a swing and a miss.

THEY LANDED SAFELY and stepped out onto the windy, rain-swept deck. Ramon was taken under care by the Senegals, looking seriously like he needed a group hug.

But just as Nolan and Batman were about to seal up the copter for the night, Twitch appeared on deck.

He said simply: "I think I've found the island we've been looking for."

Under the glare of a flashlight, as the rain continued to fall, he showed them a map he'd printed off Google. On it he'd found the island where Ramon said the woodcutters were supposed to have been taken. Then he found Big Hole Cay, the place they were most likely taken, at least for a while. And for some reason, possibly related to all the Bermuda Triangle material he'd read, Twitch had drawn a straight line from the first island to the second, revealing a line that went almost perfectly north to south. And from there, he drew a line to the east and found an island that, along with the other two, formed a perfect triangle.

"I call it the 'Bahamas Triangle,'" he told them. "And I'll bet it's just about the only island you *haven't* flown over tonight."

Nolan and Batman were stumped. They checked Twitch's map coordinates and sure enough, they hadn't flown anywhere near the cay he'd identified.

"Don't ask me why," Twitch added, "but I've got a real good feeling about this one."

With that, he handed Batman the map coordinates, thanked them, then retreated back inside the boat, getting out of the rain.

"It's just our luck that he's right, you know," Batman said. "If he'd just told me the aliens had led him to this conclusion, it would have been hard not to believe him. He operates on a completely different level than the rest of us."

"Boy, do I know that," Nolan replied.

They didn't say another word.

They just jumped back into *Bad Dawg One*, took off, and headed for the island Twitch had identified.

IT WAS ONE of many cays on the far eastern edge of the outer Abacos that was too small to have a name.

Uninhabited, covered with stunted brush and low-hanging black mangrove trees, it was roughly an eighth of a mile long and only a couple hundred feet wide, with a small beach on its seaward side tucked under a craggy, shallow sand dune.

And maybe it was the darkness, the rain, the humidity, or the fact Nolan was exhausted and his special night scope was overheating, but at first, the huge, dark shape he spotted on this tiny beach looked like some kind of sea monster covered in storm debris. In the shadows, he thought he could see its head, its tail, its massive body.

But as they got closer, things came into better focus. The object was huge and black, and it had definitely washed up from the ocean.

But it was not a sea serpent.

It was a submarine.

WHEN THEY FIRST circled the island, Nolan and Batman thought the vessel was probably an old World War Two-era sub that had washed up here decades before and had been left to rust away.

But once they got down to wave-top level, they realized that while not state of the art, it was a much more modern boat. And when Batman brought the copter to a hover right over the debris-strewn hulk, they could see a large red star painted on the conning tower.

No doubt about it. It was the missing Russian submarine, *Irktisk*. The one that was supposedly lost in the mini-hurricane.

"Hey, we actually found the damn thing!" Batman exclaimed, high fiving Nolan with his hooked hand. "This has got to be worth a couple million anyway—and that's before Bebe can work his magic."

"We'll have to cut Ramon in for a piece," Nolan replied. "Or maybe a couple pounds of inspiration will do it."

Even with so many P-3s and C-130s flying over continuously, it was easy to see why no one had previously spotted the submarine. In addition to its extremely isolated location, it was lying on the beach in such a way that debris from the storm and the tides had covered over one half of it, and blown-down or bent mangrove trees had just about covered the other half.

But even with all this flotsam in the way, they could see the sub had suffered very little damage to its hull. Certainly not enough to have caused the ship to be lost.

"I wonder what happened to it?" Nolan said zeroing in on the wreck. "It barely has a dent in it."

"We've got to check it out," Batman told him.

BATMAN PUT THE copter down on the beach next to the huge metallic hulk and they got out, carrying their M4s with them.

The sub seemed enormous up close. It stretched at least 120 feet from one end to the other. It was lying partially on its side with its conning tower tilting about 70 degrees from the ground.

Despite all the debris covering it, they could tell the sub hadn't been there very long—a few days at the most. It was still steaming in some places, and the smell of diesel fuel permeated the beach, confirming that it was a conventionally driven sub.

They went around the bow and saw that while it was slightly bent, it was clear the sub hadn't even partially sunk, nor had it been the victim of some structural problem. Other than being beached, it appeared to be in fairly good shape.

Yet there were no signs of human presence anywhere. No footprints. No evidence that anyone had gotten out or tried to signal for help.

"Did *no one* survive this?" Nolan asked.

"If they did," Batman said, "they're still inside."

They walked the length of the sub and noticed something else. There were various hatches and release valves up and down the hull, especially up near the deck. But all of them had been welded shut. Even the torpedo tubes appeared to be sealed.

"Is this how it's supposed to be?" Batman wondered.

"Maybe that's the Russian way of preventing leaks," Nolan said. "Just weld them up and hope for the best?"

They had no idea. But one thing was for certain: The welds looked fairly new, if crudely applied.

They clambered up the conning tower to the open bridge, with Batman saying: "We gotta get inside this thing."

This proved easier that they thought. Once up on the bridge, they discovered the main hatch leading into the sub was wide open. And down inside, they could see the bare glow of what they assumed was emergency lighting.

"The Russians make great batteries," Batman said. "Those things are probably meant to last for weeks."

Nolan stuck his head down the hatchway.

"Do you hear . . . music?" he asked Batman.

"You mean the music that's always playing in my head?" was the reply.

But then Batman listened for a moment and nodded emphatically.

"Yeah, I *do* hear something," he said. "Where's that coming from?"

There was only one answer. The music was coming from somewhere deep within the sub.

"You want to go down there first?" Batman asked Nolan, looking through the hatch and into the sub's interior beyond. It was a little like looking into a real, dangerous fun house. Considering the circumstances, anything could be down there.

"I've got one eye . . . and you're asking *me* to go first?" Nolan replied.

Batman held up his hooked hand.

Nolan didn't say anything; he just climbed onto the ladder and started down the hatch.

The music got louder—and it was definitely Russian music. Sad, mournful and cold. And it was coming from somewhere very deep inside the sub.

Nolan went down two levels and stopped. The emergency lighting here was more of a red tinge. It gave his special night scope fits, but gradually he was able to make out most of his surroundings.

He was in the control room, but it was nowhere near as elaborate as those he'd seen in U.S. Navy subs. This place looked like something from a 1950s sci-fi movie: all hand cranks and spinning wheels and computers with reel-to-reel tapes.

"Anything interesting?" Batman yelled to him.

"Yeah, lots of dancing girls—come on down," Nolan replied.

Batman arrived a few seconds later, and together they scanned the control deck for clues, but found nothing.

They began moving aft, heading toward the music. It was hard walking on a tilt. But after managing to squeeze through a dozen or so dense, chaotic compartments, they finally reached the crew's mess.

It was dark inside and smelled of diesel oil, human sweat and urine. Typical on an old sub. But there was another smell, something vaguely familiar to the team.

And here, they found a large, ancient-looking reel-to-reel tape recorder playing a loop of an old Russian folk song. Batman slapped the recorder once and it stopped.

At that point, it became apparent that they were standing in some dark, thick liquid.

Hydraulic fluid, Nolan thought at first.

But on closer inspection, he realized it was blood. Lots of it.

And slowly, they began to make out the shapes of bodies,

hidden in the shadows all around them. Crumpled against the bulkhead, facing inward.

Thirty-four of them in all, Russian sailors and officers.

Each with his throat slashed.

Each with his right ear cut off.

27

THE *BAD DAWG One* slammed down on the *Dustboat* so hard the small coastal freighter shuddered from one end to the other.

Nolan and Batman leaped from the copter, not even shutting off its engines.

They had to talk to Ramon.

They ran below, going right to the cabin they knew he'd be using. They found him stretched out on a bunk, half asleep, singing to himself.

Nolan roused him. "Get up, dude. Naptime's over."

Ramon came to life, smiling broadly at first. But one look at Nolan and Batman's faces, and he quickly lost his grin.

"When did you first see that submarine?" Nolan asked him.

Ramon automatically went into his Rasta act.

"You found it? Wow—far out, mon—"

But Batman grabbed his shoulder and shook him once, hard.

"Knock off the spaceman shit," he said, deadly serious. "When did you first see it?"

Ramon was stunned. He thought a moment. "Five days ago," he said. "Six, counting today, I think."

"Was it after the storm hit?" Nolan asked him.

"What storm?"

"The big *fucking* storm that went through here a few days ago," Batman growled at him. "You told us you got caught in it."

Ramon actually slapped himself upside the head. "Oh, yeah right. The storm. It was before that, I think. I run out of gas. I was drifting, out to sea. I saw the sub, then the storm came and it blew me back into the islands. I gets shipwrecked, then I gets home when the weather cleared. Yep—that's how it happened."

"OK—so now listen very carefully," Batman said. "Did you see anyone near that wreck as you were floating by? Any ships or helicopters or anyone around that island?"

Ramon thought some more, then shook his head. "No, mon, it was just me and the sea. If I saw anyone, I would have screamed for the help."

Batman looked up at Nolan, who nodded curtly. Batman pulled out a wad of cash and threw two $500 bills at Ramon.

"OK, again, listen closely," he told him in an extremely stern tone. "You keep your mouth shut about this. If we find out you've told anyone, then I guarantee, you *will* go for a ride in space—but it ain't going to be on a UFO. Do you understand?"

Ramon looked right into Batman's eyes.

"I understand, mon," he said. "One hundred and 'tirty percent."

"OK, get ready," Batman told him. "We're flying you home."

The rest of the crew was standing in the cabin doorway by now, alerted by the commotion. Even the Senegals looked concerned. They knew something big was up.

"Can you get our friend up top please?" Nolan asked Gunner and Twitch.

They immediately took Ramon by the arms and hustled him out of the cabin.

"We're going back to the *Mothership* toot sweet," Batman told the Senegals. The African sailors were already in motion. They ran up to the bridge and started the engines.

Only then did Batman take off his crash helmet and rub his weary head.

"Man, this is one *very* fucked-up situation," he said to Nolan. "What happened to those Russians? Before the storm? After the storm? Were they shipwrecked and then killed? Or were they killed and then shipwrecked?"

Nolan just shook his head. "Whatever happened to them, with the slashed throats and the cut-off ears, they died *just like* those Muy Capaz guys. And that doesn't make an ounce of sense."

He looked over at Batman. He'd never seen his friend so worried before. "What *the hell* is going on here, Bob?" Nolan asked him.

Batman began nervously pulling on his beard.

"I don't know, Snake," he said. "But I say, let's drive Beevis home and then we go find out."

They hurried back up to the main deck and headed for the helipad.

But just as they were about to climb aboard the helicopter, Nolan's sat-phone began vibrating. He took it out and stared at it for a moment. Someone was sending him a text, something that *never* happened.

"What the fuck is this?" he said.

He opened the phone and called up the message on the small screen.

It was from Crash.

He read it out loud:

"Hey Dudes. Wish you were here. Having lotsa fun. In-filled Russian cargo ship in Havana, looking for bad guys;

didn't find any but blew off ship's ass anyway. Went aboard raghead LNG carrier, looking for same. No dice, but found/dumped ton of smack to the fishes. Just returned from largest fucking cruise liner ever. We wired it for TV; if bad guys move on it, we're on them like white on rice. SEALs rule. Peace out. Crash."

Nolan could hardly believe what he was reading. Neither could Batman.

"Cargo ship? Cruise liner? LNG carrier?" Batman said. "Those are our kind of gigs. How come *they're* doing them?"

28

Aboard the Sea Shadow

IT WAS PROBABLY the most unusual mission Crash had even been asked to do.

It all started when Commander Beaux came to him shortly after Crash had sent the text to Nolan.

The ex-SEAL was in his bunk, trying to get some rest. The only sleep he'd had in the past forty-eight hours was the nap on the beach prior to the *Queen of the Seas* mission. He'd been running on pure adrenaline the rest of the time.

Beaux said he was looking for volunteers. The *Sea Shadow* was back at the small, remote, unnamed cay, hidden under the strangler figs in the island's deep inlet. But it would be leaving again soon for a more populated island nearby called Turnip Cay.

Turnip Cay, as Commander Beaux described it, was an entirely unexceptional place. A few thousand people. A few hotels. A small airport—and, of course, lots of sport fishing businesses. It was just like many of the hundreds of small islands found throughout the Bahamas.

Except it had one thing a lot of them didn't.

It had a FedEx box. A very unusual one.

And 616 had to send something that absolutely, positively had to get there overnight.

Could Crash handle it?   .

HE WENT ALONG with it, of course.

The package was going to Admiral J.L. Brown up in Naval Station Norfolk. Inside was a CD containing all the video footage Crash had shot in the past forty-eight hours. Commander Beaux said it was crucial the CD reach the admiral by noon later that day.

For security reasons, e-mailing or text messaging it was out of the question; sending it FedEx was the only other way 616 could think of. But it wasn't like they could just tie up the *Sea Shadow* at some fishing dock and arrange a pickup.

So Crash's covert mission was to bring the package ashore, walk into Turnip's main village and send it to Admiral Brown, who just happened to be in charge of all naval security systems at NS Norfolk, which meant for all of U.S. Navy Fleet Forces Command.

If Crash made it there before midnight, the package would be on the last plane out, and would be on the admiral's desk by lunchtime tomorrow.

THE MISSION, SUCH as it was, took less than thirty minutes.

It was 3:30 A.M. when Crash left. He was back in the same clothes he'd worn for the *Queen of the Seas* mission. The *Sea Shadow* sailed to a point about a quarter mile off Turnip Cay's isolated north side. Crash jumped into their rubber life raft and paddled to shore as the *Sea Shadow* headed for deeper water. He double-timed it to town and dropped the pre-marked, pre-addressed package into the special FedEx overnight box at precisely ten minutes to four. Then, as part of a smaller mission, he went into the twenty-four-hour drugstore nearby and bought a dozen blank CDs for downloading further footage from the video camera. He raced back to the beach, paddled back out and waited until the *Sea Shadow* came along and picked him up again.

It all went like clockwork.

Until Crash got back aboard the stealth ship—and he knew immediately that something had changed.

AS SOON AS he crawled in through the bottom hatch, Crash could feel a different vibe. The rest of 616 were rushing around the *Sea Shadow*. Equipment was beeping; combat weapons and battle suits were being laid out. The vessel was picking up speed fast.

Crash deflated the rubber raft and then joined the team up on the control deck. The SEALs were in crisis mode. None of the usual laughing and good-natured joking. Ghost and Monkey were piloting the ship, while Beaux, Smash and Elvis were poring over a document laid out on the control room's lighted map table. They all looked supremely serious.

"What happened?" Crash asked them.

They turned as one; for a moment, it was almost as if they were surprised to see him.

"The package?" Beaux asked him.

"All set and on its way," Crash told him.

"And were you able to buy the blank CDs?"

Crash took out the pack of compact discs and laid them on the map table. Then he asked again: "What's happened?"

"Some very serious shit," Beaux finally said.

Crash became excited. "Is it what we've been waiting for?" he asked. "The phantom pirates?"

Beaux looked especially grim. He didn't answer at first, glancing at the other 616 members instead.

So Crash asked again. "Are we on them? Do we know where they are?"

Finally, Beaux replied: "Yes—we sure do."

Aboard the USS Wyoming

U.S. NAVY COMMANDER Micas Shepherd felt a chill coming on.

He sneezed, and his eyes began watering. He felt his forehead—it seemed warm. And now, suddenly, his nose started to run.

This was not good.

He checked his watch. "Just twelve more hours," he thought aloud. "Then you can stay in bed for a week."

Shepherd was commanding officer of the USS *Wyoming,* a nuclear-powered ballistic missile submarine, one of the largest in the world. The *Wyoming* carried twenty-two Trident II missiles, each with eight independently targeted nuclear warheads within. This meant the *Wyoming* carried more than *700* times the destructive force of the atomic bomb dropped on Hiroshima. This awesome power was in the hands of the sub's 155-man crew, 15 officers and 140 sailors, and was always their number one priority.

That is, when they didn't have the flu.

Shepherd was very anxious to get back to his home port at King's Bay, Georgia. The *Wyoming* had been out for almost a hundred days, on an extended cruise that had taken them first to the Arctic Circle, then down to the South Atlantic, and finally through the Caribbean.

Crew members had begun to get sick about a week before. A flu went through the boat like wildfire; this was not H1N1, but judging from the symptoms, something very similar. The boat's medical personnel were overwhelmed to the point that the sub had to make an unscheduled stop at the Navy base at Guantanamo Bay, Cuba—of all places—to offload 113 sick people: 106 sailors and seven officers. Forty-two men stayed onboard, the bare minimum needed to get the sub back to King's Bay. But a lot of them were feeling ill as well.

That's why Shepherd was fully expecting a Navy medical emergency team would be standing by once they arrived home. There was even a good chance the entire crew would have to be quarantined upon arrival.

At present, they were about sixty miles off Miami, skirting the sea lane between Florida and the Bahamas. They were sailing just below the surface, as the sub could move faster that way.

If all went well, they were just a half-day from reaching King's Bay.

AFTER GETTING A couple aspirins from sick bay, Shepherd retired to his cabin to start writing his mission reports. He was not a minute into this when his personal communications suite started beeping. A text message was coming in on the sub's Very Low Frequency band. This was surprising because the *Wyoming* was one of a handful of Navy subs equipped with a new, highly classified communications system called Narrowband IP, which allowed submerged submarines to communicate with Navy Systems Command, the Pentagon, the White House, or with just about anyone else, simply by punching in a coded number and typing out an e-mail.

For security reasons, U.S. nuclear submarines rarely

spoke to anyone while out on patrol. Usually the first communication between a sub and its home base would come an hour before its scheduled arrival and would involve information like tide checks and how many tugs the boat would require to safely come into harbor.

Shepherd was sure, though, that this incoming message was about the ship's medical situation; he knew it was important to keep the whole flu thing quiet, which was probably why the communiqué was coming in on the old but secure VLF network.

He punched in his communication code and turned the engage key to establish the connection. But instead of seeing a sequence of security codes that proceeded any classified communication, he saw instead a one-line message: "Enacting Plan 6S-S Drill."

"What the hell is Plan 6S-S?" Shepherd thought aloud.

He reached for his operations codebook and rapidly flipped through the pages, and there it was, in a recent addendum: Plan 6S-S.

If a U.S. Navy submarine should experience or be suspected of experiencing a hostile takeover, such as a mutiny or any other kind of anomalous situation, under Plan 6S-S, a SEAL team will attempt to board the vessel in question and restore order. In cases when Plan 6S-S is a training exercise, the captain will be made aware of such an exercise in advance. But for security reasons, he may not use any communications systems to check the authenticity of the drill until the SEAL team arrives on station.

Because the command was written in typically opaque Navy-speak, Shepherd had to read it three times before he understood it.

And slowly, it began to make sense. During a recent overhaul, two of the *Wyoming*'s missile tubes had been re-made into lockout chambers for just such an exercise. These chambers worked on the same principle as an airlock on a spaceship. The SEALs would attach their mini-sub to the top of the chamber, which would then be flooded with water. Donning scuba gear, the SEALs would enter the flooded chamber, close the top hatch and make their way to the bottom. The water would then be pumped out, allowing them to come aboard. To leave the sub, the procedure was reversed. It could even be done while the sub was underway, as long as it was going no faster than ten knots.

It was simple enough, Shepherd thought. Someone wanted to make sure these SEAL entry ports worked. What else could it be? But why order this exercise now? he wondered. With two-thirds of his crew flat on their backs at Gitmo and many of those still on board, including him, feeling sick?

He couldn't imagine a worse time to do it.

"I just hope these SEALs had their flu shots," he thought.

Aboard the Sea Shadow

THEY WERE GOING full throttle.

At fifty knots, the *Sea Shadow* was rocking so violently waves were splashing off both sides of the windscreen of its forward-facing bridge.

Crash felt like he was on some kind of elaborate amuse-ment park ride—he had to hold on to something at all times so he wouldn't fall over. But he imagined this was how the police felt when chasing a stolen car.

He never took his eyes off the document spread out on the map table; the one that Beaux was studying when he told him they were finally on the trail of the phantom pirates.

He knew it would be strictly *verboten* to ask where the document came from, who sent it and why. But he *could* tell the document had been printed out on yellow paper—and yellow was always a sign of high priority in the special ops world. Crash was also sure the ship's onboard Level 3 secure computer, the place where any classified messages would come from, had generated it.

But what did it say, exactly?

Commander Beaux had slid over to the control panel to check some navigation points in this mad dash; Ghost was actually driving the ship. Crash tried to hold his tongue, taking in all the drama and wondering how it would end.

But when Beaux finally returned to the map table, he summoned the gumption to ask him more questions.

"What are the details, sir?" he asked him. "Am I cleared to know?"

Beaux went back to reading the document.

"It's called Plan 6S-S," he finally explained. "They just installed it in our advanced SEALs training. It's part of what we call the TFW package."

" 'TFW?' "

"Unofficially, TFW means 'threat from within,' " Beaux said. "It was written after that asshole went crazy down at Fort Hood and shot all those people. It's part of the new regs to prevent that sort of thing from happening again. In regard to us, if a Navy ship has been a victim of hostile takeover, or some kind of incident, someone has to go aboard and take it back. And that someone usually means SEALs."

Crash felt his eyes go wide. "Are you saying these phantom pirates have taken over a Navy ship, sir? As an inside job?"

Commander Beaux nodded grimly. "In this case, Plan

6S-S means a submarine. We don't have many more details than that, which probably means, yes, *something* is happening aboard a sub and even the captain doesn't know about it. Is it a mutiny? Or an insurrection? My guess, it's the pirates. But whatever it is, we've got to go aboard and find out."

"So, this sub is close by?"

"That's where we got lucky," Beaux said. "It's only thirty miles from us. The USS *Wyoming*. Returning to its base in King's Bay in Georgia after a three-month patrol. We're heading for an intercept point right now, as you can tell, at full speed. And when we reach it, we'll have to be ready to go onboard even as the sub is underway."

Now, for the first time, Beaux actually looked at Crash directly.

"But when we do, you've got to stay behind," he said.

Crash was crushed.

"You have to understand why," Beaux went on. "We've drilled this thing many times over. Getting into a submerged moving sub has to go like clockwork. And it's very dangerous, especially at night. And technically, you're still a civilian. I just can't have that hanging over my head if you got hurt, or worse."

Crash grew angry. "If this was the case," he said, "then why didn't you just leave me on Turnip Cay?"

Beaux just shrugged. "We needed those blank CDs," he replied simply.

Crash tried to hold his temper. But he wasn't going down without a fight.

"With all due respect, sir," he said, "I think I've proved myself with you these last two days. I've matched you step for step. Plus, like I said before, I haven't exactly been sitting on my thumbs in my years since Delta. In fact, not two months ago, we recovered an Indian Navy warship that had fallen into the hands of pirates. So I actually have some *experience* in the real thing. I certainly won't be a liability. And it sounds like you'll need all the help you can get."

There was a long silence in the control room.

"At the very least, let me run the camera," Crash implored Beaux.

Another long silence. Elvis and Monkey were hovering over the control panels. Ghost was still driving the ship. Smash was pulling out their combat gear. But suddenly they were all looking at Beaux, wondering what he was going to say next.

Then Ghost spoke up. "If he stays behind, sir, all he'll be able to do is tell Higher Authority what we were doing leading up to this point."

Beaux glanced around at the rest of the team. He had a very troubled look; so did the others. Obviously, this was a real dilemma for them.

Crash took a step closer to Beaux and said, "I *have* to go, sir. This stuff is in my blood. And believe me, I don't want to be the guy left behind to give testimony if something goes wrong."

Beaux thought about it a few seconds.

Then he turned to Smash and said: "OK—get him a suit."

THE CHASE TO catch the *Wyoming* went on for another twenty minutes. Not more than a dozen words were spoken among the 616 team members in that time. Crash had never seen a special ops team so determined, so single-minded. It was as if they were communicating with each other telepathically, talking with their eyes, their hands, via body language. These guys just never ceased to impress him.

At Beaux's request, Crash had the video cam out again and was documenting the effort to overtake the sub. More than once, though, while looking through the lens, he felt like an interloper spying on a very exclusive club. The men of the 616 were all on the same wavelength—and he was on the outside looking in.

Crash was able to read a training spec explaining how the SEALs would gain entry into the *Wyoming* using the sub's lockout chamber. It was a procedure Crash had done in training before—but in those cases, the sub was always stationary. The *Wyoming* was obviously underway, and Team 616's attempts to get inside it while in motion would be like hopping onto a moving freight train.

And even if they were able to maneuver near one of the sub's lockout chambers, the real question was, would they be able to *hook on to it*? This could happen only if someone inside the sub went through the entry procedures as well, allowing the SEALs aboard. If that happened, then at least they'd know that part of the sub was still in friendly hands.

But what if they were locked out?

That would mean, if Beaux was right, the phantom pirates would be in control of a massively powerful weapon.

CRASH KEPT ONE eye on the ship's Level 3 secure computer, waiting for it to explode back to life at any moment. But the *Sea Shadow* received no further messages concerning the situation aboard the *Wyoming*. No communiqués at all from Naval Fleet Command, the *Mothership* or any of the civilian three-letter agencies.

This told Crash the security on this thing was as tight as anything he'd ever experienced. One stray word, one errant message, any misstep at all, could spell disaster. The lid *had* to stay screwed on here, at least until the SEALs could determine if they could get into the sub, and if so, find out what the hell was going on.

This meant they were facing a blind entry—going into potentially hostile territory with little or no idea what lay behind the first door, or in this case, the first hatch. From that Crash had to wonder: What would a gunfight be like aboard a moving nuclear sub, one that was carrying twenty-two massive nuclear missiles? There were so many ins and outs and places to hide on a boat like the *Wyoming*. Cabins, storage spaces, crew areas, ladder wells, weapons rooms, vents; the missile tubes themselves.

Gunplay under those conditions would be the equivalent of the worst urban fighting imaginable, shrunk down many times in size, where one stray bullet could destroy the sub and potentially detonate some of its massive weapons—and blow up half the Atlantic seaboard.

No wonder the 616 guys were being so quiet, Crash thought.

They were probably saying their prayers.

"ABOUT ONE MINUTE to visual contact," Elvis announced, bent over the *Sea Shadow*'s control panel. "If that sub is where we think it is, we should see its scopes pretty soon."

The six of them were now dressed in both scuba gear *and* battle gear. Because they would be in the lockout chamber less than two minutes, they carried small air reservoirs attached to their belts, not the usual, full-size scuba tanks. They also wore diving masks and gloves but no flippers or wet suits. Instead, they were in camo fatigues, boots and helmets. The 616 guys also had their M4 weapons, flash grenades and a sidearm, all packed in waterproof casings. There was no weapon aboard for Crash, but that was OK with him. He had his knife—and in the environment they might be entering, fighting an unknown enemy among a forest of 800-kiloton nuclear missiles, a sharp blade might prove to be the best weapon of all.

They got a visual read on the *Wyoming* just when Ghost said they would. Using their night vision equipment, they saw it was traveling due north, barely twenty feet underwater. Its speed was down to ten knots, possibly because it was entering an area off the Florida coast with a lot of sea traffic. This speed was key, though, as it was within the range of the SDV mini-sub, meaning a hookup while underway was at least theoretically possible.

It would still be the equivalent of an aerial refueling, though—the mini-sub's speed would have to perfectly match the sub's speed, and they would have to pray the sub didn't change course, even a little, while they were hooking on.

WITHIN TWO MINUTES, Ghost had brought the *Sea Shadow* up alongside the sub, steering on a course parallel to it and matching its speed.

They were able to see it through their night scopes, but just barely. Still, it looked like a gigantic sea serpent plowing through the thick blue water. And it was huge!

Now came the tricky part.

Ghost booted the *Sea Shadow*'s speed back up to fifty knots. Meanwhile the main hatch on the SDV mini-sub, dangling between the vessel's two hulls, was opened and the vessel made ready for deployment.

According to Beaux, Plan 6S-S called for a full complement of SEALs. This meant the entire 616 team would go on board, along with Crash. To do this, they would have to climb into the mini sub while the *Sea Shadow* was on autopilot and then disconnect from it.

Ghost drove the stealth vessel to a point about five miles ahead of the sub, and then dramatically reduced its speed to barely five knots. He put the ship on autopilot, and they all went out the bottom hatches and hastily piled into the SDV mini-sub. The mini-sub quickly unhooked from the *Sea Shadow*, leaving the empty stealth ship to drift, its ultimate fate unknown. But considering the circumstances, at the moment that was not important.

The mini-sub slipped beneath the waves, and now they waited until the huge sub caught up to them. Once they saw it coming, Ghost steered the SDV down toward the great, gray hull, and keeping pace, eased into a position parallel to its starboard side lockout chamber.

Then, with the skill of a fighter pilot, he steered the SDV to the left, trying to get positioned above the reconstructed access tube. It took a few tries, and a lot of finesse, but he finally attained the desired position and came down on top of the submarine's starboard side lockout chamber. Almost immediately, their connection light blinked on.

They'd done it! They were hooked to the sub.

Not a second later, they could hear the rush of water filling the empty missile tube. The water pressure equalizer light came on inside the mini-sub connection collar and started flashing red. Once it turned green, it would mean the pressure inside the lockout chamber was at a point where the SEALs could safely open the married hatch and enter the chamber.

But then what? The SEALs weren't sure.

And neither was Crash. Obviously, someone inside the sub knew they had hooked on. And someone had started the water filling the lockout chamber.

So, was this someone trying to help them get onboard? Or was it an enemy ready to kill the rescue team before it set one foot onto the sub?

Either way, Crash thought, *someone* on the other end knew they were coming.

29

AGENT HARRY BELIEVED the USS *Mothership* was haunted.

Or cursed.

Or both.

He had a small cabin on one of the lower decks, something usually reserved for a junior officer. Besides a bunk, the biggest thing in it was the massive computer suite, complete with three monitors, all of which were streaming continuous lines of intelligence on what had been dubbed "Operation Caribe."

Harry tried to spend as little time in the cabin as possible, though. It felt claustrophobic and was always cold and damp, and anytime he managed to fall asleep there, he awoke to loud banging noises or the sounds of people talking in gibberish.

More than once he caught himself thinking, *What the hell did the Israelis do to this ship?*

To get away from it all, he'd found a place up on the *Mothership*'s bow. It was forward of the bridge, right up on the snout, not far from the starboard side anchor housing.

He was sitting here now, just before dawn, anxiously going over a stack of intelligence reports. Too many, as it turned out—and that was a problem. There was *so much* intelligence being generated by the land and the sea missions of Operation Caribe, it would take weeks to get through it all. Yet the pirate attack was supposed to happen within the next few hours.

The *Mothership* was heading east; Harry was waiting to

be bathed in the bright early morning sun when he heard an odd mechanical noise.

He looked up to see a tiny helicopter approaching from the north. It was moving at very high speed, too fast for its size. And it was heading right for him.

He knew who it was right away.

Whiskey.

"What the hell is this about," he groaned.

The copter screeched over his head, did an abrupt turn-around and then came in hard and hot, violently slamming down on the cramped confines of the *Mothership*'s bow. Harry could see Nolan and Batman Bob Graves inside. It was obvious they wanted to talk to him.

A squad of the *Mothership*'s plainclothes Marine guards hurried up to the bow to investigate the unauthorized landing, but Harry waved them away.

Nolan and Graves jumped out of the copter and approached him.

"This better not be a complaint about your fee," Harry told them.

"Hardly," was Nolan's reply. He looked around the open space of the bow. "Is this a secure place to talk?"

Harry held his hands out as if to say, Who could be listening to us here?

"Where's your ship?" he asked them.

"It's on its way," Nolan replied. "But this couldn't wait. There's some weird stuff going down, and you've got to get your head around it ASAP."

Harry just sat back down in his chair and said, wearily, "Lay it on me."

Nolan proceeded to tell the ONI agent everything that had happened to them since they'd left the *Mothership* less than thirty-six hours ago. From their weird journey that first night and losing their secure radio antenna, to finding Ramon, hearing his story, then the trip to Big Hole Cay and finally finding the Russian sub and its murdered crew. He finished the report by quickly briefing Harry on Whiskey's previous dealings with the Muy Capaz pirate gang and how the bizarre way they'd been killed matched the method used on the Russians.

"We've been trying to figure out what it all means," Nolan concluded. "We heard a few rumblings about pirates up where we just were—but then, *wham!* we find this sub, and . . ."

Harry was baffled by the news. "At the very least, we have to let the Russians know we've located their boat," he interrupted. "And that it's not too pretty inside. But . . ."

He was stumped for a moment.

". . . it's like we're dealing with pieces of a puzzle," Batman continued the thought for him. "But we're not sure if it's the same puzzle everyone else is working on."

"Exactly," Harry said. "Does this Russian sub thing have anything to do with what we're dealing with here? Or is it a separate thing entirely?"

The Whiskey guys were at a loss.

"All I can do is run it up to Higher Authority then," Harry said. "I hope someone up there can figure it out."

He stood up, gathered his things and started toward the ship's CIC.

"Actually, there's more," Nolan said, stopping him. "Also a little weird."

Harry shrugged. "I'm getting used to weird," he said.

Nolan began: "I know we don't have to regurgitate our resumé for you. But when you hired us to do this gig, you must have been aware that we had experience in saving a large cargo-type ship, in saving an LNG ship, and even saving a cruise ship."

"Yeah, so?" Harry answered.

"Well, it just seems strange to us that we weren't the ones to look into those areas," Nolan went on. "I mean, instead you sent us out to the Bahamian boondocks to find a guy who has trouble staying awake past lunch. Maybe it's an ego thing, but still."

But Harry was looking back at him like he had three heads.

"What the *hell* are you talking about?" he asked.

Batman told him: "The freighter recon in Havana? The LNG carrier off Florida? And that big-ass cruise ship? Those three things are right up our alley. Why weren't we assigned to them?"

But still Harry seemed authentically perplexed. "I'm sorry, guys. I'm just not following you."

"The SEAL team," Nolan said, reaching for his sat phone. "We know what they've been up to. Look."

He showed him Crash's text. Harry's brow wrinkled dramatically.

"Freighter in Havana? LNG carrier off Florida? The fucking *Queen of the Seas*? What the hell is this crap?"

"It's what the 616 guys have been doing," Batman told him. "Our guy is with them, remember? That's his firsthand report."

But Harry just shook his head emphatically no.

"This is not the case," he told them. "Impossible."

Nolan and Batman looked back at him, totally confused.

"Now what the hell are *you* talking about?" Nolan asked him.

"SEAL Team 616," Harry said forcefully. "I helped prepare their mission statements. Those guys are supposed to be setting out radio buoys, checking the sea lanes, interfacing with the drone fleet—and basically standing by in case we need to board a ship in a hurry. This stuff you're telling me was already taken care of. We've had that Russian freighter under surveillance for weeks. And that LNG carrier had an army of DEA agents waiting for it in Camden. And there are so many CIA operators aboard that 'mother of all cruise ships,' they're getting group rates on dinners and drinks.

"So, believe me, these things you just told me? That's definitely *not* what 616 is supposed to be doing out there."

The three of them just stood there speechless.

"Unless . . ." Harry added worriedly.

"Unless what?" Nolan asked.

"Unless . . . those SEALs know something we don't."

Aboard the SDV mini-sub

IT TOOK FIVE minutes for the lockout chamber's water pressure equalizer light to come on.

When it did, Beaux opened the bottom-mating hatch of the SDV to find just what they wanted: an empty missile tube full of seawater.

At more than twenty feet in circumference, it was big enough for all six of them to float down into at once. There was a ladder to help them get to the bottom. As they were wearing scuba breathing gear but no flippers, the ladder would came in handy.

They started their descent, Beaux going first, Crash bringing up the rear. It was a slow climb down, as each 616 member was carrying his gear in a bulky waterproof case and the water was very cold. Once they reached the bottom of the chamber, Beaux hit the fluid depressurization panel and the seawater started draining out. This took another two minutes. When the water was gone, everyone removed his breathing apparatus and handed it to Monkey, who was in charge of collecting the gear. Then, on Beaux's signal, they took their weapons out of the waterproof casings.

Following the Plan 6S-S specs, Beaux used a universal lock wrench to free the hatch leading into the submarine itself.

"Once this opens," he told them, "we move quick."

Now came a moment where everyone collected his thoughts. Crash took a deep breath and let it out slowly. This wasn't like busting in on some Somali mooks or stepping on Zeek the Pirate's hired army. This was big time. Something was wrong aboard this sub—and he prayed the 616 team, with his help, could end it quickly, for many reasons. The words bouncing around his head now were from Beaux's conversation with him about rejoining the SEALs when all this was over.

Maybe it will happen, Crash thought.

Everyone checked his weapon. Then they lowered their helmet blast shields. They waited one more heartbeat—the five members of 616 at the hatch; Crash behind them, the video camera catching everything. Then Beaux finally twisted the hatch lever free. Ghost and Smash used their combined strength to push the lockout chamber's door open. A great rush of greasy steam enveloped them.

Beaux gave them a hand signal and then he burst out of the chamber and into the dark passageway. Elvis, Smash and Monkey followed, carrying all of the team's underwater gear. But at that point, Ghost put up his hand, telling Crash to wait.

Crash froze in place. Had they spotted someone hostile on the other side of the hatch? He fingered the knife hanging from his belt.

Ghost turned and took the video camera from him. Then he stepped into the passageway and started to close the hatch on Crash, this at the same time Beaux hit the chamber's outside water pressurization panel.

The water started gushing in. Crash's first thought was he hadn't moved quickly enough. He started to push forward on the hatch—but with no emotion, Ghost and Beaux pushed it back against him, keeping him in the chamber, which was filling quickly with seawater.

Crash panicked. He jammed his hand between the hatch and the seal, stopping them from locking him in. But the water was rushing in so quickly, some of it was spilling out into the sub itself.

Crash couldn't understand what was happening. Again, he tried to push against the hatch to force it open, but now all five of the SEALs were on the other side, pushing the hatch against him. Crash tried to scream but nothing came out. He was suddenly holding on for dear life, but the hatch was closing on his hand. His fingers were being crushed; he could feel the bones breaking in his knuckles.

Then Beaux yelled to him: "Just give it up, man. It's over."

With that, the hatch was jammed so tight, Crash had to let go.

He was thrown backward and found himself totally immersed in seawater, with no way to breathe.

COMMANDER SHEPHERD WAS on the other side of the sub's lockout chamber, alone, watching all this unfold.

From his point of view, the hatch swung open and these five soaking wet men in black camos and huge helmets, and carrying huge weapons, tumbled out—while one man was forced back into the chamber to drown. It didn't make sense.

Up to that moment, Shepherd was ready to shake hands with the first man through the door—but now he realized something was terribly wrong. He felt a chill again, but this time it was different. Could there really *be* a security problem on his boat?

The SEALs pushed past him and took up positions in the dark passageway beyond the chamber.

Shepherd finally grabbed the first man out of the lock—the man he identified as the team leader.

"I'm the captain," he said. "And I must know, right now—is this a drill?"

Commander Beaux took out his handgun and shot Shepherd twice between the eyes.

"No, Captain," he said as Shepherd crumpled to the deck. "This is *not* a drill."

PART FIVE

Battle in a Big Hole

30

Blue Moon Bay

FOUR PEOPLE WERE aboard the Blackwater vessel that had been shadowing the *Mothership.*

They were the same four men who'd walked out of the first briefing for "Operation Caribe," short-circuiting the company's involvement in the search for the phantom pirates. Their ship, a fifty-five-foot ex-minesweeper, had been converted into a "research vessel." Jam-packed with intelligence-gathering equipment, it was highly automated. It took just two men to operate it; the other two men were simply eavesdroppers.

After abruptly leaving the briefing on Bunker Island, the Blackwater crew had no problem finding the *Mothership* cruising the waters of Blue Moon Bay. It was hard to miss a vessel of its size and design, especially if you knew what you were looking for.

Knowing its shadowy past, they'd stayed close to the super LSD ever since. Though they weren't involved in Operation Caribe anymore, they'd decided it was in their best interests to keep an eye on those who were. It was the nature of their business to be curious.

The four men were up on the bridge, drinking their morning coffee and meticulously going through a box containing ancient writings of the Knights Hospitallers, when two shadows cut across the chart table in front of them.

They looked up to see a pair of figures in odd blue uniforms standing on the bridge with them.

The Blackwater employees were startled. How did they not notice that the men had stolen up on them?

But then they recognized the intruders. One with an eye patch; the other with a mechanical hand.

It was Nolan and Batman.

"You guys?" the Blackwater senior man exclaimed.

"Sorry to crash the party," Nolan said. "But we need to talk to you."

The four men were still unnerved that the pirate hunters had been able to get so close to them this easily. They didn't even know how the pair got on board.

"You want to talk, do you?" the senior man finally said, regaining his composure. "You'll have to pay up like everyone else."

His remark was followed by the sound of something hitting the chart table with a thud.

It was a packet of money.

"That's twenty grand," Nolan told them. "Consider it a down payment."

The Blackwater guys were impressed. The senior man made some perfunctory introductions. His men were typical-looking hired guns, mid-thirties, obviously exmilitary special ops, shaved heads, lots of tats. The senior man's name was Russell.

"So, boys," he said. "What do you want to know? Who's banging the Queen? The midnight menu at the White House? Where Bigfoot is hiding?"

"We'd like to know why you backed out of this Caribe operation," Nolan asked him directly.

The four men suddenly lost their flair. This was *not* the question they wanted to hear. Russell pushed the $20,000 back to Nolan.

"Don't want to tell us?" Batman asked.

Russell shook his head.

"On the contrary," he said. "You don't need to pay us for that. We'll tell you for free."

He pulled out two chairs for Nolan and Batman and told them to sit down.

"Why did we drop out?" Russell said, after a few moments of thought. "It was because of that crazy-ass SEAL team."

"The 616 guys?" Nolan said.

Russell nodded. "That's them," he said. "You know those guys are just barely SEALs, don't you? They're more like part-timers or reservists. That's why their team number is so high, so no one confuses them with the real thing. Their main job is training civilian newbies in port security—this while other SEAL teams are out in the field getting shot at. What does that tell you? The 616 have a rep as being troublemakers—and not the usual drunken bar fight stuff."

"Like what, then?" Batman asked.

"Like they were suspected just recently of breaking into a bank in Virginia," he said. "And the cops suspect they've knocked off at least a dozen ATMs around Norfolk, but there's never been any real proof, because they're too slick. They've also been caught with steroids and HGH, the same stuff the ballplayers use, but even though the Navy knew, they did nothing."

"That's insane," Nolan said. "Why didn't they get drummed out?"

Russell shrugged. "If they were regular Navy, they probably would have. But I guess it's because *every* special ops guy is needed these days—the good and the bad. Look at these three crisis situations the U.S. has got going on right now and how thin everybody is spread out. The Navy can't afford to get rid of guys they've spent a couple million dollars each to train. But that's also why 616 gets all the shit duty, again while the real SEALs are off doing the authentic missions. Those 616 guys are forever doing training exercises, but they never get any real stuff."

Batman shrugged. "Well, even the dumbest guy in medical school winds up working someplace."

"Right," Russell agreed. "And I guess to the Navy's credit, they thought that by putting all the bad apples in one group, they wouldn't infect the rest of the SEAL community."

"But they wound up creating a monster," Batman said.

"Exactly," Russell agreed. "But there's more, stuff the Navy *doesn't* know about. We discovered that the small bank in Virginia that 616 broke into actually had its computer security systems compromised. Not so these guys could steal anything, but we believe they used it to hack into the U.S. Fleet Forces Command's central mainframe so they could track Navy ships all over the world."

"But why would they need that information?" Nolan asked.

"Who knows?" Russell replied. "Maybe they were planning on selling it, like the Walker family did back in the 1970s. In fact, we think they've been breaking into that same bank regularly. Somehow they learned they could hack into Fleet Command, and God knows how many other places, from this little bank's little computer. Sounds strange, but it worked for them."

"But this is really bizarre behavior," Batman said. "What's the point of it all?"

Russell opened a laptop nearby and typed in a few commands. The screen soon flashed a series of surveillance photos. One showed a line of brand-new Chevy Corvettes parked together in a parking lot. They were all the same color, all the same style. They even had similar license plates—STEAM1 through STEAM5.

"For starters, this is what they drive," Russell said.

Another series of photos came up. They showed a line of five expensive beachfront houses.

"This is where they live," he continued.

Then more photos showed the 616 team members, in Navy dress-downs, going in and out of casinos in Atlantic City. "And *this* is what they do in their spare time," he said.

"Busy boys," Nolan said.

"With expensive tastes," Batman added.

"That's only half of it," one of the other Blackwater guys said.

"What's the other half, then?" Nolan asked.

The four Blackwater guys exchanged worried looks. "Might as well tell them now," one said to Russell. "They'll find out eventually."

Russell shrugged and called up more photos. They showed the 616 team, now in civilian clothes, going into a building that didn't look like it was anywhere near their home base in Norfolk, Virginia.

"That's a TV production studio in Los Angeles," Russell explained. "These guys have been hot and heavy for months trying to get someone to do a reality show about them. That's why you never see them without a video camera. They were bugging these LA production people to the point where one producer told them, go off and do something that will be worth selling. Until then, leave us alone. They make those *Jersey Shore* punks seem bashful by comparison."

"A reality TV show?" Batman said. "Now that's *really* nuts."

"Well, it gets nuttier," Russell replied. "At that first

briefing in the bunker, do you remember how gun-shy the CIA was about saying where the chatter came from on this phantom pirate thing?"

Nolan and Batman nodded.

"Well, that's because we believe it didn't originate from the usual sources," Russell told them. "We believe it got picked up by an illegal NSA domestic eavesdrop program—in Los Angeles. Our sources are pretty sure it came from a conversation between the LA cops and a Hollywood producer who'd been caught with a suitcase full of cocaine and who was trying to get a pass by flipping on someone."

Nolan pointed to the picture of the SEALs going into the production house in LA.

"Are you saying?" he asked.

The Blackwater guys nodded.

"Same producer, same production company," Russell confirmed. "Those assholes in 616 were promising him a twelve-episode package showing how they could pull off the most spectacular anti-terrorism stunt in the world. A real-live ship hijacking along the East Coast. This was something they were going to do themselves, videotape it all, and sell it to this guy as a 'teachable moment.' The thing is, the NSA unit that picked it up couldn't put two and two together, because they shouldn't have been listening in on the LA cops in the first place. They had no idea who the producer was talking about because he never mentioned the 616 guys by name because the cops never gave him the deal. So, that night the producer hangs himself in his cell, and whatever he knows goes with him. Now, it's not like the NSA can ask the cops what's what without causing a national security scandal. But they still heard East Coast, big hijacking about to happen and so on, and so they put it out there and the CIA filled in the blank by leaping to the conclusion that it was pirates. But we're sure that producer was talking about the 616 and, I suppose, in a way, if they did something like this, they *would* be pirates."

Nolan had to stop them right there. "Wait a minute—so you're saying these guys are out there, doing all this crazy shit—for a reality show?"

The Blackwater guys all nodded.

"But it gets even *worse*," Russell said. "The coked-out producer probably would have made the deal right away, except 616 had competition. The producer thought he had an even better story to tell."

"Who was their competition?" Nolan asked.

The Blackwater guys all laughed. Then Russell looked directly at Nolan and Batman and said, "You."

"Us?"

"Yeah—you. They thought it would be a better idea to do a reality show on *you* guys. Beating the pirates at their own game, swashbuckling, and all that crap. How the 616 knew you would be invited to this Operation Caribe party—who knows? Or maybe they didn't and it came as a complete shock to them when they saw you sitting there. If so, the Navy spooks sending your guy with them must have *really* blown their minds. Has he even sent you a postcard yet?"

That's when Nolan gave the Blackwater guys the short version of what Crash had texted them about the 616's activities in the past thirty-six hours. The cargo ship in Havana, the LNG carrier, the *Queen of the Seas*. It was the same speech they'd just given Agent Harry.

"Well, don't you see?" Russell said after hearing it all. "The 616 guys must have figured it out, so they set out to do all the things you guys have done, because in their eyes, they can do them *better*. I mean, you said they've gone aboard a cargo ship, like you guys did with that first job you had. They went aboard an LNG tanker—like you guys just did. They even went aboard a cruise liner—like you guys did. They're out to impress anybody who'll listen by one-upping you."

Nolan shook his head. "This is just *too* fucked up," he said.

"Hey, it's a fucked-up world," Russell replied. "If it wasn't, no one at this table would be employed. But like everything else, it comes down to money. All these 616 guys are heavily in debt. That's really what's been driving this behavior. They live this lifestyle like they're celebrities, but they don't have celebrity money. They see all the weird shit on TV—some broad making a couple million bucks for popping out eight kids—and they think, we can do better shit than that. We're *real* heroes. But they also have empty bank accounts. That's probably why they got that ghost-boat: to enhance their hero image."

"Their *what* boat?" Nolan asked.

"Their stealth boat," Russell said. "Didn't you know about that? It's that monster Lockheed built for the Navy about twenty years ago. It might look cool, but truth is, it's just a demonstration model, and up until a little while ago, the Navy couldn't even give it away. When the 616 agreed to take it over and try to make it useful, it allowed them to go just about anywhere they wanted without anyone spotting them. God knows what they've been up to in it, but we do know they've been going in and out of the Bahamas a lot in the past couple months. On 'exercises.'"

Russell took a swig of his cold coffee. "Look, I don't have to tell you about our street cred. Our reputation, good or bad, truth or fiction, speaks for itself. But frankly, we were afraid of these guys. You'd never know it by looking at them, with the uniforms and all the esprit de corps bullshit. But from what we found out on the down-low, they're some unstable, dangerous and desperate people. I mean—consider these nuts who try to get on these reality shows. Now imagine some broke, pumped-up SEALs trying to do the same thing? No, thanks—we wanted no part of them. And *that's* why we dropped out of this Caribe thing. We felt they were capable of doing anything, none of it good."

"If that's the case, then why have you been keeping such close tabs on them?" Batman asked.

The four Blackwater guys looked mortified.

"Well, there's a reason for that, too," Russell said. "But we're not proud of it."

"Your secret is safe with us," Nolan told him.

Russell just shrugged. "We heard through the grapevine that if that LA production company passed on the SEALs, and if they couldn't get you guys on the phone . . ."

"Go on," Batman urged him.

"Then *we* were their third choice," the guy replied. "This ship. The four of us. *Spies At Sea.* Twelve episodes up front—with a nice piece of the gross on the back end."

Russell downloaded his 616 surveillance photos to a thumb drive and gave it to Nolan, along with a name he wrote on a piece of paper.

"You got someone fielding offers for you, right?" he asked. "Ask if they ever got a call from the Highlight Corporation in LA. That's the production house we've been talking about. Someone named Dr. Robert turned them on to you guys, and recommended you highly. If your answering service has been ignoring that call, then the pieces will all fall together for you. We guarantee it."

Nolan picked up the pack of money.

"You sure you don't want to be paid for this?" he asked. "You certainly straightened us out."

Russell waved away the offer.

"We look at it this way," he said. "These 616 guys are buffoons, juice-heads, and obsessed with being celebrities. But they're still SEALs. They can kill you with a paperclip, slice your heart open with a fingernail, all that crap. That's what makes them so dangerous. And I'm sure if they want to make you disappear, no one would ever find you. We're tough. But we're not *that* tough."

Nolan suddenly looked over at Batman. It was like a light had gone off over his head. Nolan was sure they were thinking the same thing.

"You do seem to have some pretty extensive intelligence on these 616 guys," Nolan said.

Russell nodded. "Like I said, we've been tracking them day by day. Phone records, credit card receipts. Travel records. Considering the circumstances, we thought it best to keep a close eye on them."

"Any idea what they were doing last Easter Sunday?" Nolan asked.

Russell was mystified by the question, but began a search of his records.

It took a while, but finally he could report only one thing: As far as their surveillance was concerned, no one in SEAL Team 616 could be accounted for on that day.

THE *DUSTBOAT* ARRIVED just as Nolan and Batman were leaving the Blackwater ship.

The coastal freighter was traveling so fast as it entered Blue Moon Bay, its bow was completely out of the water and its stern was almost getting caught in its own wake. It looked like an old-fashioned PT boat, bouncing hard across the waves, except it was much bigger and not nearly as streamlined. There was a definite sense of urgency in the way the ship was moving.

Nolan and Batman banged in, shut down the helicopter, then hurried down to the galley. Twitch and Gunner were already here, firing up the team's main computer. Nolan and Batman quickly briefed them on what the Blackwater guys had told them. Then Nolan asked Twitch to call up the old BABE file. He wanted to know if it ever included any personal information about the people who were reported missing on Easter Sunday. Of all the cases the travel agencies presented to Whiskey, the Easter Sunday disappearances were the oddest because, in addition to Charles Black denying the Muy Capaz had any involvement in them, there was absolutely *no* evidence or any clues as to what really happened to the people on those three empty yachts. Not even signs of a scuffle or missing items, as had been the case in the other pirate attacks. If anything, the disappearances that day had always looked *too* clean.

But there was nothing along those lines in the BABE file. So Twitch began scouring Google for news stories on the people who disappeared that Easter morning. It took some time and some fancy Internet wrangling, but finally, Twitch found an old newspaper story identifying the person who'd been on the *Mary C*, the first empty boat the Palm Beach marine deputies found that day.

His name was Cyril Bragger. He was a Swiss national, well known, at least in high financial circles, as an expert in helping people maintain hidden Swiss bank accounts. Further Googling found an item about him in a Zurich newspaper. It said Bragger was on an extended vacation in the Bahamas, supposedly working on a book about the lost city of Atlantis. Oddly, a work associate was quoted as saying interest in Atlantis had been a sudden passion for Bragger. "This Atlantis stuff was news to us," the man remarked, indicating that Bragger suddenly left on his vacation, never to return.

This might not have seemed so unusual if the second victim hadn't also been involved in international finance.

His name, also found on Google, was Karl Reuss; he'd been aboard the second yacht, the *Rosalie*. He was as rich as Bragger, but much more shady. Reuss ran a one-man financial consulting firm with extensive ties to the former East Germany. But even more telling, it was rumored that he'd been linked to middlemen facilitating ransom payments for Somali pirates.

The search became *really* interesting when Twitch surfaced information on the third man who'd disappeared that day, the person who had been aboard the sailboat, the *Pretty Penny*. Again, according to the Internet, he was an American named Walter Choatefellow. His job? Security analyst for a company with extensive contacts inside the U.S. military. His biggest claim to fame? Selling the U.S. Navy a study on the psychological ramifications on military personnel in the wake of the Fort Hood massacre. Choatefellow had told the Navy it was inevitable that there would be more incidents like Fort Hood, that some would probably take place aboard Navy ships, and that the Navy had better be prepared when they happened. Shortly before his disappearance, Choatefellow had sold the Navy a classified program called Plan 6S-S that promised to do just that.

Digging even deeper, Twitch discovered that the three boats in question that day were not only all leased—not so unusual in the Bahamas—but had a connection, another thing the local authorities had missed. According to the leasing companies' records, the three luxury boats were all in the same small port on North Bimini Island the day before they were found empty. Happening that day in that tiny port was a scuba tour of the Stairs of Atlantis, supposedly the remains of the mythical lost city, and how they were connected to UFO activity in the Bahamas. The event had attracted hundreds of UFO fans.

And after one more pass at the yacht leasing companies' records, Twitch came up with a fourth name of someone whose leased boat had been in that same small Bimini port that day: John Beaux. The CO of the 616 SEAL team.

It was great detective work by the Twitchman. But what did it all mean?

Twitch said: "I think that while all these fanatics were touring the Atlantis Stairway thing, these three characters were meeting with Beaux. What better way to cover up something underhanded than to hide yourself among a gang of crazy UFO people?

"I think Beaux met with these people on the yachts, conspired with them on some huge hijacking scheme, maybe even of a Navy ship, and how best to get a ransom for it. But when Beaux got what he needed from them, he and his men made them disappear, along with whoever was traveling with them, knowing the Muy Capaz would be blamed. It was a good plan—until the marine deputies got involved. So the SEALs had to kill them, too. Then, when they found out we'd been hired to go after the Muy Capaz, they couldn't take the chance that the Muy would talk to us before we iced them—so they took them out just minutes before we arrived. That's why that guy Charles Black didn't have any idea as to who killed him and his men or why."

Batman almost started laughing at the end of the explanation. "It sounds like the worst spy movie ever," he said.

Nolan agreed, then added: "But it *must* be true. It's the only explanation that makes sense. It also means those nuts killed those Russian sailors, and that they just couldn't resist lopping off their ears for trophies—that old Viet Cong thing. These guys are not only celebrity hounds, they're freaking serial killers."

Gunner exclaimed: "Serial killers. Steroids. Hollywood. Money. Pirates. All you need is five chicks living in a house punching each other and you've got a hit show."

"Yeah," Batman said. "The only problem is, our buddy Crash is caught in the middle of it."

Nolan felt his sat phone buzzing again.

He took it out and flipped it open.

It was a text message from Crash.

All it said was "blu on blu."

AGENT HARRY WAS on the bridge of the *Mothership*, waiting for yet another long intelligence report, when he heard the strange noise again.

This time, he looked to the west and saw the Whiskey helicopter coming toward him. In seconds, it reached the ship and slammed down on its bow again.

Harry was out of the bridge and down the stairs quickly. He met Nolan and Batman walking toward him.

"You guys have *got* to stop doing that," he scolded them.

But they ignored his complaint.

"Were you able to find out what those SEALs have been up to since they left here?" Nolan asked him gravely.

"I've been trying to do nothing *but* since we spoke," Harry replied. "But I'm finding it just about impossible to do because of the strict security protocol involved here. I know they've been sending in coded position reports like they're supposed to, but what missions they're actually doing, there's no easy way for me to find out. And I've been reluctant to talk to The Three Kings about it, because with the state things are in, with this pirate thing deadline approaching and zero workable intelligence on the what and where, for me to go talk trash about the SEALs now would screw the pooch with extreme prejudice."

"Well, you better start greasing him up," Batman told him. "Because we got some late-breaking news."

They showed him Crash's enigmatic message. Blue on Blue was code for Americans fighting Americans. It usually meant some friendly-fire incident, but this time Nolan and Batman were certain it had to do with the SEALs and their unauthorized activities.

"I've been trying to call my guy since this arrived," Nolan said. "Or at least get a text to him—but they keep coming back as undeliverable."

Then they briefed Harry what the Blackwater guys had told them about the SEALs, and what they'd discovered about the people on the three yachts found empty and adrift off Bimini on Easter.

"Combine all that with what we told you earlier, and what do you have?" Nolan asked the ONI agent.

Harry listened to it all with his mouth agape. Capable pirates. Rogue SEALs. Atlantis. Reality shows.

"But what you're saying is these 616 guys are practically mass murderers," he told them. "It sounds too crazy."

"That's because these SEALs *are* crazy," Nolan replied. "They're broke. They're perpetually just one step away from getting drummed out or court-martialed. They're hopped up on steroids and God knows what else. Plus, they want to be media stars. That's a perfect storm for crazy behavior."

"Besides," Batman said, "if one guy—an Army major no less—can walk into an administration building and kill thirteen people, then who's to say five unbalanced individuals can't kill fifty people? There's no limit on craziness. And either the Navy has been too dumb or too distracted to notice, but just like Fort Hood, there were red flags all over the place—until it was too late."

"We've got to tell all this to the Kings," Nolan insisted to Harry. "Who knows what the fuck these 616 guys are doing out there?"

Harry thought about it for several long moments, and then, to his credit, he agreed.

They immediately headed down to the CIC.

THE THREE KINGS were there, with their small army of sailors working the large bank of computers.

But there was an air of celebration in the room; Harry and the Whiskey guys noticed it as soon as they walked in. The Kings almost seemed relaxed; their sailors did, too. They were even laughing.

As soon as they spotted Nolan and Batman, one King said, "You guys might want to work up an invoice so we can start processing your fee."

Nolan and Batman were taken aback; so was Harry.

"What do you mean?" Nolan asked the Kings.

"SEAL Team 616 has just come through," the King who usually did the talking said. "They've just stopped an insurrection on the ballistic sub USS *Wyoming*. From all reports, these phantom pirates we've been looking for were actually crewmembers of this sub. They'd cooked up a scheme to take it over and sell it to terrorists. The SEALs just radioed in their position. They're about 150 miles south of us and they have the entire situation under control. Rescue vessels are on their way."

But now, even Harry was skeptical.

"Are you sure about this?" he asked the three officers.

They nodded in unison. "Sure as shit," one said.

"But how did the 616 know there was even trouble on the sub?" Harry asked them.

The King spokesman said: "They got word of a problem on board through something called Plan 6S-S. They went aboard via their mini-sub and retook control. Apparently the pirates brought some kind of bacterial agent aboard the sub that made a lot of the crew sick, and made it easier for them to gain control—until the SEALs arrived, that is."

Nolan and Batman rolled their eyes. "This will be hard to believe," Nolan told the Kings, "but there's a good chance the SEALs are the perpetrators of all this, that they're bullshitting you and they've hijacked that sub."

The Three Kings laughed out loud. So did the sailors manning the computers.

"Now, why would you ever say that?" one of the officers asked.

Fighting hard to control his emotions, Batman explained everything they'd just told Harry. Lots of evidence pointed to the 616 as being less than trustworthy. And as the Blackwater guys had told them, they thought the SEALs were capable of anything—even mass murder.

"We just found that missing Russian sub," Batman told them. "Everyone aboard is dead, killed in the same way as these Muy Capaz pirates we'd dealt with before any of this happened. Whoever did it got aboard that Russian sub somehow, knowing there weren't any firearms on a training vessel. It was like someone was practicing before they went out and did the real thing. It didn't make sense to us before, but now it does. These freaking SEALs are off the reservation. They're now *doing* the real thing."

But the Kings were just not hearing it.

"Sorry—but that story is just a bit too incredible," one said dryly.

That's when Nolan showed them both of Crash's messages, the one about the SEALs' activities and the latest one indicating a blue-on-blue engagement.

"This is my guy telling me the SEALs are dirty, that they're up to something and something is wrong," Nolan said. "You must know their mission statements. You must know they weren't supposed to be anywhere near that ship in Havana, or that LNG carrier, or the *Queen of the Seas*."

But still, the Kings were not impressed.

"You said yourself that these SEALs are your rivals," one said. "You want to be TV stars? You're into making piles of money? OK—fine, but don't throw these heroes under the bus just because they beat you to it."

Nolan and Batman were growing furious. "You think we're here talking trash about these guys because we want to beat them out of some TV contract?"

"Well, we have to consider where the 'trash' is coming from," another King said. "You admit you got a lot of this information from the Blackwater representatives, the same people who walked out of the initial briefing for this problem, correct? Don't you think that it might be in *their* interest to mislead you? They're your rivals, too. So why would you choose to believe them over—well, us, let's say?"

Nolan and Batman were enraged by now, but neither would back down.

"What about my guy's text messages?" Nolan challenged them. "Why would *he* want to mislead us?"

The officer shrugged. "I understand he used to be a SEAL, and wanted to be one again. Maybe he was just softening the blow, before telling you he was leaving your little club."

Nolan felt his fists clench. "So—you're saying *we're* the liars?"

The officer smiled in the most self-important way. "No—I'm saying you're civilians. And frankly, I'd expect just about anything from you. Especially with your track record."

Batman almost went over the console at him. Nolan and Harry held him back.

"Look, it's over," the main King said. "We're right and you're wrong. The *Wyoming* was the target. The SEALs have restored order. Work up your bill and get it to me."

Nolan and Batman still weren't hearing it.

"You don't even know where this Plan 6S-S order came from," Nolan told them. "Did you send it? Someone at NS Norfolk? Fleet Command? The White House? Who?"

"I don't know," the top King replied mockingly. "But you see, I don't *have* to know. I just care about results."

"Let us see these communications then," Batman said. "The ones between you and the SEALs."

The King just laughed at him. "You're not cleared for that," he said. "And in fact, as of this moment, because your contract is up, you're not even cleared to be on this ship. So, please leave before I call our security detail."

Nolan and Batman were boiling. It was such a frustrating situation, both were beyond words. But they didn't move. So as promised, the Kings called the ship's security detail. Four armed Marines showed up.

That's when Harry stepped in.

"There's no need for this," he said, waving the security detail away. "I'll escort them off the ship."

NOLAN AND BATMAN flew back to the *Dustboat*, feeling sullen and beaten.

They met Gunner and Twitch up on the bridge and briefed them on the bad turn of events. Twitch was especially livid. He immediately took Nolan's sat phone and tried to get a message to Crash, but with no success.

They were all veterans of the military; they'd all come up against the sometimes imperceptibly stupid, thick-headed behavior of the top brass. Their shared experience at Tora Bora was a perfect example.

They knew that frequently, higher-ups in the military went to any lengths to get the outcome they desired, despite a world of evidence to the contrary. Call it hubris, or stupidity, or both, it was a dangerous inclination when people's lives were involved.

But this? This bordered on criminal insanity.

They steered the *Dustboat* past the bow of the *Mothership* just in time to see Agent Harry arrive at his safe spot up on the bow. He looked as exasperated as they felt.

They watched each other as the *Dustboat* motored past.

Harry could only give them a frustrated shrug—he felt their pain. The bad news for him was, he had no choice but to stay aboard the ship of fools.

At the same time, Gunner was poring over a map of the waters south of Blue Moon Bay. Because Crash's last text had come across a satellite phone, the rough coordinates of where it was sent were hidden in the message details. From this, Gunner discovered that if the information was correct, the commandeered sub was really only twenty miles away from them, and not the 150 miles the SEALs reported to the *Mothership*. Whiskey viewed this as more evidence of deception on the part of the 616.

"What the fuck are we going to do?" Batman said, holding his head in his hands. "Those *Mothership* assholes are so twisted up in their own little world, it will be a disaster before they realize how wrong they are."

Then Nolan's sat phone started buzzing again. It startled them all, especially Twitch, who was holding it at the time. The buzzing indicated a text message was coming in. It was from Crash. His last.

Twitch punched up the message screen as the rest gathered round.

The message contained only three hurriedly typed, misspelled words: "Srry. Im drwnig."

Twitch was shocked. "Does that mean: 'Sorry—I'm drowning?' " he asked.

But no sooner were those words out of his mouth when there was a brilliant white flash—followed by a tremendous explosion.

The blast was so powerful, everyone on the bridge was thrown to the deck. The *Dustboat* was hurled back twenty feet and came close to capsizing.

Struggling to regain his footing, Nolan looked out the

port side window to see the huge *Mothership* engulfed in smoke and flames.

"What the fuck . . ." he cried.

It didn't seem real—and for a moment, Nolan wondered if he was having another Shanghai flashback.

Twitch even screamed, "Is this happening?"

But Nolan blinked twice and realized it *was* real.

Horrible—but real.

They'd been inside the ship's CIC not five minutes before.

The others got to their feet. They, too, were shaking and disbelieving. It was as if an entire magazine of bombs and ammunition had blown up aboard the *Mothership*. Except the undercover vessel was not a warship. It didn't have any munitions on board.

So what happened?

Just then, one of the Senegals cried out: *"Torpille!"*

He was pointing south and, for a second, they could all see the churning telltale bubble trail of a torpedo streaking northward.

It was moving so fast, though, that no sooner had the Senegal shouted his warning that the torpedo detonated under the already blazing *Mothership*, causing a second incredible explosion.

"Jesus!" Batman yelled, as they all fell to the deck again. "It's those asshole SEALs—they're sinking the fucking thing!"

Just before the second torpedo hit the *Mothership*, they all saw a lone figure leap from the front of the vessel into the water.

He was a very lucky man, whoever he was, because after the second torpedo exploded, the *Mothership* broke into two burning pieces and went down immediately. The twin blasts had been so violent, there was no way anyone left on board could have survived.

The team was still reeling from the second torpedo strike when another Senegal cried out, "*Une autre torpille!*"

He was right: A third torpedo was churning up the water south of them. It went past the fire and wreckage left from the *Mothership* and hit under the Blackwater vessel nearby, blowing it high into the air.

This blast also rocked the *Dustboat*, but everyone was holding on tight by now. Nolan and Twitch scrambled off the bridge, down to the rear deck and, spotting the lone survivor of the *Mothership* blast, threw him a life preserver and a rope. Now, as they pulled the survivor in, a fourth torpedo hit the Blackwater boat, just as it was coming back to the surface from the first hit. It disappeared in a geyser of flames and steam.

Nolan and Twitch pulled the oil-covered figure up from the water, only to discover it was Agent Harry. He was bleeding and his clothes were in threads, and he was screaming, "Get off this ship! *Get off!*"

But Team Whiskey had already sprung into action. Batman had quick-started *Bad Dawg One* and Gunner had started *Bad Dawg Two*. They were throwing in everything they could carry: weapons, laptops and sat phones, and screaming for Nolan and Twitch to hurry up to the helipads.

Carrying Harry between them, Nolan and Twitch ran past the first helicopter just as Batman and Gunner, in the front seats, and three of the Senegals, in the back with a lot of their hastily grabbed equipment, were strapping in. Batman hit the throttles and the copter took off like a rocket.

Nolan reached the second copter moments later. He and Twitch pushed Harry into the back with the two other Senegals and then climbed in behind the controls. They didn't even bother to strap in. Nolan immediately pulled up on the main control, and they went straight up, the engine scream-ing in protest.

Not two seconds later, a torpedo hit the *Dustboat* broad-side.

Their little ship, their home and base for their many mis-sions, disappeared in a cloud of fire and debris, sinking without a trace.

THE TWO HELICOPTERS circled the debris pools of both the *Mothership* and the Blackwater vessel, but there were no survivors.

The ships had been hit by torpedoes designed to sink aircraft carriers and other major warships. They had ut-terly destroyed the two vessels, as well as the *Dustboat*.

Harry was close to a state of shock, though. He was screaming, "I knew that fucking ship was cursed—I just knew it!"

Nolan signaled one of the Senegals to get the ONI agent to calm down, which the man did by clamping his huge hand on Harry's shoulder in a firm but friendly manner.

"You are safe," the Senegal said in his deep, broken-English baritone. "We are all safe."

And Harry did calm down—for about two seconds. Then he began screaming over the copter's engine noise and directly into Nolan's ear, "But now we're the only ones left who know what's going on. And we've got no idea where that sub is going!"

But Nolan began immediately shaking his head.

"That's not the case," he yelled back to him. "We know *exactly* where it's going."

31

THE TWO COPTERS split up.

Flying *Bad Dawg One*, Batman pushed the throttles to full power and headed north.

Nolan turned south.

They had the rough coordinates of Crash's text messages. Plus, Nolan knew the range of a U.S. Navy MK-48 torpedo was about twenty miles. Because of the warm, clear water of Blue Moon Bay, traces of the bubble trails caused by the five torpedoes were still visible.

"Follow those freaking things," Harry told Nolan, yelling from the backseat again. "They're like jet contrails. They'll point us to where those torpedoes came from."

And that's what they did.

"Crash is a SEAL," Nolan kept saying as they streaked southward, trying to give himself and the others on board some hope where none really existed. "He knows how to swim, how to maintain himself until help arrives."

"But he also knows how to type," Twitch said grimly.

The top speed of the OH-6 was 170 mph. Within a minute of leaving the devastation of Blue Moon Bay, Nolan had the copter booted up to more than 200 mph, causing the engine to absolutely scream in protest. But he didn't care. All he cared about was getting to the spot where Crash was last heard from and finding him.

IT TOOK JUST five minutes to travel the twenty miles to the end of the fading bubble trails.

The sub was long gone, of course, but Harry spotted something about one mile to the east.

"Right there," he yelled in Nolan's ear, pointing over his shoulder.

And there it was. The abandoned *Sea Shadow*. It was listing heavily to starboard and emitting a thin trail of smoke. It was the first time Nolan had seen it without its shrink-wrap covering. But it was unmistakably the famous stealth boat.

They continued south for about a half-mile when they saw something else. Also listing heavily and riding atop the waves, it was the SEALs' mini-sub.

And about a half-mile south of *that*, they finally saw him. He was facedown, his bright blue battle suit sticking out from the greenish-white Caribbean waters.

It was Crash.

"God damn," Nolan whispered as he dove toward the floating body.

He pulled the copter up just above the waves and circled once. This was now a recovery operation—that much was clear.

But just as Nolan was about to go right down to the surface, without warning, Twitch opened the copter's door and jumped out.

At first, Nolan thought he had fallen out. But then he saw Twitch hit the water and start swimming madly against the prop wash toward Crash's body.

"What the hell is he doing?" Harry yelled.

Nolan was furious. What was the point of this? That two of them get killed today?

Twitch reached Crash's body and, incredibly, he flipped him over and began administering mouth-to-mouth resuscitation, even as he was fighting the sea's rotor-induced waves.

Nolan had never seen anything like it. He turned to the Senegals, who were just as astounded.

"*Fou homme*," one said.

Crazy man.

But in a split second, Nolan recalled how it was Crash who'd saved Twitch from the rough seas off an Indonesian island after Twitch had just completed his dangerous undercover mission against Zeek the Pirate. It was also Crash who had pulled Twitch out of the hellhole of the Walter Reed Army Hospital, just seconds before Twitch was about to take his own life.

Maybe this was Twitch's way of finally paying Crash back.

Nolan maneuvered the copter down far enough so Harry and the Senegals could grab Twitch and Crash and drag them into the passenger compartment. Twitch never missed a beat. He continued giving Crash mouth to mouth, even though his colleague's face was blue and his eyes had rolled back into his head.

Whether his own fragile mental state had finally caused him to snap, or he just refused to give up on a friend who never gave up on him, Twitch never broke the rhythm of blowing into Crash's mouth, stopping, giving him a series of chest compressions, and then listening for a breath, before starting all over again.

Nolan pulled up off the water and put them in a slow orbit about 200 feet high. He was devastated; they all were. But on his mind at the moment was just giving Twitch a respectful amount of time before signaling the Senegals to gently pull him away and convince him that their friend was really gone.

So Nolan orbited for a minute, during which Twitch did not slow his frantic pace one bit.

Finally, Nolan nodded to the Senegals, who quietly urged Twitch to stop.

But Twitch pushed them away.

Another half-minute went by, Nolan did a few more orbits, and the Senegals tried again.

But again, Twitch resisted—with a little more anger this time.

The Senegals. They immediately tried again—and were startled when Twitch pulled out his service revolver and aimed it at them.

"No fucking way I'm giving up!" he screamed at them.

"It's over, Twitch!" Nolan yelled back at him.

But Twitch just ignored him and kept up with the heart-breaking resuscitation procedure.

Nolan was at a loss what to do.

He yelled back at Twitch again—gave him a direct order, but again was ignored.

"Your friend is dead!" one of the Senegals finally yelled in Twitch's ear. "Let him go peacefully."

That's when Twitch finally did stop, but only long enough to say, in perfect French, which Nolan had never heard him speak before: "*Nous sommes Whiskey. On ne mort pas!*"

We are Whiskey. No one dies.

But he was wrong.

Crash was dead.

And it was at that moment that Twitch finally realized it. He just fell away from the body and buried his head in his hands. Harry took off his jacket and used it to cover Crash's face.

They would never know exactly how Crash drowned, how he got out of the sub's lock-out chamber, or how the flooded SDV became detached from the *Wyoming*.

But it didn't make any difference. At least not to Nolan.

He turned the helicopter sharply and screamed, "*Someone's* going to pay for this!"

Then he lined up the SDV mini-sub within his gun sights and opened up with the copter's twin 50s. The two long streams of bullets tore into the vessel with fiery accuracy, blowing it to pieces.

Then the *Sea Shadow* appeared in his sights. He opened up on it, too. It took only a five-second burst before the hundred-million-dollar ship blew up, scattering debris for hundreds of feet in all directions.

Then Nolan turned again, this time toward the north, angrily pushing his throttle to full forward.

Behind him, on the horizon, a line of black swirling clouds was growing steadily.

Another storm was coming.

32

Naval Command Center
Norfolk, Virginia

ADMIRAL J.L. BROWN sat in front of the communications console, nervous, mouth dry, barely able to stay still.

He was in a large, spare, windowless office known as the Rubber Room. Located in the basement of the main administration building for the vast NS Norfolk complex, it was the nickname for the base's blast-proof intelligence bunker. The occupants of the floors above him—the hundreds of officers, sailors and civilians of the Fleet Forces Command—were responsible for watching over all U.S. Navy ships operating between America's East Coast and the Indian Ocean.

That number included roughly half of the country's forty-plus nuclear submarines.

And now one of them was missing.

BROWN WAS FLEET Forces Command's top security officer. In his early sixties, with the look of a college English professor, he was charged with making sure all the ships under NS Norfolk's control stayed safe while at sea and were protected whenever they were in port.

Arriving at work shortly after 0900 hours, Brown learned there'd been a disturbance on the submarine USS *Wyoming*. The first report said a sailor on board had either gone berserk or had tried to lead some kind of insurrection. Brown knew the *Wyoming* had made an unscheduled stop at Gitmo Bay the day before to offload about two-thirds of its crew due to extreme medical issues. At first he was sure this trouble report was related to the sub's unusual situation and had nothing to do with the ongoing, highly classified Operation Caribe.

The good news, though, learned in a follow-up report, was that the unpleasantness aboard the *Wyoming* had been quelled almost immediately. This was thanks to the quick intervention of a SEAL team that had gained entry to the sub by enacting a new, still obscure security drill known as Plan 6S-S.

Even Brown had to go to his operations codebook to see what Plan 6S-S was all about. But at that moment, he was grateful that it had worked. And he was confident that the Navy could keep the whole incident under wraps until the inevitable follow-up investigation.

In fact, the first call Brown made after hearing about the SEAL team's heroics was to the Navy Personnel Office at the Pentagon, asking how fast he could propose the SEALs for some kind of commendation.

But then, shortly before noon, Brown received an unexpected FedEx package. Inside, he found some disturbing video footage, apparently shot by the same SEAL team that had boarded the *Wyoming*. It showed them doing things in connection with Operation Caribe that they simply had no business doing. Boarding a Russian container ship in Havana

Harbor. Intercepting a Yemeni LNG carrier off the coast of Florida. Surreptitiously going aboard the gigantic cruise liner, the *Queen of the Seas*.

At the end of the footage was a message, typed on a piece of yellow classified action paper that read: "Now you know what we can do."

That's when Admiral Brown realized something might still be wrong aboard the USS *Wyoming*.

NS NORFOLK HAD been trying to establish communications with the *Wyoming* most of the morning. But other than that one brief message, sent by the SEAL team stating that the problem had been resolved, there had been nothing else.

Then, at exactly noon, a communiqué from the sub arrived via a VLF text message. It asked if Admiral Brown wanted to speak to the SEAL team leader by sat phone. A reply message was quickly sent to the sub confirming Brown was standing by and providing the number of his personal secure phone.

That's why Brown was now in the Rubber Room. He was anxiously awaiting the call from the sub.

It came at 1400 hours. Brown was amazed the communication line was so clear. He knew he was talking over the *Wyoming*'s new Narrowband IP phone system, but it sounded like he was talking to someone in the next room.

The caller identified himself as Seal Team 616 leader, Commander Dogg Beaux. He explained that he was speaking from the *Wyoming*'s CAAC, the control and attack center, and transmitting with help from the sub's communication specialist.

Brown bluntly asked the condition of the submarine.

"Everything is fine, sir," was Beaux's reply. His voice was calm, polite. "No problems at all."

."Are you able to continue to King's Bay?" Brown asked him.

"We are," came the reply.

Brown was immediately relieved. "It's probably best not to discuss the 'internal situation' until then, is it?" he asked.

But there was no reply to this.

"When do you expect to arrive in King's Bay?" Brown went on.

There was a short silence. Then Commander Beaux spoke again: "We will arrive after a few requests of ours are met."

Brown chuckled loud enough to be heard over the phone. It was common practice when one branch of the Navy did a favor for another, that an exchange of something such as ice cream was obligatory.

"How much Rocky Road do you and your men want?" Brown asked, hoping it was that simple.

But there was another brief silence.

Then Commander Beaux replied, "About a hundred million dollars worth should do it."

THE CONVERSATION FOR the next five minutes was one-sided and bizarre.

Commander Beaux did all the talking. He explained, calmly and rationally, that the *Wyoming* was in his hands temporarily and that he and his men had seized it to prove a point: A U.S. Navy nuclear sub *could* be hijacked by real pirates with just a little know-how and the right equipment. Beaux said his team was looking at the situation as an opportunity, a "teachable moment"—a way the Navy could learn how to prevent a real submarine hijacking. And their payment for providing this service would be $100 million, plus full immunity from prosecution, as well as exclusive rights to any TV or movie deals resulting from their actions. Beaux insisted the price was a bargain. In return, his team would give back the sub, release the crew and tell Naval Command exactly how they did it. At that point, they would become private contractors for the Navy, to which Beaux added that he knew how the Navy had no problem hiring ex-special ops guys these days.

But then Beaux went on to tell Brown that all of the sub's defensive systems were operating, and he claimed he would be able to see and hear everything Naval Command did regarding the situation. He said he could detect any U.S. Navy search aircraft that might be dispatched to look for them. He also stated that, while he considered playing a little cat and mouse with the Navy all part of the exercise, if he discovered any special ops teams were activated, or called back to deal with him, he would have to escalate the matter.

With all this in mind, he suggested the admiral promptly reach a decision on his demands.

Brown was stunned. Despite all the bullshit and blather, the fact was the *Wyoming* had been taken over and was being held for ransom, no different from what the Somali pirates were doing a half a world away.

So the threat of a pirate action off the U.S. East Coast *had* been real, he thought. It's just that the phantom pirates were some of the Navy's own.

Brown was not alone in the Rubber Room. There were a dozen people with him, doing their best to stay quiet and undetected. They were from NCIS, the JAG's office and the FBI. Most notable for their absence was anyone from ONI.

The two FBI men had been rushed up from Operation Caribe's Land Mission office in Miami in anticipation of the hijackers getting in touch with NS Norfolk. Upon arriving, they'd told Brown that three ships connected to Operation Caribe had been torpedoed that morning in the Bahamas and that the hijacking of the *Wyoming* was most likely a related event. This only ratcheted up the tension in the Rubber Room.

The FBI agents were experts in hostage negotiations, and all during Brown's conversation with Commander Beaux, they kept slipping him notes containing messages such as *Keep him talking. Keep him on the line. Get him to talk about his family.*

And, of course, the entire exchange was being recorded and piped through a speaker phone. All this so everyone in the Rubber Room could do their best to measure the gravity of the situation and listen for any clues that might resolve it.

Noises detected in the background on Beaux's side of the conversation were key. The voices of the crew, what machinery was running and what was not. These things could tell a lot about conditions aboard the sub.

After listening in for a few minutes and hearing a lot of background clatter in between Beaux's sound bites, one naval officer scribbled a note to Brown that read: "The sub is definitely submerged and underway."

To which Brown scribbled back that, despite Beaux's warning, every available antisubmarine asset on the East Coast should start looking for the *Wyoming* immediately.

But everyone in the Rubber Room also knew finding the sub would be a tall order. The U.S. Navy had spent billions of dollars over the years making its nuclear submarines super quiet. Specialized rubber gaskets separated every one of the millions of nuts and bolts aboard every sub. Every moving part within every machine on board was coated with top-secret sound-damping sealants, rendering them silent. Every member of the crew wore special sneakers.

Hundreds of sensors inside and outside the boat's hull made sure everything on the sub stayed quiet. U.S. subs were designed to fool the anti-submarine forces of Russia and China at the very least. They were built so well that even U.S. forces would have a hard time locating one. A U.S. sub on the loose could hide just about anywhere in the millions of square miles of ocean and, because it was nuclear powered, it could stay under water for weeks or even months at a time, if necessary.

But, as Brown finally said to Beaux: "You know we'll find you eventually. Your supplies are already low, you'll need food at some point and you'll have to surface. What happens then?"

"I intend to get this done way before that," was Beaux's enigmatic reply. "So, let's all profit from this situation. Because if we go down that negative path and draw this thing out, the circumstances could be dire."

The experts were now silently pleading with Brown to keep Beaux on the line. But Beaux was too smart for that.

"Can you define 'dire' for me, commander?" Brown asked him. "Are you thinking of harming the crew, things of that nature?"

Beaux never lost his cool. "The only difference between this sub and the majority of the Navy's other ballistic boats," he said, "is that we only have twenty-two Trident missiles on board and the rest have twenty-four."

With that, Beaux ended the conversation.

But not necessarily the transmission.

Aboard the Wyoming

"ARE YOU SURE they can still hear us?" Beaux whispered to the sub's communications specialist.

"I'm sure they can," the sailor replied quietly. He pointed to the switch on his communications console that showed the Narrowband IP's phone line to NS Norfolk was still open.

Beaux said to the sailor: "Stand by."

There were about twenty other crewmen crowded on the sub's control deck. Each was at his station or watching over someone performing their duties. Another twenty or so sailors were being held in the passageway nearby. All of them were under the eye of a SEAL holding a gun.

Just as they had been during Beaux's phone conversation, the two sailors who were working the sub's steering yokes nearby were verbally counting out their depth numbers: "We are at nine hundred feet and holding steady . . ."

The helmsman was calling out his numbers: "Seventeen knots, true . . ."

The electrical officer was checking his equipment and announcing minor fluctuations in power. Sonar men were calling out contacts: "Range—three miles off port." The electronic warfare officer was keeping track of his equipment, as was the weapons officer. In effect, more than a half-dozen conversations were going on at once, the normal chatter of a submarine making its way through the ocean depths.

Through it all, Beaux remained seated at the communications suite. He had a prepared script in front of him.

It contained all the talking points he'd wanted to get across to NS Norfolk: The sub was under his control. This was a teachable moment. The payment demand. The circumstances of escalation. The blanket immunity and the worldwide TV and movie rights.

He put a check mark next to all these things.

Unchecked, though, was a section that began with: "If you doubt our resolve, look for three holes in Blue Moon Bay."

Beaux scratched out the comment. "Better I left that unsaid," he whispered to himself.

Beneath it was another section left unchecked. It read, "We regret the loss of Commander Shepherd."

He crossed out that section, too, as well as one that read, "We regret the loss of the torpedo officer."

He looked at his watch. The Narrowband IP phone line had been open without any direct communication from him for about a minute. He decided that was enough. He nodded to the communications specialist, who reached over and flipped the switch, finally ending the transmission.

Ghost was standing nearby, M4 assault rifle in hand. Beaux looked up at him and nodded.

Ghost yelled, "All quiet!"

Every sailor at his station immediately stopped what he was doing. Some slumped forward in their seats. Others simply collapsed.

"Thank you, gentlemen," Beaux said, not bothering to look up from his notes. "Your group performance was worthy of an Oscar."

Beaux then said to Elvis, "Check around up top, will you? We haven't done that in a while."

Elvis walked past the sub's periscope and out of the control room altogether. He climbed the ladder up through the sub's massive conning tower to the bridge above. He stopped before he reached the main hatch, though. What was the last depth reading that had been called out? Nine hundred feet below the surface? And what had the helmsmen said was their speed? Seventeen knots?

Elvis smiled and finally opened the main hatch. Not a drop of water came in on him.

He poked his head outside—and felt only the warm breeze on his face.

What he saw was not the rolling waves of the Atlantic,

but many overhanging branches belonging to dozens of strangler fig trees. And around him were the waters of a large rectangular lake, much of it hidden from view by these same dangling tree branches, suggesting a thick Louisiana bayou. The underside of the sub was resting on the lake's smooth, muddy bottom. The lake water covered the remainder of the hull to a point about five feet up to the conning tower, and again, the overhanging strangler fig branches hid the rest.

The sub's ballast tanks were full. If the *Wyoming* had to move, all they had to do was blow these tanks and the sub would gently come off the bottom. Then they could turn it around and be on their way.

Not that they were planning on leaving anytime soon.

Not when they were in the perfect hiding place.

Elvis had to hand it to Commander Beaux. He'd found them the ideal spot to stash the *Wyoming*. Totally isolated, absolutely uninhabited. Few people even knew this place existed or paid attention to it if they did. And, anyone who might have visited here recently was long gone by now.

Big Hole Cay.

No way it could have a better name than that.

DESPITE HIS CALM performance on the phone with Admiral Brown, Commander Beaux knew he had an unexpected problem on his hands.

Almost all of the *Wyoming*'s remaining crew members, the people he was counting on to run the sub's critical functions, were sick. In fact, many were *deathly* sick.

It had taken Beaux nearly two years to plan this undertaking. Absorbing everything he could get his hands on about ballistic subs, including stolen classified material, he knew what was needed to make them run. Depth limits, speed limits, communications arcs, tolerances to ocean temperature layers, even how many meals the galley could serve in a day. He knew how to keep the secondary battery power on. He knew how the reactor worked. He knew the basics of how the Trident missiles were fired.

But never did he think, when the day came that they finally hijacked the sub, it would have only a bare-bones crew aboard, with most of them so sick they could hardly stand.

It almost seemed like a blessing in disguise at first—that was the ironic thing. Watching over forty sailors was much easier than watching over 150. In fact, the *Wyoming*'s entire skeleton crew could fit on the control deck, or in the passageway nearby, which greatly helped the 616 team keep an eye on them. Getting the sub to Big Hole Cay, and before that, using selective brutality to force the weapons crew to show him how to fire the torpedoes—all of it had gone like clockwork for Beaux.

But in the time since arriving here, nearly half the remaining crew had been taken to sick bay, ravaged by the flu. And the other half, those twenty-odd sailors still performing their duties, were getting increasingly ill. Wearing flu masks and sometimes coughing so hard they lost their breath, they were at their stations only because the SEALs were holding M4 assault rifles on them. While being in a sort of a collective state of shock, the sailors were soldiering on, hoping the Navy could somehow get them out of this bizarre blue-on-blue hostage situation before they all died. But many had trouble just keeping their heads up.

The result was that Beaux and his men were forced to run a lot of the boat's operations themselves. The nuclear reactor had been taken off-line because all the sailors normally on duty to service it were sick. But, there were other critical areas that had to keep functioning for the plan to work: environmental systems, communications, secondary electrical units and the ballast tanks. And, to keep the threat alive, 616 had to maintain the Trident missile launch console and keep enough power in reserve should things really deteriorate and they be forced to use it.

Beaux was no fool. He knew this endeavor wasn't going to be easy. He knew some blood would have to be spilled and that he would run into unanticipated problems.

But again, never did he think he'd wind up stealing a submarine full of sick sailors.

THIS SITUATION BECAME critical several hours after breaking off communications with NS Norfolk.

Beaux was down to sixteen sailors still at their posts by that point, way below the minimum required. In an effort to fix the problem, he made his way down to the *Wyoming*'s sick bay, carrying his M4 assault rifle with him.

The sub's only corpsman was helping a sailor onto a cot when Beaux arrived. The sick bay was packed with men on bunks or fold-out cots or, in some cases, on blankets stretched out on the cold deck. The place reeked of illness.

"I need more people to get back to work," Beaux told the corpsman directly. "There's got to be some in here who aren't as bad off as the others."

The corpsman just shrugged. He'd probably gotten over the shock of the hijacking sooner than everyone else simply because he was so busy treating the sick.

"You're looking for malingerers, then?" he asked Beaux.

"I'm sure there's a few," Beaux replied.

The corpsman just shrugged again. "There is only one member of this crew who hasn't shown full-blown flu symptoms yet," he said. "And that person is me. I doubled the dose of vaccine I took before I came on board, plus I'm the only one walking around with surgical gloves, and that makes a difference, probably more than the flu masks. But

I'll be honest with you—I'm feeling fatigued and weak. My throat is sore, and my stomach is beginning to act up. So, it's only a matter of time for me, too."

The corpsman had a hot plate on his desk. A small pot of coffee was heating on it, enough for one cup. Beaux nonchalantly poured it for himself—he *had* to stay awake, and the team had no more amphetamine pills. He started to walk into the infirmary, intent on finding one or two able bodies, but the corpsman stopped him.

"Can't go in there with any airborne irritants," he told Beaux, pointing to the steam rising out of the coffee.

Beaux begrudgingly surrendered the cup. "Make sure I pick it up on the way out," he grumbled, finally disappearing into the sick bay.

Once he was out of sight, the corpsman cleared his throat, retrieved a mouthful of phlegm and spit it into the coffee.

"Will do, asshole," he said.

33

Big Hole Cay

THE HURRICANE HIT at sunset.

Everyone inside the *Wyoming* heard it coming, this unexpected storm. The thunder sounded like artillery. The lightning caused all the electricals onboard to blink. The wind was so fierce, it seemed to be making the seventeen-thousand-ton submarine sway.

Most disturbing, though, rain could be heard pelting the sub's hull. Like a continuous barrage of machine gun fire, it was hitting all sides at once.

And that meant something was very wrong.

The *Wyoming* was built to be silent, especially when submerged. It was soundproofed, inside and out, top to bottom, stern to bow. So why did everything outside sound so loud?

Having no luck getting any more sailors back to work, Beaux was in the CAAC going over the Trident launch procedures when the commotion started. Leaving Smash, Monkey and Ghost to watch those few crewmen still left on deck, he retrieved a trouble light, grabbed Elvis and together they climbed the conning tower ladder to the bridge above.

The noise outside grew the higher they went. The sound of the rain alone was deafening. Then, just as Beaux was about to open the top hatch, the sub moved dramatically to the left. It shifted so violently, at first, both SEALs thought it was an earthquake.

"Damn!" Elvis yelled. "We're ninety-five percent underwater. Even a two-hundred-knot wind shouldn't be moving us like that."

Beaux pushed open the top hatch—but the weather outside was so fierce, it nearly slammed the heavy cover back down on their unprotected heads, a blow that would have killed them both. It took all their combined strength to force the hatch back open and lock it in place.

Then they had to crawl up onto the tilted sail platform. Finally steadying themselves against the ferocious gale, they stood up and looked around.

Beaux couldn't believe what he saw.

He screamed: *"What happened to all the water?"*

It was true. Even in the darkness, they could see the lake's water level had dropped to almost nothing. No longer five feet up the sail, more than *two thirds* of the submarine's hull was now exposed. It was like someone had pulled a plug at the bottom of the lake and the water was draining out.

This was why the rain sounded so loud from the inside: so much of the hull was now above water. This was also why the *Wyoming* was at a tilt. Resting on the slippery, muddy lake bottom, with hardly any water to support it, the hurricane winds were blowing it over.

Fighting the severe gusts and rain, Beaux aimed the trouble light back at the channel opening 100 feet beyond the sub's stern. This was the place the 616 had widened on the backs of the twenty day laborers in the run-up to the *Wyoming*'s seizure. Expanding the mouth of the channel had been necessary to get the sub into the lake.

But now he saw the channel opening was clogged with trees, beach debris, sand and mud, effectively damming it and drastically reducing the flow of water into the lake.

Beaux spun Elvis around and pointed out the situation to him.

"What the fuck?" Elvis yelled over the storm. "That's impossible!"

Had the hurricane blown the trees down, felling them perfectly over the opening? Or had a great swirl of flotsam washed ashore and completely jammed the gap? Both were highly unlikely—yet there were no other explanations.

Then, in the midst of all this, they saw something else. Not at the clogged channel opening, but at the far end of the sub's deck itself. Caught in the trouble light's beam, close to the suddenly exposed tailfins.

There was a man down there. He was soaking wet, wearing a tie-dye shirt, ragged pants, a knit hat jammed on top of dreadlocks, and jammed on top of that, of all things, a welder's mask. In fact, he was welding something on the sub's tilted hull.

"What the fuck?" Elvis yelled again.

"Who the hell is that?" Beaux screamed. *"What's he doing?"*

Then two more men appeared on the sub's tail, both also soaked to the skin. Barely visible through the sheets of rain, they were wearing brightly colored African dashikis.

Neither SEAL had brought his assault rifle, so Beaux grabbed Elvis's .45 automatic and aimed it at the men. But before he could squeeze the trigger, the bridge was suddenly awash in orange sparks. Someone was shooting at them! In an instant, dozens of tracer rounds were ricocheting off the top of the sail, one of them blowing the trouble light right out of Beaux's hands, another destroying the sub's periscope.

Both SEALs tried to duck—but it was too late. They heard one especially loud *crack!* and a bright flash of orange went by them. The next thing Elvis knew, he was looking down at his left hand.

It was covered with blood—and holding his severed right ear.

IT WAS ALL Beaux and Elvis could do to retreat back down the conning tower ladder. Dripping wet and shaking, they staggered into the control room, which like the rest of the boat, was now at a pronounced slant. Elvis was bleeding profusely and still clutching his ear.

The other SEALs were shocked.

"What *the hell* happened up there?" Monkey yelled at them.

"We don't know," Beaux shot back. "The water is running out of the lake. We're almost totally exposed. And there's some crazy guy down on the deck with a welding rig. *And* someone started shooting at us!"

The three other SEALs exchanged troubled looks. The sick sailors still on duty just listened in, confused. The water is running out? People on the deck? People shooting at them? What was Beaux babbling about? They were supposed to be in the middle of nowhere.

"Wait a minute," Smash urged them. "Are you *sure* about all this?"

Beaux *was* sure—and he knew it was a disaster in the making. When Team 616 attacked the Russian training sub a week before—a target of opportunity if ever there was one—they'd first disabled it by planting a charge near its exterior propeller shaft while stalking it in their mini-sub. When the Russian captain beached his injured, unarmed vessel, the 616 first sealed all its escape vents, and then broke inside. They practiced rounding up the crew and securing the boat, and—when their impromptu training exercise was over, well, the witnesses just had to go. But that sub had also been off-kilter, because of how it wound up on the beach, and moving around inside it had been extremely difficult. Now the SEALs were facing the same thing here, but on a much grander scale. Even worse, the low water level meant they didn't have the depth needed to blow their ballast tanks and leave here if they wanted to.

But most troubling of all, *someone* was out there. . . .

Smash was still disbelieving. "How can this be possible?" he exclaimed. "We checked out this place a million times. There's not supposed to be *anyone* around for miles."

Monkey examined Elvis's wound and said: "Maybe someone was hunting? Some rifle shots can go a long way."

Elvis was instantly furious. "Hunting? At night? In a *fucking* hurricane?"

The sub's corpsman was on hand, checking the ill sailors being made to stay at their posts. He gave Elvis a cursory glance then retrieved a towel from his medical bag.

Out of sheer desperation, Elvis turned to the corpsman

as he was applying the towel to his wound and asked: "What do *you* think happened?"

The corpsman just shrugged and replied, "I think someone tried to shoot your ear off—and succeeded brilliantly."

ELVIS WAS TAKEN to the sick bay, where the corpsman stitched him up as best he could. There was no hope of re-attaching the ear, but Elvis insisted the medic keep it in the infirmary's icebox.

The corpsman was loath to give Elvis a bunk that would be better used by a sick sailor, so he took the wounded SEAL down to the torpedo room, one level below. It was a relatively roomy compartment, one of the few places aboard the sub that actually had both head- and legroom. It was used occasionally as the sick bay's annex.

The corpsman set up a cot right next to the starboard-side torpedo tube and helped Elvis lie down. Elvis complied without a word, keeping his assault rifle close by.

Then the corpsman left, intent on flushing Elvis's severed ear down the toilet.

Elvis tried to lie still, praying sleep would come. "Maybe I'll wake up and it will all be a bad dream," he thought.

And he did drift off after a few seconds, only to be startled awake by a loud noise.

It took him a few moments of painful listening before he realized someone was banging on the torpedo tube.

From the inside.

UP IN THE CAAC, three of the four remaining SEALs had climbed into their battle gear. Flak jackets, body armor, Fritz helmets, extended ammo belts. They were ready to deal with the bizarre situation outside.

Who was the strange man on the sub's deck and what was

he welding? How did the channel mouth get all jammed up? And who was shooting at them? Beaux, Ghost and Smash were going up top to find out and to defend their position, leaving Monkey behind to guard the sailors on deck.

But just as they were ready to climb the conning tower ladder, all the lights on the submarine suddenly went out.

They'd heard a dull thud an instant before they were plunged into darkness. It took a few seconds before the sub's emergency lights finally blinked on. But they sent little more than a dull, greenish glow throughout the control room, casting eerie shadows everywhere.

"*Now* what's happened?" Beaux bellowed.

No one seemed to know. Beaux turned to a young ensign, the highest-ranking crew member still on the deck, and demanded an answer. The ensign guessed that with the reactor turned off and the submarine relying purely on battery power, a short circuit had occurred somewhere in the power bus.

So, how could they fix the problem? Beaux pressed him. The submarine equivalent of a tripped circuit breaker had to be pushed back in place, was the ensign's reply. Exactly where that breaker was located, though, was the question. There was so much redundant wiring on the *Wyoming,* it could be in one of a dozen places.

Beaux's head began pounding. His stomach was starting to ache. He didn't need this, not now, not ever. He barked at Smash to go with the CAAC's electrician to locate the tripped breaker. Then he reaffirmed that Monkey should remain on deck and watch the sailors.

Then he and Ghost headed for the bridge to deal with the problems outside.

THE *WYOMING* WAS built in sections. The nose contained the sonar equipment. The next section carried the torpedoes. Then came the CAAC, the crew's quarters, the reactor, and the forest of Trident missiles. Toward the back of the boat was the maneuvering room, the atmospheric control room and the engine room. All of them contained some sort of circuit breaker.

Smash and the electrician made their way through each compartment, aided only by a single flashlight. It took twenty long minutes, walking the whole way on a tilt. But after examining all the breakers and finding none had tripped, the electrician said they had to check out the main electrical room, way at the end of the boat.

It was here they finally found the cause of the blackout—and it had nothing to do with circuit breakers.

The sub's primary power cable, looking like an anaconda and nearly a foot around, was lying on the electrical room floor, smoking and in pieces.

It had been blown in two.

SMASH AND THE electrician quickly headed back to the CAAC, barely able to navigate the darkened passageways. Along the way, the sailor told Smash that to repair the severed cable would take days, and that was under the best conditions. But until then, they could not access any of the power stored in their batteries, nor could they restart the reactor.

This meant the only electricity available to them would have to come from a handful of small diesel generators that were normally used only for short periods of time when the sub was in port. And even with these generators running, everything aboard the sub, from the air circulators to the ballast tank blow mechanisms to the missile launchers, could only draw about one-tenth their normal power.

Smash and the electrician reached the CAAC where the sailor went about starting the auxiliary generators. Then

Smash climbed the conning tower ladder to report the bad news to Beaux.

He opened the hatch to find himself in the midst of a gun battle—with a ferocious storm going on around it. Bullet rounds were ricocheting all over the open bridge. Beaux and Ghost were cowering in one corner, their battle suits drenched, trying to return fire, but failing miserably. Their trouble lights had been shot away. The wind was absolutely howling. The rain was coming down in buckets.

Fort Apache . . . in a hurricane.

That's what it looked like to Smash.

Clearly 616 was in a fix. The bridge itself was narrow with a lot of thick, bulky cover around it. Like a parapet on a castle wall, it would be almost impossible to get shot up here if one was properly behind cover. But, it was just as impossible to return effective fire, as doing so made the shooter woefully exposed in all directions. Yet whoever was shooting at them, 616 *had* to defend their position somehow—that's what their SEAL training told them to do. And the bridge was the only place they could do it from.

Trying his best to be heard above the appalling conditions, Smash yelled his report across to Beaux. The 616 commander was not happy to hear it.

The boat's main power cable? Blown in half?

Sabotage . . .

Beaux immediately suspected the submarine's crewmen were responsible.

He pulled Smash out onto the bridge and gave him his M4.

"Provide counter fire when needed," Beaux yelled to him before starting to crawl down the hatchway.

Smash stopped him, though. "But, sir," he yelled over the gale. "*Who* are we shooting at?"

Beaux just shook his head and said, "I got no idea."

* * *

BEAUX QUICKLY RETURNED to the CAAC, feeling like his whole body was on fire.

Despite the auxiliary generators being turned on, the control room was much darker than before; even the emergency lighting was beginning to fade. Beaux dropped his battle gear and checked himself for any hidden wounds. Finding none, he tried to get his thoughts straight, but was struck with a sudden wave of claustrophobia. The darkened, tilted boat was throwing off his equilibrium, making him dizzy. It took a couple minutes before the unpleasant feeling finally passed.

His body behaving again, he managed to grill the electrician's mate about the damaged power line. The sailor confirmed what Smash had told him. The cable had been blown in two, cause unknown.

"Was it done on purpose?" Beaux asked him sharply.

But the sailor didn't reply. He simply put his flu mask back on and returned to his station.

This convinced Beaux the cable had indeed been cut. But all the ailing sailors on the control deck were under guard *before* the lights went out. None of them could have sabotaged the power line.

This meant someone laid up in the sick bay had to be responsible.

Beaux marched back down the dark passageway to the infirmary and confronted the corpsman a second time. The medic denied anyone had left the sick bay, saying no one was strong enough to. But Beaux brushed his explanations aside and made a pronouncement instead: Until the person who cut the cable came forward, the corpsman was to withhold all medication from every sailor under his care. If that meant some of them died, then so be it.

The corpsman just shrugged on hearing the edict.

"That's not a problem, sir," he said. "Because we ran out of medicine a long time ago."

BEAUX HAD TO see the damaged cable for himself.

With Monkey still guarding the control room, the SEAL commander made his way through the murky passageways, heading aft toward the power locker. It soon became tough going. It was extremely cramped and trying to walk on a tilt made a bad situation worse. The sub's emergency lighting was of little help, too, being so dull and lifeless. And while Beaux had a flashlight with him, it started to fade about halfway to his goal, forcing him to shut it off.

At one point, it became so dark, he had to get on his hands and knees and feel his way along the slanted passage. His claustrophobia returned, the fear running through him like a knife. In the midst of the anxiety attack, he heard weird noises all around him. People mumbling, whispering, crying softly—and someone walking close by as if with a peg leg. All this on top of the sound of bullets and raindrops hitting the exposed hull. But anytime he stopped and listened closely, the strange noises went away.

It took a long time to reach the electrical room. When he finally arrived, he turned the flashlight back on and discovered the power line really *was* blown in two—and the destruction was worse than he'd thought.

He knew no sick sailor had done this. Only a trained saboteur could have destroyed the cable, probably using an explosive charge.

That only meant one thing: Someone *else* was aboard the sub.

BEAUX TRIED TO rush back to the CAAC, but with his flashlight barely working, he was forced to rely on the feeble emergency lights for illumination. They were more hindrance than help.

He became lost almost immediately, crawling through some areas he knew were not part of the sub's regular passageways. After what seemed like forever, he felt a door in front of him. Hoping it was the portal to the next section, he opened it to discover it was an equipment locker close to the torpedo room. As the door opened wider, he was touched by something warm and wet.

He tried the flashlight one more time and in its weak glow, he found a body hanging inside the equipment locker, held in place with electrical wire, not three feet away.

Beaux collapsed against the far wall and immediately vomited. He remained there, flashlight off, for a long time. Only when he regained his composure did he turn the failing flashlight back on and direct it back at the bloody body. That's when he realized it was Elvis.

His throat had been slashed and he had multiple stab wounds in his chest. Most disturbing, his other ear had been cut from his head and stuffed deep into his mouth.

BEAUX SCRAMBLED ALL the way back to the CAAC, tripping and injuring himself many times. When he finally reached the control room, the only SEAL there was Monkey. Ghost and Smash were still up top.

Monkey was startled to see him. Beaux was in a full-blown panic, not the usual state of affairs for the 616 commander.

"What the hell is it now?" Monkey asked him.

But Beaux could barely talk. Monkey made him sit down and only then was he able to croak: "They're inside the boat. *Someone* is inside the boat. . . ."

Monkey immediately checked the clip in his assault rifle. "I gotta go get Elvis then," he said, starting to run off.

"*No!*" Beaux yelled, stopping him in his tracks. "Go up top with the others. I'll take care of things down here."

Monkey thought the order was puzzling, but he complied. Once he had gone, Beaux's fear slowly turned to anger. His perfect plan was coming apart at the seams and he needed someone to blame. He scanned the control room, his eyes falling on the young ensign, the last officer remaining on deck.

Beaux took out his .45 automatic, staggered over to the junior officer and put the muzzle against his head.

"Open the security safe and get me the missile launch keys and codebook, now," he told him.

The ensign hesitated just for a moment . . . so Beaux pulled the trigger, shooting him through the temple. The young officer crumpled to the deck.

Then waving his gun in front of him, Beaux looked at the rest of the shocked sailors and said, "Who's next?"

34

NS Norfolk
0200 hours

IT HAD BEEN twelve hours since Admiral Brown had spoken to Commander Beaux.

Except for trips to the head, Brown had not moved from his seat in the Rubber Room, praying for the phone to ring again.

In the meantime, despite a lot of bad weather, a growing fleet of search planes was scouring the Atlantic and the Caribbean looking for the *Wyoming*. So, too, was every available U.S. Navy and Coast Guard ship. But so far, there were no results.

Brown had even arranged to have some spy satellites drawn away from other missions to join in the search, but again, he knew what they were up against. U.S. subs were so quiet, they were almost impossible to detect while underway. And the experts in the Rubber Room were convinced the *Wyoming* was underway.

What Fleet Forces Command faced now was waiting for whatever supplies the sub still had on board to run out, forcing the hijackers to reveal themselves. But that could still take days, even a week or more. And in his previous phone call Beaux had indicated that whatever was going to happen, was not going to take that long.

Everyone with a need to know had been briefed on the *Wyoming* problem, right up to the White House. But this was just one more crisis on the President's plate. There were still dangerous situations ongoing in North Korea, in Iran and on the India-Pakistan border, all of them involving rogue elements trying to get control of nuclear weapons. When word of the *Wyoming*'s seizure reached the White House Situation Room, only one definitive question came back: Is this connected to the other three crises? Brown had to reply that no, he didn't believe so. So the White House basically replied: "Keep us apprised, but solve it on your own. We've got our hands full already."

After that, an idea was floated around the Rubber Room that maybe the best way out of the dilemma was to quietly agree to the hijackers' demands. Pay them the money, get the sub and the crew back, then deal with the fallout later. After all, that's how the majority of Somali hijackings were resolved.

As time dragged on, opposition to this idea became less and less.

THE RUBBER ROOM had already gone through numerous pots of coffee and two deliveries of food that no one bothered to eat. It was now 2 A.M. and, resigned to a long stay, Brown was about to request some cots be brought to the basement office when his phone rang.

The caller ID indicated it was coming in on Narrowband IP.

It was Beaux.

The FBI men started their recorders. The other experts gathered around, pens and paper at the ready. The room became absolutely quiet.

Brown answered the phone.

Beaux's opening comment was: "I thought we had a deal, Admiral . . ."

Brown was thrown for a moment. "I'm not sure what you mean," he replied.

"I told you what would happen if you sent any special ops teams against us," Beaux said. "That was the agreement."

But Brown really *didn't* know what Beaux was talking about. He looked at the gang of experts and shrugged. They all shrugged back. The Navy had no idea where the sub was. How could they send any special ops units against them?

"I assure you, Commander," Brown said, "we have not dispatched any special operations forces anywhere. How could we? We don't know where you are."

"I don't believe you, Admiral," Beaux shot back. "One of my men has been killed already, someone set off a bomb inside the boat, and we're in the middle of a God damned firefight outside. These aren't freaking ghosts doing these things. So you *must* know where we are!"

The people in the Rubber Room were more confused

than ever. A SEAL had been killed? A bomb had gone off on the sub? Gun battles outside? Where the hell *were* these guys?

Beaux started coughing, and didn't stop for ten long seconds. This was noted by the hostage experts. Finally, he spoke again. "I'll be honest with you, Admiral. Before all this started I would never have fired these nuclear missiles—at my own country or anyone else's. But I can't guarantee that anymore."

Brown said, "But to do that, you need the launch codes."

Beaux replied, short of breath, "I *have* the codes and the launch keys—*and* the weapons officer's firing mechanism. And after some persuasion, I managed to convince one of the crew members to show me how it all works."

There was another long coughing spell. A FBI man put a note in front of Brown. It read: "He's sick. Probably the flu."

Beaux recovered and went on: "Now, let's stop playing games. In an effort to hurry this thing up, we might be willing to adjust our demands. We can come down to fifty million dollars for our fee, and we'd be willing to split any profits from any TV broadcast or movie production with a charity, possibly for the families of people killed in unfortunate sinkings earlier. But we still insist on total immunity from prosecution."

Another FBI agent passed a note to Brown. "He's bending. Keep him talking."

But then those in the Rubber Room heard a loud noise coming from the other end of the phone. Something had just happened aboard the sub.

Beaux's tone changed instantly. "If you say there are no Special Forces guys around us, what the fuck do you think that was?"

More sounds in the background. Gunfire—and explosions.

Then Beaux said, "Back these guys off, Admiral! I'll fire these goddamn missiles and maybe I'll start shooting sailors, too. Call off your special ops guys or else!"

And with that, Beaux hung up.

Brown just looked around the room at a dozen stunned, bewildered faces.

"Who the *hell* are they fighting?" one of the FBI men asked. "And where?"

At that moment, one of Brown's aides came into the room. He had a freshly burned DVD in hand.

"You should see this, sir," he said. "Everyone here should."

He fed the DVD into one of the computers, and they were soon looking at aerial footage taken above the unmistakably clear waters of the Caribbean.

"We just got this from our drone unit," the aide explained. "It was shot yesterday. It shows a special ops team working on Operation Caribe recovering the body of one of their members. Apparently Team 616 killed this guy before they took over the *Wyoming*."

The footage, cloudy, shaky, and in black and white, showed a small helicopter diving down to the surface of the water to pick up what appeared to be a drowning victim. The helicopter then fired on two vessels nearby, identified in the video footage as "Abandoned by hijacking suspects." Then the video ended.

"What special ops team are we talking about?" Brown asked the aide.

"They're private contractors," the man replied. "Those Team Whiskey guys? You know, the whole ex-Delta Tora Bora thing?"

Brown felt his heart sink to the floor. He knew all about Team Whiskey from his contacts in ONI.

"Those guys are crazy," he moaned. "They've been off

the reservation for years and were only called back because we were all so shorthanded on this Caribe thing. But they're like the freaking Band of Brothers. If these SEALs killed one of them, they'll be relentless in getting their revenge."

"So these Whiskey guys probably know where the SEALs are? . . ." one of the FBI men asked.

Brown nodded grimly. "They must. But believe me, from what I know about them, they're not going to call and tell us. If one of them has been whacked, they'll want their own pound of flesh, no matter what."

The FBI man said, "Are you saying that wherever the hell they are, this Whiskey unit would risk a nuke launch just to get payback?"

Brown thought for a long moment, worry lines creasing his face.

Finally he said, "We'd be crazy to bet against it."

PART SIX

The End of Whiskey Justice

35

TEAM WHISKEY KNEW the SEALs would come to Big Hole Cay.

It was the final piece of the puzzle. The last bit of mystery to fall in place.

The SEAL team's perplexing behavior in the last few months all made sense now. Sneaking in and out of the Bahamas, cruising these strange waters in the dead of night. All the planning, the subterfuge, the machinations. The murders. All of it, just to make this weird little island the center of their universe.

Their plan *was* simple. They'd stalked then hijacked the *Wyoming*, and instead of hiding in the ocean where they knew they would eventually have to surface and be spotted, they found this place and hid it here, among the outer islands of the Abaco Bahamas, where no one would ever think to look for it.

Except Whiskey.

THE TEAM WAS here long before the sub arrived—and in that time they'd come up with a plan of their own.

It wouldn't be easy. There would be hurdles. Their sat phones were fading, a combination of weak batteries and the massive oncoming storm. No one in the team had slept or eaten in almost two days, meaning they were all running on pure adrenaline. And their copters were so low on fuel, they barely had thirty minutes flying time left between them. Maybe just enough to go for help, but not much more.

But that was OK—Whiskey didn't want any help. It would have taken hours to get anyone to believe their story anyway, and they had no desire to wend their way through the bureaucratic minefield of U.S. military intelligence. They'd just gone through that bullshit exercise with The Three Kings. They weren't about to make *that* mistake again.

No, this one they wanted to do themselves. On this little island, out in the middle of nowhere. With their limited resources, no sleep, in the middle of a hurricane.

They wanted to do it this way because, if their plan worked, they'd be able to spring a trap that even the *uber*-devious 616 would find impossible to get out of.

And once their enemy was ensnared, Whiskey planned to get its revenge in spades. Not just because the traitorous SEALs had stolen the *Wyoming* or killed scores of people on the *Mothership*, the Blackwater vessel, the Russian sub and God knew where else—

Whiskey wanted retribution because the 616 had killed one of their own. Their friend. The guy who'd put Whiskey back together. The guy who'd saved their lives many times over.

This was personal.

They were doing this one for Crash.

WHISKEY KNEW EARLY on that once here, attacking the *Wyoming* directly would not work. Forcing their way inside the sub and fighting amongst the cramped cabins and compartments would be like the worst kind of urban warfare. Plus, as the *Wyoming* cost more than $1 billion, the Navy probably wouldn't appreciate Whiskey shooting it to pieces.

More important, though, the team had to think about the sub crew's safety, plus the twenty-two nuclear-tipped missiles onboard. They also had a time element hanging over their heads. Whiskey knew they *had* to execute their plan quickly—and not just because everything they intended to do would work better under inclement conditions, and eventually the cover of darkness. It was because once the weather cleared, there was no telling what might transpire, including the possibility of the Navy finding the sub on its own.

Whiskey *did not* want that to happen—at least not until they were able to get their hands on the SEALs themselves and mete out their own brand of justice.

WHISKEY HAD ESTABLISHED their gun positions while it was still daylight, long before the sub arrived— and as it turned out, they'd placed them perfectly. There was a particularly thick grove of strangler fig trees near the lake's north embankment, about a hundred feet away from where the sub would eventually come to rest. Thick vines ran horizontally along this bank, many entangled with patches of green moss. There was so much vegetation, it turned out to be the ideal spot to hide two of the team's portable .50-caliber machine guns.

Farther down the lake's embankment, close to where the sub's bow would eventually be, was a trench that ran off into a small cavern. This cavern, in turn, housed one of the island's mysterious blue holes. The trench and the cavern were almost impossible to see from the middle of the lake, a weird topographic trick.

This also made it difficult to detect the 30mm cannon that had been taken from *Bad Dawg One* and relocated here.

HIDING IN THE forest that afternoon, the team watched as the sub squeezed itself through the widened channel opening, stopping under the overhanging strangler figs and then sinking to the lake bottom, leaving only half its sail poking above the surface. The team waited until the skies began to darken in earnest, a combination of the approaching hurricane and the coming of night. Only then did they move to spring their trap.

The rusty tools left by the twenty day laborers on the beach nearby had turned out to be godsends. Once the sub had hidden itself and the first rain began to fall, the team had taken a 300-foot, half-inch-diameter cable from one of the copter's emergency winches and had strung it back and forth across the channel mouth, wrapping it around posts they'd pounded into either side of the opening. They pulled this cable tight, then placed any tree or branch of substantial size they could find against it, upright at first. When enough trees were impaled vertically, the team had added more horizontally. With the pressure of the water flow keeping the trees in place against the cable, the weave they created slowly began to resemble a wall.

They'd next added mud, sand, and beach debris washed up by the coming storm. The more stuff thrown on the blockage, the less water came through the channel. Within an hour, all water flowing into the lake had stopped. And about two-thirds of whatever water was left in the lake had gone out the much narrower opening on the other side of the island.

It didn't seem like it should have worked—but it did. That's because the idea had come from the Senegals, residents of a country where water could be so scarce, people learned how to use everything at their disposal to quickly capture it or, when need be, control it.

That's why the team had dubbed the dam *Senegals' Bridge*.

* * *

THE HURRICANE HIT full force shortly after the sub was trapped.

The winds arrived first, then the rain, the thunder and lightning. Hiding in the forest, Whiskey was quickly soaked, as was all their gear, including their copters. But they'd pressed on because the next step was a major one: preventing the SEALs from launching the sub's nuclear-tipped missiles.

Having Agent Harry along had come in handy here. He wasn't the same person as before. He'd snapped after the SEALs sank the *Mothership,* and he'd yet to snap back. He wanted revenge on the SEALs now as much as Whiskey did. This had become personal for him, too.

Because of his position in the ONI, Harry knew about sub-launched nuclear missiles. They worked in a curious way. Generally speaking, once the firing sequence had been initiated through a series of keys being turned and codes being inputted into the launch computer, tanks on either side of each missile tube were filled with water. Controlled explosions beneath these tanks quickly turned this water into steam. The steam was so powerful when shot into the confined area of the tube that it forced the missile out, literally expelling it into the air for a dozen feet or so. The moment the missile started falling back to earth, its own rocket engine ignited, sending it on its way.

The bad news here was that even though Whiskey had drastically lowered the water level of the lake, the SEALs could still launch a missile if they wanted to. They could still flood the missile tube side tanks with water and set off the explosion to create the steam and push the weapon out of its silo. As soon as the missile fell even one iota, its engine would light and off it would go.

So, how could Whiskey prevent this?

Harry had come up with the answer. To avoid accidents, the hatches above any ballistic sub's missile tubes were designed so if there were any resistance to opening, the missiles would not fire. If Whiskey could somehow keep the missile hatches shut, the world would be spared a possible nuclear catastrophe.

Ideas such as piling rocks atop the sub were discounted as impractical; because the island was mostly coral, few rocks here were bigger than a pebble. Besides, Harry claimed all that was really needed was a shim welded into the right spot on each missile hatch hinge. If done correctly, the shim would create enough resistance to prevent the hatch from opening and thus a missile from launching.

That's where Ramon came in.

Batman had used about half the team's remaining gas to fly to North Gin Cay, stir Ramon out of a pot-induced slumber, explain the situation as best he could to him, and then make him an honorary member of Team Whiskey. Ramon had gathered his welding supplies and they'd flown back to Big Hole Cay at top speed just before the weather became really bad.

As soon as the water went down Batman had delivered Ramon and his gear to the submarine's stern and he started welding the half-dollar-size shims onto the missile hatch hinges, sealing them in place. Once discovered, the only spot from which the SEALs could fire on him was the open bridge, and Whiskey and Ramon's two Senegal bodyguards had that covered, blasting the SEALs whenever they showed their faces.

It had taken a few of these one-sided battles before Ramon felt safe doing his work. But after a while, and a little bit of inspiration, he'd ceased to notice the gunfire going on around him.

* * *

ONCE PART TWO of their plan was in motion, Whiskey had concentrated on part three: rescuing the sub's crew.

Harry was very helpful here, too. Again, he knew about the inner workings of ballistic submarines and especially how cramped they were, despite their size. He also knew that if the reactor were taken offline, the SEALs would have to rely on power stored in their batteries for electricity. Should that source be interrupted, the hijackers would be forced to use a handful of small maintenance generators to work all their environmental systems, including the emergency lights and the air circulators. While, in theory, these generators could supply enough electricity to work the nuclear weapons too, in this scenario, the SEALs would find themselves prisoners of their own prize—enclosed in a dark, congested space, running on ten percent power, with foul air and little illumination. Under those conditions, it was hoped 616 would become so distracted, they'd let down their guard on the crew.

But this still meant someone had to sneak aboard the *Wyoming* to work a bit of sabotage on its electrical supply and then organize the evacuation.

Nolan was the first to volunteer for the job, but was voted down because he had only one good eye and moving inside a darkened, now off-kilter sub would be too time consuming for him. Batman couldn't be the infiltrator either because he had only one hand. And Gunner was too large to move stealthily around the confined areas of the sub, as was the stocky Agent Harry.

That left Twitch.

BUT HOW COULD he get onboard?

Harry had that answer, too. The ideal portal would have been through one of the *Wyoming*'s two lockout chambers, the same means of entry the SEALs had used to take over the sub. But the lockout chambers' close proximity to the conning tower made going through one of them too dangerous.

That left only one other place of access: the torpedo tubes.

The tubes were basically horizontal lockout chambers. Each had a muzzle door that opened outward to allow the torpedo to go on its way before closing again. This door was attached to the hull by a hinge, but it had no locking mechanism, so getting into it from the outside would not be a problem.

It was at the other end, the place the torpedo was loaded, where it got dicey. There was a breech door here and once Twitch went in, there was no way Whiskey could know if this door would be open or closed, locked or not locked. And if it was open, who would be on the other side? Friend or foe?

It had been a risky proposition, but they all agreed it had to be done. And unstable as he was, Twitch was raring to go.

So shortly after Ramon started his work at one end of the sub, Twitch went in at the other.

BY THE TIME Twitch set out, the lake was nearly drained. But, because of the sub's slant, the starboard torpedo tube was still below the water's surface.

Armed with a .45 automatic, a knife, two hand grenades and his night vision goggles all wrapped in a waterproof bag, the diminutive team member had slowly made his way to the front of the sub, using the darkness and the horrific weather as his cover.

Diving into the water, he'd gone under, found the starboard torpedo tube and opened its muzzle door with a tug. The rush of water filling the void actually sucked him into the tube, but just as they thought it would, the water drained away through a flood valve as soon as the muzzle door closed behind him.

From there, he'd faced a forty-two-foot crawl. The torpedo tube was dark, greasy and horribly claustrophobic, definitely *not* a place for Twitch's troubled psyche. At one point he'd become so disoriented, he wasn't sure which way was up or down.

He'd pressed on by pushing with his elbows and his knees in a painfully slow wormlike motion. However, the effort took a toll on his artificial leg. He did everything he could to keep the prosthetic attached, but by about halfway in, the brace that held it in place had snapped in two.

Still, he'd reached the breech door somehow. But then came the ultimate question: The door was closed, but was it locked? Twitch gave it a slight push, but it didn't move. He tried again—still nothing. He'd fumbled around for some kind of latch or internal opening device, but there was none.

He'd faced a huge problem then: If he couldn't get into the sub, how the hell could he get out? It had been hard enough crawling headfirst into the tube. He couldn't possibly crawl out backward, push out the muzzle door and fight against the resulting rush of lake water coming in.

He'd tried to listen for any noises on the other side of the breech. Harry had told him that, because of its size, the torpedo room was sometimes used as an overflow sick bay. But Twitch had heard nothing, as the hatch was made of thick steel. So, he'd done the only thing he thought he could do. He pulled out his long, razor-sharp combat knife and banged on the breech door with its blunt end, praying someone friendly on the other side would investigate.

And someone *did* open the door.

But it was not a sailor, and he was not a friendly.

It was the SEAL named Elvis.

There was a weird moment when their eyes met and Elvis realized he'd seen this person before—at the Bunker briefing and later inside the *Mothership*'s CIC.

Elvis had exclaimed: "What the hell are *you* doing here?"

Woozy from his head injury, Elvis had assumed anyone knocking on the other side of the breech door was an enemy trying to get aboard the sub. But along with the shock of seeing someone he knew, he just didn't have enough time to raise his assault rifle, point it inside the tube and pull the trigger. There were just too many moving parts required for that.

Twitch had been quicker. He'd lunged forward with his knife and caught Elvis just under the jaw, twisting it twice. Elvis went to the deck immediately, dropping his weapon. Twitch fell out of the tube, landed on top of his victim, and stabbed him twice in the chest, brutally but not fatally.

It was only then that Twitch noticed the renegade SEAL was missing his ear. This caused him to flash back to the night when Whiskey raided the Muy Capaz's camp. All the pirates had had one of their ears lopped off by the SEALs before they were killed.

The *same* SEALs who had just killed the guy who had saved Twitch's life less than a year ago.

Though Elvis had begged for his life, Twitch cut off his other ear and stuffed it deep into his mouth to prevent the SEAL from alerting others.

And though he would have preferred drowning him, the same way his friend Crash had died, Twitch had used his combat knife to finish the job.

TEN MINUTES AFTER hanging Elvis's body in the equipment locker, Twitch found himself on the sub's lower level, inside its electrical locker. Agent Harry had told him where he could find it, but the journey was almost unbearable. His artificial leg kept falling off and no matter what he did, he couldn't get it to stay back on. As a result, he'd been forced to use Elvis's purloined assault weapon as a crutch. Luckily, he neither saw nor heard anyone while making his way below.

Twitch had done a double up to blow the power cable, placing two grenades together, then pulling the pin on one. The power locker was made of reinforced steel, so he'd been well protected from the blast, and the sound of the double explosion had been muffled somewhat. He allowed himself a fist pump of triumph when all the lights on the sub went out.

But he also knew someone from 616 would soon come down and investigate the problem and he did not want to run into that person on his way out, especially with his balky leg. So he'd hidden in the shadows nearby and waited.

Two figures arrived at the power locker about ten minutes later. One was a member of the crew, an electrician. The other was one of the rogue SEALs, the one they called Smash. It was all Twitch could do to not attack the traitor. True, it would have meant one less asshole to deal with later, but after having already killed one SEAL, doing in another would have surely alerted the rest of 616 before Twitch had fulfilled his most important mission: the crew's escape.

So he'd waited in the murk until the two men departed. Then he'd begun making his way back up to the sub's higher levels. But that's when things really started to go awry.

Bold as it was, Whiskey's plan had been hastily conceived. For one, no one ever took into account that night vision goggles didn't work well in complete darkness, the prevailing condition on most of the sub once the main power cable had been blown. A victim of his own success,

Twitch had a hard time in the pitch-black passageways, limping mightily, with no clue what was around the next corner.

He was supposed to get to the sick bay next, as the thinking was that a lot of flu-ravaged crew members would be located here. But it was just too dark to find it. So, again falling back on his Delta training, after every few steps, Twitch had come to a halt and started sniffing the air.

And after a few minutes, he detected the unmistakable smell of antiseptics.

Then he just followed his nose.

THERE WERE TWENTY-SIX sailors in the *Wyoming*'s sick bay, a place built to hold a dozen.

Many had not eaten in days due to flu-induced vomiting and diarrhea. Others had severe sore throats and swollen necks. Some had so much fluid in their lungs they were slowly drowning. With the lights out almost everywhere, the deplorable conditions in the sick bay had only gotten worse.

Commander Beaux had left the infirmary not too long before, telling the corpsman not to give the sailors any more medication. It had been a moot order, though, because the sick bay had already run out of medicine.

That was the lowest point for the Navy medic. He knew then *none* of the sailors would survive. All of them in the infirmary and still on duty up on the CAAC would continue to get sicker by the minute until they finally dropped dead. And there was nothing the corpsman could do about it.

Into this swirl of misery limped the small, compact Hawaiian man whose name the corpsman would later learn was Twitch Kapula.

He was covered in grease and blood, was carrying a

prosthetic leg under one arm and using a bayoneted M4 assault rifle as a crutch under the other. He looked quite sick himself, especially the way he practically fell into the darkened sick bay.

The corpsman was startled to see him.

"Who the hell are you?" the corpsman had asked him.

"I'm here to get you out," Twitch announced in reply.

The medic was floored. It had never occurred to him that someone might actually come to rescue them.

"How many of you are onboard?" he'd asked Twitch anxiously.

"Just me," was the reply. "I'm it."

The corpsman laughed at him. "You're kidding, right?"

The greasy, bloody little man had looked him straight in the eye and asked: "Do I look like I'm kidding?"

The corpsman pulled him to the back of the sick bay, out of sight of the passageway. He let Twitch quickly explain who he was. The corpsman soon realized that their rescue force wasn't exactly the 82nd Airborne.

"Do you have a plan, at least?" the corpsman asked.

Twitch said he did. "I'm going to move all of these guys down to the torpedo room and they're going out the starboard torpedo tube, one at a time."

The corpsman was floored. "*That's* the plan?"

Twitch just nodded again. He asked: "How often do the SEALs check on you?"

"That asshole Beaux was here a while ago," the corpsman told him. "You probably came close to passing him on your way. But besides him, no one else lately. I think most of them are up on the bridge, in the middle of a gunfight. I treated one for a gunshot wound and put him in—well, in the torpedo room."

"Consider that guy out of the equation," Twitch replied

sharply. "And my friends outside are keeping the others busy up top. So this is our window of opportunity. We got to take it."

The corpsman then examined Twitch's prosthetic leg.

"What happened to your appliance?" he asked.

"I tore the brace sneaking in," Twitch explained. "I'll have to leave it here for the time being."

Then Twitch looked around the darkened infirmary again and said, "Show me the sickest guys."

The corpsman just shrugged. "They're all really, really sick."

Twitch took a deep breath and let it out slowly.

"OK, you'll have to stay here," he instructed the corpsman. "And if anyone comes down here checking on you, you'll just have to fake it somehow, at least until we get most of them out."

Then, without another word, Twitch picked up the nearest sick sailor, draped him over his shoulder and staggered away, once again using the M4 as a crutch.

And this he did, one man at a time, for the next hour, until all of the sick sailors had been moved.

36

IT WAS NOW four in the morning.

The storm was still raging outside the sub. Inside, it was still dark and full of weird noises and ghosts. Or at least that's what Commander Beaux believed.

He was sick. He was vomiting. His neck was swollen, and his chest felt like an anvil was pressing on it. His skin had even turned a shade of blue—all symptoms of the H1N1-like virus sweeping the sub.

After last talking to NS Norfolk, he'd spent an hour close to the CAAC, in what was once the captain's cabin, ostensibly reading over the Trident launch book, the document he'd killed the young ensign to get. He was so ill, though, he could barely think straight. He had no idea what was happening up top, and he just didn't have the guts to go back below and cut down the body of his old friend, Elvis.

His grand dream was slipping away—and being replaced by a nightmare. What he'd hoped would be a smooth, clean operation had turned into a nonstop gun battle with a bunch of phantoms on the outside, and maybe something even worse on the inside.

The sailors still on duty on the control deck were useless at this point. Beaux could see them from his doorway and they were just as sick as he, if not worse. They'd stayed at their stations only because the last remaining petty officer alive told them to, so as not to risk getting anyone else killed by 616.

But clearly, it was all for show.

IT WAS ONLY that he wanted to get out of the foul smelling control area that Beaux finally managed to reload his M4, put on his flak jacket and head back up to the open bridge.

He could barely climb the conning tower ladder without stopping on every other rung; this is how weak he'd become. When he finally reached the top, he stopped, took a deep breath, and then pushed the outside hatch open.

He was greeted by the combined roar of the violent storm and the fusillades of bullets flying overhead. Ghost, Smash and now Monkey were up here, still pinned down, still firing only sporadically and still hitting absolutely nothing in the dark. They looked at him with a mixture of surprise and disgust—like someone who'd run from a battle and then for some reason decided to return.

Beaux took advantage of a lull in the gunfire to climb out of the hatch and crawl over to where the others were huddled. They looked just as disheartened—and just as sick—as he.

Another spray of tracer fire went over their heads, causing all four to hug the cold, wet, tilted deck. Each man cursed the exasperating situation. This was not the norm for them. They'd been in battle now for more than two hours, and they *still* had no idea who they were fighting against.

Their mysterious enemy was some kind of special ops unit—that much was obvious. But were they *other* SEALs? That would present the ultimate horror show for Beaux and company. They'd never been popular within the tight-knit SEAL community; to have fellow SEALs sent to take them out would be impossible to bear.

The gunfire eventually died down long enough for them to talk.

"How's Elvis doing?" Monkey asked Beaux. "Have you checked on him lately?"

"Elvis is dead," the 616 commander replied starkly, at last revealing what he had seen below. "I found him an hour ago. Whoever blew up the power cable gutted him down near the torpedo room."

The other SEALs looked back Beaux in disbelief.

"Why *the fuck* didn't you tell us?" Ghost yelled at him.

"Why would I?" Beaux shot back. "Do you feel better now that you know?"

More gunfire went overhead. Then they were quiet for a long time.

Finally Smash mumbled: "We shouldn't have torpedoed those ships, man. That's when it all started to go wrong."

"And we shouldn't have killed the captain," Monkey added.

"We shouldn't have killed *anyone,*" Ghost declared harshly. "That's what brought us all this bad karma."

Another barrage of tracer fire went over their heads.

"I know it looks bad," Beaux told them. "But I believe we can still come out on top in this thing."

The others glared at him, incredulous.

"Really? How so?" Ghost asked snidely.

Beaux pulled an envelope from his pocket. Within he showed them four keys and the step-by-step procedures for launching the Trident missiles, including the final launch codes.

"I'm very close to knowing how to do it all," Beaux said. "And I mean, really *doing* it. It's easier than you think."

"You're not serious?" Ghost challenged him. "You always said us doing a launch would just be a threat, nothing more."

"Well, now it's gone from 'threat' to 'bargaining chip,'" Beaux replied, trying to catch his breath. "I told that to Norfolk. And now we have a tool that we can use to get out of this mess."

"But why?" Ghost asked, growing angry. "Haven't we done enough?"

Beaux just shook his head. "Look, we launch one missile," he explained. "It goes into the sea or someplace. At least they'll know we're serious. They'll call off these SOF guys, we get out with our lives, and I'm convinced, *still* do some kind of movie deal."

"But you don't know where a missile will go if we launch it from here," Ghost snapped back. "I'm no expert, but to just fire one randomly—there's no way you can tell where it will come down, is there? Especially with the boat already sitting cockeyed?"

Beaux began to reply, but was suddenly interrupted by a noise louder than the screaming storm and the roar of gunfire.

It was mechanical. A whirring sound. Getting louder.

A helicopter?

In a hurricane?

It appeared an instant later. Coming out of a flash of lightning, it was an OH-6 gunship.

It unleashed a wild burst from its .50-caliber machine guns. The barrage sailed harmlessly over the tilted bridge, but the copter was flying so slow, it was obvious the people inside *wanted* the SEALs to see who they were.

The pilot was clearly visible. Hokey blue uniform. Rock star haircut. Huge oversized battle helmet, and designer sunglasses even though it was night. He was looking right at them. And the copter itself looked like a souped-up hot rod with a rotor and weapons attached.

The SEALs had seen it all before—*that* was the problem.

"I don't *fucking* believe this!" Ghost yelled over the storm. "Is that those pricks from Team Whiskey?"

"But they're supposed to be dead," Monkey yelled back. "All of them!"

Beaux watched the copter disappear back into the storm. "Son of a bitch," he said. "They really *are* ghosts. . . ."

They'd all thought that Whiskey had gone to the bottom of Blue Moon Bay along with the Navy's undercover ship and the Blackwater vessel. But they'd been wrong. Somehow, the private special ops team had escaped the carnage . . . and managed to find 616 here.

That's when a noise like an explosion went off inside Beaux's head. It hurt his ears, it had been so loud, so violent. Suddenly, it all made terrible sense to him. NS Norfolk really *didn't* know where they were or who was shooting at them—because Team Whiskey had not told them. And

Whiskey hadn't been sent here by anybody—they'd figured it all out on their own. Had they been in the employ of the Navy, they would have called in help once they'd found the sub. They would have surrounded the island with Navy ships. They would have had fighter-bombers loaded with precision-guided weapons circling overhead. They would have half the 82nd Airborne landed on the island by now.

But they'd done none of that.

Why?

Because they were here for a different reason. They weren't here to take the sub back.

They were here to avenge the death of their guy named Crash . . .

And that was very bad news for the 616.

Beaux just collapsed to the wet and oily deck. For the first time in the whole episode, he was actually, truly frightened for his life.

"Man, we really fucked up," he murmured. "Not killing all those guys for good was a big mistake."

Now it was starting to dawn on the other SEALs, too, what was really going on here.

Whiskey had played them perfectly. They'd kept them occupied up on the bridge for the past two hours because not to fight back from here meant not to fight at all, and that just wasn't in their genes. But while the 616 had been up here, doing a "more balls than brains" routine, Whiskey had been working its dark magic around and below them.

The ghost on board. The sabotage. Blocking the channel. Killing Elvis.

"God damn, I'd rather have Delta Force coming after us than these assholes!" Ghost cried out. "They're never going to let us out of here alive, because we whacked their bud!"

The copter reappeared at that moment, this time from the opposite direction. It spit more .50-caliber rounds all over the bridge. The bullets didn't hit anyone, but the SEALs were caught in a tsunami of tiny shrapnel. It was like getting hit with a spray of thumbtacks. Suddenly they were all cut on their hands and faces.

"He's right!" Monkey yelled. "They're not trying to kill us! They're just trying to wound us!"

"These guys are bastards," Ghost said, toying with a white handkerchief in his back pocket. "Cruel—but *smart* bastards . . ."

Monkey panicked. He pushed himself away from the others, suddenly stood up and began desperately searching for some way off the sub. Beaux jumped up and threw him back to the deck, hoping the Whiskey gunship wouldn't see them.

The OH-6 was gone, swallowed up again by the storm. But Beaux saw two disturbing things nevertheless. First, the Rastafarian was still on the deck and still welding. Between the storm, the darkness and the bullets flying everywhere, Beaux still could not tell what the hell he was doing. And as soon as the two armed guards in dashikis spotted him looking down on them, they raised their weapons and began firing.

At that moment, Beaux spun around and caught a glimpse of the front of the sub. He was shocked to see, illuminated by another flash of lightning, a gang of people in the shallow water near the lake's shore, running through a culvert—and suddenly disappearing.

This vision lasted only an instant, and in the crackling light, it was hard to make it out clearly. But Beaux was sure that at least some of the people he saw were *Wyoming* crewmen.

"Jesus—they're escaping!" he yelled, ducking just as the gunship came out of nowhere and covered them with another storm of razor-sharp shrapnel.

"Now I know how King Kong felt!" Monkey yelled, his hands and face horribly cut and bloody.

Beaux pulled Smash over to him.

"Get below!" he screamed at him. "See what the fuck is going on—but come right back!"

Smash didn't argue. He scrambled over to the hatchway and was soon sliding down the ladder. He was glad to get out of the gun battle and out from the storm, but he was not looking forward to walking the dark passageways knowing at least one Whiskey infiltrator was probably still aboard the sub.

Once back down on the control deck, he did a quick scan of the CAAC. The sailors here were all so sick, he couldn't imagine any of them going anywhere.

So, he slowly made his way down the dark, debris-strewn passageways expecting someone to stab him in the heart at him at any moment.

He arrived at the sick bay unscathed, though, but he was in for a shock.

The infirmary was empty.

"What the fuck?" he whispered. "They're *all* gone?"

37

THE ONLY THING harder than Twitch getting into the *Wyoming* would be getting the sick sailors out.

The water level on the submarine was now about four-fifths down the hull and still dropping. Gunner and two of the Senegals were huddled near the bow, staying low in the muck, anxious as to how it was all going to play out. They could hardly see each other in the dark and wind and rain; the hurricane was now blowing across the island at indescribable force. They'd been waiting out here so long, with no way to communicate with Twitch on the inside, they were wondering if any sailors were going to be rescued at all.

Then, without any warning, a dark figure slid out of the nearby torpedo tube and tumbled awkwardly into the water.

The Senegals immediately retrieved this person and brought him to the muddy bank. He was a young sailor, covered in grease and still wearing his flu mask.

"A lot of people are behind me," he gasped. "But a lot of them are sick, too."

And that's how it began. In the midst of the thunder and lightning, sailors began falling out of the tube one after another. Gunner and one of the Senegals were waiting in the water as they came splashing down, a drop of six feet. Some were strong enough to wade to the muddy bank themselves, a stone's throw away. Others had to be pulled to safety.

As soon as they reached solid ground, the other Senegal helped them down the culvert and into the blue hole cave. Here they were out of the elements, and there was a fresh water spring from which they could drink.

One of the first sailors to escape grabbed the Senegal on shore and told him: "I don't know who you people are— but you just delivered us from Hell."

To which another sailor said: "And your friend inside deserves a medal—if they give medals to crazy people, that is."

THE FIFTH SAILOR to come out of the tube was the boat's environmental systems engineer.

He seemed relatively healthy, so Gunner had one of the Senegals hustle him along the channel's bank to the team's main weapons dugout. Gunner knew Nolan would want to talk to him.

Nolan and Harry had been sitting in the vine-entangled dugout for more than two hours now, firing at the SEALs anytime one of them stuck his head up from the bridge. Their barrages had been so intense, they'd not allowed any of the 616 guys to squeeze off more than one or two shots at a time before taking cover again. Nolan and Harry had been firing lots of random bursts, too, just to keep the SEALs off balance.

The sailor practically fell into the nearly invisible weapons pit, getting snarled in the strangler vines as he arrived. Nolan and Harry quickly introduced themselves, not that it made much difference. They were both wearing battle suits, head to toe, with blackened faces and night vision scopes attached to their oversized helmets.

Nolan asked the sailor the situation aboard the sub. The man tried to distill it as best he could.

"Everyone was really sick on the way home," he began. "Bad flu. Then the SEALs came aboard, killed the captain and stuffed his body somewhere. We all thought it was a drill, at least at first. Then they made us tell them how to fire the torpedoes—they killed the defensive weapons officer right in front of us, so the junior XO told us to do whatever these guys wanted. So, we did. And eventually we wound up here."

He looked out on the dark, storm-swept island and added: "Wherever the hell 'here' is."

"What about the nukes?" Nolan asked him. "Are they still operational?"

The sailor nodded grimly. "And those guys have the launch code book, too, because we heard they just shot our ensign a little while ago to get it. So they probably know *how* to do a launch—even though there's actually a few different places you can do it from. My guess is they probably studied up on submarines before they pulled this stunt. We could tell some things were screwing them up, but they also knew a little bit about how to run a submarine."

Nolan used his special night vision scope to scan the back of the *Wyoming*. Ramon was still up there, doing his welding. He had at least a half dozen hinges still to do.

"Have they been in touch with anyone on the outside?" Nolan asked the sailor.

"They've been talking to Norfolk on the IP phone," he replied. "I'm sure the Big Brass got no real idea what's going on here, but Beaux told them he'll use the missiles if he doesn't get what he wants—which is a huge money payment, a TV show and immunity from prosecution. They also want you guys to stop attacking them."

Harry laughed maniacally. "Like *that's* going to happen," he roared, opening up again. Every time he pulled his trigger, he yelled at the SEALs: "Show yourselves, you assholes! You chicken motherfuckers!"

"So is your plan to try to force these guys to give up?" the sailor asked Nolan. "Read them their rights, that sort of thing?"

Nolan shook his head slowly. "We're going to wait them out," he said. "But when they do give up, we're going to make them pay for what they did."

"They killed a good friend of ours when he didn't have a chance," Harry interjected, talking more like a member of Whiskey than one of their ONI adversaries. "So, we're going to kill them the same way, while they're helpless and don't have a chance in hell of escaping. Do you have a problem with that?"

The sailor laughed darkly. "Are you kidding?" he said. "Just get me a front row seat. Any idea *how* you're going to do it?"

"We're going to line them up and shoot them," Nolan declared simply. "Like a firing squad. One at a time, each guy who makes it out of there alive. And we're going to videotape it so the whole world will see."

"Right on!" the sailor exclaimed.

"Or we might hang them," Harry said suddenly.

Nolan shrugged. "Well, right," he said. "We might hang them instead. . . ."

"Or we might drown them." Harry kept talking. "Or slice their throats. . . ."

Nolan was getting slightly annoyed—in Whiskey's overall plan, the means of the SEALs' execution had yet to be decided. "Yes, maybe we'll do *all* of those things, and electrocute them, too," he said. "But whatever the way, they're going to pay for what they did to our friend. And in the bargain, you guys get your payback, too. Just like everyone else they've fucked with in the past few days, all the people they killed. The score will be settled—but it will be settled our way. That's our goal."

"But how long will you wait for them to come out?" the sailor asked.

Nolan adjusted the ammo belt in his M4. "Until Doomsday if necessary," he replied defiantly. "We know they're diehards, so it might be a while before they realize they have no other choice. That's why our guy in the copter just let them know *who* we are, finally, just to freak them out a little more. We're hoping them knowing it's us firing at them will make them panic and do stupid things—like trying to negotiate with us. Or at least that's the plan; we'll see if it works. But no matter how long it takes, we'll be here."

That's when the sailor looked out at the sub and noticed something. "Well, I hate to say this, but you might have your dirty work done for you way before that."

"What do you mean?" Nolan asked him.

The sailor pointed to a spot just in front of the sail. There was a closable vent there and puffs of nasty black exhaust could be seen shooting out of it.

"There's an auxiliary generator right below that vent," he said. "Those fools have been running it and a few others full blast ever since the power cable was cut. The problem is, they're not built for that. They're more for use when the ship is in dock, during repairs, things like that. And they're always supposed to be properly ventilated, which at the moment, none of them are. I guarantee that one in particular is going to burn out at any minute, and when it does the fumes will be like poison. They'll go right through the boat, because the air filtration system isn't really working and the vents can't handle it all. It will produce a cloud of carbon monoxide inside and whoever is breathing it in will see some smoke, but they might not realize what's happening until it's too late. They'll just drop to the deck and it will be like going to sleep."

This was *not* something Nolan wanted to hear. He wanted the 616 to suffer more than that. But he also had another, bigger concern.

He asked the sailor: "When that generator goes, how long will it take for the fumes to poison the entire boat?"

The sailor shrugged. "Ten minutes maybe—twenty tops."

Nolan immediately looked to the front of the sub.

"Damn," he said. "I hope all the friendlies are out by then."

38

BATMAN WAS FACING an unusual problem for a combat pilot. He was low on fuel, but still had plenty of ammunition left. That didn't happen very often.

Like the rest of Whiskey, his mission since taking off about ten minutes ago was to keep the SEALs on the open bridge pinned for as long as possible, this to prevent them from firing at Ramon and his security party, as well as the sailors coming out of the torpedo tube. It was also his job to finally let the SEALs know who they were dealing with, a bit of psy-ops that Whiskey was hoping might hurry the inevitable simply by screwing with 616's collective heads.

But doing these things in the OH-6 in hurricane-force winds had been a real chore. One of the Senegals was with him, and the normally cool customer was holding on for dear life. Batman was, too. He was just grateful the plan didn't call for him to fire directly at the SEALs. That would have required a sustained hover, tricky to do under these conditions, especially if the SEALs were firing back at him.

So, while they might have looked threatening to the 616 guys trapped atop the conning tower, it was all Batman could do to keep the helicopter in the air.

He'd made about a dozen passes on them, wounding them, scaring them, and per the plan, generally fucking with their heads. But now he had only enough gas for a few more sweeps. He hoped all the sailors would be safely out of the sub before then—and that Ramon would be done by then, too. He really didn't want to have to land this copter once its tanks were dry, then get into *Bad Dawg Two,* and use it to provide air cover until it, too, ran out of gas. But that was a definite possibility.

He turned sharply and went to fly over the sub's bridge

again. He was about 100 feet away and coming down fast when he saw one of the 616 guys suddenly jump up out of cover and into plain view.

It was hard to tell who in Whiskey fired first. Nolan and Harry opened up from their dugout. The Senegals protecting Ramon fired from down on the deck and Gunner even fired the 30mm cannon from down near the sub's bow.

But Batman was closer—and more accurate.

At first he thought the SEAL was going to take a shot at Ramon down on the deck, so he didn't even think about it. He squeezed off a burst from his twin 50s and watched the rounds tear into the renegade SEAL's body.

It was only then that he realized the man had attached a white cloth to his rifle and had actually been waving it at the helicopter.

It was too late though. The SEAL was blown off the bridge and into the water below where he was quickly swept downstream.

Batman pulled the copter up and over the bridge a moment later, missing it by inches.

"God, was that a flag of surrender?" he asked his white-knuckled Senegal passenger. "Did I just screw up the plan?"

"Ne vous en faites pas," the Senegal replied, once they had regained level flight. *"Un de moins meurtrier pour noyer tard."*

Don't worry about it, he said. Just one less murderer to drown later. . . .

BEAUX WAS SHOCKED that Ghost was so suddenly gone.

Like Elvis, he'd known the guy for years—they all had.

But that was the final straw. It was totally useless to be

up on the bridge, trying to do battle with Whiskey, while God knows what was happening in the sub below. The 616 team had already lost two men, with absolutely nothing in return. SEAL training or not, this strategy would not come to any good end for them.

Sick, dizzy and deflated, Beaux had had enough. On his order, the last of his command collected their weapons and scampered back down the conning tower ladder, slamming the hatch behind them. Their defense of the boat from up top had ended in abject failure.

They wearily climbed down to the control deck and dropped their weapons, helmets and ammunition.

Then they dragged themselves into the CAAC, only to find that all the sailors they'd left at their posts, unattended, were now gone.

IT WAS TOTAL confusion in the torpedo room.

Twitch had led the last group of sailors out of the CAAC, this while the SEALs were still battling Whiskey up on the open bridge.

Luckily, he didn't have to carry any of these guys. Most could walk, and those who couldn't were helped by those who could. The remaining sailors arrived in the torpedo room just as the last of the sick bay sailors was going out.

It took another ten minutes but once all of the CAAC sailors had gone, only the corpsman and Twitch remained. The *Wyoming* would soon be empty of friendly forces— and anything could happen after that.

"You go first," the corpsman told Twitch. "I'll push you along if you need any help."

But Twitch shook his head. He had one more thing he had to do.

"No, you go," Twitch told the medic.

The corpsman was taken aback. "Aren't you coming?" he asked Twitch.

Twitch said, "Not yet. I have to go get my leg. I need it. . . ."

Before the corpsman could say another word, Twitch disappeared back into the dark sub.

39

ADMIRAL BROWN HAD just finished his eighth cup of coffee when his phone rang.

It surprised everyone in the Rubber Room. The FBI experts had predicted that after their last conversation, Beaux would not call back for hours, if at all.

But it was now 5 A.M., and the phone was ringing.

Brown waited for the tape recorders to be turned on and then answered by pushing the button for speakerphone.

"We are ready to adjust our demands downward," was how Beaux started off the conversation, his voice sounding totally burned out.

"I'm listening," Brown replied dryly.

Beaux was obviously reading his response. "I think we've all learned some lessons here," he said between coughs. "We could draw up a set of security guidelines to prevent something like this from happening again. We could also give you intelligence on how an enemy could hide a ballistic sub close to the U.S. shoreline without being detected."

"These things might be useful," Brown said, stringing him along. "But our concern is the welfare of the men assigned to that boat."

"The crew is no longer on the boat," Beaux replied quickly.

A gasp went around the Rubber Room.

"They are safe, you mean?" Brown asked eagerly.

"They are no longer here with us," Beaux said. "So, I guess in a sense, they are."

A wave of relief washed over those gathered around Brown.

"So you're altering *all* your demands?" the admiral asked him.

"We can come to some agreement on that, yes," Beaux said. "This has never been about money. And we'll even be willing to stand trial. People like prison interviews, don't they?"

An FBI man passed Brown a note. It read: "Ask him what he wants in return exactly."

Brown relayed the question and Beaux replied immediately. "Forget everything else. You've got to do one thing and one thing only: Get these freaking Whiskey guys off our backs. We know now they're the ones who have us surrounded—in fact, they're out there flying around, rubbing our noses in it. They *want* us to know it's them, even though they've brutally killed two of my men already and they're not doing your boat any favors, either. Now I'm sorry, Admiral—we realize now you didn't send them. We realize now that it was probably out of your control. So we're not blaming you. But seriously, we're ready to throw in the towel here. So please get word to these guys somehow and tell them to back off. They'll get paid no matter what—damn it, *we'll* pay them, if that's what it takes. Anything just to stop them from messing with us."

Brown and his experts were silently celebrating—even

though the Whiskey problem was totally out of their hands. But they weren't about to tell Beaux that.

"OK, how about this?" Brown proposed. "You tell us where you are and we'll come get you."

"Now, that's a deal," Beaux said, obviously relieved. "But you'll have to hurry . . ."

"We will," Brown assured him.

They could hear Beaux let out a long sigh.

Then he said: "OK, Admiral, we are at—"

But at that moment, everyone in the Rubber Room heard the sound of a huge explosion coming from Beaux's side of the phone.

Then the line went dead.

NOLAN AND HARRY finally stopped firing their weapons.

Their dugout was awash in empty shell casings and depleted ammo clips. Five minutes had gone by since they'd seen any movement from the sub's bridge. It was obvious the SEALs had retreated inside.

"I guess they finally figured it all out," Harry said.

Nolan took off his helmet and wiped his tired face.

"Thanks to Batman," he said. "But at this rate, there'll be no one left for us to whack."

Their job was done here. They prepared to split up. Nolan would move to the front of the sub to help the last of the escaping sailors. Harry would climb up the sub's tailfin and join the two Senegals protecting Ramon on deck.

But before they crawled out of their dugout, Harry fired off one last burst, hitting the sub's communications antennas. A pair of long, thin tubes sticking out of the top of the conning tower, they'd somehow survived the onslaught. Both exploded now into sparkling bits of metal and glass.

"Just so they won't be calling out for any more pizza," Harry explained.

NOLAN MADE HIS way down the muddy embankment, joining Gunner and the two Senegals near the front of the sub.

The last of the sailors were just coming out of the torpedo tube; Nolan helped several get to shore. As sick as they were, they were all grateful—some were even crying—happy that they were finally out of the terrifying U-boat.

The sub's medic was the last man out. Nolan and the Senegals caught him before he hit the water and helped him to the channel bank. The man could barely hold himself up. He collapsed to the mud, overwhelmed with relief.

Except for one thing.

Twitch was not behind him.

"Where's our guy?" Gunner yelled to the corpsman over the howling wind.

The medic reported: "I wanted him to go out in front of me, but he told me to go first. Then he ran back into the sub."

Nolan and Gunner were stumped. What the hell would have made Twitch stay on the sub?

"His leg," the corpsman went on. "He left it in the sick bay, so he went back for it. The problem is, the sick bay is just one level up. He *should have* been right behind me."

At that moment, Nolan saw Agent Harry up on the deck near the conning tower gesturing wildly at him.

He was pointing to the generator vent just in front of the tilted submarine's sail, the one the environmental systems guy had told them about. A column of solid black smoke was now rising out of the opening.

"Is everybody out?" Harry was yelling down at them. "Because this is looking serious. . . ."

Nolan froze. If the environmental systems guy was right, the fumes from the burned-out generator would fill the sub with deadly toxic fumes in twenty minutes.

And Twitch was still inside.

Nolan would have throttled his wayward colleague if he were in front of him. Getting another prosthetic leg was not a problem. Yet, knowing Twitch as Nolan did, that fake leg was probably his most prized possession. It had been with him even before he'd been sprung from the hellhole of Walter Reed Hospital's Building 18.

But if Twitch wasn't out of the sub by now, something must be wrong.

And that meant only one thing.

Nolan had to go in and get him.

"So close," he griped to Gunner, shedding everything he had on him except his knife, his .45 automatic and his special night-vision scope. "We were so *fucking* close. . . ."

NOLAN WADED INTO the depleted lake and made his way through the wind and rain to a point right under the torpedo muzzle door. Gunner and the two Senegals followed him in; one Senegal handed him a *dashi,* a large kerchief that Nolan tied around his nose and mouth. This would be his only protection from the creeping toxic fumes.

Gunner and the Senegals then boosted him up to the torpedo tube. It took some doing, but Nolan finally managed to squeeze inside.

He began shimmying down the greasy pipe, hoping he wouldn't run into someone unfriendly coming the other way. The tube was awful inside. Slimy, because so many sweating and coughing sick guys had come out, and bloody, because some of them had also been bleeding.

It was also pitch black, so Nolan had no idea when he'd

run out of tube. One moment he was crawling along, the next he was falling in space.

He hit the torpedo room's deck hard, landing on his shoulder. Painfully getting to his feet, he adjusted his specially adapted night-vision scope and took a look around. The torpedo room was a mess. Overturned cots. Bloody litter and bandages everywhere. Piles of ripped and oily clothes, stripped off by the sailors before they went out the tube. The place smelled horrible.

He quickly found his way out and started moving aft. Navigating was difficult, as his night-vision scope was working at only one-third power due to the almost nonexistent lighting. The biggest problem, though, was how cramped the tilted passageway was. Trying to get through it on an angle was almost impossible in some places. Plus he was beginning to smell smoke.

He finally turned the first corner and was suddenly looking at a body. It was hanging in an equipment locker right in front of him and at first he thought it was one of the sub's crewmen. But on closer inspection, he realized it was the SEAL named Elvis. He'd been brutally stabbed, his throat was slit, and one of his ears was stuffed in his mouth.

Nolan knew immediately whose work this was.

Twitch . . .

The dead man's eyes were wide open, though. He seemed to be looking at Nolan and saying: *Why would you ever come to this horrible place?*

NOLAN MOVED ON. He'd only been inside the sub for about three minutes and the smoke was already getting more noticeable. Up one level and past the crews' quarters, he finally found his way to the sick bay. It, too, was dark, smelly and in disarray. He searched the place twice, but couldn't see anything resembling Twitch's artificial leg.

His .45 automatic out, scanning the darkness in front of him, he resumed moving aft. The sub was a mess just about everywhere he looked. Because of the tilt, anything not secured had spilled on the deck: water, coffee, oil and lots of unidentifiable fluids. It was as if the *Wyoming* had been seized weeks ago, not just a day earlier. And with each step he took, the smell of smoke got stronger.

He reached the CAAC to find it was in the worst shape of all. Smashed equipment, discarded flu masks, expended ammo clips, with blood splattered everywhere. The smoke was getting thick in here.

He scanned the control panel, looking for anything that might shut down the balky generators. But most of the controls had been either smashed or damaged by liquids, including blood.

That was the condition of the missile launch console. It had been ripped apart, as if someone had clumsily tried to cross the wires inside to make it work. But two of the keys needed to launch the missiles were in their respective locks and they'd been engaged. That could only mean the SEALs had attempted to launch at least one of the Trident missiles, maybe more.

"These guys *are* nuts," Nolan whispered.

He moved to the center of the CAAC, stopped and just listened. He prayed that he'd hear Twitch shuffling down the passageway nearby, like some old haunted soul, looking for his lost leg. Then they could get the hell out of here.

But no such luck.

NOLAN FOUND HIS way to the sub's missile bay. He'd been inside the *Wyoming* for about ten minutes at this point, halfway to when the seeping smoke would become overwhelmingly toxic.

He moved very cautiously in here, scanning everything around him before taking a step. There was no mystery why they called this place the Forest. It was a vast hall with twenty-four vertical tubes, each resembling a thick metal tree covered with control boxes, wires, cables, and assorted switches and buttons. They were all painted gray and festooned with radioactivity warning signs. Viewed through his night-vision scope, the place looked like the set of a science-fiction movie. The smoke was even thicker down here, though, rising up from the deck like a lethal fog.

Ten steps in, he stopped and just listened again. Amid the sounds of machinery struggling to stay alive and a cacophony of electronic beeps and burps, he heard three odd things: a voice alternately whispering and cursing somewhere among the missile tubes, someone snoring loudly and the sound of metal tapping on metal. It made for an eerie combination.

He crept to the center of the Forest, cranking his night-vision scope to its highest possible power. He followed the trio of strange noises for about ten more steps—and that's how he found Twitch.

His missing colleague was sitting on the deck, tucked between two missile tubes. His weapons were nowhere in sight. He was swearing softly as he tried to reattach a broken strap to his prosthetic leg. But his face was covered in blood; both his eyes were closed and swollen. His hands were so cut up, he was having trouble just holding the leg brace, never mind trying to fix it. Clearly, he'd been severely beaten.

Nolan's first instinct was to grab him and carry him out of this place—but he stopped himself, a wise choice.

First, he noticed a thin wire wrapped around Twitch's neck. Then he saw a shadowy figure was sitting beside him, propped up against the missile tube wall. It was one of the three remaining SEALs, the one nicknamed Monkey. He was sound asleep and snoring.

The wire around Twitch's neck was attached to the trigger of Monkey's M4 assault rifle, which the SEAL was cradling in his arms. If Twitch moved too far in any direction while Monkey dozed, the M4 would blow his head off.

In the background, near another pair of missile tubes, maybe twenty feet away, Nolan saw the last two SEALs, Beaux and Smash. Both had M4s slung over their shoulders. They were also holding a cigarette lighter over a manual of sorts and were jabbing buttons attached to one of the launch cylinders.

Still in the shadows, Nolan studied them closely. What were they doing exactly? The rescued sailor had told him in the dugout that there were several different places on board from which to fire a nuclear-tipped missile. Did that mean they could be launched from down here, just by pushing the right button?

The smoke was getting thicker now, as was its sickening smell. Nolan couldn't tell whether the SEALs even knew the burnt-out generator was filling the sub with deadly fumes. As it was, all three of them already looked like zombies. Yet they'd managed to catch Twitch somehow—and with all the sub's crew now gone, he was their last remaining hostage.

Nolan steeled himself. There was no way he could sneak back out and return with reinforcements, not with only a few minutes of breathable air left in the sub.

He had to free Twitch now.

He finally stepped out of the murk, holding his .45 automatic out in front of him. Monkey woke up and saw him right away. The SEAL looked very nasty up close. Gaunt, sunken eyes, pasty white skin; the sores around his mouth and nose were obvious even through the night-vision goggles. He was either suffering from the acute flu, or being slowly poisoned by the fumes. Or maybe both.

He was also slow in reacting. He just stared up at Nolan, puzzling over him in the dark. Nolan must have looked like a monster to him, the dashi wrapped around the bottom half of his face, his patch and the night-vision scope covering his eyes, his clothes stained with grease and blood, surrounded by the smoky gloom.

But then Monkey's eyes fell on Nolan's .45 automatic.

"Don't go shooting that thing off in here," he told Nolan in a weirdly passive voice. "We got twenty-two live missiles, and just one bullet could—"

But Nolan didn't let him finish. He squeezed his trigger and shot the SEAL right between the eyes. His head came apart and splattered on the deck.

"So much for The Plan," Nolan thought grimly.

Nolan saw Beaux and Smash, alerted by the gunshot, spin around and look toward him; both appeared dazed and confused. Again, they were armed with M4s, but they didn't have night-vision goggles, meaning they couldn't see Nolan as well as he could see them. But they could certainly detect his shadow in the faint glow of the green emergency lights.

Nolan had to move fast. He grabbed Twitch, tore the wire from his neck and retrieved Monkey's M4. Then he started dragging his badly beaten friend away.

But which way to go? Between the smoke, the dark, and the tightly packed missile tubes, Nolan wasn't sure where he was. Every direction looked the same. He wasn't even sure which way he came in. When Nolan was a kid his favorite attraction at the amusement park had been the House of Horrors. Now he was in one for real.

By pure luck, he stumbled onto an aisle that was slightly wider than the rest; it also had a red line running down the middle. Nolan began dragging Twitch along this aisle, even as he could see the ghostly shadows of Beaux and Smash moving through the Forest parallel to him. And through it all, Twitch was *still* trying to reattach his artificial leg.

The two SEALs began taunting Nolan.

"Throw us your weapon and we can talk about this," came Beaux's distinctive twang. "Nothing is so bad that we can't hash it out. . . ."

Nolan responded by firing his .45 twice in the direction of the SEALs. The bullets ricocheted wildly around the missile compartment, causing an earsplitting racket.

"You're *fucking crazy,* man!" Smash yelled, ducking behind a tube. "One bullet in the wrong place and this boat will go up and take half the East Coast with it."

Nolan fired two more shots at the disembodied voices. Again, the bullets crashed loudly around the missile tubes, throwing sparks everywhere.

"You're going to kill us all!" Beaux yelled. "Be reasonable! We can *all* get out of here in one piece."

But Nolan wasn't really listening. He was desperately looking for some way out of the missile hall. He still couldn't tell forward from aft. Not that it made much difference. Considering how intense the smoke was getting, returning to the front of the sub, to the conning tower or the torpedo room, would be suicidal.

So what could he do?

There was only one option left. Nolan knew the Forest contained two lockout chambers, one of which the SEALs had used to come aboard in the first place. If Nolan could find them, maybe he could use one to escape.

Perhaps attuned to his thinking, the SEALs opened up on him with their assault rifles. Nolan hit the deck, shoving Twitch behind him as the barrage went overhead. He raised his pistol and squeezed off a shot, only to hear his clip pop out.

Damn . . . His pistol was out of ammo.

Nolan threw the .45 away and raised the M4 he'd taken from Monkey. He squeezed the trigger; the weapon bucked once, firing a single round—and then *its* ammo clip popped out.

"Son of a bitch," he cursed.

The rifle was *also* out of ammo. It'd had just one bullet in it all along.

It was at that odd moment, with them pinned down and defenseless, that Twitch came out of his fog. Suddenly he seemed aware of what was happening around him. Or so Nolan thought.

Because at that point, Twitch looked up at him and asked, "Are we still in Shanghai?"

Dozens of bullets were zinging off everything around them, lighting up the near darkness. Nolan could only imagine this was how the SEALs felt when Whiskey had them pinned down atop the conning tower earlier. He just hoped the missile compartments could take a bullet or at least deflect one. If not, they could all be turned into radio-active dust at any moment.

Nolan knew the lockout chambers were located among the forward tubes—he just didn't know which ones. Using the light created by the SEALs firing at him, he finally regained his bearings and spotted the forward part of the Forest. He started dragging Twitch in that direction, trying to keep both SEALs in sight as they continued firing in his direction, with no idea that he was now without a weapon.

"We'll cut you in on the deal—our team and your team," Smash was yelling, as the gunfire died down. "We'll give you points on the movie."

"And that's on the gross, not the net!" Beaux echoed.

Nolan finally reached the forward part of the missile compartment. But he soon discovered none of the tubes here was marked any differently than the rest. There was nothing indicating which tubes were the lockout chambers.

So he randomly selected one tube and yanked open its hatch, only to find a huge Trident missile inside. Suddenly Beaux and Smash renewed their barrage. Their bullets went over his head and started ricocheting off the missile poised inside the tube.

Nolan quickly pushed the hatchway closed, then held his breath.

He waited about five seconds—and nothing happened. No explosion, no sound of the missile taking off. No start to Armageddon.

Then from the darkness, he heard more taunting.

"If we have to shoot you we might all go up together!" Beaux yelled.

"Then no one wins!" Smash added.

Nolan pulled Twitch along again and made it to the next tube. He yanked this hatch open—only to have a body fall right into his arms.

The corpse almost embraced him. It was so close, Nolan could read the nameplate over the left breast pocket: COM-MANDER SHEPHERD.

The *Wyoming*'s captain . . .

He'd been shot in the head and the wound had swelled to grotesque proportions. The smell was unbearable. Nolan dropped the body immediately. It hit the deck with a sickening crunch.

He almost lost it right there. But he shook off the horror when he realized there was only one tube to go before he ran out of choices.

He yanked its door open—and a small gush of water came out, soaking both him and Twitch. But this was a good sign. There was no missile inside; instead Nolan could see a metal ladder that led straight up to the deck.

He stuck his head inside the launch tube, but his heart sank when he heard people and equipment moving around the silo just above him. He knew who it was: Ramon, his welding gear and his armed guardians.

He thought he could actually see the glow of the arc welding light seeping through the seams of the hatch.

"God damn," Nolan cursed, looking up into the empty tube

The only way they had to get out of the sub—and Ramon was right above him, about to weld it shut.

RAMON'S ACETYLENE TANK was running low.

His back was hurting. He was soaking wet. Until just minutes before, a gunfight had been raging around him. *And* he was in the middle of a hurricane, welding.

But he hadn't had this much fun in his life.

"One more to go, mon," he said to Agent Harry and the two Senegals still watching over him. "One more shim and dis boat is sealed."

Ramon jammed the small metal piece into the missile hatch and fired up his torch. He wiped the rain from his eyes, flipped down his mask . . . but suddenly the missile hatch began to move.

"Jesus, mon!" Ramon cried out. *"What is this?"*

He and the others watched in astonishment as a bloody hand emerged from underneath the hatch. It was like a horror movie happening right before their eyes. A monster inside the sub was trying to escape. But was it real? Ramon freaked out. He went to step on the hatch and sever the fingers, when Agent Harry yelled for him to stop.

Something else was being jammed between the hatch seal and the lid.

It was a piece of white plastic—with a boot on it.

Twitch's fake leg.

Harry pulled up the hatchway to see Twitch's bloody, distorted face looking up at him. Below him was Nolan, trying his best to push his lame colleague up and out of the lockout chamber.

The strange thing was, they really *did* look like creatures from a horror movie.

"What the hell happened to you guys?" Harry yelled at them. "Everyone thought you'd be coming back out the torpedo tube!"

"Just pull us out, will you!" Nolan yelled back. "We've had two freaks on our ass and I've been boosting Junior here for the last forty-eight feet!"

The Senegals reached down and lifted Twitch out of the tube, allowing Nolan to get to the top rung of the ladder.

But just as he was easing himself out, something grabbed onto his leg.

He looked into the hole and saw Beaux was right behind him, arms wrapped around his right leg, trying to pull him back down.

This shouldn't be, Nolan thought. With bullets flying and the two SEALs just inches away from catching them, he and Twitch had dashed into the empty missile tube, locking it with just seconds to spare. They'd heard Beaux and Smash banging on the hatch door as they began their mad climb up, but were sure they'd finally left them behind. Now, in this moment of terror, Nolan saw Beaux no longer had his M4 with him. Had he and Smash expended their ammo shooting open the silo's lock?

It made little difference now, though, as the 616 commander was laughing crazily and tightening his grip on Nolan's leg. Nolan tried kicking him away with his other leg, but Beaux still hung on tight. Nolan tried to hit him with his fist, but the rogue SEAL was just out of reach. Meanwhile, Nolan's friends on top, with the wind and the rain still swirling around them, were trying their best to pull him one way, with Beaux pulling him in the other. And the SEAL was winning, because he had such a tight grip on him. Making it worse, Smash was on the ladder right below Beaux and now he had hold of Nolan's other leg.

The desperate tug of war seemed to go on forever—with Nolan caught in the middle and losing. It was like he was being pulled back down to the underworld by the devil himself.

Is this how it ends? he thought. *After such a perfect escape?*

Finally, Ramon took action. He re-fired his torch, leaned almost all the way into the hole and with one of the Senegals holding his feet, put the flame right next to Beaux's throat.

"Let go of my friend," he growled. "Both of you—or this guy gets his gullet fried."

Beaux had no doubt this crazy-looking man would burn him. So both he and Smash immediately let go of Nolan. But because the people up top were still pulling on him, Nolan came shooting out of the missile tube at high speed, knocking over Harry and the other Senegal, with all of them landing in a heap on top of Twitch.

Nolan rolled off the pile and collapsed on the sub's tilted deck for a few seconds, fighting hard to catch his breath. The rain was pelting his face, the wind was still blowing fiercely—but at that moment, he couldn't recall anything feeling so beautiful.

"One more moment," Harry said to him, finally helping him up, "and it would have been curtains for you."

Then Ramon started calling out from below. He was still headfirst in the missile silo, still holding his lit welding torch.

"Do you even want these dizzles now?" he asked. "Or

should I drop them back where they belong and then seal this coffin?"

Nolan recovered enough to stagger back to the missile tube and look down. He saw Ramon with his welding torch clenched between his teeth, one hand holding Beaux and the other holding Smash.

"*Fucking hey* we still want them!" Harry yelled, also peering down the tube. "There's only two, but that's okay. It still means The Plan is back on schedule. And *that* means it's payback time—for all of us. . . ."

The Senegals looked to Nolan. He hesitated just a moment, but then said: "Yes, OK—pull them out."

With that, the two Senegals reached down and roughly pulled the SEALs to the deck. Both hijackers were visibly disoriented and terrified. Ever since Whiskey let it be known that they were the ones who'd found them and the *Wyoming* here, it was clear that if anyone from 616 was ever captured outside the sub, only a horrible death awaited them.

In fact, Harry already had his pistol out. He shoved it so far into Smash's temple, it broke the skin and the SEAL started to bleed.

Ironically, in the midst of all this, the rain had suddenly stopped. Morning had come, and the hurricane was moving off as quickly as it had arrived. There were even signs the sun was about to break through on the rapidly clearing horizon.

"Perfect weather for a firing squad!" Harry roared.

Word had spread of what was happening on the deck and a group of freed sailors had gathered on the lake's muddy bank nearby to watch the drama play out. Harry's call to action elicited screams of support from them.

"Drown them!" someone yelled from the bank.

"No! Burn them at the stake!" came another voice.

"No—*hang one! And make the other walk the plank!*"

Harry buried his pistol even deeper into Smash's head wound.

"I say we do them right here—right now," he growled. "No ceremony. No bullshit. No last words. Quick justice, just like we planned. . . ."

An even louder cheer erupted from the muddy bank. Smash began to weep openly. Harry's finger started to squeeze his trigger.

But then Nolan calmly reached over and moved Harry's pistol away from the SEAL. "As much as I want to do this," he said, "we just can't . . ."

Harry looked back at him in total bewilderment.

"Can't what?" he asked. "Shoot them up here you mean?"

Nolan shook his head. "Can't shoot them at all," adding quickly: "Or hang them or burn them or drown them."

Harry just didn't understand—and neither did the growing crowd of sailors on the bank.

But strangely enough, Ramon understood, and so did the Senegals. And Twitch. And even Batman and Gunner, who were standing in the shallow water nearby.

Ramon said, "We kill them like that, mon, we become as bad as they is."

Nolan looked at the others and just shrugged. "Exactly . . ." he said.

But Harry was devastated. "I'm so confused," he moaned.

Nolan collected his thoughts, then spoke again. "We're better than this. All of us—because we're Americans, in spirit if not in body. I know it seemed like a good idea at the time, freaking these guys out, screwing with their heads, and intending to get our pound of flesh when we finally got our hands on them. But we have to remember *who* we are, and what country we call home—and what the hell we've been fighting for all these years, two hundred and thirty years and more. Fighting these traitors, defending ourselves against them—that's a different story. But if we pop these guys now, taking justice into our own hands, then we're no better than the tyrants who run Iran or North Korea or the Taliban or bin Laden and his mooks. Like our very good friend here just said, if we kill them now, like this—we become like them. No . . . *We're* civilized. They're *not*. We're Americans—and now they're not. And that's what makes all the difference."

The sailors on the muddy bank were stunned at first. But slowly, Nolan's words began to sink in.

"We'll turn them over to the Navy," he went on. "They'll get a trial—and *then,* they'll get their punishment, guaranteed. But until then, we'll do this the right way."

Many of the sailors on the bank started to applaud. A few even cheered. And though a few remained silent, Nolan had given them all something to think about.

Standing near the muddy bank, watching it all, Batman lit up a damp joint, took a puff and passed it to Gunner.

"That was an interesting speech," Batman said, letting out a lungful of smoke. "Especially from a guy who's not allowed to step foot inside the U.S."

At that moment, the sun finally broke through on the horizon, bathing the top of the tilted sub and illuminating Nolan in particular.

Harry took note of the atmospherics and just shook his head. "Oh for Christ's sake!" he exclaimed. "If you got the Almighty doing your special effects, how the hell can I argue against that?"

Harry then turned back to the still confused but much relieved SEALs, now sitting on the slanted deck, their hands tied behind them.

He leaned down and spit in both their faces.

"What do you know?" he hissed at them. "Today's your lucky day."

40

THE SUNRISE TURNED out to be especially spectacular that morning. The hurricane was entirely gone thirty minutes later, taking its wind and rain and heading north to brush the Atlantic coast, but ultimately to die at sea.

After binding and gagging Beaux and Smash and then lashing them to the sub's top tail fin, the Whiskey team, plus Harry and Ramon, went down to the blue hole and helped sort out the sick sailors from the very sick ones. But even the crewmen who appeared the most ill were starting to look better. Maybe it was being out of the sub and out of danger, or maybe it was the water from the mysterious blue hole, but everyone seemed to be improving, including Nolan and Twitch. When Ramon told them the blue hole's water was rumored to have healing powers for both mind and body, both men drank a gallon each.

THE FIRST C-130 appeared over Big Hole Cay around 10 A.M.

It was a Coast Guard plane out of Miami. It circled a few times, then dropped three flares. Nolan had exactly three flares left in *Bad Dawg Two*; he fired them in reply.

The C-130 wagged its wings and flew off.

THE FIRST NAVY copters arrived about an hour later. There were five of them in the initial wave. Three were filled with heavily armed Shore Patrol police; another was carrying Navy investigators, engineers and medical personnel. The fifth copter was the command aircraft.

The CO of the landing party was a Navy captain from Fleet Forces Command named Billias. Sitting in the cabin of his large Sea Stallion helicopter, he listened to Whiskey's account of what had happened, first warning everyone involved that they would still have to do a full debriefing starting the next day on a Navy ship yet to be determined.

This debriefing would take at least a couple days, but as Billias told them, the team couldn't complain very much. After all, Whiskey was still on the clock.

Batman asked him how the Navy finally figured out where to look for them. Whiskey sure didn't call them—even if they had wanted to, their sat phones had crapped out long ago.

"Someone on a passing airliner saw the sub in the lake and asked the pilot about it," Billias replied dryly. "They thought it was a new amusement park."

Meanwhile, Navy investigators dressed in hazmat gear had gained entry to the sub. They confirmed there were two dead SEALs inside, plus three dead sailors, including Commander Shepherd.

They also reported, after killing the balky generators, that the sub was more or less intact. The reactor was unharmed, as were the Trident missiles. This meant the Navy still had an aura of plausible deniability surrounding the incident. One of its subs had simply run into a little mechanical trouble east of the Bahamas, no big deal. That would be the official story—at least for the time being.

Unofficially, Billias told them the Navy was thrilled that Whiskey didn't destroy the sub in order to save it, like they did the Indian Navy warship, the *Vidynut*, in another adventure.

The weirdest thing of all, though, was that some of the Navy SP police had recovered the body of the fifth SEAL, the one nicknamed Ghost. It had washed up at the opposite end of the island.

Whiskey had told the Navy investigators that he'd been blown off the bridge during the battle for the sub. Yet when the SPs found his body, it had been torn apart, right down to the bones. These were not wounds consistent with someone who'd been shot.

"It's the chickcarnie," Ramon said, on seeing Ghost's gruesome corpse. "The monster that lives out here. They wreak havoc on anyone who disturbs their nesting place, dead or alive. He's been out there all night watching us."

It sounded crazy—yet no one had any other explanation why the renegade SEAL's body was found in that condition.

THE NAVY FINALLY finished with Whiskey by mid-afternoon.

More Navy helicopters had landed by this time. One took Beaux and Smash away to a high security lockup in, of all places, Guantanamo Bay.

"Haven't you heard?" Billias told Whiskey. "It's where we put all the professional terrorists."

Two Navy repair ships were on the way to Big Hole Cay. The naval engineers were already studying ways to disassemble the Senegals Bridge, intent on letting the water back into the lake gradually and, with any luck, floating the sub out for a tow back to King's Bay.

Meanwhile, Whiskey asked for and received full tanks of aviation gas for their gunships. While they were all aware of the formal debriefing the following day, they told the Navy there was something they just had to do first.

So, after bidding farewell to the three dozen or so sailors they helped free from the *Wyoming,* the two Whiskey copters finally took off from Big Hole Cay.

BATMAN WAS FLYING *Bad Dawg One*; Nolan was piloting *Bad Dawg Two.* The Senegals, Agent Harry and Ramon were all with them—as well as another passenger.

Crash's body had been wrapped in plastic and temporarily buried on Big Hole Cay, away from the fighting. It was now lying on the floor of the passenger compartment of *Bad Dawg Two*, a borrowed U.S. flag draped over it.

The two copters flew west until they reached the coast of Florida. Night was just falling.

Using Agent Harry's directions, they found a military cemetery right on the coast near Fort Lauderdale. They landed on a beach nearby, and climbed up to the darkened graveyard. The four remaining Whiskey members carried the body. The rest of the group carried some of the rusty shovels from Big Hole Cay.

They found an empty spot and dug a grave, with everyone pitching in, including Harry and Ramon. Adhering to an ancient custom from their country, the Senegals dug with their hands.

Then they finally laid Crash to rest.

There were no prayers, just five good minutes of silence. Crash had no family, so he would stay here, in good company with other fallen heroes, until his friends could make more permanent arrangements.

When they were done, Harry used a sat phone borrowed from Billias to call ONI headquarters in Washington. He asked for the status of the three other crisis points around the world.

The reply was brief. "No nukes have gone off anywhere in the past forty-eight hours," he said. "So things must be heading the right direction."

So, positive news all round.

It was time to leave. The group headed back down to the copters on the beach, but Batman and Nolan stayed behind for a moment.

"Well, you got your wish," Batman told him. "Bad way for it to come about, but at least it happened."

Nolan didn't know what he meant.

"You're on U.S. soil," Batman explained. "For at least a little while anyway."

Nolan looked around and took in a long breath of the warm air.

"Yeah, I guess I am," he said.

He reached down and took a bit of dirt from Crash's grave and put it in his pocket.

Then he said, "I guess this will have to do—for now."